Illuminating Gracie

LISA C. TEMPLE

*For my mother and father, Ellen and Ted Cheek,
who have always seen the light in me - even when
no one else could.*

. . . . let your light shine before others, that they may see your good deeds and glorify your Father in heaven.

Matthew 5:16

. . . . beauty is not in the face; beauty is a light in the heart.

Kahlil Gibran

. . . . darkness cannot drive out darkness; only light can do that.

Martin Luther King, Jr.

CONTENTS

Prologue

Part 1 THE GARDEN

THE ANGEL LOCHEDUS SAT, HEAD BOWED, DEEP IN THOUGHT. HE WAS enjoying the solemn stillness of the garden – the reflection of the pregnant moon on the rippleless pond. This place, it reminded him of another garden - the garden where it all began - the garden of perfect serenity and unparalleled peace, until evil had invaded its borders, shattering its immaculate calm and peerless purity.

The battle between good and evil had raged throughout time. Even though he knew how it would all end (for it had been written), it made the fight no less desperate – no less heartbreaking. No, this place was not the perfect garden where it all began, but he loved it just the same. Maybe fighting for something with all your heart and all your strength made that something sweeter – more precious.

He was preparing for a different kind of battle now, the loss of which could mean his very soul. As he looked out over the water, his mind drifted back to the fire fifteen years ago. After centuries of performing the least favored of all tasks, Lochedus' heart had grown unbearably heavy with the pain inherent in its performance. He had known, even then, that he shouldn't feel that way because, after all, the souls he'd been taking were going to an infinitely better and more permanent place. But having suffered a devastating loss of his own, his grief had merged with the suffering of the survivors, leaving him feeling despondent and wondering if things could ever be the same. He'd hurt right along with the loved ones left behind, and without his partner by his side he had no balm for his loneliness and despair.

Because he was an angel, Lochedus carried the power of life and death in his touch. With the wave of his hand, he could calm an angry sea or rain down terrible destruction on the heads of the guilty. He could grant peace to the troubled and visit devastating disease on the deserving. But no matter how hard he tried he could not, that night, pull himself from the depression that threatened to tear him apart. It had taken the touch of a small boy to do what a mighty angel could not and the far- reaching fallout from the child's selfless act would echo throughout eternity.

Through the years, Lochedus had checked in on the boy, quietly keeping vigil – never speaking, only watching. Not one time did the boy acknowledge his existence or seem to see him again. Not even in his darkest hours did he call out for help. That is, until tonight. The boy, now an old man, didn't beg for his own soul, but for the soul of another – the one he loved most in the world. And now, the angel would move Heaven and Earth – and Hell if he had to – to help the one to whom he owed so much.

With a sigh, he pulled himself back to the present; the sudden change in atmosphere signaling the arrival of the one who stood before him now. The air, only moments ago motionless, whipped with a violent fury and the trees surrounding the white-capped pond bent double as if seeking escape from the angry blowing. The angel lifted his head, nodding a resigned greeting to the intruder.

"Must you always be so dramatic, brother?" he asked. "I was enjoying the peacefulness of the night."

The interloper chuckled, impervious to the escalating elements. "The calm before the storm, you mean, Lochedus?"

The angel, irritated now, stood, planting his feet firmly despite the violent lashing wind and driving rain. He shouted to be heard over the squall.

"Don't forget the rules, Beladona."

"Yeah, well, the rule book has already been tossed out the window on this one, don't you think, little brother?" Beladona punctuated his retort with a sarcastic roll of his eyes and an arrogant curl of his perfect top lip. "In fact, you seem to have forgotten all the principles you once stood by. There may be hope for you yet!"

Irritation replaced serenity as the angel fought to maintain his temper, not willing to allow his brother the satisfaction of knowing he had gotten to him. After all, that's what Beladona did best. Lochedus wouldn't give him that. He would remain calm if it ended him. Right then, he felt as if it might; but he succeeded in sounding unmoved – even nonchalant – when he replied.

"You know nothing of hope, Beladona, and you know nothing of me. I would proceed with caution." Lochedus managed a sarcastic smile of his own, though inwardly he was shaking.

His cool reply elicited the desired response. His traitorous brother considered it a personal defeat if he failed to evoke anger, and without another word he turned on his heel and stalked off, ignoring the near tornadic conditions that swirled around him.

When his brother was at last out of sight, Lochedus took a long trembling breath. He was angry with himself for his weakness. He knew what lay ahead and knew what was required of him. There was no room for weakness. It would be a fight, and fight he would, until only peaceful gardens remained.

Part II THE MANSION

THE OLD MAN'S ARMS AND CHEST ACHED EXCRUCIATINGLY, AND HE prayed for the strength to keep pumping the heart of the old woman to whom his heart had belonged for many years.

He had no way of knowing that, at the moment, the body he was feverishly working over was only a shell. The soul of the woman he loved had been ripped from its housing and was, even now, hurling through a vortex – a black hole devoid of time and space.

The old woman was angry, as she so often was. She was feeling cheated, as she often did. And, she was very, very scared – for her, a way of life and, now, apparently death. She had heard of near-death experiences many times. They almost always involved brilliant warm light and achingly beautiful colors. They also included flashbacks of the temporarily deceased's life.

Where were *her* bright lights – *her* rainbow of colors – the playback of *her* existence? She shouldn't be surprised, she thought. After all, why should her death be any different than her life?

It could have been a minute or a millennium – she had no way of knowing – but at last she could see a pinpoint of light at the end of the long tunnel. And then it was over. The black void simply ceased to exist and was replaced by a blinding light that bathed her, surrounded her, and moved in her and through her. Though the light was without form, a voice spoke, and she somehow knew that she was hearing the light itself speak.

"Stop!" it commanded, and her insides quaked with fear.

Afraid to answer, but afraid not to, the old woman asked in a trembling voice that was no more than a whisper, "Stop what? I don't understand?"

"Still your petty thoughts . . . do not think . . . LISTEN!" The voice thundered and it seemed to the woman as if her very soul shook.

"You have squandered your entire life with needless fear and wasted anger. Instead of looking outward – toward those around you – you have focused all your thoughts inward. You have constantly obsessed over what you feel, what you need, and what you lack, and have never spent a moment's time concerned with those things in others.

"But your talents were given to you to multiply. To do that, you must give of yourself. Though given much, you have given nothing; and just as a beautiful flower that is planted in a barren desert will wither and die, so too has your soul withered and died.

"But Fortunate One, because of a love pure and unconditional – a love far greater than you have ever given or allowed yourself to receive – you are being offered a second chance.

"Open your heart to love and give all to aid another. In doing this, you will help them find their true destiny and, in turn, find yours.

"This will not be an easy task. Because of the way you have lived your life, you have opened yourself up to evil, and evil will not give up easily. There will be help from both the earthly realm and from this one; but, in the end, it will come down to you.

"Time is short to accomplish your task, so go back now with a grateful heart, to the one who saved you."

The old woman had no opportunity to ask questions or even give her thanks, because the second the light spoke its last word, she was flying through the darkness again.

Slowly, she became aware of a painful pounding on her chest. At first she was typically livid; but then she remembered and opened her eyes to see the face of the man who saved her – the face of the only one who had ever really cared for her – and she knew that he was the one to whom all was owed.

Going against her every instinct and fighting to get over every wall she had built so carefully around herself, she shakily sat up and threw her arms around the old man's neck. For a long time they just cried – and then they made their plans.

Chapter One

PROBLEM CHILD

ON A FRIDAY NIGHT AT 7:15, MOST GIRLS MY AGE WOULD BE HEADED out to have fun. I, on the other hand, was doing the food delivery thing for my sister-in-law again. My life? Not ideal. Understatement!

After four painfully long months in this backwoods metropolis, I'd made exactly one friend – March Ann Mayham – and if she was tied up "family functioning," food delivery was about my only option for weekend excitement. Even with March Ann, things never got too exciting, but at least together we could share the boredom. The problem was that, unlike me, she actually had a life – a close family, other friends, after school activities. In fact, she had so much of a life, I couldn't figure out why she had gone out of her way to befriend me. She probably felt sorry for me.

Generally speaking, just the thought of a pity friendship would have driven me crazy, would have forced me to do something so stupid or rude as to send her running in the opposite direction. But loneliness has a way of making you accept things you normally wouldn't. So, with March Ann I was on my best behavior. I kept my sarcasms to a minimum and tried to act with some civility. One had to make sacrifices in small communities.

One of the many charming aspects of *this* lovely community was its propensity for life-threatening weather including flash floods, thunderstorms and, my personal favorite – tornadoes. Since moving from Atlanta, Georgia, to Lake Martin, outside of Tallassee, Alabama, seventeen weeks and three days ago, I had spent umpteen hours in basements, school hallways, and on one particularly memorable day a Walmart dressing room, all in an effort to prevent becoming a sad statistic on *WSFA's Doppler Weather Report*.

I was fervently wishing I was in a basement, hall or dressing room tonight. Anywhere but where I was – the middle of nowhere – surrounded by nothing but empty fields, frightened-looking cows and trees bent in two by what I believe is commonly referred to as "gale force winds."

One, two, three, four, five; one, two, three, four; one, two, three; one, two; one . . . I counted down, a habit I had begun, out of the blue, several years ago. I suppose it was a method of "self-soothing" when finding myself in particularly stressful situations like this one. At least, that was what Edgar had said. Edgar was the shrink my parents had forced on me when they decided that all my little idiosyncrasies were getting out of hand and too much for them to handle alone.

I didn't see what the big deal was. So what if I spouted off a few numbers, locked doors repetitively, checked under my bed eight to ten times a night before falling asleep. Whom did it hurt? I just saw myself as a slightly over-cautious girl with a penchant for numbers. Edgar – Dr. Bower, that is – said that my explanation didn't "add up" (his idea of a joke), because I could not really be considered cautious when I took unnecessary chances with my life like driving forty miles over the posted speed limit or climbing out of a third story window in a thwarted attempt to meet a guy I had only known online. A living, breathing oxymoron – that's what he had called me – a paranoid risk-taker; an underachiever with a near genius IQ; a girl who craved friendship, yet did all in her power to run friends away. The end result wasn't an oxymoron, just a moron – a very lonely moron.

Well, whatever my issues were and the reasons for them, I was in full counting mode now, probably because I was scared to death. The gusts of wind whipped at my car with such force that I could barely keep it on the road. My windshield wipers did little to combat the sheets of rain and seeing three feet in front of me was becoming a problem. I made the decision to pull over on the shoulder of the road until things slowed down. If the storm got any worse, I might even have to abandon my car and make a mad dash for the ditch running parallel to the right side of the narrow highway. I had listened to enough storm warnings to know that in the event of a tornado, the last place I wanted to be was in a car or a trailer.

After about five minutes of sitting on the side of the road, the rain began to dissipate a bit and the winds lessen. As I eased off the shoulder back onto the narrow highway, my headlights caught the glint of some type of reflection fifty yards or so ahead, to my left. As I closed the distance between the car and the mysterious lights, I was comforted to see three bright white poles topped with red reflector dots, which served to mark a small dirt lane lined with enormous water oaks. I had been so freaked out by the storm that I had completely forgotten about the directions my sister-in-law had given me – directions that stipulated that I turn left onto the dirt road marked by three reflector poles.

Weak with relief, I carefully turned from the paved road to the dirt one while mentally cursing the mud bath my poor car was taking. Four months ago, turning onto a dirt road would have been a sure sign to plug in the GPS, but this wasn't Atlanta, and dirt roads weren't the exception, but the rule. So despite a distinct feeling of unease, I began creeping down the tree-lined, limb-strewn, dark-as-pitch path alternately praying, cursing and counting until, at last, I spotted a glimmer of light through the fog 100 yards or so in the distance.

An eerier feeling I couldn't remember ever having as I made my approach toward the source of the lights. Visibility was very poor even though the rain had abated considerably, so I was practically on top of the house before I realized exactly what I was seeing.

It was a house, all right, but not just any house. It was really more like what I would call a mansion. It was a huge old French manor with a stone façade and elaborate arched windows, and though I'm sure it had been quite grand at one time, it now had the look of a home that had seen much better days. While it wasn't what I would call dilapidated, it was certainly unkempt.

The overgrown weeds and general disrepair of the place gave it a whole "spirits in residence" vibe, and the fog and mist emanating from the ground around it only increased its unearthly haunted-house feel. I was a pair of stiletto heels and a tube top away from a bad B-movie, and even though I knew turning around and leaving the way I came would be reasonable – even sensible – I pulled on up to the intimidating old place and parked a few yards away from the steps leading to the massive front doors.

I was still not fully committed to a course of action, so I sat waffling between getting out and making my delivery or turning around and taking off. As was so often the case in my life, food played a major role in my decision-making process. If I retreated now, the Blue Plate Special occupying shotgun in my ancient Cutlass would go to waste. Normally, I would have no problem scarfing down the turkey, dressing, peas and pie but the ten pounds I had added to my already chubby frame over the past six months, no doubt, attributed to my general lack of appeal to my fellow students at All Saints High (well, the counting probably didn't help, either); so I had made a decision to cut back on the groceries in an effort to shed the excess weight.

Not wanting to waste perfectly good food or be tempted to do something even more drastic – like eat it – I made the decision to carry out my appointed task. Opening the car door, I leaned down to make sure my shoestrings were securely tied. I wanted to be ready in case zombies, werewolves or the like were lying in wait for me, and a hasty retreat was called for. Once satisfied that my footwear was secure, I grabbed the food and headed up the brick stairs to the aged wooden doors centered in the face of the mansion.

Lights burned dimly through the foggy glass of ancient-looking lanterns. They cast a soft glow onto the bronze knockers mounted in the center of the impressively enormous doors. Quietly counting, I took a final deep breath and, summoning my usually non-existent courage, I raised my hand to lift the knocker and announce my arrival to the occupants therein. To my surprise, before I could grab the metal ring, the right door flew open with a loud *thuuunk*.

I half expected a bug-eyed hunchback to greet me with, "The master will see you in the conservatory," but that wasn't how things happened. Not even close. Instead, a rotund little old lady, gray hair flying, hands on hips and clearly perturbed, met me saying, "Well, don't just stand there! Come on in, Grace, I've been waiting a long time for this!"

What the heck did she just say to me?! I couldn't believe it. I had driven through a virtual tornado to get food to this old woman and that's the thanks I get? Well, maybe not a tornado, but conditions were favorable for a tornado to develop. That's what the *Doppler Weather Report* had said. Didn't she listen to the news? Or, better still, didn't she look out one of the hundred or so windows in this house? Didn't she know what I had driven through so she could dine fine tonight?

I pointedly checked the ticket on her bag and then glanced down at my watch. It was just as I thought. She had ordered the food at 6:35 and it was now 7:25; I doubt Dominos could have done it any faster. I would say the old lady had a bit of an instant gratification problem. But then, to be fair, time was probably more of an issue at eighty than at not quite eighteen.

Gritting my teeth, I chose to take the high road. I bit back the caustic remark in my head and, instead, responded in the voice I reserved for old folks and functional idiots. "Ohhhhh, I'm so sorry I didn't get your food here fast enough! Pleeease forgive me."

Her response served to irritate me even further.

"Save the sarcasm, Grace, and get on in here. You look like you've been through a war."

Though miffed at her dig at my appearance, I dutifully followed her across the marble foyer, through a gorgeously appointed dining room and into a cozy wood-paneled library filled with floor-to-ceiling shelves lined with leather-bound books that I was willing to bet included many first editions and collectors dreams. The walls of the room were punctuated with oil paintings that were, even to my untrained eye, obvious masterpieces, and the hardwood floors were covered in antique oriental rugs woven in deep, rich jewel tones.

I found it rather odd that the inside of the home was so immaculately furnished while the exterior seemed unkempt and weathered with age. I couldn't quite put my finger on it, but something about the house – or really something about the whole scenario – just felt off. Creepy. A chill ran through my body, and I caught myself mumbling a number sequence under my breath. After a moment I managed to reign in my fears and get back to appreciating the elegance with which I was surrounded.

For the first time in quite a while, I wished my mother was with me and not just because I was sure any ghosts in the area would be more frightened of her than she was of them. I wanted her with me because she would have truly loved seeing this house. The limestone floors, foot-deep crown moldings and oriental rugs combined with fine French and English antiques and important-looking art to create an overall ambience of style, refinement and class. Too bad that "ambience" was completely shattered by what my father would have called a "big-mouthed broad."

"Don't just stand there with your mouth hanging open, girl. We've got a lot to talk about. We might as well sit down and get to it!"

"Uh . . . we do?" I stammered, trying hard not to look like the "country come to town" that I surely was. I was trying to figure out what we could possibly have to talk about when her shrill voice sounded off again.

"Grace! Would you wake up and sit down?" she barked, pointing toward a sumptuous velvet settee flanked by two deeply carved Chippendale chairs. Confused but compliant, I sat down on the plush cushion and awaited further instruction. None was forthcoming, because without a word the old lady took the bag of food from my hand and exited the room.

Great! Now that I'm in this crazy old woman's library, I wonder whether she is going to do me in with the rope, revolver or candlestick. I was trying to stay calm and think rationally, but panic was winning the day.

All of my life, my family had joked that I had multiple personalities. I don't think they had any idea just how right they were. Tonight those personalities were at war inside my head. There was the "not-a-care-in-the-world girl" wheedling with: *A sweet, rich old lady wants you to sit down and chat; what's the problem? Maybe she is childless and needs an heir.* My second personality – the over-the-top paranoid – screamed: *Get the heck out of this Bates Motel before Sybil gets back with the arsenic and lace.* Finally, the quiet, sensible and, by far, least dominant part of my personality rationalized: *Okay . . . okay . . . remain calm. You bet this is a bit strange, but no one is killing anyone. When the old lady gets back, just politely give her the bill and tell her you have to go because you have more stops to make.*

Naturally, the sensible part of my personality drew the short straw and I started frantically debating between chatting up and charming the old lady or hitting her over the head with an Imari vase and making a run for it. Unfortunately (or fortunately), neither option presented itself, because when she came back, she wasn't alone. The old woman was accompanied by an equally old, though better physically preserved, gentleman. His neatly trimmed snow-white hair and ramrod straight posture brought to mind the many military men with whom I'd been surrounded throughout my life. He was tall and fit and, despite his age, emanated a quiet strength.

"Grace, this is Willem. Willem has worked for me for many, many years. I thought it important to include him in this discussion."

"Ma'am, if this is about the food taking too long to get here . . . uh . . . there was a big storm going on," I stated defensively.

This was just plain crazy. Was she bringing in the old guy to scold me or to kill me? The man seemed as confused as I was.

"Food . . . you ordered food, Mrs. B.? You know what the doctor said about your diet. I'm assuming Grace here didn't bring a salad with her."

How did these folks know my name? They were talking about me as if they knew me. I felt like I was having an out-of-body experience and I had to fight to keep from hyperventilating.

"Oh, hush, Willem, it was a good excuse to get her here." She silenced him with a withering look.

Ok . . . ok . . . that's it! I jumped up. I had officially had enough – enough of these crazy old folks, enough of this crazy night and enough of this crazy town. Actually, come to think of it, enough of my life period, because as messed up as this night surely was, it was more exciting than most of my weekends, and that was just plain pitiful.

I was leaving this house now! If these two nuts were *real* nuts, then I would find out soon enough and at this point I just didn't care anymore. I was heading toward the library doors when Mrs. B.'s piercing voice rang out.

"Willem! Stop her! Do something!" She sounded frantic, which, of course, alarmed me even further. I steeled myself, ready to do battle if necessary.

Willem, in response to the old woman's command, blocked my exit by stepping in front of the library doors. He held his hands out in front of him, not in a threatening way, but almost apologetically.

"Gracie, please," he pleaded, using the name that only my father used. "Don't go. I know you don't understand, but if you will give us a minute, you will."

Poised in my best "fight or flight" position, I hesitated long enough to look into Willem's face. What I saw there stopped me dead in my tracks. This was not the visage of the crazed killer of my imagination. It was a face lined with age but positively radiating love and compassion. While the old lady's crow's feet and furrows appeared chiseled into her skin by a lifetime of misery and disappointment, Willem's had an altogether different look to them. They were lines etched by love from years of living and laughing.

I briefly wondered how he had managed that while laboring under the old crone for so long.

"Please, Gracie," he pleaded softly. "We seem to have gotten off on the wrong foot somehow. If you wouldn't mind sitting down for just a minute, *I* will explain."

He had put the emphasis on "I," obviously sensing my distrust of his employer. I immediately felt calmer, almost strangely so. I had heard about all of the old woman's screeching I was going to, but Willem was different. He just seemed so kind and sincere. I would listen to what he had to say. I walked over to the settee and perched on the edge of the cushion, looking up into Willem's weathered face, waiting for his explanation of the craziness that had come before. I chose to completely ignore the old lady.

"Gracie, there is a simple explanation for why we wanted to meet you," Willem offered. "You see, we thought . . . well, Mrs. B. and I wanted, uh . . ."

"Oh for gosh sakes, Willem! Let me handle this. We wanted a girl for the summer!"

"What?!" I, along with all my inner voices, screamed. Once again, I was on my feet, my brain going into "hypermode." My paranoid inner voice was yelling: *I knew it, I knew it, I knew it – they are freaks! Run! We have got to be faster than the two of them.*

Even my saner self was encouraging me to get out of the house. The daredevil in me was strangely silent, perhaps, for once, squelched by the two more cautious sides of my personality. But, horrification had frozen me to the spot. I couldn't move a muscle.

The old battle-axe was quicker to figure out the source of my shock than Willem. "Oh, for goodness sake, Grace, get your mind out of the gutter," she sniped.

Willem quickly clued in and backed away in dismay, shaking his head from side to side. "Oh, Lordy, no, Ms. Grace, I didn't . . . I mean we aren't . . . I . . . that's not what I, uh, we, meant."

Red-faced and stuttering, he started and restarted his explanation, finally settling on, "Gracie, what Mrs. B. meant to say was that she, well we, will be here at Lake Martin for the next several months. While here, Mrs. B. will be requiring the services of an assistant. We were hoping that you might consider taking the position."

I was looking at them both like they had suddenly grown additional heads. "Uh . . . why . . . why . . . I mean, why me?"

I was certainly relieved that their intentions were honorable, but I was totally confused. Why did they talk *to* me and *about* me like they knew me? Was this some odd case of geriatric omniscience – while most senses were failing others became enhanced – or was something else going on here? Why would they want to offer me a job when they knew nothing about my skill sets or me? I knew the pickings were pretty slim around these parts, but surely they could do better than me . . . in the dark . . . blindfolded. I wondered if they had me confused with some other more worthy girl. I was almost positive that there wasn't another Grace Bennett in the area, but then again, I didn't get out much.

I was just about ready to open my mouth and tell them some type of mistake had been made when my practical personality banged on my brain. *Wait just a minute, Gracie girl; you do need a job this summer. That is, unless you really want to spend three miserably long months working for St. Pat.* I must have shuddered slightly at that thought, because Mrs. B. gave me a strangely knowing look and spoke up again.

"Well, what do you say, Grace? When can you start?"

I thought her attitude was a bit presumptuous. Though my first instinct was to say, "Sign me up," my pride caused me to take a different tack. I looked her straight in the eye and asked, "Well, that depends. What's the pay and what are the benefits?"

Pay and benefits – ha! As if I was weighing all my many options! I would have been really proud of myself for sounding like "the Donald," if not for one thing. When I looked into that old woman's eyes, I felt the strangest sensation – a jolt really – that I couldn't begin to decipher. It was like the feeling one gets when they see someone they haven't seen in a long time but are really happy to have run into. How strange. I knew I had never met this old woman before, and I was equally certain that if I had, I would not have liked her. Momentarily taken aback, I began mumbling numbers under my breath in an attempt to regain focus. Maybe I was imagining things. It certainly wouldn't be the first time. But I didn't think it was my imagination, because our eye contact seemed to have had some effect on the old lady, as well.

She had no trouble moving past it, though. "Oh, I see; you're entertaining other offers of employment, are you, Grace?" Her tone was loaded with sarcasm. "I guess you would prefer working for Patty."

What was going on here? How did this woman know so much about my family and me? The hairs stood up on the back of my neck. I would have been overcome with fear if her bombastic barb hadn't made me so mad. Before things could get out of hand, Willem stepped into the mix.

"Excuse me, Grace. Would you mind giving Mrs. B. and me a moment to speak privately?" Without waiting for a reply, he took the old woman by the elbow and half-guiding, half-pushing, escorted her from the room.

Never one to stand on the rules of etiquette, I tiptoed to the door and strained to hear the conversation taking place between the two old folks. My job was made easier by the fact that neither of the two could hear very well themselves. They didn't realize that, without even trying, I could pick up most of their conversation.

"What in the world are you doing, Mrs. B., trying to run her off?" Willem demanded.

"I'm doing nothing of the kind, Willem. But, honestly, she is very irritating. And look at the way she is dressed. She is a mess!"

That witch! That hag! The nerve of her, talking about me behind my back like that! Who did she think she was? Obviously she hasn't taken a good look at herself in any of the antique mirrors around here. I glanced down at what I was wearing – my standard uniform: black T-shirt with band logo, dark jeans and red Converse sneakers. What was wrong with the way I looked? I felt my face flame with anger. I would have stormed out of the house that very minute if I hadn't heard Willem's soft reply to the old woman's insulting statement.

"No, ma'am; she's not a mess. She is absolutely beautiful."

My anger melted into a big puddle at my feet as warmth flooded my body. I knew I liked that Willem – clearly a man of taste. That was far more than I could say about the "lady" of the house. She had rubbed me the wrong way since she'd first opened her big ol' door. Clearly, she had some pretty strong feelings about me, too.

Having calmed down a bit, thanks to Willem, I began to think through the situation. I didn't like Mrs. B., nor did she seem to like me. But for some unfathomable reason, she wanted me to work for her. I realized that I was going to have to change the way she felt about me or she might just change her mind. I couldn't let that happen. The idea of working for Patty at the Martin's Nest had been tolerable, if just barely, a few moments ago, but now that same thought was unbearable. I guess the difference was hope. The mere mention of other gainful employment had opened my eyes to the possibility of escape – escape from the misery that I called my life.

In the back of my mind, I had another reason for wanting to work for the old couple. There was something mysterious going on here – something that wasn't readily apparent. I wasn't sure what it was, but I was sure I wanted to find out. Maybe solving the mystery was just the remedy for my boredom, the antidote for my doldrums.

I made a decision on the spot. I was going to do everything I could to get the job; everything I could to keep Mrs. B. from changing her mind. I was going to calm down and employ tact. My mother was known for saying, "You catch more bees with honey," so I was going to sweeten up fast. It wasn't going to be easy; I didn't do "sweet" well. But if I *didn't* want to spend the summer playing "Hazel" at the bed and breakfast, which I didn't, and if I *did* want to find out what was going on at "Casa del Crazy," which I did, sweet I was going to be!

With those thoughts in mind, I dashed back to the settee and was seemingly relaxed and all smiles when the two old folks strolled back into the room.

Chapter Two

WITH ARMS WIDE OPEN

"HEY, MRS. B., I MEANT TO TELL YOU HOW MUCH I LOVE FRENCH AND English antiques. Those are Chippendale, right?" I said, indicating the pair of chairs next to the settee on which I was now settled. I silently thanked my mother for the years of enforced antique education. I had spent many a weekend with her, tromping through estate sales and flea markets. I wasn't sure whether Mrs. B. bought my feigned interest or whether it was just that Willem's "little talk" was having the desired effect, but either way, she was receptive to my flattery.

"Well, as a matter of fact, they are, Grace. I see you have a good eye for furniture." Relaxing a bit, she again broached the subject of my employment. "Grace, I am sure you are wondering why we called you in reference to this position."

Yeah, the thought had crossed my mind! "Uh . . . well . . . yeah . . . I mean, yes ma'am. I was kind of curious, you know, how you and Mr. Willem, you know, knew about me." I was suddenly a nervous wreck, massacring the Queen's English with aplomb. Naturally, the old hag didn't miss an opportunity to make a dig.

She raised an eyebrow and started with, "Well, ya know, uh . . . Grace."

"Mrs. B!" Willem boomed. "Please!"

Realizing that the old lady was making fun of me, I mentally prepared a verbal assault of my own, but she quickly corrected herself.

"Quite right, Willem. Excuse me, Grace. Old habits die hard."

A little bewildered by the whole exchange, I kept quiet and waited for her to continue, and she did.

"You were wondering how we came to know of you. It was through your typing teacher, Mrs. Fowler. We asked for a reference, and she supplied your name, saying you were the best typist in any of her classes. She also said that your computer skills were top notch and that you had a flair for the written word."

I was surprised, to say the least. I mean, thanks to my father, I definitely knew my way around a keyboard. He had insisted on it. It was about the only thing he had ever really *made* me do. He would say, "Gracie, if you ever get down on your luck and need to make money, you won't last a day waiting tables. You just don't have the personality for it. You *will* learn to type, girlie; that way, I know you will never starve."

It just so happened that I enjoyed typing and I enjoyed computers. Unfortunately, I *did not* enjoy authority, thus, my surprise that Mrs. Fowler had recommended me.

The old lady ignored my shocked look, pursed her age-lined lips and continued, "I came to Lake Martin for a reason, Grace. I spent several years here as a girl and thought it the perfect place for my purposes. You see, I'm working on my autobiography. While it is close to completion, there are certain areas of it that need fine-tuning. I'm afraid I just don't have the skill or patience necessary to go it alone, and I was hoping that you could help me with the editing and whatnot. Do you know shorthand?"

I shook my head. "No, not really, but I have my own system I created for note taking. It won't be a problem. Transcription is no problem, either. What other tasks will I be helping you with?"

I was getting excited. This job sounded much better than making beds and delivering food for the bed and breakfast. It certainly sounded more glamorous. I felt like Lois Lane.

Willem jumped in to field my question. "Your other duties will be varied. While we are here, we are very much wanting to keep a low profile – not always easy in a small town."

"No kidding," I agreed.

"Anyway," he continued, "it will be up to you to help us maintain that privacy by handling things that might require a trip into town."

When he spoke of town, he could have been speaking of any number of small hamlets in and around the Lake Martin area. But, generally speaking, "town" to a Lake Martin resident meant either Wetumpka or Montgomery. If a person was just looking for a decent-sized grocery store, Wetumpka would do; however, if a girl wanted a good day of clothes shopping, she was going to be driving to Alabama's capital city, Montgomery. Luckily, neither was very far. You could make it to Wetumpka in twenty minutes and Montgomery in forty-five.

I was thrilled at the prospect of running errands and going into towns. I didn't really care what I would be going for, just that I would be going. I did feel like I should be asking some questions, though. I didn't want to seem uninterested. I turned to Willem and asked, "What type of things would I be doing in town?"

He smiled and answered. "Oh, you know nothing big; things like buying groceries, going to the post office and the drugstore. Just routine stuff."

It didn't sound routine to me, it sounded like Heaven. I would have the opportunity to operate independently of my family, like a real person. It would be like having a home of my own – a really *big* home. I couldn't believe my good fortune. Two hours ago, I was depressed and angry at the thought of spending the entire summer underneath the thumb of my goody-two-shoes brother and his holier-than-thou winsome wife, but now . . . now things had changed. I was to be a "Girl Friday" to a very worldly and fascinating woman of means. My summer had just gotten a lot more interesting.

And Mrs. B. – the old dear – I'm sure her bark was much worse than her bite. We would be great friends. She might even be like the grandmother I never really knew. I did have a few more questions, though in truth I couldn't imagine an answer that would have dampened my enthusiasm. Unless the two old people asked me to murder someone, I was taking the job.

"This all sounds great, and I am very excited. I do have one problem. Uh . . . my car, well, it's kind of a clunker. I hold my breath every day and pray that it won't break down or fall apart. I was wondering . . ." I hemmed and hawed around, not really sure what to ask or how to ask it.

Willem quickly interrupted. "Of course, we will work all of that out. We wouldn't expect you to drive your car. If you agree to take the job, Gracie, we will have you sign some papers regarding Mrs. B.'s privacy and then we will go over all of the little details."

"May I ask what the job pays before I make a decision?" People usually found out that information before they actually took a new position - didn't they?

Mrs. B. was the one to answer my question this time, though she didn't seem entirely pleased to be doing so. "Money . . . so unpleasant . . . but I suppose you do need to know. I was thinking $3,000 a month, but you would be considered contract labor, so you would be responsible for paying your own taxes – very important."

I didn't really hear anything past "$3,000 a month." Did she really say that? Three thousand dollars a month – that was . . . uh, $750 a week . . . like, $150 a day . . . assuming I would be working a five-day week. I was struggling to divide eight into $150, when Mrs. B. interrupted my calculations.

"Is that satisfactory, Grace?" she asked.

Was she kidding me? Satisfactory? Uh . . . yeah! I was afraid that she would change her mind or lower the number if she saw how shocked I was, so I managed a semi-coherent answer.

"Uh . . . yeah . . . yes, ma'am. Perfectly satisfactory," I quickly replied.

Was it my imagination or did her smile seem a little mocking?

"Oh, good," she enthused. In that case, Willem, why don't you make us all some tea, and we will do the paperwork and go over a few details."

"Yes, ma'am!" Willem enthusiastically agreed. The old man was beaming: smiling ear to ear. "I'm so glad we've got this settled. You'll be a welcome addition, Ms. Gracie! That's for sure." Slightly bowing, he left the room to go prepare the tea.

Now alone with my new employer, I felt nervous – scared that I would say something wrong, resulting in the retraction of her unbelievable offer. Unconsciously, I started quietly counting, making it to eight before she interrupted.

"Grace, may I ask why you do that; why you count under your breath?" She asked the question not in a mean way, but as if she were merely curious.

I surprised myself by answering truthfully. "I honestly don't know. It's just something I started doing a few years ago. It seems to help me when I'm . . . uh, you know . . . kind of nervous." I didn't mention my therapist's theories or my Obsessive-Compulsive Disorder diagnosis. I didn't think my visits to the shrink came under the heading of "Things to Mention to a New Employer." I braced myself for what I was sure would be a sarcastic reply, but this time she surprised me.

"Well, we all have our coping mechanisms. I've had many in my life – some more unhealthy than others. My doctor thinks that exercise is a great stress reliever. Perhaps, we can both benefit from the regimen he has laid out for me."

Exercise – ugh – never one of my favorite things. It wasn't that I was endearingly clumsy like the girl in one of my favorite romance novels, nor was I particularly athletic, either. I suppose, if the truth be told, I was just plain lazy. I had never been attracted to the idea of purposely sweating. But if sweat was necessary for a job that paid $3,000 a month – sweat I would.

I was trying to come up with a reasonably enthusiastic response to her exercise suggestion when Willem came back into the room, weighed down with an elaborate tea service that I was almost certain was sterling silver.

Placing the tremendous tray on the table in front of the settee, Willem set about pouring the steaming liquid into exquisitely delicate, gold-banded china cups. He then laid out sumptuous linen napkins monogrammed with letters so fancy as to be unreadable. The dainty china cups and elegant starched napkins looked strange in Willem's huge gnarled hands, but those hands were steady as a rock and looked practiced and sure in the task before them.

As the two old folks and I sat sipping our tea, we made small, uncomfortable conversation, as if by silent agreement choosing to delay more discussion of my recent employment until after our refreshments.

I wondered, yet again, about the odd set of circumstances that brought me to this moment, and wondered even more still about these two eccentric elderlies and their strange familiarity with me, apparent since I first entered the doors of the remote mansion. It wasn't just that they knew my name. It was something far deeper and more profound. I had a sense that they *knew* me – the *real* me. And try as I might, I couldn't shake the feeling that there was something bizarre going on. So, as I sat drinking tea and making small talk, I was also inwardly analyzing the night's events trying to ascertain what, if any, reason I might have for the apprehension that threatened to overcome me.

Much of my life, the past three years, had been spent on what I call my "paranoid pursuits:" locking, unlocking then relocking doors; turning oven knobs off, on, then off again; repetitively looking under beds and in closets. These are not the healthy actions of the reasonably cautious. No way. They are, instead, the compulsive habits of the seriously paranoid. I had accepted that about myself. Accepted yes; understood, no. And, because I didn't understand *why* I did what I did – all those crazy compulsions – it was easier for me to label my current fear as paranoia. I could dismiss my unease as unfounded, irrelevant and trivial, and casually sip my Earl Grey while waiting to hear more from my mysterious new employers.

Despite my level of comfort, I was somewhat relieved when Mrs. B. excused herself, saying that she was suddenly tired. She said that Willem would review with me the employment contract and answer any questions I might have. She again emphasized the need for absolute privacy and my expected discretion, and with that wished me a good night and swept from the room with all the drama of a 1920s movie queen.

At least, that seemed to have been her intention. Sadly, the result was something far less glamorous. Her cinematic sweep was interrupted when she tripped on the corner of an oriental rug. Willem was on his feet immediately and, checking her fall, helped her to the library doors – all the while apologizing for an imagined wrinkle in the carpet that the old lady was loudly proclaiming his fault.

Attempting to cover what would surely have been an inappropriate giggle, I fake-coughed into my linen napkin and then looked back at Willem to make sure he had not caught my faux pas. What I saw in his face both surprised and embarrassed me. Willem was staring down at the irritated old woman with a look of pure unadulterated worship. I had never seen anyone look at another person with such love – such adoration. Certainly, no one had ever looked at me that way. I was embarrassed because I felt like a voyeur, peering into the deepest recesses of Willem's heart.

I quickly glanced away, pretending a sudden fascination with the pattern on my empty teacup, but my mind was buzzing with this new information and the questions it raised. Were Willem and Mrs. B. in love? A couple? They certainly didn't act like a couple. If they weren't together, did the old woman have any idea about Willem's feelings for her? Did she have feelings for him? One big question I had was *why*. Why did Willem have such love for this woman? I mean, she wasn't very pleasant, nor was she very attractive. What could Willem possibly see in her? And then there was the most important question of all – why did I care?

Lost in my thoughts, I guess I didn't hear Willem say my name the first time, because he touched my arm and, smiling down at me, said, "Ms. Grace, are you all right?"

My face flushed crimson. When he looked down into my eyes, I felt he could read my every thought, hear my every question. Maybe he could because he had a funny little grin on his face when he continued.

"Your body was here, but your mind was a million miles away, Gracie. You okay, love?"

"Oh . . . yeah . . . I'm fine. I guess I was just trying to absorb everything. So much has happened tonight. I'm really excited and very grateful for this job. I just can't thank you enough."

I wasn't a hugger – never had been – but I had an overwhelming desire to give Willem a big embrace. Of course, I wouldn't do it. I barely knew him, but there was something so . . . so . . . huggable about the old man. An aura of goodness radiated from him. It was impossible not to be affected and your mood not be lightened, when around him. Well, maybe not impossible. He didn't seem to have that effect on Mrs. B. I wondered, again, how the two oldsters came to be together. They were as different as daylight and dark – black and white – Heaven and Hell. One day, I hoped to hear their story, but for now I would settle for hearing about my new job.

Willem settled in beside me on the small sofa, and we fell into easy conversation. Without the stress of Mrs. B.'s subversive negativity, I found myself opening up to Willem in a way I had never opened up to anyone before. I was completely comfortable with him, and in his presence I was completely comfortable with *me* – a concept with which I was totally unaccustomed.

I suppose it was this unexplained comfort level that caused me to lay bare my soul. I had always played my cards close to the vest, so to speak, keeping my feelings completely to myself. In fact, the mere mention of feelings usually caused my insides to run hot and cold. I could handle expressing joy, during the unusual periods in which I actually felt it, but hurt – hurt was something else entirely. My pain was *my* pain, no one else's, and I had a lot of pain. Of course, it came out in all kinds of bizarre ways – sarcasm, anger, OCD – but that didn't matter to me. As long as no one knew what was really going on inside, I would be okay. I was in control. Now, I was letting go of that control with a man I barely knew. I had no explanation for my abandon, nor any hesitation. He simply asked me to tell him about myself, and I did. I mean I *really did.*

I told him all about the eleven schools I had attended in my seventeen years. How, because my father had been in the Air Force, I had never really spent enough time in any one place to make real friends. With very little, if any, prodding on Willem's part, I told him of my parents' decision to move back to this area, after my father's retirement. I explained that my mother's family – now all passed away – were from Wetumpka, and that my parents had met when my father was stationed at Maxwell Air Force Base in Montgomery.

Prattling on, I told him about my brother and sister-in-law, with whom my parents joined forces to open up a bed and breakfast at Lake Martin. Then, to my horror, I began to cry, relating my father's decision to take an additional civilian assignment for one year in Kuwait and my mom's subsequent agreement to accompany him – leaving me in the "capable hands" of my sibling and his oh-so-irritating wife.

Through this virtual explosion of information, Willem sat and listened. Willem didn't listen the way most adults did – as a form of waiting – waiting to get in their two cents worth. No, Willem was different. He listened in a quiet, immersed way, somehow communicating through his silence genuine interest, even empathy. He had that rare quality of making the other person feel as if they were the most important, interesting thing on earth, and, for me – a girl starved for attention – he was Superman, Dr. Phil and Granddad all rolled into one.

When I finally finished my diatribe, he waited, as if making sure that I had nothing left to say, and then he took my hand and spoke a single sentence: "Gracie, you are exactly where you are supposed to be and everything is going to be all right."

A single sentence – a single simple sentence – eighteen words, yet those eighteen words, within me, released a tidal wave of emotions so strong that I could barely remain upright in its path. And after that wave came ripples of peace so soothing and pure as to be all encompassing. For the first time in my life, I acted without fear, without shame and without doubt. I reached out to this savior of an old man, placing my arms around his weathered neck and my head on his strong shoulder, and wept and wept and wept.

Finally, having no tears left to shed or any need or desire to shed them, I let go of him and wiped my nose on my sleeve. I was surprised at my own complete lack of embarrassment. "Well, I guess I'm ready to sign that contract now, if you'll still have me, that is," I said with a giggle, feeling lighthearted and cleansed.

Before Willem could respond, a voice boomed over the intercom system I'd noticed earlier next to the library doors. "Willem! Willem! If Grace is through with her little 'breakdown,' kindly inform her of the dress code while working here."

I waited for the familiar surge of anger that would normally arise within me upon hearing such a remark. Astonishingly, no such anger arose. Instead, seeing the twinkle of humor in Willem's eyes, I winked at him with one puffy lid and responded toward the squawk box. "Well, Mrs. B., my Chanel suit is at the cleaners, but I'll see what I can come up with."

Dead silence greeted my comment for just long enough to cause my stomach to drop to my shoes, but then, to my great relief, Mrs. B.'s bodiless voice responded with an intonation not totally devoid of humor. "Oh . . . a joke . . . I see . . . clever girl. Well, good night."

"Good night!" Willem and I chimed in unison, both on the verge of laughter. Willem, his face alight with merriment, grasped me in a one-armed hug so tight I could barely breathe.

"Gracie, love, I think you are going to be very, very good for the old girl! A blessing, to be sure!"

I found myself smiling until my cheeks hurt. I smiled through Willem's review of the employment contract and smiled even when he explained the need for me to work some nights and weekends. I just felt so incredibly happy. My joy increased exponentially as each job benefit was listed: a cell phone, a gas allowance, and best of all, a credit card of my very own. Of course, I understood that the cell was so that Mrs. B. and Willem could get in touch with me at all times, the gas was for their errands, and the credit card was for expenditures on their behalf. But that didn't dampen my spirits one bit. For the first time ever, I felt grown up, mature, taken seriously, and I was thrilled.

Walking me to my car, Willem asked a last question. "Gracie, I know you have a few weeks left of the school year, but would it be possible for you to work Saturdays and some afternoons until you finish up? I don't want you to get behind in your schoolwork, though."

"Actually, we have Monday and Tuesday off this week for teacher in-service days," I explained. "Even after this week I can come anytime you need me. No problem, no problem at all. Schoolwork isn't an issue." I answered quickly and honestly. Doing the work had never been a problem. It was *being told* to do the work that was the problem. And wanting to be *at school* to do the work, yeah, that was a problem, too; but the work itself – not a problem.

Right then and there, I promised myself that I would suck it up and do what was expected of me. I was actually teetering precariously on the edge of summer school, thanks to my inability to get to class on time in the mornings. Truancy had resulted in a failing grade on a couple of pop quizzes in my homeroom class. I had better actually hit the books for the next month, if I didn't want to blow history. And I didn't want to blow history. Not now that I had something far better to do with my summer than sit at a desk. Sitting at a desk might have been preferable to making beds and dusting for my sister-in-law, a.k.a. Saint Patty – Our Lady of Perpetual Perfection – but it wasn't better than my new gig. Not by a long shot.

Chapter Three

DREAM WEAVER

SAYING OUR GOODBYES, I GAVE WILLEM A FINAL HUG AND WITHOUT looking in the backseat, even once, settled in behind the Cutlass wheel, strapped up and took off. I carefully pulled from the paved drive back onto the red dirt road. As I looked back over my shoulder at the mansion, I was surprised to see how "non-spooky" the house appeared to me now, amazed at how quickly my perception had changed.

Clipping along, I one-handedly went through my 70s metal collection and selected Sabbath's *Heaven and Hell* CD. For the past few years, my musical taste had leaned toward darker music, and the night seemed particularly appropriate for it, despite my good mood. Having cranked up *Neon Knights,* I felt, rather than heard, the telltale *thump, thump, thump* that signaled a flat tire.

You have got to be kidding! I thought to myself, instinctively moving the car toward the side of the dirt lane. The fearless joy of a mere moment ago evaporated instantly as I looked back toward the manse, realizing that the porch lights that had guided me toward the place had now been extinguished. Because the music that had been rocking my world now sounded discordant and scary, with a trembling hand I turned the radio off and again looked over my shoulder, straining to see down the dark stretch of road.

It wasn't a far walk back to the house – maybe 150 yards or so – but as I looked left and right into the pitch dark woods that flanked the narrow lane, every ounce of my newfound bravado fled, leaving in its wake a racing heart and pounding pulse.

Don't be a loser, Grace; I chided myself, attempting to bolster my courage by using the tried and true "humiliation/degradation" technique. *Get your butt out of the car and walk back to the house! Willem will help you.* At snail-speed, I turned the ignition key to the off position, unhooked my seatbelt, and opened the door of the car. I'd put one foot on the still-wet earth when a terrifying screech sounded from somewhere deep within the bowels of the woods to the left of me. Scared witless, I forcefully pulled the door back toward me, unfortunately forgetting the foot that was in its path. Now maimed, I reopened and closed the door, making sure that all my body parts were inside and all the locks were pushed down.

Wonderful, Grace! Now you are broken down and crippled! This was actually the plot for at least a hundred horror movies I'd seen over the years. Except for one thing: I wasn't a hot blonde. I hoped that would be enough to save me. Maybe I should just honk the horn and flash my lights. Surely that would get Willem's attention and he would come running. There was just one problem with that idea – it would wake Mrs. B., as well. I didn't think that could possibly be a good idea.

If I walked to the house, I could lightly knock on the front door and since Willem probably hadn't had time to turn in yet, he would answer with Mrs. B being none the wiser. This was definitely the better option, all except for the whole "walking down the dark scary road" thing. Common sense told me that if I didn't want to come across as some paranoid lunatic to my new employers, I needed to "woman-up," get out of the car and walk to the house.

Regrettably, my brain and body were just not in agreement. I wanted to get out of the car and walk – I really did; but my legs just would not move off of the seat in cooperation. So, at an internal impasse, I waited, hoping for some miracle to take place, thereby negating my need to make a decision.

But, passively hoping for a miracle and actively expecting a miracle were two very different things; therefore, you could have knocked me over with a feather when one came walking down the road. At first, I thought what I was seeing was some kind of optical illusion created by the interplay of bright headlights and total darkness – a shadowing of a sort. Then I had a worse thought: *was I hallucinating?* It had been a very stressful night. Could drastic mood swings cause people to see things? I didn't have long to contemplate the issue because whatever it was – answered prayer or fear fulfillment – it was getting closer – fast.

When I first spotted the lone figure, it was at least seventy-five yards away. Then, in what seemed to be the blink of an eye, *he* was standing almost directly in front of my car, one hand shielding his eyes from the bright headlights and the other on his blue jean-clad hip. What in the world was this guy doing way out here?

Lord, pleeeease, I prayed, *let this guy be a Good Samaritan, willing to help me, rather than a Freddy Krueger wannabe who'd failed to get the hot-blonde memo.* Fighting panic, I readied myself to start blowing my horn at the first sign of evil intent. I watched as he slowly walked from the front of the car to my passenger door, motioning for me to roll down my window.

As anxious as I was, I would have had to be dead to be oblivious to the guy's looks. I had really just caught a glimpse of him, up close, in my headlights, but it was enough to know that he was tall, dark and handsome. When he leaned over to look in my car window, my interior lights allowed me a slightly better view of his face, and what I saw confirmed my earlier instincts – he was exceptionally gorgeous. I wasn't stupid. I wouldn't let down my guard just because he was hot. After all, I'd heard of Ted Bundy and was savvy enough to know that not all crazies looked like Charles Manson. But there was no denying that beauty had its privileges, and I felt some of my tension slip away in the wake of the beautiful boy's extraordinary green-gold eyes.

For some reason, my mind was operating with exceptional clarity in the crisis. I was scared, but not panicked - really almost calm. My underused gray matter categorized my fears and weighed my options, spending no time on needless counting or multiple cortex conversations. I decided to risk cracking my window just a bit and when I did, the boy, sensing I felt threatened, backed up a bit from the side door before saying his first words.

"Well, hey there, gorgeous! It must be my lucky night! You seem to be a damsel in distress."

He again leaned in slightly toward the window affording me a longer look at his unusual eyes that appeared, at once, bright green and butterscotch gold, mile high cheekbones and movie-star-white smile accented by a single perfect dimple. He was dressed in faded Levis and a black T-shirt – nothing special really - but I knew beyond a shadow of a doubt that if I lived to be a hundred, I would never see another boy as pretty as the one that stood before me now.

Pretty – that was the word for him, but not in a feminine way - far from it. There was an indefinable quality about him that raised him above mere "handsome" status. Millions of guys had dark wavy hair, white teeth and beautiful eyes, and many guys were gorgeous. But this boy, he was something different – something that couldn't be printed on a page or described with words. His looks transcended such futile characterizations.

And when this other-worldly creature – this angelic Adonis – leaned in my window, flashed his bright smile and called me "gorgeous," that's when I knew with absolute certainty that this was all just a dream. The isolated mansion, the strange old folks, the new job, the cleansing catharsis, and the sexier than sexy boy were all just a part of my slumbering subconscious.

The urge to cry was overwhelming. I should have known from the beginning that what I was experiencing wasn't real. Things like tonight just didn't happen to me. I wanted to lie right down on the hallucinatory highway and never get back up again, but the urge to keep going – keep experiencing my break from reality – was too strong. Usually when I figured out I was dreaming I would wake right up, but not this time, and I was glad. If this was a dream, I was going to make it last as long as I could. I was going to embrace my somnolent gift and see where it took me.

Praying that the night was still young, I looked up at my manly mirage through the crack in the car window. He was leaning in closer, looking back at me, clearly puzzled, and waiting for a response. I guess "dream boy" didn't know I was on to him. I quickly decided that if I was sleeping, I wasn't going to waste time with fear or bashfulness and I rolled my window all the way down before responding.

"Well, hey yourself, handsome. I guess if I'm the distressed damsel, that would make you my knight in shining armor, and I've got to say, your timing is impeccable. I'm guessing I have a flat tire, and wouldn't ya know it, not a spare in sight." I was having a grand time. As dreams go, I would give this one an A-plus. The hero in this little nighttime drama was spectacular!

He responded to my teasing tone with a flirtatious smile. "I left my cell back at my place, but if you want to walk with me, we can call a service. It might be too late to get anyone out here tonight though; in which case I could give you a lift home, and we could see about getting that tire fixed in the morning."

"Well, that's awfully kind of you," I said, batting my lashes, which seemed non-existent compared to the thick dark fringe that surrounded his almond-shaped eyes.

He responded precisely the way any proper dream boy would. "I'm just glad I came along when I did. It's not safe for a pretty girl like you to be out in the dark this late and all alone."

I thought it rather strange that, despite my sleeping state, I could still feel goose bumps rise on my arms and a shiver run down my back, but still certain I was in deep r.e.m., I ignored the tiny trickle of apprehension, unlocked the door and got out of the car.

"So, where to?" I asked and was surprised when he pointed toward the mansion. This was an intriguing dream, to say the least. He must live with the old folks.

"Hmm . . . nice twist," I observed as we began walking toward the big house.

"I'm sorry, what did you say?" he questioned, as he chivalrously matched my short strides despite his much longer legs.

"Oh," I laughed. "I was just saying, nice twist; that you live with the old folks. My subconscious is quite creative. This is a great dream!"

Not slowing his step, he asked, "A dream . . . uh, you think you are having a dream?" He seemed genuinely confused for a moment before bursting out in laughter. "Well, I have been known to have that effect on women, but let me assure you, honey, you are very much awake. Why would you think you were . . . having a dream, I mean?"

I ignored his question completely. Of course he would say that. He would disappear if I woke up; better for him if I kept sleeping. "So, you live with Mrs. B. and Willem, huh?"

This time he ignored me and, just before we reached the edge of the paved drive to the mansion, he started veering sharply to the left rather than heading for the front doors. Lengthening his strides, he arced away from the side of the house. He was walking a little ahead of me now, suddenly in a hurry.

I raised my voice a bit. "Don't you go through the front door?" I asked. I was starting to feel a dull throbbing in my injured ankle and a clammy cloak of foreboding settle over my body, causing my breath to shorten and my knees to tremble.

"Shhh!" he cautioned. "I really do not want to wake up those two. And, to answer your question, I don't go in the front door, or any other door in that place. I live in the guesthouse at the back of the property."

I was beginning to get the suspicion that I had made a terrible, terrible mistake. Dread curled in the pit of my stomach like a cobra as I came to the sudden realization that I was not dreaming, but was very much awake. I was not in a sleep-induced fantasy but rather a wide-awake nightmare. Though mood swings were fairly common for me, the pendulum of highs and lows was fast catching up to me, and I stumbled – nearly falling – with sudden fright and exhaustion.

"Whoa there, sweetheart, are you okay?" His solicitous manner, so appealing before, now sounded sinister.

"Stop calling me those stupid names! What's with you?" I half-screamed with the fear that was almost choking me.

He whipped his head back at me and for the briefest of moments, even in the dark, I could have sworn I saw twin flames of fury in his eyes. But then, as if sliding a mask into place, the anger was gone, replaced with laughter.

"Well, you've never told me your name. I don't know what to call you. Come to think of it, I've never told you mine, either – bad form on my part – my apologies. Please allow me to introduce myself. I'm Merchison Spear – Merc to my friends. And you are?"

He came to a stop a few feet in front of where I stood frozen with anger, fear and indecision – afraid to move any farther. My brain was working again, analyzing my options. As close as we were to the house, I could probably scream loud enough to wake Willem. At this point, I would even settle for the old woman. I felt so alone and vulnerable. How could I have been so stupid? I wasn't sure if "Merc" was a bad guy or not, but whatever he was I was totally at his mercy. I found myself, yet again, attempting to determine if I was being paranoid or sensible – *my* eternal question. Either way, I wasn't going to tell him my name – not yet. Not until I knew exactly who he was and what he was doing out here. I dodged his question and ventured a query of my own.

"So, you are a friend of Mrs. B.'s and Willem's?" I remained immobile, refusing to move until I got some answers.

His voice held a note of irony when he responded with, "I don't know if I would say that."

His answer led to my inevitable response. "Then what *would* you say?" I knew if his intentions were pure, I was being very rude, but I didn't care – I needed some answers. I strained to see his face in the dark, hoping his eyes would give me the assurance I needed.

"I would say we have a business relationship. I pay them money and they let me live in the guesthouse attached to the property. We don't socialize. We don't run with the same crowd."

Sarcasm dripped as thick as molasses from his mouth and I had the uncomfortable feeling that my new friends/employers – Mrs. B. and Willem – were somehow being insulted. Of course, I'd thought of a few choice insults for the old woman myself tonight. She seemed to possess a talent for irritation. But, for some odd reason, I didn't like the idea of this guy putting her down. And Willem . . . well, when it came to Willem, Merc better just tread lightly. I wouldn't put up with a single bad word about the old man. To me, Willem was an angel.

Merc had said that he didn't run with the same crowd as Willem and Mrs. B. and I certainly believed that. I didn't get the impression that the old people ran with any crowd. And this boy, I would guess, could run with the crowd of his choosing. At any rate, this was a pretty strange conversation to be having at this particular place and time, but I was trying to get a feel for him.

Merc – assuming that was his real name – was probably a nice guy trying to do a good turn; however, there was just something about him that superseded his startling good looks. I was by no means some crystal rubbing, mantra-chanting, "earth child" who sat around candles and Ouija boards chatting up spirits and raving about auras, but if I was I would say Merc was surrounded by an aura of danger. No, it was more than that really. There was a darkness – a sense of evil – around him that was almost palpable. If I had more faith in my own instincts, I would probably have run for the hills.

Lord, listen to me; I sound like a crazy person. Next thing you know, I'll be sharpening stakes and dodging full moons. *Get a grip, Gracie girl. You've been reading way too many supernatural romance novels.* I was letting my grossly overactive imagination get the better of me. How often did I get an opportunity to be alone with a gorgeous guy? Easy answer – NEVER! If I wasn't careful, I was going to blow my chance to get to know Merc with all my paranoid delusions.

"Look," he broke into my thoughts, "Are you going to at least tell me your name?"

He closed the narrow gap between us and was now only inches away from me – close enough for me to smell the cologne he was wearing. It was musky and woodsy and something else I couldn't place, and altogether very, very sexy – even seductive.

As if able to read my thoughts, he leaned in even closer, affording me full access to his aroma, and in a husky, almost whisper beseeched, "Please . . . tell me your name."

I have no logical explanation for my body's reaction to his hushed entreaty. My pulse flew matching my heart rate, while every pore and fiber of my skin went on high alert, going hot and cold virtually simultaneously. For once, I was grateful for the dark and the cover it provided my blushing face.

The worst part of the whole thing was that I had the distinct feeling Merc not only knew what embarrassing reactions his close proximity caused in my traitorous body, but he *intended* on eliciting just those responses. Whether it was my sapped energy from the drama of the night or my own sad lack of experience in the area of male/female relations, I had no resources available to me to mount a proper defense against him. In all honesty, I couldn't imagine why I should. After all, I knew plenty of girls that would have been on this guy like "white on rice." Why should I get bogged down with details and unanswered questions like: Who was he *really?* Why was he being so nice to me? Why hadn't Mrs. B. and Willem mentioned him?

Why should *I* look a gift horse in the mouth? If this "uber-hot" boy wanted to be my "knight in shining armor," why shouldn't I let him be just that? I had never been anyone's "damsel in distress," and it certainly wasn't because I had some feminist axe to grind. No, that wasn't it at all. It was because no one had ever applied for the position. So now I was going to ignore the warning bells, silence my fears and pack away my paranoia. For once, I was going to be the one with the romantic story to tell at the lunch table on Monday, instead of the one listening on the far fringes and replying with the obligatory "oohs" and "ahs" to the stories told by all the braver, more beautiful, more fortunate girls.

Having solved my inner conflicts, I answered him with a breathless and what I hoped was sexy voice, "Grace, my name is Grace."

I wanted him to say something like my name was beautiful. That would play well with the lunchtime listeners. But, to my surprise, he seemed almost irritated.

"Ha . . . ha ha," he barked a short laugh. "Yeah, that's about right. Well, come on, *Grace* – let's get you home."

I was a little disconcerted by his reaction. *Huh . . . weird. What should my name have been? Veronica . . . Candy . . . Jinx?*

Never one to keep my mouth shut, I opened it, ready to ask him if he preferred stripper names, but before I could get a word out Merc's whole body stiffened and he jerked his head sharply to the right. I strained to see what he saw or heard to create such a reaction in him. The only thing visible was the dim outline of the tremendous back portion of the mansion that was softly lit by landscape lighting buried deep in the bushes.

I looked at Merc, wanting an explanation for his behavior. "What's the problem? Did you hear something . . . somebody?" I whispered. If he *had* heard something, then he had better ears than I. Of course, I *was hyper-focused* on the visual treat that was standing next to me. A hurricane could have blown through, and I might not have noticed.

"Quiet!" he hissed and at the same time grabbed my arm and pulled me toward a scraggly grouping of azalea bushes running down the side of the house. He crouched down, none too carefully, taking me with him.

"What is it, Merc? You are kind of freaking me out. If anybody is out here, I'm sure it is just Willem. He might have spotted my car or heard us. No big deal." I was rambling a bit, suddenly nervous and puzzled by Merc's covert actions. Why were we hiding?

"Would you *please* lower your voice, Grace," he chided. "I really, really, do not want to bump into the old man tonight." His voice was heavy with irritation and something else that almost sounded like fear.

"Why?" I snapped, though carefully keeping my voice hushed. "Do you owe the old folks rent money or something?" *Lordy Lord, I really am going to have to look into charm school.* I just could not keep the sarcastic barbs from spilling out of my mouth like toxic waste. If I kept this up, my romantic rendezvous would take on all the excitement of a AAA Motors towing.

Merc was practically begging now. "Grace, I will explain later if you could just, for now, PLEASE quit talking. Things are not what..." He abruptly stopped speaking and with a resigned sigh stood up. I awkwardly followed suit, curiously peering around, searching for what, or rather *who,* had gotten Merc so twisted.

"Fantastic . . . just super," he mumbled, suddenly sounding like a little boy who was about to stomp his feet with frustration.

Men really are all just alike – young or old, gorgeous or geeky – they are all just big ol' babies!

Rolling my eyes, I attempted to respond in the patient voice I'd heard my mother use with my father all my life. "What's fantastic, Merc?" I had yet to see or hear anything, but clearly Merc was upset about something; his breath sounded heavy and erratic in my ear. It was only a second before the source of his apprehension rounded the back corner of the mansion carrying a high-beam flashlight and whistling what sounded like Otis Redding's *Dock of the Bay.* Momentarily blinded by the bright light, I squinted trying to make out just who was headed our way.

"Evening," the stranger began speaking when he was a few yards away from us. "My grandfather sent me out here to find you."

My eyes finally adjusted, allowing me to see a boy of about my age smiling at me with an easy lopsided grin. His eyes crinkled with good humor and, if it was possible, I knew I liked him on sight. Merc stood stiffly by my side, not moving or speaking, and it was easy to surmise that he did not have the same congenial feelings regarding the cheerful newcomer.

"Granddad said you were having some car trouble and asked me to make sure you got home safely." The boy glanced sharply at Merc and then, as if deciding he was unworthy of further attention, returned his focus to me. "Grace, I'm sorry I wasn't able to meet you earlier this evening. We are all sure glad that you are going to be working for Mrs. B. I know we are going to have a great summer!"

His smile was infectious and, on further inspection, I realized he was absolutely adorable. He was about six feet tall with almost shoulder-length straight blonde hair that he wore tucked behind his ears. He was broad-shouldered, lean and muscular – all in all a fantastic-looking boy.

I smiled back at this cute guy, amazed that he was to be a part of my summer package as well. Neither Mrs. B. nor Willem had mentioned him. I did a quick inventory of my current circumstances. I was standing next to a mansion, sandwiched between two gorgeous guys who were both determined to help me. The phrase "embarrassment of riches" sprang to mind. I stood there with my mouth hanging open like a big-mouthed bass, trying my best to figure out exactly what to say and what to do. I had never found myself alone in the dark with even one good-looking guy, much less two. I finally settled on the simple approach.

"Willem and Mrs. B. didn't mention anyone else was living with them." *Come to think of it, they failed to inform me of the Greek god living in the guesthouse, either. I wonder what other little pop-up toys they have waiting for me.* I was beginning to love this job, and I'd yet to work a single day!

The boy laughed, a beautiful sound – robust and full of merriment. Even in the dim light I caught a twinkle in his bright eyes. He was a chip off the old block if I had ever seen one.

"That doesn't surprise me in the least, Grace," he said. "Granddad is usually so busy dancing to Mrs. B.'s tune that he seldom has time to think of anything or anyone else." There was no malice or complaint in his voice when talking about the old lady. He'd obviously inherited more than beautiful eyes and a contagious smile from his grandfather.

"Oh, by the way, I forgot to mention I'm Locke Wingard. He laughed again and winked right at me before continuing. "Maybe short-term memory loss is contagious – a hazard of living with old folks."

I got the feeling the boy laughed a lot and I liked it. I laughed with him, realizing that the sweet-faced blonde had the same effect on me as Willem did. Five minutes in his presence and my doubts and fears had vanished. I felt completely safe. What an amazing quality to possess.

Throughout our conversation, Merc had not uttered a single word, or for that matter moved a muscle. It was as if he was flash-frozen to the spot. A quick peek at his face confirmed my earlier suspicion – he was seething with anger. I had no experience whatsoever with soothing a man's ruffled ego, and in fact I wasn't sure Merc's anger had anything to do with me at all. Nonetheless, I felt compelled to try and calm the tension that Locke's sudden appearance had caused.

I definitely felt like accepting the ride with Locke that Willem had somehow known I needed and thoughtfully arranged, would be my better, safer option. Merc, despite his obvious irritation, was probably relieved that he wouldn't be saddled with my problems tonight. But even so, I couldn't help feeling both disappointment and guilt at the thought of telling him "thanks but no thanks." I sincerely hoped that this wouldn't be the last I saw of him. Though, if I was honest with myself, I would have to say that I was being ridiculously unrealistic in thinking there could ever be anything between us. The surreal events of the night had given me a sense of empowerment, I guess; made me feel as if anything was possible. But despite the good fortune that had befallen me on this red dirt road, I was still the same girl with the same less-than-stellar physical qualities. And girls like me didn't date guys like Merchison Spear. It just did not happen. I will admit getting a job like the one I was given tonight was highly unusual as well; however, my typing and writing skills put it in the realm of improbable but not impossible. I possessed no such physical characteristics – nothing that would recommend me to a boy such as the one that now stood, barely concealing anger, right next to me.

I wondered why Merc was so angry. I felt reasonably certain that it had little to do with me, and everything to do with his relationship with the residents inside the mansion. There was obviously some weirdness going on between Merc and the old folks; between Merc and Locke, too. I hoped that whatever it was didn't prevent me from, at least, being his friend.

I vowed to try to get to the bottom of what was going on between the new people in my life. A good place to start was Locke. He didn't seem like the type that would have a single secret. Nope, he was an open book, for sure, and one I looked forward to "reading;" but before I could start, I had to deal with the issue before me – gracefully saying goodbye, for now, to Merc. I turned to him ready to thank him profusely for his kind offer of assistance, but before I had the chance he took the initiative by addressing Locke for the first time.

"It looks like you and your 'grandfather' have this well in hand," he spat through clenched teeth and then spun on his heel and headed off into the darkness without a word to me.

My heart plummeted and my cheeks flamed red. I couldn't believe he had not even said goodbye to me. He'd just tossed me aside like a dirty sock. Crestfallen, I shouted into the darkness a weak, "Thank you, Merc," but received no response in return. I stood next to Locke, struggling to put the words together to form a sentence – just to say something that would help me move past my moment of abject embarrassment.

I was still struggling when yet another miracle happened. In what seemed like only a moment, Merc returned and, without a word to either Locke or me, shoved a note into my hand and once again silently stalked away.

Aware of the blonde boy's eyes watching me but unable to garner the self-control needed to wait, I unfolded the paper and read the beautiful words haphazardly scribbled on the paper: *Breakfast – Tomorrow morning – Pick you up at 9:00*. I read and reread the words as my stomach found its way to my throat and back again. I could not believe it; Merc and me, having breakfast – *together*. It really was a miracle!

Chapter Four

OH, WHAT A NIGHT!

A THOUSAND THOUGHTS BARRELED THROUGH MY BRAIN, NOT THE LEAST of which was what to do about the boy curiously looking at me – Locke. He didn't seem to share the same distaste for Merc as Merc had for him, but I still felt more than a little awkward standing next to him trembling with anticipation over my newly scheduled date.

"Date" – what an interesting concept, and one completely foreign to me. This would be my first – my breakfast with Merc – and what a way to break into the whole business of dating, with a guy that could easily pass for a movie star. In fact, off the top of my head, I couldn't think of a movie star who could hold a candle to Merc.

What a night! In what alternate universe would the boy standing next to me now be an afterthought – someone to be dealt with rather than dreamed about? With a silent sigh, I forced myself to put the note away and deal with the situation at hand – getting home. After all, I had a lot to do before my breakfast with Merc and I had to be at home to do it.

Locke must have sensed my desire to get moving, because he turned to me with a big grin and a fake British accent and quipped, "Your chariot awaits, my lady – right this way."

He really was so darn cute. Until a few hours ago, riding in a "chariot" with a guy like Locke Wingard would have been a dream come true for me. Now, I still wanted to get to know him, but my real attraction was for Merc. Of course, I was probably being plain stupid to think that, despite Merc's invitation, I had even the smallest shot with him. But why else would he ask me out? In truth, it made no sense at all. Nothing about this night made any sense, and I was suddenly in a hurry to get home and go over the night's happenings scene by scene.

"Thank you, my Lord," I responded with my own English lilt. I had actually practiced speaking with an accent after watching *Harry Potter* a number of times. I fancied myself pretty good at it.

I followed Locke behind the house and through the side door of a massive four-bay garage. Only one car occupied the huge area, but from the looks of it the automobile deserved its own private palace. It was a limousine – long, sleek and black – just like the ones I had seen in the movies and when occasional dignitaries visited bases on which our family had, from time to time, lived.

"Wooow!" I exclaimed. "So this is Mrs. B.'s idea of being inconspicuous?"

"Yeah, Wil . . . uh . . . Granddad said the same thing. He's hoping to talk her into buying something a little *quieter*."

We laughed together and I couldn't help feeling an attraction to this uncomplicated, happy-go-lucky guy. He just had a way about him. He made me feel good. It shouldn't surprise me that I was attracted to him. After all, he was *attractive*. Up until tonight I'd never felt a romantic pull toward anyone, and now I found myself drawn toward *two* distinctly different-looking, different-acting boys. Of course, I had to account for the fact that I had never really been alone with any male except my brother for more than a few minutes. I mean, maybe I'd been alone in a classroom taking a makeup test with a guy or something, but that was about it.

Locke and I talked and laughed all the way back to the Martin's Nest. I enjoyed his company so much that it felt like we had known each other for years. I couldn't believe it when he told me that though there were only a few more weeks left in the school term, he would be finishing up his junior year at All Saints High. He said that by starting this semester – no matter how late – he would be allowed to participate on the sports teams in the fall.

"You must be pretty good in ball if you are willing to start a new school this late in the year," I pointed out. "I would have jumped at the chance to have some time off. What sport do you play?"

"Pretty much all of them," he grinned. "But that's not the only reason I want to go on and get started at All Saints." His voice took on a more serious tone as he continued. "To tell you the truth, Grace – I like school. Or maybe I should say I appreciate it. There was a time in my life, before my grandfather found me, when I was tossed from foster home to foster home and school to school. Many times, in fact, I never got to go to school at all. I guess I just fell through the cracks of the educational system." He shrugged. "I'm thrilled to be in school – to learn. I think learning is a gift and I intend to soak up everything I can. I hope to get a scholarship to college."

I was slightly taken aback by what he had to say. I even felt a little guilty. I had always taken school for granted. I certainly hadn't appreciated it. To me, school was a necessary evil, at best.

"Will you be trying to get a football scholarship?" It didn't even occur to me that a guy that looked like Locke would be awarded benefits based on anything other than athletics. I was knee-deep in football country in Alabama. Folks ate, breathed and slept football. It wasn't a sport; it was a religion a million members strong, at least. One of the first questions people around here asked was, "Are you for Alabama or Auburn?" The state's oldest rivalry. Sometimes it was even the teachers doing the asking so I was more than a little intrigued when Locke responded the way he did.

"Heck, no – I'm actually wanting to get a philosophy degree. I'm hoping to get scholarship money based on my grades. Fortunately, my last foster family had me in a pretty good school so I've been fairly stable for the last two years, and my GPA is high. I'm really going to have to work hard this next year, though."

I couldn't help but be impressed. This guy had his life all mapped out. It sounded like he'd had a tough time of it too, though he hadn't let that hold him back. I suddenly had a picture go through my mind of Locke and me studying together at the huge dining room table in the mansion, or maybe the pair of us walking down the halls of the high school, chatting and laughing like close friends.

But who was I kidding? It wouldn't take five minutes for the female vultures of All Saints High to descend upon a hottie like Locke. He, unlike me, would be instantly accepted into the ranks of the school royalty, while I sat like a serf watching from the gallery. But even though I had only just met Locke, I knew he would be nice to me at school. I mean, it wouldn't be like he would ignore me or anything. He wasn't that kind of guy. But just as Mrs. B. and Willem didn't run in the same circles as Merc, I didn't run in the same circles as someone like Locke. I was smart enough to know that and prideful enough not to let it bother me – or at least not to let it *show* that it bothered me. Oh well, there were only a few more weeks left of school and then I would have the whole glorious summer with Locke and with Merc. Things were definitely looking up.

I gave my new blonde friend directions to the bed and breakfast and before I knew it we were driving down the winding road leading to the front doors of my lodge home.

"You know, Grace, the mansion is pretty cool, but for my money, your digs are even better. What an awesome place to live!" He was staring down toward the dock, which was still lit up by the electric torches my brother and father had installed several months ago.

"Thanks Locke. It's okay, I guess." In truth, I hadn't paid that much attention to the bed and breakfast. I was so angry about having to move in with Pete and Patty that the surroundings just didn't do much to capture my attention. Also, in my mind, water equaled shorts and bathing suits, neither of which I would go near; so living on a lake felt like the worst kind of torture to me.

Locke gave me an odd sort of look before shrugging his shoulders and commenting, "Well, to each his own, I suppose, but I think it's beautiful out here."

Neither of us had mentioned Merc on the ride home. I figured Locke was not any more comfortable talking about him than I was, but right before I got out of the car he decided to bring him up.

"Grace, I'm absolutely sure that this is none of my business because I've only known you a few minutes, but I need to say something to you about that Merc."

I felt my body tense, wondering what was coming next. "Okay, Locke. What is it?"

"Well, it's like this, Grace," he started. "I don't know the guy, and I'm not in the habit of bashing people I don't know; but there is just something about him that I don't trust. I realize that girls tend to be into the whole rich/good looking thing, but rich and good looking doesn't always equal safe. I admit I feel a little sorry for him losing his parents and all – I can identify with that. But it doesn't change the fact that something just seems off with him. I've seen a lot of things in my short life, Grace – bad things and good things, bad people and good people – and while I don't think Merc is 'bad people,' I do think he has a darkness about him."

He paused for a moment, trying to gauge my reaction, and when I didn't respond he kept going. "Another thing is that Granddad . . . he seems to have some reservations about him, too. I've tried to ask him about it, but he won't really go into it. So, I don't know," he shrugged. "I guess what I'm trying to say is to be careful, and if you ever need me – just holler and I'll be at your side in a flash."

I was startled by the serious tone that suddenly colored Locke's voice but also flattered that he seemed to care about me. At least I knew a little more about Merc now than I did before. It didn't surprise me much that he had money – he had that air about him. But I wasn't expecting to hear that he was an orphan. I wondered if that would account for some of his "darkness" – the darkness I'd felt all around him and Locke had picked up on, too.

As much as I wanted to, I stopped myself from quizzing Locke about what he had just told me regarding Merc. I was curious but didn't want to seem too nosy or overeager. I wasn't going to let his warning prevent me from having breakfast with Merc, but I would be on my guard with him, trying to get to know him a little at a time. That is, if he hadn't forgotten all about me by the morning!

"Thank you, Locke. I *will* keep that in mind. I really do appreciate it." I tried to match my tone to his more serious one, but he was finished with serious and, instead, broke into a huge grin.

"Great! Well, let's get you inside. I bet your family is wondering where you've been. He opened the car door but turned back to me before adding, "By the way, I'll take care of getting your tire changed in the morning. I know Mrs. B. and Granddad were hoping you would come by tomorrow anyway. Would you like me to pick you up?"

"Well . . . I actually have some plans in the morning. I'll just have someone drop me off at the mansion, probably around eleven, if you think that will be okay." I hoped he hadn't picked up the little bit of hesitation in my tone, but when I looked at him I knew he had. He chose to ignore it, though, and instead responded lightly.

"Yeah, that sounds fine, Grace."

He came around to the passenger side of the limo and opened my door for me. He had clearly taken his grandfather's instructions seriously because he walked me all the way to the front door. He had almost made it back to the long black sedan when Patty and Pete came walking up from the car park area.

"Grace, we were worried to death about you! Where in the world have you been?" Pete demanded. "We thought you were swept away by the storm." He pointed toward Locke, who had by this time returned to my side looking for all intents and purposes to be my protector. "Who, may I ask, is this?"

Patty put a hand on Pete's arm, obviously trying to calm him down while at the same time trying to figure out what was going on. Her head swiveled from the limo to Locke to me. If Pete hadn't been so mad, I might have laughed out loud at the look of utter bewilderment on her face.

"Well . . . what do you have to say for yourself, young lady?" Pete yelled.

That did it. I began giggling. "You did *not* just call me 'young lady,' Pete . . . did you?"

My laugher caught both Patty and Pete off guard. I guess I hadn't laughed too often around them since moving in. They both stood there staring at me like I'd lost my mind, so Locke took the moment of silence to jump in.

"Hi!" He stepped forward with hand extended toward Pete, who reticently took it in his. "I know you must have been so worried about Grace. Her car broke down on my family's property while she was delivering food to us. We should have called you; it was really thoughtless of us not to. I'm Locke Wingard."

Embarrassed by his display of anger, Pete vigorously re-shook Locke's hand and then, turning to Patty, made proper introductions. "Locke, this is my wife, Patty. Please forgive us for being so rude. We really were worried, what with the bad weather and all."

After warmly shaking Locke's hand, Patty turned to me. "I'm sorry, Grace. I should have never sent you out in such a storm. I just wasn't paying attention to what the weather was doing." She then shifted her attention to Locke. "Locke, thank you so much for taking care of Gracie. We really owe you one. Would you like to come in and have some tea or coffee?"

I was torn. I really liked Locke and any other time I would have jumped at the chance for him to come into my home and drink tea. But I needed some time to myself – time to prepare for my breakfast with Merc.

Once again, Locke seemed to read my mind, because he declined the offer. "Thank you so much for the invitation, Patty. I would love to, but I know my grandfather is expecting me back and I don't want him to worry. I sure would like to come back again, though. Your place is just beautiful."

"Anytime, Locke," Pete offered while beaming at the compliment. "And, again, thank you so much for helping out Grace. We will get the car picked up in the morning."

"No, no – Grace and I have all that worked out already. But I hope to see you guys soon. Have a great night!"

I walked to the car with him, joyfully aware of Pete and Patty's eyes burning a hole in my back.

"Grace," Locke started, as he opened the limo door. "I was wondering if you wanted to go on a picnic tomorrow afternoon? It's supposed to be a really pretty day. I thought it might be fun."

This cannot be happening to me! I was so stunned I couldn't formulate an answer right away. I finally choked out a weak, "sounds great," before turning and floating into the doors of the Martin's Nest.

It came as no surprise that Pete and Patty were full of questions about my night. Any other time, I would have reacted badly to what I would have viewed as an invasion of my privacy. But this wasn't any other night. This was the greatest single night of my life, so I behaved in a way totally uncharacteristic of my normal self. I told them everything – well, almost everything.

I actually enjoyed telling them the story, and they seemed to enjoy hearing it, laughing in all the right places, commiserating with my fear or confusion in others. I skimmed over the part about my tearful breakdown and didn't go into any detail concerning my instincts regarding Merc's dark nature, but other than those minor deletions I was quite forthcoming. To say my brother and his wife were bewildered by my sudden change in nature might be an understatement; they were floored. But they took it all in stride, clearly thrilled at whatever happened to have created such a drastic alteration in my normally irritable, unsociable behavior.

They both put up a good show protesting my change of employment plans for the summer. I knew they would far prefer hiring someone with housekeeping experience or at least someone willing to make up a bed without putting up a fight, but they had gone along with Mom and Dad's suggestion to hire me just to keep the peace. Now they would have the opportunity to get a real "household technician" and no one would be mad at them – a really good thing for two people-pleasers like Pete and Patty. It was a win-win for them, but they were careful not to act too happy about it. They were genuinely pleased for my good fortune, and, for once, I headed up to bed light-hearted and happy with all the world.

My normal nighttime routine consisted of a two-pronged procedure designed to put both my body and mind at rest. The first part of the operation was a long and piping hot bath, which when completed left me nearly comatose and as relaxed as I was ever likely to be. The second involved security and was a complicated series of checks and rechecks of my closet and windows. These checks were followed by a full-scale maintenance inspection of the ceiling fan in my room, performed to insure no loose blade separated from the fan base and decapitated me in the dead of night while I lay sleeping.

My bedtime routine was written in stone, but this was a night of firsts and by the time I finished relating my story to Pete and Patty, I was so tired that I had little energy left for any more than a little water thrown on my face and a cursory glance around my room and under my bed. I did decide not to test my luck any further by risking a beheading, so I turned down the thermostat and turned off the fan. As predicted, sleep was difficult with excited recollections playing in and around my brain. When I finally dozed off, my slumber was haunted by strange flashes of images that I couldn't decipher or, if I could, I couldn't remember.

Chapter Five

FRIEND OF THE DEVIL

LOCHEDUS KNEW THAT THE OTHERS WERE WAITING FOR HIM, BUT HE WAS drawn, as he so often was, back to the place he felt most at home. It didn't even matter to him that he knew his brother would be waiting for him there, ready with his barbs and innuendos designed to create in Lochedus doubts and insecurities. Being who he was – a son of the Most High – did not make him immune to such tricks; it just made him a little more aware. He had barely made it through the gate when the expected voice, rife with arrogant disdain, broke through the darkness.

"I have to say, brother, you have more of a talent for subterfuge than I would have imagined. Are you sure you are fighting for the right side?"

Despite his best efforts, Lochedus felt his resentment rise but, with a deep breath and a quick prayer, he managed to harness his escalating enmity and answer in a voice that, for the most part, camouflaged his feelings. "There is just one true side, Beladona, and you are not on it. For the record, I do not employ 'subterfuge' – that is a tool for the lost."

"Oh, reeeallly?" The dark boy drew out his words in an effort to antagonize his brother. "Then you don't consider presenting yourself as someone you are not, deception? It sounds to me as if you are deceiving yourself, Lochedus – and poor, poor Grace."

Lochedus fought desperately to remain in control. It literally made him sick to hear the girl's name come out of his brother's mouth. He tried counting the way Grace did and, to his surprise, after a moment he was calm enough to continue. "I am deceiving no one, Beladona, but to explain it to you is simply not a priority for me. Let's just say my intentions, unlike yours, are pure."

Lochedus couldn't help feeling a little proud of himself, though he knew pride to be a slippery slope. He felt he was holding his own in the verbal sparring match with Beladona – not an easy thing to do. But bitter banter and sarcasm were the tools of the wicked so he had little skill employing such devices and his confidence was short-lived.

Like fingernails on a chalkboard, his brother's rancorous voice purred a response, "Hmmm . . . what is it that they say the road to Hell is paved with? Oh, yes . . . I remember . . . good intentions."

Sensing a triumph was near, Beladona stepped from the inky recesses of the garden to stand directly in front of Lochedus before continuing. "And, if your motives are only good and pure, then why haven't you enlisted the help of the Heavenly Hosts? Methinks the angel do protest too much!"

Too late, Lochedus realized that he had never enjoyed a moment's victory against his brother's vicious "wordsmanship." He wasn't supposed to. Feeling defeated, he fled his beloved garden with his brother's malevolent laughter ringing in his ears.

Chapter Six

JANE

STRIDING THROUGH THE DIMLY LIT COURTYARD OF THE MANSION, Lochedus made a conscious effort to shake off the ominous mood brought on by the confrontation with Beladona. He knew he should be accustomed to his brother's rhetoric by now, but he was a sensitive soul and the evil words that flowed so easily from the mouth of his brother hurt him deeply. He didn't want the two old people inside the house to be damaged vicariously by his darkened mood, so he paused before breaching the French doors to the living room, to pray for confidence and peace.

He was so engrossed in his own thoughts and prayers he did not, at first, notice that he was not alone.

"Lochedus, why are you so troubled?" The familiar loved voice bathed over him like a warm shower, immediately refreshing and rejuvenating his soul.

He turned to see a statuesque, beautiful black woman dressed in a flowing robe of perfect white. On her forehead, she wore a jewel-encrusted band of pure gold accenting her large topaz eyes and high cheekbones. Her ebony skin glowed with vitality and an inner light unlike any found on earth.

"Jane!" he cried, flinging himself into her arms. "I can't tell you how glad I am to see you."

The woman laughed, returning Lochedus' exuberant hug. She took him by the arms, pushing him back so that she could look down into his face from her six-foot-six-inch height. The smile she bestowed upon him was full of affection and indulgence, such as one gives to a naughty but much beloved child. "Hello love, you are looking very . . . modern." She eyed his blue jeans and plaid shirt with a mixture of humor and confusion.

Lochedus returned the laughter, glancing down with a look of surprise, as if only just noticing that he was, indeed, wearing clothes at all. "Oh . . . these old things. I just had them hanging in the back of my closet." He did a quick spin around, suddenly feeling lighter and more carefree than he had in days.

The woman burst into gales of laughter that filled the courtyard. "Silly boy, enough of the doom and gloom! Surely you know what to expect from one such as Beladona. You simply cannot put any credence in his words. Your motives are pure – aren't they?" She grasped his shoulders with both hands and her tone grew more serious. "Do not let him convince you otherwise. Your 'brother' works for the author of lies; never forget that. Besides, Beladona is not your real problem. He should be the easy one."

The young man's eyebrows shot together as he looked at Jane, genuinely perplexed. "What do you mean, he is not my problem? Then who is, pray tell?"

Jane placed a calming hand upon the boy's arm, sending by her very touch waves of peacefulness throughout his body. "Certainly Beladona is a problem, Lochedus, but he is a known entity – always easier to deal with. You must be most cautious of the unknown – those parading as good, when indeed they are not. And don't forget as long as one has a heartbeat, they have a soul capable of saving. Nothing is ever as simple as black and white, dear one. You must be diligent, patient and forgiving. You must be constantly seeking ways to turn hatred into love."

The majestic black angel's voice lost its softness as she gave him a look that spoke volumes. "You are here for a reason. Make sure you never forget that and make sure you don't confuse earthly feelings for heavenly ones."

He'd not been trying to hide his motives, but he hadn't exactly been forthcoming either. One look from Jane told him that nothing was hidden from her. She knew everything, yet she was still willing to help. With reverence and appreciation, he sank to his knees and kissed the hem of her robe in supplication.

She leaned over as if to kiss the top of his head, but instead put her lips to his ear and whispered urgently, "Be careful, Lochedus. This mission you have chosen is a difficult one and more important than you know. There is great controversy between our kind regarding the plan, so be cautious and watch your back." With a furtive glance she looked around before continuing. "You will be living among humans, but you must never allow yourself to think like one. There is danger for your soul down that path. You will be susceptible to all the human frailties that as angels we do not possess. Greed, lust, pride and jealousy will bring you low, Lochedus, and you must constantly guard against them."

She took his hands and lifted him up from his kneeling position to stand face to face with her. "I don't know if I will be allowed to return to you again, but I will be watching and praying. Be strong, my brother, and never forget who you are."

She evaporated instantly into the night air, leaving Lochedus feeling both relieved and apprehensive at once. But he took her words to heart, and like a soldier who'd been issued orders for battle, he straightened his shoulders and marched into the mansion.

Chapter Seven

BREAKING THE LAW

I WOKE AT 6:45 AM TO THE SOUND OF MY CD PLAYER/ALARM CLOCK blaring "Rock Me Like a Hurricane." Feeling excited, if not completely rested, I headed straight for the shower and let the hot, then cold, water do what my fitful night's sleep had not. Finally feeling completely alert, I slathered baby lotion from head to toe, wrapped a big fuzzy towel around me, and headed for the unpleasant task that lay before me – wardrobe selection.

For most girls my age, picking out clothes was something to look forward to – to relish. For me, it was a different animal altogether. It was a wholly unpleasant, even dreaded activity. Over the years, I had simplified my misery by limiting my selection to what amounted to a uniform of black or dark blue T-shirts bearing my preferred band's logo; hoodies or sweatshirts – same color palette/ same subject; jeans – black, indigo or slightly lighter if I was feeling slightly slimmer; and Converse tennis shoes. The tennis shoes I wore came in a wide range of colors and patterns. I loved bright colors, but I was just very aware of the tragedy of hot pink and green madras on wide hips and wasn't about to make that mistake! Every ensemble I chose, every time, was designed to cover up, to camouflage, to create the illusion of a taller, thinner me. In actuality, my choices *did* create an illusion – an illusion that I was immersed in a gothic lifestyle. That was okay with me, just as long as I looked like a taller, thinner "Goth."

Despite the uniformity of my wardrobe, it still took me over an hour to select just the *right* black T-shirt and jeans for my breakfast with Merc and my picnic with Locke. I hadn't missed the "dress code" comment made by Mrs. B. either, but I would just have to explain to her that I hadn't had the time or the funds to buy anything new yet.

I screamed, "Hallelujah!" as a few light water drops hit my bedroom window, giving me the needed excuse to top my jeans with a raincoat. There was nothing like a slicker to cover up the sins of *my* flesh. After dressing, I blew dry my long, curly hair, taking the time to use the diffuser so that my curls would fully form rather than deteriorate into a big, frizzy mess.

I was putting my blow dryer back in the bathroom drawer when I spotted the box of makeup I hadn't touched since moving to Alabama. Thinking this was a pretty good time to pull the Maybelline out of mothballs, I grabbed the crate of powders and goos and headed to my bedroom to sit at the antique dressing table that had been passed down from my Grandma Kate.

I had just started the arduous, and somewhat fruitless task of seeking out and curling my barely-there eyelashes, when Patty walked into the room.

"Hi, Grace!" she said, propping her little bitty self against the doorframe of my bedroom. She was dressed in purple-and-white striped nylon running shorts and a purple baby "T", looking every bit of 100 pounds soaking wet. "I just wanted to tell you I hope you have a great time on your dates today. You must be so excited! Two gorgeous guys – what fun!" she enthused.

I eyed her enviously, desperately hoping that she and her shorts would be nowhere around when Merc picked me up. "Yeah . . . thanks, Patty." I was trying hard to sound upbeat – to overcome my jealousy. She *was* always so nice.

But then she uttered the phrase that would send me right over the edge – the phrase that every chubby girl knew well and hated. "You know, Grace, you don't really need makeup. You have such a pretty face."

OH, NO, SHE DIDN'T!!! I couldn't believe she had actually said it. Didn't *she* know that *I* knew what that statement really meant? Roughly translated, it meant your face may be tolerable enough, but your body is a disgusting blob. I was 100 percent certain that no one had *ever* spoken those words to a thin girl. Not ever. I mean, what would the harm have been in saying, "Grace, you don't need makeup because you are so pretty?" Would the "truth police" come knock down her door and arrest her for including me – in all my entirety – in the compliment?

Well, thanks to St. Pat, my "pretty face" was purple with anger and embarrassment as I disgustedly threw the mascara back into the box, got up from the chair and slammed the bedroom door closed in her shocked, hurt little face.

One, two, three, four . . . I started counting, trying to calm down, trying to get to my happy place – the one I'd been in last night.

I knew I had overreacted to Patty's remark just a little, but now none of that mattered. What mattered was that in a very short time, the man of my dreams – the man of *every* girl's dreams – was going to come to my home to pick me up for breakfast.

Or was he? There it was – the thought I had not allowed myself to entertain. It had always been my experience that if things were too good to be true, they usually weren't; true, that is. It just made no sense whatsoever that Merc would have any interest in me. I had tried my best not to look the proverbial gift horse in its mouth, but I was nothing if not analytical, and the whole thing just did not hold up in close analysis.

So that was my train of thought and what was really bothering me. Sure, the "pretty face" comment ticked me off, but the truth of the matter was I was scared – plain and simple. I was petrified that Merc wouldn't show up at my door, as promised, to take me to breakfast and perhaps even more frightened that he would, because that would mean that something was terribly, terribly wrong with him.

I didn't consider there to be any alternatives to those two scenarios. I didn't dare – not even once – entertain the notion that a guy as beautiful, as dynamic, as sexy as Merc could possibly find me, in any way, appealing. And as long as I was deadly honest with myself and understood the way things were right from the very beginning, then I eliminated the possibility of getting hurt – really hurt.

So that's pretty much the way I lived my life. I never expected anything but the worst from myself or from other people. That way, no one – including myself – could ever really let me down. I had kind of lost sight of that mindset last night and allowed myself to hope, if only for a moment. Now I had my feet planted firmly back on the ground of reality, and I was confident that when that car did not pull down our drive and Merc did not knock on our door, I would be all right – just fine – because it would be nothing more than what I had expected all along.

It was 8:55 – five minutes before my scheduled date with Merc – when, glancing out the picture window of the inn, I spotted Pete hammering a loose railing on the pier and decided to walk down and talk to him. Sure that Merc would stand me up, I faced the embarrassing task of asking my brother for a lift to the mansion. Normally, I wouldn't think twice about asking Pete for help. He was a helpful kind of guy. But I realized that my recent run-in with Patty might have put him in a slightly less than cooperative mood. Maybe, I thought, she hadn't had time to blow the whistle on me yet, and I could get a commitment out of my brother before he found out about my churlish behavior toward his beloved.

I reeled out a few numbers for good measure, forced a smile on my face, and headed for the door, praying that I would not pass Patty on the way out. That's when I heard it – the ding, ding, ding of the chime that sounded every time the front door of the bed and breakfast opened. Scrupulously careful not to get my hopes up by reminding myself how many *other* people it could have been,

I threw up a quick prayer, counted to five, and headed for the front desk.

My footsteps faltered just before I rounded the corner that would bring the reception area into view. I mentally cursed my lack of foresight in not arranging for Patty to be on another part of the property well in advance of Merc's expected arrival. It wouldn't have taken much; Patty was susceptible to suggestion. I didn't make the suggestion because I didn't really believe for one minute that Merc would actually keep our date.

But saints be praised, Merc had shown up, and now I stood just beyond his view listening to my irritatingly adorable sister-in-law greet him doing her best impression of Scarlett O'Hara.

"Good Morning, Suh! Welcome to the Martin's Nest. How may I help you?" Her words were innocent enough, but the delivery was pure Belle.

"Good Morning," returned the deep, beautifully cultured voice that I'd played over and over in my head since last night. "I'm here to pick up Grace for breakfast. Is she around?"

I could only imagine the astonishment Patty felt upon realizing the boy with whom I was to have breakfast was one and the same as the Greek god standing before her. It wasn't like guys came around here looking for me on a regular basis; and now a boy comes strolling in, looking better than a body had a right to, asking for me – Gracie. Yeah, I would say St. Patty of Perfection was experiencing something roughly equivalent to hyperbolic shock. As annoyingly sweet as Patty surely was, she had been born a "have," while I was firmly ensconced in the world of "have nots." And, try as she might, she simply would not be able to completely mask her stupefaction at the realization that I had crossed the line between our two camps.

That brought up a whole interesting issue, which I had actually given some real thought while lying in my bed last night. Of course, this would only become a *real* issue should I begin spending time with Merchison on a regular basis. But assuming I had the chance to "keep company" with the gorgeous boy (admittedly, a huge assumption), I had a decision to make. Should I take every opportunity I could to show off my prize to those around me – flaunting my new "friend" for all the world to see – or should I keep him all to myself?

I found myself smiling at the thought of the looks on all the girls' faces at All Saints High – all the girls who had at one time or the other looked down their cute little Southern noses at me. This was my chance to prove to all of them that I was just as good, even better, than they were. And the boys – the ones who had never given me a second glance – would be forced to wonder what they had missed in me if a guy like Merchison Spear – so obviously superior to even the best of them – chose me, Grace, to be his companion.

Unfortunately, there was a Side B to this album, which might make Side A not worth the playing. Yep, there was most certainly a downside to parading Merc all over town. Once I'd let my genie out of the bottle, I might not be able to put him back in again. I had to consider the distinct possibility that Merc had shown an interest in me only because he hadn't met anyone else in the area. Simply put – he might be lonely. And if that was the case, parading him around every young single girl in the community could be a very big mistake.

I knew the girls around here – barracudas, the whole lot of them. Any one of them would steal her best friend's beau without hesitation if she were so inclined. They certainly wouldn't think twice about going after Merc right in front of me. I was no competition for most of them, either. I'd been all over the world and, if I was being honest, I would have to say that the girls around here were among the prettiest I had ever seen. I would love to think that Merc had seen some "indefinable something" in me that set me apart from all the others, but I thought it far more likely that he just hadn't had the time or inclination necessary to develop friendships in the area thus far.

Of course, for all its purported "Southern charm," Tallassee and the little towns surrounding it were as closed-off societies as I had ever lived in. The classes were well embedded and virtually impenetrable. Well, impenetrable to someone like me. But I suspected that looks and money such as Merc possessed would operate as twin battering rams in breaking down the walls of this small-town, Peyton Place caste system to allow him entrance. I could only assume that Merc's exile from the Tallassee elite was self-imposed, so as tempting as it was to up my social credibility by putting him on display, I knew I had better think twice before parading him around the downtown Dairy Queen on a Saturday night.

Merc's note hadn't mentioned where we would be eating, so I guess part of the decision would be out of my hands. Either way, this very well could be my one-and-only date with the boy, so there was no sense in over-analyzing the issue this early in the game. Nevertheless, I knew seeing St. Pat's reaction would be fun and with that thought in mind I pulled on my raincoat, fluffed out my hair, and rounded the corner to greet my breakfast partner.

I had been trying to convince myself all morning that my recollection of Merc was flawed – that he wasn't really all *that* good looking. I had only seen him in the dark, and I had been very nervous. But as he stood in the entranceway of my home, with the warm sunlight illuminating every square inch of the room, I could see that my memory had not begun to do him justice. His thick dark hair was windblown and slightly damp, and he was dressed simply in faded jeans and a white T-shirt. He wasn't just good looking – he was flawless. All my planned greetings fled my mind, leaving me virtually unable to put the words together to form an intelligible sentence. With a crooked smile and a knowing look, he greeted me.

"Hi, Grace! I hope I'm not early. I wanted to make sure I could find the place in the daylight."

I wondered what that meant. Had he found this place at night? Come to think of it, I had never told Merc where I lived, and I certainly didn't see him asking Locke for directions. I stowed the comment in the back of my mind for more careful examination later and, finally finding my tongue, greeted him. "Hi Merc! I hope you didn't have any trouble finding me."

He shook his head. "Not a bit – came right to it. You all must love living here. The Martin's Nest is just beautiful." He looked from me to Patty, making sure to include both of us in the compliment.

A flush of pure pleasure coursed through me at his words. Granted, I would have preferred him point out *my* beauty, but that would have been too much to ask and probably more than a little insincere, so I would settle for a compliment to my home. I was quite pleased with the look on Patty's face. She was clearly impressed with Merc's polished manners and erect bearing, marking him as more than just a pretty face. He was clearly the whole package, which probably, in Patty's mind, added to the mystery of what exactly he was doing here with me.

We accepted his kind words in unison. "Thanks!" I realized I really had no other choice but to introduce Merc to my sister-in-law.

"Patty, I would like you to meet Merchison Spear." I hadn't meant to go all "White Gloves and Party Manners," but I guess I was just reacting to the changes I immediately detected in Merc's behavior. Last night he was quick with the "honey" and "sugar" and came across as a laid-back party boy. This morning that boy was gone, replaced by a much more formal young man. The rakish flirt of the evening before now displayed a more refined, yet equally appealing, old-world charm.

That charm certainly seemed to be working on Patty and for one horrifying moment I thought she might curtsy. Thankfully, she simply dimpled prettily and responded with the modern Belle's curtsy equivalent – the hair toss.

"I'm so pleased to meet you, Merchison. You must be new around here; what brings you to our neck of the woods?" Patty's near waist-length blonde hair *was* beautiful and her signature toss was designed to bring attention to just that beauty – normally to great effect. So I almost cackled out loud when Merc chose that precise moment to let me know that his mischievous side was alive and well.

Ignoring her attention-getting move completely, as well as her attempt to pry into his background, he turned to me and after wolf-ishly winking, replied with a repeat of what he had told her earlier. "Oh, I'm here to beg Grace to join me for breakfast." Then almost as an afterthought more formally added, "It's very nice to meet you as well, Penny."

OMG! He didn't just call her the wrong name! His conspiratorial wink left little doubt in my mind that he misspoke intentionally.

To Patty's credit and my dismay, she merely laughed and corrected him sweetly. "It's Patty, actually – Merchison – but my mother did used to say I was like a bad penny – always turning up."

What the heck was *that* supposed to mean? Honestly, Patty could be such an airhead. Merc laughed right along with her but I noticed a strange, almost hostile, look flash in his eyes – just for a moment – then it was gone again. Had I imagined that? I didn't think so, but since I couldn't think of any good reason why Patty's remark should elicit a hostile reaction I marked it up to my overactive gray matter.

Feeling a little uneasy and having done my mannerly duties, I decided the best course of action was retreat. I considered, if only briefly, taking Merc down to the pier to introduce him to my brother but I didn't want to appear to be rushing things – making too big of a deal over my date. Instead, I turned to him and suggested we head out.

Merc again politely told Patty – getting her name right, this time – that it was nice meeting her, and we made for the door. His hand was on the doorknob when Patty's voice slowed our exit.

"Merc, I hope Pete and I will get to meet Mrs. B. and Willem soon. I know you live on their property and you probably bump into them from time to time. Please let them know we would love to have all of you over for dinner. In fact, would next Friday be good for you?"

I could have cheerfully cracked open the 12-gauge, loaded it up and shot her right where she stood. She might have had no way of knowing that Merc and the old folks didn't exactly get along but the invite was still way out of line. There were many reasons why a dinner with all the parties wouldn't be a good idea but those reasons paled in comparison to my biggest grievance. Patty's invitation to Merc could easily look like some sort of contrived attempt on my part to engineer a second date. I was mortified; but I needn't have been, because Merc – a.k.a. my hero – handled the problem with one fell swoop.

"Gosh, Patty, that is awfully kind of you but, unfortunately, Mrs. B. is not in very good health and she is actually a bit of a recluse. That was one of the main reasons she decided to hire an assistant – to hire Grace, that is. She doesn't get out. Believe me, I wish she would. I think it would be good for her. I think we are all hoping Grace will be a good influence on her, maybe get her out some." He flashed his blinding smile, full of warmth and concern over the poor dear woman from whom he rented his apartment.

I was blown away. Merc did a perfect imitation of a doting, caring friend and neighbor. One would have thought him a beloved grandson or nephew, even. He was clearly an accomplished liar – a fact I knew I should be concerned about but couldn't help feeling grateful for at the moment. My relief was short-lived because, to my surprise, Patty didn't seem to buy the line Merc was so beautifully peddling.

"Oh, really? Well, I see. That is unfortunate. I'd like to call and extend the invitation, just the same," she persisted. "Or maybe I could drop off some casseroles and say hey."

I gritted my teeth in anger. *God, casseroles!* The Southern woman's answer and excuse for everything. If a Belle wanted information, she got it with Poppy Seed Chicken Surprise or Aunt fill-in-the-blank's Sweet Potato Soufflé. This thing was getting out of control – quickly. I felt like I was in the middle of a verbal sparring match between Merc and Patty. It was all done ever so politely, but it was a contest just the same.

"As kind as the thought surely is, Patty," Merc parried, "Mrs. B. doesn't handle drop in company very well. I'm afraid the old dear might be rude to you. She wouldn't mean to be, you understand; she just gets flustered and sometimes it comes out all wrong. You know, it might be a good idea to drop a note to her by Grace. Then maybe Grace and I, together, can talk her into getting out – joining all of us for dinner. I have to warn you, though; she can be a stubborn old girl."

Merc's little speech rang with sincerity and affection and I found myself almost buying into his act. I could not believe it when Patty opened her mouth, yet again.

"Well, I don't know, I would still like to at least call her," she insisted. "After all, Grace will be spending quite a bit of time with this 'Mrs. B.' and we know nothing about her at all. Come to think of it, I don't even know her last name. What is it?"

"Oh, for gosh sake, you are not my mother, Patty," I bellowed in a most unladylike fashion. I didn't care because enough was enough. Who did she think she was? After the "pretty face" comment, she was dang lucky I had bothered introducing her to Merc at all. You would think she was twenty years older than me when the fact was she was barely five years my senior. There might have been some small part of me that was embarrassed that I hadn't bothered to get Mrs. B.'s full name myself last night, but for the most part I simply did not appreciate Patty's condescending attitude and nosy Nellie questions. I wasn't sure where Patty's motherly concern was coming from, but I wasn't about to let this precedent be set! I was going to nip it in the bud, and fast!

Determined to make a statement, I grabbed Merc's hand and literally pulled him out of the door before he could begin to respond to Patty's question or even say goodbye. Once outside, my eyes were immediately drawn to a small, bright-red sports car that I was certain could only belong to Merc. I didn't know much about cars, but I knew just by looking that this was a pricey one. It was flashy, it was hot – it was Merc.

I was trying to formulate some clever remark about my date's wheels in order to divert attention away from the little confrontation with Patty. I didn't want Merc to think that my family was a bunch of rednecks that constantly fought with each other – even if it was true.

I eyed the candy-apple convertible with considerable appreciation before turning to Merc. "Your car is gorgeous! What kind is it?"

He ran a hand down the side of the car with a huge grin. "Thanks! I have to admit, I love it. It's a 1957 Ford Thunderbird. I cleaned out my savings to get it, but I think it was worth it!"

I thought that I could die happy if Merc ever looked at me the way he just looked at that car – like it was the most gorgeous thing in the world - like he couldn't live without it. Clearly, the Thunderbird was important to him. I guess that made him a typical guy; though I didn't really think there was anything typical about him. Unfortunately, Merc's attention didn't stay on his much-loved car for long.

"Well, meeting Patty was certainly interesting," he remarked tentatively, as if fearing I might re-explode at the mention of her name.

"Yeah, well . . . I'm sorry about that little scene back there. Patty's not too bright and sometimes she can just drive me crazy." I glanced over at Merc, praying I wouldn't see the star-struck look in his eyes that most guys got when first seeing my sister-in-law.

"Really? Not too bright?" He raised an eyebrow. "I didn't get that feeling at all. She seems very perceptive, to me."

Jealousy blazed through my body like a house on fire. I'd always known that I couldn't compete with Patty in the looks department; however, I had always felt equally certain that she was no match for me in brainpower. Now Merc had effortlessly popped that bubble with one well-placed comment. I wasn't even sure how to respond, so I decided to change the subject.

"It really is nice out today." And, in truth, it was. The morning shower was over and the whole world seemed to glisten. The still-wet leaves of the cedar, birch and oak trees twinkled like diamonds in the morning sun, and the green water of Lake Martin sparkled so brightly that it was difficult to look directly at it without squinting.

The light morning breeze blowing through the trees made the temperature for now tolerable, even pleasant. But I was all too aware of how quickly that would change. In another hour or so, the humidity and temperature would climb to such a level as to make retreat to an air-conditioned cabin or car necessary. That is, unless you wanted to jump into the lake, which would require a change of attire - out of my uniform and into something with far less mate-rial. That was not happening – not now, not ever.

I wished I had the confidence to strip down and jump in; I just didn't. The thought of getting into a bikini – or even a one-piece

– in front of anyone, much less Merc, made me sick to my stomach. I also never wanted to be one of those girls who went into the water in a big ol' T-shirt. They might as well wear a sign on their back saying "Fat Chick" or "Big Girl." So I was stuck watching all the thin, confident people have fun.

Looking across the lake, I spotted our boat – full of some of those aforementioned thin people – headed for our dock. I had absolutely no interest whatsoever in standing with Merc watching the two bubbly blondes I knew to be on board bounce down the pier, so I nudged things along a bit.

"So are you ready to go?" I asked with fingers crossed. "I have to go by the mansion at some point, so we should probably head on." I didn't want to put an end-time on our date, but I wanted even less to have to introduce Merc to the buxom sisters soon to be on dry land. Thankfully, he took the hint.

"Hop in." He gave me a killer smile and opened my door, motioning for me to get in the car.

Before I knew it, we were speeding around the narrow country roads, taking hairpin turns without even slowing down. My heart was racing faster than the car, though I wasn't sure whether it was from fear or excitement - probably a little of both. I wished desperately that I had brought a scarf and sunglasses so I could do the whole "Grace Kelly" thing, but instead I spent a great deal of time pulling my hair out of my lip gloss while trying to remain looking cool. Merc only slowed the car one time, when we came up behind a large orange refuse truck blocking the right side of the road shedding its workers to pick up large limbs and trash from the storm the night before. He didn't sit still for long though, and just the second there was a tiny gap in the oncoming traffic he gunned his engine and swerved around the large vehicle, leaving the angry workers shaking their fists and heads behind him.

We drove on another five minutes or so before he said a word to me. Finally, when we came to a fork in the county road we were on, he stopped.

"I have a little surprise for you, Grace."

When he looked at me with those amazing amber eyes and said my name, I quit breathing completely.

"When I realized what a beautiful day it was," he continued, "I decided to stop and get some donuts and bagels and something to drink. I thought it would be more fun to drive and eat than go sit in a Cracker Barrel or something. Does that sound good to you?"

He could have suggested that we eat on the floor of the Mini-Mart and I would have agreed just to be with him; so riding around with him in his fabulous convertible was a no-brainer. I was a little disappointed that we probably wouldn't see anybody. I was also a little paranoid that he didn't want to be seen with me, but I tried to push that thought from my mind and just enjoy the experience.

"Sure, Merc ! That sounds perfect," I chirped, while attempting to make some sense out of the mess that was my hair.

"Great!" He hung a right onto the highway and then took an almost immediate left onto a dirt road. Pulling to a stop, he reached into his glove box and pushed a button that popped open the trunk of the little car. "I'll be right back," he said.

After a few moments of rambling around in the back of his car he returned with the promised box of donuts and bagels, along with a large silver thermos and two plastic goblets.

"I realize we are technically old enough to drink, but I don't really consider champagne alcohol. I thought some Mimosas would be a nice treat to celebrate your new job and our new friendship. You don't think there is anything wrong with having a little champagne with me, do you, Grace?" He asked.

He favored me with a heart-melting smile that would have made me agree to torturing kittens. I had never had a drink before and had never heard of a Mimosa. I guessed it was some type of champagne from what he had said. Alcohol was the big forbidden fruit in my home. My grandfather had been an alcoholic and my father was a firm believer in the disease theory that said it ran in families. The only time I had ever seen my father drink was after he returned home from a tour in Iraq when I was fourteen years old. He pretty much stayed drunk for about six months. Finally, after my mother threatened to leave him, he cleaned himself up and put the alcohol away for good. Now, there was a zero tolerance for liquor policy in my home. One would think it would take quite a bit of time and persuasion to defeat my years of anti-alcohol indoctrination. Sadly, all it took was a single dimple and some amazing golden-green eyes.

"No, I don't think there's anything wrong with just a sip or two, as long as I don't get drunk. I don't think Mrs. B. would appreciate my showing up for work wasted." I nervously giggled while silently praying that I wouldn't have some type of allergic reaction to the champagne. My father had always said our family had an allergy to alcohol. I hoped he had been exaggerating because the last thing I wanted was to break out in hives or start vomiting or something while I was with Merc.

"Oh, don't be silly." He scolded. You could drink every drop of champagne I brought and probably not even feel it. Besides, the orange juice will dilute the champagne. Trust me, you won't even get tipsy," he laughed.

For the briefest of moments, a picture of Adam and Eve in the garden flashed through my mind with Eve holding out the apple to Adam saying, "Trust me, Adam." Have Mercy! All my dad's lectures over the years had really done a number on me. I quickly reminded myself that Dad wasn't here now. He and Mom had dumped me with St. Patty and Perfect Pete. As far as I was concerned, that disqualified him from taking up space in my head or conscience. I determinedly forced the picture from my brain and reached for the bubbling glass Merc was holding out to me.

After pouring a glass for himself, Merc turned to me and asked quietly, "Well, Grace, what shall we toast to?" He wasn't laughing anymore. His face was inches from mine and he was staring at me in a way that made me want to flinch away. I wasn't used to such close scrutiny and I was afraid he was taking note of my every flaw. He, on the other hand, became only more perfect under intense inspection. At the moment, I was painfully aware of the sea of differences that separated us.

I wanted to look away from his beautiful stare but his "mood" eyes — moments ago amber now seafoam green - had me locked in a mesmerizing grip from which there was no escape. He leaned in even closer to me, and I thought that he was going to kiss me. I stopped breathing completely, closed my eyes and waited for the magic to happen. But it never did.

Massively mortified, I finally lifted my lids, hoping that he wouldn't be looking at me like I was some kind of idiot. He *was* looking at me but not with disgust. He was staring at me intently with an expression that read somewhere between bemusement and bewitchment. It took an amazing amount of restraint not to turn away. I had always dreamed of basking in the warm gaze of my heart's desire. But in reality it was very difficult — almost painful — to open oneself up to that extent. I felt stripped naked and laid out bare. To add to my discomfort, Merc seemed as shaken as I by our closeness.

After what seemed to be an eternity, he leaned away from me and in a strangled voice tinged with forced gaiety said, "Let's toast to beginnings."

He held his glass to mine and I noticed that his hand was slightly trembling. I didn't know what was going on, but the mood had definitely changed in the car. We both struggled to throw off the unsettling feeling and after clinking our glasses Merc drank the entire contents of his in one gulp. I tentatively brought the plastic goblet to my lips, laughing nervously at the bubbles tickling my nose, and prepared to sample my first taste of alcohol.

Just like my first kiss, this new experience was to be indefinitely delayed because at that precise moment the blue lights came into view.

"Damn," Merc muttered under his breath, as he looked first in his rear-view mirror and then over his shoulder.

Panicked, I looked at Merc, hoping to see the calm on his face that would indicate a minor inconvenience rather than a major catastrophe. I wasn't well versed in traffic laws as they pertained to alcohol but I was praying our obvious sobriety would prevent us from being hauled to the clink.

"Damn," he repeated with a tone to his voice that sent a cold chill down my spine.

I turned to him and what I saw – the dark look on his face – filled me with far more dread than the siren or blue lights. Merc wasn't frightened. He wasn't worried. He was absolutely, positively furious. I had never seen such a look of blind rage on a person's face, and it scared me to death. Tears filled my eyes as I struggled to find the words that would calm him down. I didn't know how much trouble we were in, but I did know that striking a police officer would only compound the problem, and Merc looked as if he was moments away from doing just that.

Thankfully by the time the tall, thin, salt-and-pepper haired sheriff reached Merc's driver's side door, Merc's look of rage was gone and in its place was a sheepish, apologetic look. In my shock I had unfortunately dropped my Mimosa onto my lap, the car seat and the floorboard. Conversely, my date had magically produced a driver's license and vehicle registration card.

How did he do that? I never saw him hide his glass, get his wallet or open the glove compartment. Yet there he sat with license and registration in one hand and nothing in the other.

If the appearance of the sheriff surprised me, the next person on the scene blew me away. As Merc was asking the sheriff what the problem was, a second figure appeared in my peripheral vision.

"Excuse me, Officer, may I speak with you for just a moment?"

I recognized that voice. *Oh Lord . . . PLEASE . . . tell me that isn't who I think it is.* I slowly turned around in my seat only to see that it was exactly who I thought it was. It was Mrs. B. and she was talking to the sheriff.

I was almost scared to look over at Merc, afraid that the sudden appearance of the old woman would cause his frightening temper to re-emerge. With my heart pounding and my head down, I peeked through my hair to see him, still holding his license and registration, barely containing laughter.

"Mrs. B., I presume?" he said, struggling to maintain his composure.

Wait a minute . . . what's wrong with this picture? I knew that Merc wasn't close with Mrs. B. in the way I had led my family to believe, but had he never met her or at least seen her on the property?

"You mean you don't know her?" I hissed under my breath. This probably wasn't the best time to ask for an explanation, but I did have a few questions.

I heard Mrs. B.'s piercing voice raise an octave and I could only assume that the sheriff had said something that displeased Her Highness – poor, poor man. He had no idea what was about to hit him. She looked so harmless, but nothing could be further from the truth.

"She's quite a bird, isn't she?" Merc laughed as he calmly unscrewed the top of the thermos and took a quick sip before closing it back tightly and tossing it behind the seat. "No sense letting good champagne go to waste."

My eyes bugged out, shocked at his action. He really was one cool customer.

"Aren't you freaking out? We could go to jail. There are laws against drunk driving in this state – in every state. Mother's Against Drunk Drivers has worked hard to have tougher laws enacted."

A M.A.D.D. representative had spoken at the school recently. I might not have listened to the whole thing, but I did catch the highlights.

"I'm not sure of all the details," I whispered frantically. "But I know we could be in big trouble. I remember something about an open container law." I was completely unnerved by the entire situation. Merc, however, seemed almost giddy now – completely unconcerned.

"Grace." He put his warm hand on top of mine, and I was ashamed to realize that even in the current crisis the mere touch of his hand could send my pulse into overdrive. "We are not drunk. And though we did – or rather *I* did – technically break the law, your new employer appears to have things well under control."

He reached up and pushed my hair behind one ear and my stomach did three flips.

After my breath returned, I looked behind me to see Mrs. B. and the sheriff shaking hands. For the first time I noticed the car that had pulled in behind the sheriff's car. It was the long, black limo and at that very moment Willem was opening the driver's door and getting out. I wished the earth could have opened up and swallowed me whole.

I continued to gape in horror as Willem strode straight past the sheriff and Mrs. B. and came to a stop right next to where I sat in the convertible. I wanted to hide under the seat or in the trunk – anywhere to keep from having to look into Willem's disappointed eyes.

"Hello, Gracie," he said while opening my door. "How about I give you a ride to work this morning?"

I flushed red to my roots but managed to stammer, "I don't know . . . what about Merc? Am I in trouble?" I glanced back at the sheriff's car, too humiliated to look at Willem.

"*You* are not in trouble. *Merc,* however, will not be available to drive you anywhere." Willem's tone left no room for argument.

Willem may have been speaking to me but he and Merc seemed to be having an entirely different, unspoken and highly unpleasant conversation; the old, stern eyes locked in a death match with the young defiant green ones. It was a few seconds before anyone spoke again.

"Sorry about this, Gracie," Merc apologized, and for a minute he sounded both confused and despondent. He leaned over and kissed my cheek, surprising me and infuriating the normally unshakably sweet Willem. "Maybe I could pick you up after work and take you home." He offered, failing to pick up on the fact that he had pushed Willem way too far.

Willem's response was lightning-fast and almost violent. He grabbed my hand in one of his huge hands and my purse in the other, pulling me out of the car and slamming the door shut. In a voice barely above a whisper but far more lethal than I thought possible for Willem, he responded to Merc's offer for me.

"We have already taken care of Grace's car problem. You need not worry yourself about anything as it pertains to Gracie right now. You have your own issues to deal with – don't you?" He then leaned into the car so that his face was only inches away from Merc's and whispered something I could not make out.

I fully expected Merc to react to Willem violently. I don't know what I would have done if he had. I loved Willem but I was incredibly attracted to Merc. It was most inconvenient for me that the two seemed to have some real problems between them. I was going to have to find out the reason behind their animosity toward each other.

I knew that Willem would have definitely preferred me to just walk away from the car and not look back but I just couldn't do it. I turned to Merc, with my hand still in Willem's, to say goodbye.

Merc's face had gone white as a sheet and he was staring at Willem as if he had seen a ghost. Things were getting stranger and stranger. I wished I knew what Willem had said to Merc because it clearly upset him. Feeling the tug of Willem's hand, I shook off my own confusion and said goodbye to my dream date, trying hard to convey as many messages as I could in as few a words as possible. I wanted him to know I had enjoyed myself and that I really, really wanted to see him again. I couldn't say that – not with Willem right there; I was hoping my tone of voice would say what my words could not.

"Merc, I had a good time, despite what happened. I appreciate your willingness to help with my car, too; I really owe you one." That was the best I could do under the circumstances. I hoped I would have another opportunity to see the boy who was looking more like a true Romeo with every minute that passed. The stage was set and the players all present and accounted for. I just prayed I wouldn't have to drink any poison to be with my man.

Merc's response to my short speech – or lack thereof – left me feeling as if my little Shakespeare fantasy was just that, a fantasy. He didn't thank me or even acknowledge my thanks. He just sat there, staring straight ahead as if I'd never said a thing.

Aghast at his snub, I allowed Willem to usher me to the back of the waiting limo. He politely helped me into the backseat and then closed the door and walked over to where the sheriff and Mrs. B. were still talking. I strained to see if I could make out anything that was happening among all the adults or, even more importantly, between the adults and Merc.

Finally, realizing that I wasn't going to figure out anything from inside the car, and knowing it would be inappropriate for me to get out, I settled back into the plush leather seat and for the first time took notice of the sumptuousness of my surroundings. With the exception of the short ride in the front seat with Locke last night, I had never been anywhere near a limousine. I had heard kids at different schools I had attended talking about renting them for proms and dances, but since I had never been asked to a dance before, what to ride to one in had never been an issue for me. I mentally added this to the list of new experiences I'd had over the past twenty-four hours. Of course, I would have preferred experiencing a limo ride as a prelude to a date rather than an alternative to a patrol car but, as my mom was fond of saying, "Beggars can't be choosers."

I lay my head back against the buttery leather and closed my eyes, silently counting in an attempt to regain some sense of control over my rising panic.

I knew my chief concern *should* be retaining my new job. It would be the height of pitiful ignorance to place more importance on a guy I barely knew, and would probably never see again, over well-paying gainful employment. I desperately tried to recall the incredible sense of excitement and satisfaction I had felt when leaving the mansion last night. I had been on Cloud 9 and now that jubilation was being overshadowed – rendered unimportant – simply because a good-looking (okay, great looking) guy had paid me a tiny bit of attention.

I hadn't even been asked to *choose* between the old folks and Merc. In fact, at this point, I had no idea whether I had either one to choose from any longer. But I had a strong feeling that I was standing dead in the middle of two distinctly opposing forces; and before it was over with, I was going to have to make a choice.

One, two, three, four, five . . . How had things gone so wrong so quickly?

One, two, three, four . . . What was going on outside the limo?

One, two, three . . . Would I ever see Merc again?

One, two . . . Would I still have a job when the old people got in the car, or would I be re-sentenced to the bed and breakfast for the summer?

One . . . Could all I had gained over the past few hours be cruelly taken away from me in the space of a few short minutes?

Counting was not helping me and I couldn't take the suspense a minute longer. I lurched forward onto my knees and crawled between the two facing bench seats, trying to get a better look through the window divider that separated the passenger seats from that of the driver. Unfortunately, that was the precise moment that Mrs. B. chose to enter the car.

Embarrassed beyond belief, I scrambled from my knees and took the bench nearest to where I had been caught crawling. I braced for the worst, holding my breath and waiting for what I was sure would be a blistering firestorm of criticism from the old lady.

I watched Willem help Ms. B. into the car and then fold his long frame in behind her, taking the seat directly across from mine. I wondered if he chose to get in the back to protect me from the old woman's sarcastic wrath.

"Lovely to see you again, Grace," Mrs. B. remarked sweetly. Though the expected sarcasm was present, there was also something else in her greeting, something far from expected – humor.

Until that moment, I hadn't looked at her; afraid of the anger I would surely see. But now that I did, I couldn't believe my eyes. She was trying her best to keep from laughing. I didn't understand exactly what was happening, but I was greatly relieved just the same. I intended on taking full advantage of the unexpected turn of events.

"I'm really sorry about all of this. Honestly I am," I started. "I promise nothing like this will ever happen again. That is, if you still want me for the job. I sure hope you do."

I tried to remember all the things my father had drilled into my head over the years. I sat up straight. I looked the old woman in the eyes and tried to impart sincerity and trustworthiness – both traits that had been called into question by my actions of the morning. If I was going to manipulate this thing to my favor I needed to appear as earnest as possible.

"Yes . . . well, let's not dwell on the past," she said with an imperious wave of her hand. There was a twinkle in her eye that I found, if not frightening, certainly unsettling. "We've all made mistakes, my dear," she added with a wink.

I couldn't believe my good fortune . . . until Willem jumped in with both feet.

"Some more than others, Mrs. B." His face was beet red as if he was fighting fury.

I wasn't sure whether he was mad at me or the old lady or both. Were they playing good cop/bad cop with me? If they were, they had reversed the roles. It was disconcerting, to say the least. I wasn't sure what to do, so I finally went the way of the coward. I sat back and let the old folks battle it out.

"Oh, please, Willem. No harm was done. Grace didn't drink anything; you said so yourself. And even if she had it wouldn't have been the end of the world. I'm not sure that balance isn't preferable to abstinence anyway."

"Balance? Balance? Are you serious, Mrs. B.? And who is going to teach Grace that balance . . . you?" Willem was raising his voice, clearly upset; I realized the relationship between the two old people was far more complicated than that of employer/employee.

And what was all this talk about "teaching me balance," for Heaven's sake? Not for the first time in the last twenty-four hours, the hair on the back of my neck stood up. Something really, really weird was going on but whatever it was, I was drawn to it all like a moth to a flame.

Both adults seemed to remember my presence at the exact same moment, but it was Willem, with a sheepish look, that addressed me directly for the first time since putting me into the car.

"Please excuse our manners, Gracie. Mrs. B. and I have been together for so long that we forget – or I forget – my place sometimes. We may have a funny way of showing it but we are both just concerned about you and what's best for you. We may not always agree on what that is, though."

This was beyond bizarre. They were talking to me like I was their child and they were divorcing parents. How could they care so much about me when they had known me for less than a day? I was getting a very spooky feeling but I wasn't sure what to do about it. I was absolutely positive that they meant me no harm. Even Mrs. B., for all her snipes and criticisms, wasn't out to get me. I knew that. So I saw no reason for not hanging out, collecting a paycheck, and finding out exactly who these people were and who they were to *me*.

"I understand, Willem. It's no big deal," I said with a conviction I didn't really feel at the time.

He reached across and patted my hand, giving me a sweet smile. "Well, we'll just drop all this for now. If I'm not mistaken, you have a lunch date you don't want to be late for."

I heard Mrs. B. make a "hrmpph" sound and looked over in time to see her rolling her eyes.

"Oh, yes, by all means, let's not forget Grace's picnic with Locke." Her sardonic personality was back in full force.

The way she had said Locke's name left me wondering whether she had something against him. I couldn't imagine anyone disliking Locke, but if anyone could, it would be the old lady. It was just one more thing to think about – to wonder about – to try to figure out. My nondescript, non-interesting life had suddenly become a puzzle to solve.

With a withering look shot at Mrs. B., Willem left the backseat in order to get behind the wheel and drive us to the mansion. I was grateful that the old woman decided to close her eyes and take a nap rather than talk to me. Willem was quiet, too, so I followed suit and used the short time in the car to mentally prepare for my next date.

As we pulled to the front of the house, Willem popped out of the car ready to assist us in getting out. It didn't feel right to sit waiting for him to open a door that I was more than capable of opening myself. As I put my hand on the handle, a very much awake Mrs. B. grasped my arm with a surprisingly strong grip.

"Grace . . . listen to me! Don't let anyone keep you from your heart's desire. You and only you know who that person is. Don't let someone else's fears become yours. If you want your life to be happy and fulfilled, you have to do what is necessary to get what you need. Do you understand me?" She was staring directly into my face with an urgent look, demanding an answer to what was obviously not a rhetorical question.

I was so shocked by her sudden outburst that it took me a moment to answer, which gave Willem time to open the back door of the limo. From the look on Mrs. B.'s face I knew that this was not a discussion she wanted to have in front of the old man. Even so, she seemed to desperately need some physical sign that I understood what she had said to me, so I simply nodded my head in assent. Seemingly satisfied with my response, she took Willem's proffered hand and departed the car without a backward glance.

After my disastrous date with Merc, my first impulse was to follow Willem into the house and beg him for a ride home. I would have liked nothing better than to have some time alone. It would have been good to be able to think through everything that had happened. But upon closer reflection I realized that running away and not going through with my date would be both selfish and counterproductive. I didn't have the same fears about Locke as I had with Merc. I knew he would show up with figurative, if not literal, picnic basket in hand. I also knew that I would have a good time. Locke would make sure of it. Though I had no practical experience in the area, I had always heard that the best way to get over a guy was with a guy. The old adage, "If you can't be with the one you love, then love the one you're with" seemed particularly apropos at the time; so, game on.

Chapter Eight

WHEELS OF CONFUSION

I FOLLOWED THE OLD COUPLE INTO THE HOUSE AND EXCUSED MYSELF TO freshen up for round two. I walked into the powder room, marveling that it was actually bigger than the space I slept in. It was lavishly decorated with a pair of shell-shaped sinks with gold fixtures. Above the sinks hung twin antique mirrors in the center of which was an ornate sconce dripping with crystals in the shapes of teardrops and flowers. A separate sitting area was arranged with a small, silk-covered sofa and delicately carved French salon chairs. The walls were painted in an aged red stamped with gold fleur-de-lis.

I knew people paid thousands and thousands of dollars to cre-ate the appearance of "old," but I was sure this was no illusion. Unlike the exterior, everything was well kept and immaculate, and it was the real thing. It was like stepping back into time, into an old French manor house – only with working plumbing. Mrs. B. had done well in choosing this mansion. It wasn't like she herself exuded class but she sure gave it her best shot. She tried really hard to come across as some "lady of the manor." She might have been able to pull it off if it weren't for that big ol' mouth of hers. She had all the trappings of wealth, though; and in this world that went a long way. I would love to have known where all her money came from. Had she inherited it, married well or made it herself? It would have been interesting to find out, but I would have to save that for another time because right now Bachelor Number Two awaited.

I didn't know what Locke had planned but I decided to opt for lip balm rather than lip gloss this time around because it took me a good ten minutes to get the streaks of sticky pink goo off the sides of my face and out of my hair from the convertible ride with Merc. I was just finishing with the cleanup project when I heard raised voices coming through the vent mounted near the ceiling. Once again, I was the beneficiary of the poor hearing of the elderly. This time, though, a young voice – that of Locke – was a part of the mix.

"Do you have any idea what the two of you have done?" Locke may not have been deaf, but his voice was raised – only in anger.

"I don't know why you are making such a big deal out of this. It wasn't like Willem had a conversation with him or anything," Mrs. B. bit back, sounding exasperated.

Willem spoke more quietly than the other two; I had to strain to catch his words. "I know you're angry but honestly, we didn't have much of a choice. Something's not right. I can feel it in my bones. The boy is in trouble; I'm sure of it, which means so is Gracie. I mean, what was I . . . ." He cleared his throat. "What *am* I to do?"

A thrill of fear ran down my spine at the strange, frightening conversation. I looked around the area, furiously searching for something I could stand on so that I could get closer to the ceiling, and was relieved when I spotted a low-slung leather bench across the room. After dragging it under the vent, I took off my shoes and climbed aboard just in time to hear Locke's response to Willem's words.

"You are supposed to trust me, Willem. I won't let anything happen to her." He spoke more gently this time. "And trust him, too; the boy will protect her with his life."

"But, I don't think Merc…" Willem started.

I didn't require a bench to hear the old lady's abrasive voice cut in. "Of course he will protect her, and he is much stronger than you give him credit for, Willem. You both are overreacting, as usual."

Protect me from what? I wanted to scream but I couldn't and still continue listening, so I kept quiet and stood on my tiptoes, trying to get as close as possible to the vent while maintaining my balance.

"Overreacting? Is that what I'm doing?" Locke fired back. "You really have no idea what you are talking about. There was a reason why I told you both you could not leave this property and you definitely could not interact with the boy. Now everything has changed and all bets are off." Locke's words were tinged with bitterness. "And not that you probably care, old woman, but now everyone's future is in jeopardy – even mine."

I couldn't believe what I was hearing. I didn't understand any of it, but I understood enough to be frightened. There was definitely something mysterious going on in this house and I seemed to be smack dab in the center of it. I didn't hear anything else for a minute and I thought they had finished talking. I had carefully climbed down off the bench and grabbed my purse, ready to head out in search of Locke, when I heard Willem's contrite voice one more time.

"We really are sorry, Lochedus, but you need to understand that I'm going to do whatever I have to do to protect the girl. I will not let her be hurt or worse in order to protect myself. I won't."

My knees almost buckled underneath me. "Hurt or worse" – is that what he'd said? What in the world had I gotten myself into? And what had he called Locke? It sounded like Lockadus or Lockedus. The problem with eavesdropping was that you couldn't ask the speakers to repeat themselves.

Part of me thought I should just ask them what they were talking about. After all, they *were* talking about me. That was rude, wasn't it? So maybe I shouldn't care if they knew I'd listened in. But I couldn't get past the social taboo against eavesdropping. I mean, I didn't care that I *was* invading their privacy; I just cared that they *knew* I was invading it. So I decided not to mention what I had heard and just keep my eyes (and ears) open for any signs of danger. A smart girl might leave the place and never come back. I *was* smart but I still preferred a little danger rather than a lot of loneliness.

I gave myself a final once-over in the mirror, pinching my cheeks in a sad attempt to give my dull-as-dishwater complexion a little boost. Black might shave a few inches off my hips but it didn't do a thing for my skin tone. I bent over at the waist, giving my hair a final useless toss, and headed out the door – and straight into the arms of my waiting date.

"Locke – hey!" I exclaimed, feeling like I'd gotten caught with my hand in the chocolate chips. I felt like he would have no way of knowing what I had overheard, but that didn't keep my face from reddening in guilt and embarrassment.

Showing no sign of suspicion, Locke returned my greeting, "Grace – I was just looking for you." He gave me a quick hug and a big smile and then added, "Wow, you look great! I really love your hair that way."

Again my face turned crimson, this time at the warmth and sincerity of Locke's words. His compliment made my head slightly swim. Merc had said something nice this morning, as well; but somehow it was easier to believe coming from this boy. He had a way of making every word out of his mouth seem like the Gospel.

"Uh . . . thanks," I mumbled. "So . . . where to?" He wasn't carrying an actual picnic basket but he did have a rather large knapsack thrown over his shoulder, so I figured he was ready to roll.

"Oh, it's a surprise." His lopsided grin had a touch of mischief in it and his eyes sparkled with good humor. If there was anything sinister afoot, you would sure never know it from Locke's face. Maybe it was he, rather than Merc, who was the consummate actor.

As was my gift, I managed to push the overheard conversation almost completely from my mind. I *was* a little worried about exactly what he had planned – not because I feared for my life, but rather for my dignity. I prayed that whatever we were doing didn't involve anything athletic. It was "unseasonably cool" for Alabama but "unseasonably cool" in Alabama usually equaled hot as Hades anywhere else; so hiking or the like would undoubtedly be a miserable experience and would result in my looking like an uncoordinated wet rag.

We bumped into Willem and Mrs. B. in the kitchen as we were grabbing some sodas to add to the mystery contents of Locke's backpack.

"Everything is ready out back, Locke," Willem said with a sly smile that only added to my nervousness. "You kids have a great time – and be careful."

I thought back over the conversation I'd just overheard and Willem's seemingly innocent remark took on sinister significance.

Mrs. B. snorted ungracefully before adding her less than heart-felt wishes to Willem's. "Oh, yes, by all means, have a wonderful time – on my dime."

I wondered what she meant by that comment. Was she paying me for the afternoon or was she paying for the surprise Locke had arranged? My raging insecurity even had me wondering if she might be paying the handsome blonde to take me on a date but I quickly eighty-sixed that thought, realizing that she probably didn't like me enough to foot the bill for my enjoyment.

My stomach quivered anxiously as I wondered, again, just what Locke had come up with. Whatever it was, he and Willem both seemed excited about it; so, taking a breath for courage, I grasped Locke's outstretched hand and followed him from the kitchen into the courtyard.

Like everything inside the mansion, the courtyard was a stunning place, abloom with multitudes of flowering bushes and varying shades, shapes and sizes of greenery. Brick pavers led to a small but lovely three-tiered fountain made delightful by stone cherubs playing in the falling waters. A stucco wall covered in ivy, gold-blooming confederate jasmine and honeysuckle enclosed the entire area, and a delicate fragrance filled the air in a most enticing way.

As breathtaking a sight as the courtyard was, it did nothing to alleviate the keen awareness of my hand in Locke's. I hoped he wouldn't notice the sweat that slickened my palm and, if he did notice, that he would assume the heat of the noonday sun brought it on.

I found myself wishing that I were the type of girl with the type of body that could pull off a strapless sundress or a pair of white shorts and a pastel halter top. I felt the beads of sweat forming on my upper lip and under my mass of hair and cursed my penchant for sweets that rendered me forever doomed to suffocating black and denim.

I was so busy with self-flagellation, I failed to notice what Locke had retrieved from the bench behind the fountain until he was standing in front of me grinning from ear to ear.

"You're going to need to put this on," he said, while handing me a bright red biking helmet.

"Uh . . . what is it?" I stared at the offensive item in his hand and played dumb. It was worse than I had even envisioned. We would apparently be riding bikes – not something I had done much of for a good reason: it required a significant output of energy.

"Locke," I started. "I don't mean to complain, but I'm not so good on a bicycle." I felt like a complete idiot admitting I'd yet to master a skill most four-year-olds had accomplished.

"Grace," Locke soothed, "just have a little faith. I promise you are going to be just fine."

Having faith wasn't my forte, but I tried to put on a brave face for Locke's benefit. He seemed so excited.

After strapping on his own helmet, which on him somehow worked, Locke turned to me. "Okay, Little Miss," he laughed playfully, "your turn." He gently placed the helmet on my head, tucking the strap underneath my chin. I was almost glad there wasn't a mirror around. The sight of my round red face might have served to depress me to the point of paralysis.

"I look like an idiot," I pouted.

But Locke was having none of it. "You, my girl, are a vision. You really have no idea how pretty you really are. Now stop stalling, and get ready to ride!"

I knew I would play that comment over and over in my head for days to come, but right then there was no time because he disappeared for just a minute and came back riding a tandem.

"A bicycle built for two," I squealed. "I can't believe it!" I had wanted to ride a tandem ever since I was a little girl and had seen Paul Newman and Kathryn Ross ride a double-seater in the rain in *Butch Cassidy and the Sundance Kid.* As a young girl, my favorite thing had been to watch movies with my dad. He liked old westerns, so I watched old westerns – anything to be with him. And the bike scene in *Butch Cassidy* had been my first exposure to romance. I had never forgotten it. Now, Locke comes riding up on a tandem; it was just too perfect. It really was just *too* perfect. Almost like he knew. I internally rolled my eyes at myself. My paranoia was working overtime.

"Well, don't just stand there. Get on," he badgered good-naturedly.

I held my breath, sucked in my stomach, and got on the bike.

It took me a few seconds to get the hang of things but once I settled down and got into a rhythm, we were pedaling down the country lane, laughing and talking like school children. Even the weather cooperated, with the cool winds blowing through the large water oaks that lined the property, offering enough of a breeze to keep us comfortable. Every once in awhile Locke would point out a tree or plant and tell me its name, sometimes even saying what it might be used for or its healing properties.

I was surprised at how much ground we covered and even more surprised when Locke said that Mrs. B. owned all of it. I attempted to dig a little into the old woman's background but other than telling me her last name was Brunatelli, Locke wouldn't share any details, saying that he didn't feel comfortable doing so because she was such a private person. Taking the hint and not wanting to do anything to ruin the lighthearted mood of the afternoon, I dropped it. I didn't really much care if the old lady was the former Mrs. Sadaam Hussein, as long as she paid me $3,000 a month plus expenses. As if it never happened, I completely pushed aside the overheard conversation between the old folks and Locke and threw myself into the spirit of the day with great abandon.

Periodically throughout the afternoon my mind would drift to Merc, and my heart would contract and my stomach would do a funny little flip. But I would remind myself that this time yesterday I would have sold my soul for a date with a guy like Locke and I needed to concentrate on the proverbial "bird in the hand" rather than dream about the elusive one in the bush.

There was something so innately "good" about Locke, and maybe that was the problem. I didn't feel "good" enough for him. But even though Merc didn't radiate the blonde boy's wholesomeness, in my heart I knew I wasn't nearly good enough for him, either – just in a different way.

After riding around on the bike for about forty-five minutes we cut through a particularly dense area of the woods, over a small creek and down a narrower path than the ones we had been on. I thought we were just winging it and that Locke didn't have any particular destination in mind for our lunch, until his excited announcement.

"Well, we're here!" he said, while hopping off the bike but still holding it balanced for me.

"Here" was a very small clearing bordered by a circle of large trees abloom with delicate pink flowers. The trees were close enough together that their branches met and interlaced in the middle, creating a ceiling of a sort. It was hard for me to believe that nature had created such a perfect room and decorated it more beautifully than the finest French salon.

"Oh, Locke," I exclaimed. "How did you find this spot? It's amazing!"

"I'm glad you like it, Grace," he answered, his beaming face proving the truth of his statement. "I have to admit, though, I didn't find it – Willem did."

His confession caught me off guard. "Really? You've got to be kidding! How in the world did he have time to find this place? Y'all just moved here – right?"

Locke's face hinted at guilt, like he had said something wrong; but he quickly recovered and answered my question. "Oh, yeah, yeah . . . we've only been here a few weeks, but Granddad – he's a hiker and a biker. Where do you think I got the tandem?"

My mouth dropped open as a picture of Willem and Mrs. B. pedaled through my mind. I couldn't help but giggle at the thought. "PULEEZE, don't try to tell me that the old woman rocks the backseat of this thing." I looked down aghast at the bike I was straddling; I could barely co-pilot it. It was preposterous to think of Mrs. B. on the seat.

We both broke out in laughter, each imagining pictures of the old lady on the tandem.

"You remember the mean old lady on the bicycle in the *Wizard of Oz?*" I asked while gasping for breath.

The deer-in-headlights look on Locke's face told me that he had no idea what I was talking about.

"You know, Locke," I persisted. "*The Wizard of Oz* – the green witch – surely you've seen the movie."

"Oh . . . yeah . . . sure, I remember," he said, but his laughter rang false to my ears.

I could tell he had no idea what I was talking about and had obviously never seen the movie. I felt sad for him. When I was little, Pete, Mom, Dad and I would all pop popcorn, snuggle up together and watch movies – classic movies like *The Wizard of Oz*. I wondered what other things my new friend had missed out on by being an orphan. I had a sudden nostalgia wash over me, missing my mom and dad. Again I reminded myself that they had abandoned me and pushed them to the far recesses of my mind; they didn't deserve to be anywhere else.

I was anxious to move past an awkward moment so I pressed for further bike details. "So, why would Willem have a tandem?"

"I think he just found it on the property and decided to fix it up. He likes to tinker around with stuff. He's pretty good at it, I think." He reached over and took my hand and helped me off the bike.

"That's kind of neat. Are you like that, too? Can you fix things?" I asked, suddenly remembering an article I'd read on dating tips that said a girl should try to ask a boy about himself – his likes and dislikes, etc.

"Hmm, not really – well, kind of. I guess I'd like to think I'm good at fixing some things, but maybe not things like bikes or toasters." He gave me that "Lockesque" smile – the humble lopsided one that felt like it should have been followed with an "aw, shucks."

"So if you don't fix toasters or tandems, what do you fix?"

He thought for a minute before answering. I got the feeling that the response out of his mouth wasn't the one in his head. "This and that, I guess – just nothing too technical."

That wasn't the way the article said things would work. According to the writer, men loved to expound on their talents. I felt like I had to pull the words from Locke; probably because he seemed, at heart, to be shy.

I watched him as he began unpacking his knapsack. First, he laid out a red-and-white checked cloth, securing it with rocks he'd found around the area. Then out came the food: pimento cheese and peanut butter and jelly sandwiches, small packs of chips, brownies, and sodas. He even brought a portable CD player so we could listen to tunes while we ate. I couldn't believe this lovely boy had gone to so much trouble for me. I should have been thrilled, but instead I was suspicious. Why *would* he do all of this for me? It just didn't make any sense at all. Did it have anything to do with the snatches of conversation I'd overheard? Was he trying to "protect" me from something?

He looked over at me watching him and smiled brightly. "I tried to remember everything but, to be honest, this is my first picnic; so I hope I covered all the bases."

I laughed, trying to shake off the dark feeling that had come over me unexpectedly. "I think you definitely did, Locke. I can't believe you went to all this trouble just for me." As always, I said what was on my mind.

I knew I sounded a little pitiful and insecure, but I couldn't help myself. At the risk of sounding redundant, things like this just did not happen to me – Grace Bennett. Things like this happened to other girls – pretty girls, popular girls - but not to me. I kept waiting for the other Converse to drop.

If Locke picked up on my mood, he didn't let on. He just smiled sheepishly and confessed, "Well, I really can't take all the credit. Granddad made the sandwiches and brownies. But I did think of the music all by myself." He pointed proudly to the CD player like a kid who was showing off a good grade on a test.

God, he was cute! I just wanted to pick him up and squeeze him. Granted, I didn't get the same weak-all-over, heart-beating-out-of-my-chest feeling I got when I was near Merc, but I did think Locke was an amazing guy. I just had to find a way around all my insecurity. I also had to find out what was really going on. I knew in my heart of hearts that Locke, Willem, and even Mrs. B. were good folks; but I also knew there was some other hidden agenda behind their actions. That agenda was feeding my insecurity and that wasn't a good thing. I needed to know the real story. I needed to ask Locke. I just had to wait for the right time and until then keep it together.

Locke was curiously studying my face as if trying to read my thoughts. "Grace – you okay there?"

"Uh huh, sure. I'm fine. Sorry about that; I just kind of zoned out for a second. I do that sometimes." I laughed, trying to play things off before getting serious. "Listen Locke, I want to thank you. No one has ever done anything like this for me before. It's great – you're great." I could feel the tiny prick in my eyes that signaled the possible onset of tears. I swallowed hard, trying to stop the emotion. Crying would have been humiliating – pitiful – sad. I wasn't good at expressing emotion. I never had been. I usually made a joke to get through the times when my feelings were threatening to take over, but I couldn't think of a single thing to say.

Sensing my distress, Locke quickly came to the rescue – sweet as always. "Well, I bet you are just saying that so I won't get jealous. Heck, I'm your second date today!" He had meant to lighten the mood, but the mention of my morning with Merc created an awkward moment between us. This time, I was ready with my usual sarcasm.

"Ab-so-lutely! I'm just a guy magnet. I spend my life flitting from one dude to the next! That's me!" And just like that we were teasing and cutting up again. Emotional crisis diverted, at least for the moment.

"Pimento cheese or PBJ?" Locke offered, holding one in his right hand and the other in his left.

"I guess pimento cheese sounds good, but I like either one." I was a little uncomfortable at the thought of eating in front of a good-looking guy.

"Why don't you have one of each," he offered.

"Goodness, no! One is plenty. I couldn't possibly hold two." Okay; major deception. I could easily eat three with room left for dessert, but I wasn't going to say that.

He handed me the pimento cheese and unwrapped one for himself. After popping open a can of soda he cranked up the tunes, choosing a group I wouldn't normally have listened to on a bet but found myself enjoying.

"Who's the artist?" I asked, surprised at how appealing I found the upbeat tempo of the music. Normally my taste ran to a much darker place.

"You like 'em? They're one of my favorites. The group's called *Half Priced Hearts*. I found them on the internet and downloaded some of their stuff. It makes me feel good."

We both lay back on the cloth, tapping our feet and snapping our fingers to the beat, acting like total goofballs. After a few minutes the track changed to a slower, more melodic selection, and our moods, as if by agreement, changed as well.

Neither of us said anything for a while as we let the strains of the music wash over us. I never would have believed that I could relax to the point of almost sleeping next to a gorgeous boy, but I was at the sandman's door when Locke's voice brought me back to consciousness.

"Hey, Grace. You awake?" His voice was just above a whisper, and I prayed that I hadn't been snoring.

"Yeah, Locke," I answered serenely. I felt like I was in a dream – a perfect boy and a perfect afternoon. Sure, I had some unresolved questions but, all in all, this had been a fantastic date. Maybe Locke was going to ask me out. I didn't know what I would say because of my feelings for Merc, but it would sure be nice to be asked.

"Why do you try so hard to make people not like you?"

Oh, Locke, you know I like you, but I also like Merc and . . , WAIT – what did he just say?

"What did you say?" I jumped to my feet, spilling the soda I'd balanced on the cloth next to my right hand.

"Wha . . . Grace . . . you seem upset. Did I say something wrong?"

The look on his face was priceless. It was somewhere between abject fear and complete confusion. Eliciting such strong emotions in a boy would have normally made me feel kind of powerful, but with Locke I just felt bad.

Taking a deep breath, I forced myself to calm down and behave rationally; not easy for me considering I had gone (in my mind) from prospective girlfriend to loner lunatic in the space of a moment. I grabbed some napkins and started mopping up the mess I'd made with the drink. I cleaned in silence until I could get myself better in control.

"Why do you think I don't want people to like me?" I finally asked.

"It's not rocket science, Grace," he began carefully. "You are pretty, but you try hard not to be. You are very smart, but by your own admission you don't excel or even try in school. You have a great sense of humor, but you use it to make fun of yourself or other people. It seems to me that you hide your light under a bushel instead of letting it shine. I was just wondering why?"

I felt the blood rushing from my face and a buzzing start in my head, rolling down my body in waves until every inch of me was throbbing. I felt like I was breathing through gauze and the entire world looked bleached – stripped of color as my vision narrowed to a point. I knew I should be thinking about something – about what Locke had said; but I couldn't concentrate.

I heard distant shouting. Was it one voice or two? I couldn't tell. And then I was falling. Not onto the hard ground, but into arms – strong but gentle – like landing on the most perfect cloud. Right before everything went black, the thought occurred to me – I'm home.

How long had I been out? A minute? An hour? I didn't know. Where were the strong arms that had caught me when I was falling? Now I felt nothing but blades of grass through cheap material. I couldn't move or speak, but I could hear. I'd been right – there were two voices.

"What did you do to her?" The first voice demanded.

Was it possible? The voice sounded like Merc's. Why would he be here?

"I didn't do anything to her." Locke sounded hurt and defensive. "I was just talking to her - that's all."

"Well, you must have done something or said something to cause this. She obviously fainted." It *was* Merc! What was he doing here – talking to Locke – yelling at Locke?

"I told you. I didn't do anything. We were just talking. But while we're asking questions – why are *you* here? What were you doing – spying on us? Or did you just drop by to bring us a cocktail?" The sarcasm sounded all wrong coming out of Locke's mouth. It just wasn't his style.

It was Merc's turn to sound defensive and very confused. "No, of course not." He answered haltingly. "I just wanted to make sure Gracie was all right. I intend to keep making sure she is protected. I don't know what you are talking about or what you're doing here with her, but you aren't taking her – not for a very long time."

Fingers of apprehension spread down my body. If I hadn't already been lying on the ground, I would have fallen. *Take me where? Protect me from whom?* I wanted to scream. I should have known all along that this whole thing was to good to be true. Tears threatened to spill out from under my lids and I prayed they wouldn't notice. What could these people possibly want with me? I had kept myself calm with assurances that they meant me no harm. Now, Merc was accusing Locke of wanting to take me somewhere. Where? Why? All I could think to do was keep still and keep listening.

Locke's incredulous voice broke through my fearful musings. "Wait one second! You think I'm here to take Grace?"

"Why else would you be here, 'Locke'? Do you think I don't remember you? That I don't know who you really are – what you really do?" The way Merc spat out Locke's name left me wondering if he, too, knew him by another name.

"That's not why I'm here." Locke's voice was almost a whisper, and it held some type of emotion I didn't understand. I wished I could see his face, but I was scared to open my eyes.

Merc lowered his voice, no longer sounding angry or accusatory, just confused. "If you aren't a danger to Gracie, then who is? The old lady? Willem? And why are you all here – in this place – with her?"

"Look, son, I've answered all of the questions I can for now. Just know that none of us are here to do anything but help and protect the girl. You know that danger is headed your way and, trust me, you can't handle it alone. So if you want to be with her you'll have to take our help whether you like it or not."

Maybe it was hearing Locke call Merc "son" or maybe I was just sick of being a bystander in my own life; either way, I'd had enough! I sat straight up, ready to rock and loaded for bear. Unfortunately, I rose with such gusto that I nearly knocked Locke clean out.

"Ow!" he cried, falling backward onto his butt. "Grace, thank God – you're okay!" he said, rubbing his head furiously where I'd banged him on lift off.

"Uh . . . sorry, Locke," I apologized, looking around, completely puzzled.

Locke, who had shifted to his knees, was fussing over me, brushing my hair back from my face and even placing two fingers on my neck to check my pulse.

"You really gave me a scare, Grace. I feel just terrible about saying what I did. I guess I'm a little too blunt sometimes."

I sat open-mouthed, craning my neck from side to side, trying to figure out where Merc had gone.

"I'm going to finish packing things up and then get you back to the mansion. It's pretty hot out here. I'm sure you will feel better in the air-conditioning." He was waving a paper plate in front of my face, trying to cool me off.

"Locke?"

"Yes, Grace?" he answered. His kind, caring blue eyes gazed into mine with transparent concern.

"Where did Merc go?" I demanded. I had to know. This time, I had no intention of pretending I hadn't heard the conversation. If my life was in jeopardy, I needed to know why and from whom.

I'd always envied damsels in distress, thinking how wonderful their lot in life must be to have some strong knight to love them and fight all their battles for them. But in the cold light of reality, I realized I just wasn't cut out for the part. I couldn't just stand by helplessly watching others take risks for me while I sat in my ivory tower (or French Chateau) drinking tea and filing my fingernails completely oblivious to the peril.

Locke hadn't answered me, so I repeated the question more firmly. "Where did Merc go, Locke? I need to know where he is and I need to know what is going on." I suddenly felt brave – strong – like Joan of Arc ready to take on whatever ominous enemy lay in wait for me. I wished I had a horse.

And there it was again: the blank look, the deer-in-headlights, innocent-as-a-newborn-babe look Locke had perfected. "What are you talking about, Grace? Merc hasn't been here. You must have hallucinated when you were passed out." He was lying. I was sure of it. That is, until the strangest thing happened.

As Locke gazed deeply into my eyes, I felt myself begin to question my heroic resolve. In fact, I began to question everything. The whole afternoon was fast becoming a surrealist canvass splattered with the paint of my emotional extremes. Should I believe my new friend, thus rendering my semi-comatose state only a fertile field for my vivid imagination, or should I take a stand and demand an explanation for that which I knew, in my heart, to be true?

It probably sounds strange to say avoiding confrontation was a part of my basic DNA makeup; I fought with my brother and sister-in-law on a daily basis. But that was different. I knew they loved me (or were at least bound by holy matrimony to tolerate me). Locke was different. I wanted him to like me and, to me, that meant submission and blind allegiance.

Everything in my life – every emotion and decision – was rooted in fear. I didn't try in school because I would rather not try and fail than try and possibly not succeed. I didn't put myself out there to make friends because I couldn't stand the thought of rejection; better I do the rejecting first. And now - with Locke - I would rather act as if I believed his lies instead of call him on them and take the chance of his walking away. And Merc – he was the biggest fear of all. From the first moment I laid eyes on him, I knew that a rejection from him could be potentially devastating.

There were times when the power of my thoughts could be so disturbing – so depressing to me – that it would actually dim my view of the physical world. At first, I thought that's what was happening. It took me only the space of a heartbeat to realize that it was not my damaged psyche at fault. The sky had actually darkened to almost black.

It's a humongous cloud, blocking the sun – everything will brighten up again in a minute, I assured myself. I looked nervously around our little nest, which had earlier seemed so cozy and intimate, only to find that now its barrier of tightly-spaced trees and overhanging branches made me feel claustrophobic and caged in. I watched apprehensively as Locke walked with a determined step to the edge of the circle, where he stood staring intently into the dark woods – his shoulders set in what looked to me to be a defensive posture.

"Locke?" I whispered loudly, though I had no idea why I felt the need to lower my voice. He didn't answer, but continued to peer into the darkness. "Locke?" I repeated, raising my voice, to ensure, this time, I wouldn't be ignored.

With an exasperated huff, he paced back to my side, a worried expression on his normally sunny face. He didn't speak but just stared at me as if trying to come to a decision of some kind. Instinctively I kept quiet, sensing that he couldn't be pushed, and finally he seemed to make up his mind.

"Grace," he started. "I think we need to leave – now. We aren't going to take the bike – it's too dark. We are going to go on foot, but we need to move fast."

Utterly unnerved, I mutely shook my head in assent. Without even a backward glance at the helmets, knapsack or bikes, he grabbed my hand and began roughly pulling me toward the opening in the trees where we came in.

"Locke, what's wrong?" The bubble of fear welling up in my throat caused my question to come out as a croak. He didn't answer but tugged even harder, very nearly lifting me off of my feet and causing my angst to transform into full-blown panic. Though I kept moving in order to keep my arm intact, I didn't go quietly into the night.

"Locke!!! What's out there?" I enunciated each word in an effort to relay the seriousness of my concern.

As if just realizing that there was a human being attached to the appendage he was yanking on, Locke paused, looking back at me with palpable intensity. This was not a boy I had seen before. This was a man – poised for trouble, alert to danger.

"Grace," he answered through gritted teeth. "I don't have time to explain right now. Will you PLEASE just do what I'm asking of you? PLEASE!"

I resented his fifth-grade-teacher tone but the encroaching darkness caused me to reserve any feedback. We reached the small creek we'd crossed on the way to the picnic and without as much as a "Mother, may I?" Locke scooped me up and into his arms and carried me through the shallow water. It was a true testament to the depth of my apprehension that I didn't make a single sound of protest and instead wrapped my arms tightly around his neck, giving only mild regard to his opinion of my weight.

I *was* greatly relieved when my feet again hit solid ground, yet I was even more relieved that Locke appeared unscathed by his unexpected display of masculine virility. He had snatched me up as if he was lifting a piece of paper or, at the risk of sounding cliché, a feather. It would have been nice to take the time to bask in the awareness that he had sustained no personal injury from lifting my load, but there was no time for prideful reminiscence because no sooner had he returned me to a standing position we were off again– hand in hand – moving through the woods at a rate exceeding any pace I was comfortable with or accustomed to.

I'm not sure at what point I began to notice that the sweet pine aroma that normally permeated the woods had given way to a horrific odor akin to rotten eggs – or maybe a dead body. I wasn't sure what it smelled like; I just knew it was sorely testing my gag reflex, causing me to cough and gasp and adding to my already taxed lung capacity.

"What in Heaven's name is that smell?" I panted out through my hand that was covering my mouth and nose.

Locke paused, sticking his nose in the air and taking a deep sniff. "Sulfur, definitely sulfur."

"Huh . . . What?" I had a thought rush through my mind about a television show I'd seen once on alien abductions. The abductees, almost to a man – or woman – recalled smelling sulfur around the areas from which they were taken. OMG – were we running from aliens? Something bizarre was going on, that was for sure. I prayed that I wouldn't end up like one of those nut jobs with tin foil on their head hanging out at the gates of Area 51.

"'Locke..." I began.

"Not now, Grace," he huffed.

Well! The bloom was certainly off the rose in this little romance. Danger or not, I didn't like one little bit the condescension in Locke's exasperated voice.

I did find myself strangely appreciative for the years of enforced gym laps that allowed me to keep moving for another twenty minutes. But P.E. training aside, I was poorly prepared for an afternoon marathon and simply could no longer keep up the grueling pace Locke had set for us.

"Wait . . . Locke, please . . . I've got to stop for a minute."

He turned and looked, not at me but past me, into the woods, searching for the danger I had yet to understand.

"Just a little farther, Grace. I can carry you if you can't make it."

I was so exhausted, I was almost tempted to let him but the fleeting image of Locke in a back brace at school on Wednesday stopped the thought dead in its tracks.

"Thanks, but no thanks," I declined. "I guess I can make it a little bit farther."

Thankfully, it was only a short distance before the woods began thinning considerably and the now-gray sky became visible. I would have never imagined that I could be so grateful for a dusty, red dirt road, but the moment our feet hit the familiar path that led to the back of the mansion we both let out a tremendous sigh of relief.

I bent over, putting my hands on my knees, and tried to catch my breath. I found it unbelievably irritating that while I was drenched in sweat and just short of an asthma attack, Locke stood next to me fresh as a daisy and not a bit winded. Even his golden locks hadn't a strand out of place. But the thing that made me the craziest – literally drove me to the brink of insanity – was the look on his face - his smooth, dry-as-a-bone, dumb-as-a-rock face. It was not the look of a hunted man – fearsome and determined – as it had been moments ago. It was the look I had seen *ad nauseum* since meeting Locke last night – the sweet, affable, airheaded good ol' boy look. I wanted to slap it off his face.

Standing there on that red clay road, dripping sweat and spitting nails, I didn't care one whit whether Locke liked me or not. If he tried to tell me that I had misunderstood things, that we had not been in any danger, that we'd torn through the woods like the Devil himself was after us for no good reason – then there was going to be Hell to pay for the golden boy. I didn't run for anyone – not even a guy. If he played dumb, I was going to knock the stupid right off of him.

"Locke," I started, in a voice of barely restrained violence. "Now that we are 'safe,' I would like to know exactly what we *weren't* safe from."

Maybe it was my tone of voice, or maybe he had just had enough of the farm boy routine, but for whatever reason he let the act slip for a split second, giving me a view of the real Locke Wingard.

His admittedly stunning but vaguely vacuous visage morphed into something else altogether – the image of a calculating con-niver – a manipulator – a liar; and I knew beyond a shadow of a doubt that the next words from his mouth would be a contrived creation devised to throw me off the scent of the real truth. A giant clap of thunder boomed overhead and white lightning turned the sky a paler shade of gray, causing me to jump and giving red carpet treatment to Locke's impending opus.

"It was a wild animal – a wolf, I think. But it could have been a bear. Whatever it was, it was huge. I know it was. I caught a glimpse of it through the trees and even though it was dark, and I couldn't tell exactly what it was, I could tell it was massive. It must have smelled our food. It was really stupid of me to take us so far into the woods. I'm really sorry. I hope you can forgive me."

He put an arm around me and pulled me toward him. Ducking his chin down into his chest, he looked up at me through his silky blonde lashes with pleading eyes. "You do forgive me, don't you, Grace?"

Sidestepping both his embrace and his question, I pulled a rubber band from my jeans pocket and busied myself taming my perspiration-soaked hair into a ponytail. I didn't trust myself to respond to him. I was far too angry. He probably thought I was still just upset and scared from our near "animal attack." He didn't get that I didn't believe a word of his story. He didn't get that I was somehow immune to his startling good looks. And he definitely didn't get that it was hard to lie to a liar. He thought he could manipulate me – maybe they all did. They were going to find out that two could play the game. But they would find out on my time schedule – not theirs. I would play along; let him think I bought his little act. Then I would begin my own investigation. My plan required that I have some help and I had a pretty good idea who to ask.

Chapter Nine

LIAR

LOCKE STUDIED MY FACE INTENTLY, SEARCHING FOR ASSURANCES THAT I believed his story. I could play dumb with the best of them. I'd had a lot of practice doing it over the years.

"Animal attack, huh? "Wow! We were lucky to get out of there with our lives! I had no idea there were wolves and bears in these woods. We should tell Pete and Patty about it. We have guests staying on our property; there could be legal problems. We could get sued if somebody gets eaten." I widened my eyes, mimicking Locke's "concerned look." I had to bite my lip to keep from laughing and I sped up so he couldn't see my face.

"Actually, it's probably not a good idea to tell anyone about this. Not until we know exactly what we are dealing with. We wouldn't want to start a panic," he hedged, stretching out his pace to match mine.

I guess he hadn't completely thought through the consequences of his little story. He probably thought I would just squeal and fall into his arms, the grateful, rescued damsel wildly appreciative of her brave knight. Fat chance! I couldn't help sticking the knife in a little further – make him really work for it.

"I don't know, Locke. I think we have a responsibility here to do the right thing. I think we should call the sheriff – let him know what we think is running around in these woods." I gave him my "brave face," the one I had perfected over the years for various reasons (somehow I'll get through the death of my grandmother, Mr. Teacher, and when I do, I'll take your makeup test).

"The problem is, Grace, I don't really know what I saw and until I do, I think we should hold off telling anyone. I'll go back out there tonight – armed, of course – and try to check for prints."

He had nothing to worry about. I wouldn't be telling anyone about running from a bear in these woods. They would think I'd lost my mind. Or, it would confirm to them the already long-held suspicion that I was crazy. There were no bears in these parts. I wasn't sure about wolves, but I was pretty sure there weren't any of those, either. But I wasn't planning on telling Locke that.

"Okay, Locke – good idea. You go out and check for signs of big game and let me know what you find."

He jerked his head around to look at me, studying my face quizzically, trying to decide if I was making fun of him. My face was a perfect mask of sincerity, and after a moment he looked away seemingly satisfied.

Another clap of thunder shook the ground and large raindrops begin spattering the dirt road, making a mess of my already trashed jeans and shoes. I quickened my pace, rounding the corner that brought the house into view.

I wasn't really surprised to see Willem standing at the wrought iron gate of the courtyard waiting for us. I *was* kind of surprised at the getup he had on: a long black slicker, rain boots and hat and, in his hand, a giant black umbrella that looked big enough to shield a small sports team. He ran out to meet us halfway, pulling us in under the umbrella, though it was by this point a fruitless gesture.

"Hey, kids. I sure didn't think it was going to storm today. Let's get you two inside before it gets any worse." He wrapped his surprisingly strong arm around me and at once I felt the safety that had eluded me for the past two hours.

Passing on the umbrella, Locke ran ahead of us. We caught up with him as he was stripping down at the back door. As he pulled off his soaked T-shirt, I was reminded of the disparity between ourselves once again. He looked like an ad for Abercrombie & Fitch: wide shoulders, smooth perfect chest that tapered down to a slim waist, and washboard abs. Locke's body – like his face – was flawless and very, very predictable. As he leaned over to untie his sneaker laces, I couldn't help noticing that the perfection of his front side also extended to his back. Why wasn't I more impressed? I should be salivating at this little peep show, but I wasn't. He ran his hands through his wet hair, and I could have sworn he flexed. FLEXED! Oh, please. His performance left me completely cold. It didn't do much for his grandfather, either.

"Oh, for God's sake, boy – put your shirt back on!" Willem demanded as he began shedding his boots, hat and coat. "Nobody wants to see all that."

Locke looked over at me as if he expected me to disagree with Willem's statement. He was getting no support from this side of the fence. Instead, I quietly removed my shoes and socks and began picking the leaves off them.

Seeing he would get no help from me, he fired back at Willem. "Well, you have enough clothes on for both of us. Are we expecting a hurricane?"

I noticed an irrigation of irritation running under the exchange between Locke and Willem. It didn't seem like playful banter – it was harsher. The relationship between Locke, Willem and Mrs. B. was perplexing, to say the least. It was going to take some keen insight and investigation to figure it all out. While sticking my nose in where it didn't belong was a life skill of mine, insight wasn't a strong point, so I was going to need some help. I was willing to bet Merc knew more about all these folks than he let on. I needed to ask him. It sounded like as good an excuse as any to see him again.

Willem's voice interrupted my thoughts. "It wasn't my idea to put all this stuff on. Mrs. B. wouldn't let me out the door without it, silly old bird."

"Oh, yeah," Locke responded sarcastically. "She's a real Florence Nightingale – always fussing over you – ha, ha, ha." His laugh had a mean edge to it that put my back up and didn't sit right with Willem, either.

"You know, 'Locke,' (and there it was again, that ironical tone he used with Locke's name) you would think you would be kinder – more compassionate or something."

Willem sounded puzzled, as if he was trying to figure out something that was bugging him about his grandson. He could join the club. I was trying to figure out Locke, too. One minute he seemed like the nicest, sweetest guy in the world, and the next he was something entirely different. Maybe I wasn't the only one who didn't know the real boy. I couldn't exactly talk to Willem about it, though. After all, he was his grandfather, and blood was thicker than water. I certainly didn't want to say anything to offend him. I would just have to watch and listen.

Locke ignored Willem's remark and left the kitchen to go upstairs to get changed. He was rounding the corner, headed for the stairs, when he ran into a much-offended Mrs. B.

"OH, MY WORD!!! Are we using the kitchen as a dressing room now, boy? Would you kindly go upstairs and not come back down until you are appropriately clothed?" She ran her eyes up and down his body, clearly no more impressed with what she saw than I was and, before Locke could answer or even move, she added an additional dig. "You know, you really are terribly transparent."

"What is that supposed to mean, old woman?"

I couldn't believe he had called her that to her face. I had certainly thought of her as "old woman, old hag, old fill-in-the-blank" but I would have never had the guts to say it. In fact, as abrasive as she was, the manners that had been instilled in me since birth precluded me from ever talking to an elderly person with such disrespect. I guess they didn't teach those sorts of things at the orphanage, and that was a crying shame for Locke because he was walking on some exceedingly dangerous ground.

"How dare you speak to me like that? Who do you think you are talking to, young man?" Her pudgy face was red with anger and, unless I missed my guess, humiliation. I actually felt bad for her and disgusted with Locke.

"Who do I think *I'm* talking to? Who do you think *you* are talking to?" Locke was equally angry, his beautiful face turning almost ugly with rage. "You are on very thin ice!"

Willem quickly stepped around me and stormed over to where the young man and old woman stood, nose to nose, looking as if they were about to exchange fists.

"Whoa, whoa, whoa you two – not another word. I mean it – not another single word. Are you forgetting we have company? Now, Locke, you go on upstairs and put on some clothes. And, Mrs. B., why don't we sit down with young Gracie, have a cup of tea, and find out how the picnic went?"

I had almost forgotten what had happened in the woods because of what just happened right in front of me. It was clear to me that Willem had wanted to stop Locke and Mrs. B. before they said something in front of me that I shouldn't hear.

Watching the fuming Locke head for the stairs, I envied him the ability to escape. I guess I was on sensory overload; too much had happened. I needed to try to sort things out in my head and come up with a game plan. I couldn't do it around these people. I'd never had much of an ability to make up my mind about things – always wishy-washy, flipping from one extreme to the other; but around the residents of the mansion (and Merchison Spear), my extremes were even more extreme than usual. I required space to calm my spinning mind and settle things out a bit. Maybe I'd make some lists. I had always heard they helped.

"To tell you the truth, I'm really not feeling real well right now. I think it would be better if I head home. If you need me to do anything for you, I will be glad to come back tomorrow - first thing. After the experience Locke and I had in the woods, I am just drained and could use some time to recharge my batteries." As an afterthought, I added, "I bet that's why Locke is acting so weird, too. He's probably just upset."

I saw the old man and old woman exchange a concerned glance before Willem asked, "Grace – what experience in the woods?"

Heck! I should have kept my mouth shut – at least for today – if I wanted to go home. Now I was going to have to explain what happened, even though I didn't really know what happened myself.

"Well, first I fainted. And then we saw something – or really, Locke saw something – out in the woods. He thought it might have been a giant bear or wolf. Then it got really dark and it started smelling really bad. I don't know; it was weird. We just got out of there fast. We left your bike, Willem. I'm sorry about that. Locke thought it would be faster on foot."

I knew I wasn't making any sense. I was just babbling. The old couple sat slack-jawed, looking at me like I'd just confessed to a murder, horror painted on their old faces. Horror but, strangely, not surprise.

Willem recovered first. "Oh, no, Gracie - are you all right?" he asked, while pushing me toward a bar stool in front of a long, black granite-topped island in the middle of the kitchen. "You must have been scared to death. Is that why you fainted? From fear?"

Willem's face was a mask of grave concern and I immediately felt bad for even mentioning what had happened. All of the drama might have been better left for the young people, except for the fact that I was pretty sure the two old folks knew all about what was out in the woods. Call it instinct – a feeling – whatever. I just knew that I had somehow fallen behind the looking glass when coming to this mansion last night, and much like Alice I was the only one who didn't know at least some of what was going on. They knew something, all right, and they were worried about it.

Even Mrs. B. was unusually sweet, fussing over me like a mother hen. "My poor dear! How horrible for you. Would you like to lie down?" She practically ran to the fridge to make me a large glass of iced tea, loading it up with lemon and sugar. "Drink all of this," she demanded. "No hot tea – you need something cool.

You mustn't get dehydrated. The sugar will restore your energy. You don't want to pass out again."

I flushed furiously. I wasn't accustomed to being the center of anyone's attention. That is, unless I had done something wrong or caused trouble of some kind.

"I really am fine," I assured them, drinking down the tea in a few gulps. "I feel much better. Don't worry about what was in the woods, either. It was probably nothing more than Locke's and my imagination."

I was trying my best to downplay the situation in order to keep the old folks calm. I would hate for one of them to have a heart attack or a stroke. I didn't know CPR – except for what I'd picked up on television.

At the same time, it was kind of nice to have such a big deal made over me. It made me feel, I don't know – loved, I guess. Not that my own family didn't love me because they did; but Mom had Dad, and Pete had Patty, and I had a lot of time alone.

Mrs. B. and Willem could certainly fill a gaping hole in my life. I never knew any of my grandparents. But in order to bond with the *Casa De Crazy* residents, I was going to have to know a lot more about who they really were. My tendency would be to throw caution to the wind and embrace my new "old" friends and their young compatriots wholeheartedly. But while I didn't trust my feelings about these people – they were all over the map on this thing – I did trust my survival instinct, and it was telling me to proceed with caution.

All of us sat quietly, each alone with our thoughts until Locke finally came down the stairs fully dressed and back in good humor, if only temporarily.

"What's everybody looking so glum for?" he asked, as if the argument with Mrs. B. had never happened.

"Gracie was just telling us about what happened during your picnic, Locke," Willem offered, his voice even and measured, his eyes telling a different story.

Locke shot a vicious glare at me, all traces of his return to Pleasantville erased. I looked down at the travertine floor and begin silently counting the tiles. I hadn't realized he had been intending on keeping the afternoon's events a secret from the old folks. He should have been more specific.

"It was no big deal, really," Locke echoed my false sentiments of moments earlier.

"I can't say I agree with you there" Willem said. "But we will discuss it later. Grace needs to get home."

Willem turned to me and said, "Grace, your tire has been fixed, but I honestly don't feel like you should drive yourself home – what with fainting and all. Why don't you let Locke give you a ride?"

I had no desire, whatsoever, to get in a car with the steaming blonde boy. He was furious with me for telling Willem and Mrs. B. about the incident in the woods. I didn't think I could handle a confrontation right then.

"Thanks, Willem, but I'm fine to drive. I feel much better now. I think Mrs. B.'s iced tea did the trick. I'll need my car for school on Wednesday, anyhow."

To his credit, Willem didn't put up a fight. I think he knew I'd had enough of his grandson for one day. Mrs. B. must have known too, because when it came time for me to leave she asked to walk me to my car. She didn't strike me as someone who took too many extra steps, so I figured she had something on her mind and I was right.

We walked silently to the driveway, and she watched as I got into my car and buckled my seat belt before finally saying what she had to say.

"Grace," she began, "you undoubtedly have picked up on some, shall we say, 'weirdness' in my home. I want to ask you for a favor, and then maybe give you a little advice."

I sat patiently waiting for her to continue until I realized that she was waiting for me to give her some sign of encouragement.

"Okay, Mrs. B., I'll do what I can, and I'm always up for advice." That was a big lie. I didn't do advice well, and I felt sure she knew that. But the woman was my boss. A little sucking up seemed not only appropriate but advisable.

She barked out a short, ironic laugh and then turned almost fully around, craning her neck from side to side – as if looking for any hidden eavesdroppers. I wasn't about to tell her that the one voted "Most Likely To Listen" was sitting in the car waiting for her to share her pearls of wisdom. Whatever those pearls might be, her surreptitious glances made it clear that she meant them for my ears only.

My mind darted back to this morning in the limo when Mrs. B. had told me to listen to my heart. Not exactly news-making advice – really rather cliché but she had seemed quite sincere at the time, so I didn't think it the best idea to ignore her. I didn't want to disregard her guidance anyway, since it seemed to line up with my own desires. I did wonder if tonight's speech would be much the same as this morning's: cryptic and evasive rhetoric – answering no questions, only giving rise to new ones.

The old lady seemed satisfied that she wasn't being stalked and finally got down to what she wanted to say.

"Grace, I really don't have time to go into much detail with you but I want . . . no, I *need* you to know a few things, the first being that you have nothing to fear from me or Willem. We would never do anything to hurt you. In fact, we would like nothing better than to help you and make your life better. Believe me when I say it is very important to me that you are happy, Grace. I know I'm a bit of an old nag, but I care about you – a lot – and so does Willem."

I would have to be the Tin Man not to be a little moved by her speech but, touched or not, her words just added to my confusion. Why would she and Willem care so much about me? I also couldn't help noticing that she didn't mention Locke in her blanket declaration of good intent. Did that mean that he meant me harm? Now was my chance to ask.

"I appreciate you and Willem wanting good things for me; I really do, Mrs. B. I like you both an awful lot, too. But, to be honest, I don't know you very well, nor do you know me, so I really don't understand why you give a flip about me. People who have known me my whole life barely tolerate me, so how could you feel so strongly for me? Also, I couldn't help but notice that you didn't mention Locke. Is he somehow a danger to me?" I was asking about Locke, and he was important, but whom I really wanted to know about was Merc.

She chose her words carefully, as if having to think about each one. "Honey," she began, the endearment sounding strange coming from her lips, "I know you have trust issues. I understand that. I can only repeat what I said to you this morning, which is you must listen to your heart. It's an acquired skill, Grace, but a very valuable one. Deep down inside of you, you know with whom to place your trust and, more importantly, with whom to place your heart. I didn't mention Locke because he is a bit of a conundrum. I believe he wants to do the right thing; he just may not know the best way to go about it. He is experiencing some new feelings and emotions that he doesn't know what to do with right now. He will figure it out."

She placed her veiny, ice-cold old hand on top of mine before continuing, "You don't worry about Locke. Willem and I will handle him."

I started to interrupt her, but she just went right on talking. "Grace, it isn't Willem's grandson you are really worried about, is it? I know you have questions about the other boy on the property – Merchison Spear. I can't tell you that he isn't dangerous because I believe that he is. But – and this is a big but – I believe he very well could be worth the risk."

This definitely wasn't what I had expected her to say. "What kind of danger?" I asked. "I feel completely in the dark here, Mrs. B. – like I've wandered behind the looking glass; and I need to know what I am dealing with."

My heart was flying a million miles an hour. I guess up until now I had fooled myself into thinking I was imagining things – blowing things out of proportion. Now, this strange woman was confirming my worst fears. I didn't do danger. I wasn't sure I could make an exception, even for someone as amazing as Merchison. The old lady had said to listen to my heart, and my heart was telling me

I needed to know more. I was beginning to get irritated with all the cloak-and-dagger stuff.

"I've already said too much, Grace. It isn't my story to tell. I'm just trying to give you the benefit of my experience. A little danger is better than a lot of safety if being safe means being without the person with whom you were meant to share your life."

Share my life? I just met the guy! I was just hoping for a second date; maybe, in my wildest fantasy, a dating relationship. But sharing my life with Merc? I'd barely spent an hour with him, total, and while he was certainly spectacular looking, even I wasn't so shallow as to decide my entire future based on those looks. I had to admit, though, that something way, way deep down inside of me had felt warm and right when she'd said those words. Could that be my heart? Is that what I'm supposed to be listening for? I had no practice with such things. I tended to use my head, not my heart. Maybe I could use a little of both and see what happened.

"I just don't want to be flying blind. I need some answers." I was almost pleading, but I could tell by the set look on the old woman's face that she wasn't budging.

"Just remember what I've said, Grace." She cocked her head to the side as if just thinking of something else. "And Grace . . . one more little piece of sage wisdom: Relax. Life doesn't have to be so hard. Everyone isn't out to get you. Real danger is rather obvious – not really so subversive as you would believe it to be."

Well, that certainly cleared everything right up! At the beginning of our talk, she had said she wanted to ask something of me – a favor – and then give me some advice. I wasn't even sure which part was the favor and which part was the advice. I was fantastically flummoxed.

Hoping to prolong the conversation, I asked, "You said you wanted to ask me a favor. Was there something else you wanted me to do?"

Her face screwed into the yellow-toothed half-grimace/half-smile that I found so frightening. "Apologize to Patty. She really does love you."

I almost swallowed my gum. "What . . . how . . .?" I stammered.

She didn't answer but only turned and walked away, all the while laughing in short staccato bursts that eventually degenerated into a dry hacking cough that sounded like a two-pack-a-day smoker. In complete disbelief, I sat watching her until she closed the front door behind her before finally buckling up and heading out.

Chapter Ten

NIGHT MOVES

I HAD TO FIGHT THE URGE TO TURN AWAY FROM THE MAIN ROAD AND head farther into the woods in search of Merc's bungalow. I managed to overcome my baser instincts, but that didn't keep me from creeping along at a mile or two an hour in hopes of recreating the magic of last night. I stretched the short drive out as long as I could but once there I had to face the fact that I wouldn't be seeing my dream man again – at least not tonight.

I drove the rest of the way home like a zombie, avoiding all thought of any importance (like how in the world Mrs. B. knew about my fight with Patty) until I made it to my own bedroom and into my bed where I could spend hours of uninterrupted reflection – reviewing every second, in minute detail, of the last twenty-four hours.

I felt like all the answers I so desperately needed were locked away in my brain – yet unexamined – waiting for me like a word on the tip of my tongue that I just couldn't remember. It was a nagging, persistent intuition, and it was telling me that all the events of my crazy weekend were somehow intertwined and that with some intense examination and a little luck, I could figure it all out.

After all, I had cut my teeth on Nancy Drew and Hardy Boys, who were replaced in fourth grade by Agatha Christie. When most twelve-year-old girls were poring over *Seventeen* and *Teen Glamour*, I was cracking cases with Scott Turow and David Baldacci. I knew my way around a mystery, and I was anxious to try my hand with this one. Of course, I wanted to do so at a safe distance. I didn't like folks throwing around words like "danger." They scared me. But if I could get a handle on the real story, I would know what and whom to avoid, and that seemed like a good place to start.

I was going to make that list – bulleting all the people and events, the funny feelings and odd looks, the strange coincidences and double entendre – and attempt to link them together into some type of cohesive explanation of the last two days. I didn't have faith in many things about myself, but I did believe in my brain. As underused and flighty as it might be, when it's truly been needed, it has never let me down. I was going to put it to work now drawing some conclusions that would aid me in the decisions I would make in the coming days regarding the old couple and the two gorgeous guys. All things considered, I had much to be grateful for. My life was definitely looking up. At least I wasn't bored anymore. I might even get around to apologizing to Patty P. I wasn't in any particular hurry on that one though; it wouldn't hurt her to stew a bit.

As I drove into the parking lot of the Martin's Nest, I was disappointed to see that the area had been spared the rain so the guests and innkeepers – Pete and Patty – were out in full force. They were laughing and talking on the deck as they cooked burgers and dogs on the grill and watched their kids play down on the banks of the lake, shooting bottle rockets and tossing a Frisbee.

My stomach growled and I realized that I hadn't eaten anything but a pimento cheese sandwich and a half a bag of chips all day. If I kept this up, I might actually lose a pound or two. There was no better diet in the world than unrequited love, so I was probably destined for a size four.

I was hoping to pass by the side of the group unnoticed, not even the allure of grilled food tempting me enough to forgo my deeply embedded antisocial instincts in favor of uncomfortable small talk; however, I was forced to play nice for a few minutes because Patty spotted me as I attempted to quietly skulk by.

"Grace, there you are. We were just talking about you. How did your dates go?"

She emphasized the word "dates" – in the plural – and I saw the bimbo twins give each other a quick look that, no doubt, meant how did she get one date, much less two? The bimbo twins were a pair of bottle-blonde, thong-wearing, ridiculously endowed *Girls Gone Wild* rejects who had been staying at the inn with their parents for almost two weeks. I avoided them at all costs because being in their orbit just made me feel bad. Their very presence highlighted all that I was not. When I would bump into them on the property, they went out of their way to be sweet, but I knew it was just a cover for the wicked hearts that beat within. Now Patty had given them perfect fodder for their cruelty.

I took a deep breath trying to calmly recall Mrs. B.'s words about Patty. "Everything was fine - thanks. Sorry I can't stay and talk I've got a paper due and I'm pretty beat Y'all have fun. Goodnight." There, I'd said it; and pretty sweetly if I do say so myself. I was almost to the door when Patty ruined my self-adulation.

"You're going to do schoolwork? Will the wonders never cease? I don't recall your ever touching a book, Grace. I guess miracles do happen!"

My Lord, the girl had no filter at all! At least Pete had the good sense to put a warning hand on her arm. I would have preferred he break it, but that probably wasn't going to happen so I would just have to defend myself.

"Yeah, well, there's always a first for everything, Patty. For instance, one day you may learn to keep that big ol' mouth of yours shut!" With that, I stomped off in a wake of shocked gasps and uncomfortable titters of embarrassed laughter. My response had been an overreaction, but I was tired, hungry and confused. Like everything else about Patty, her timing was perfect.

One particularly loud guffaw sounded eerily familiar and strangely out of place, but as I spun around to identify its source I was greeted by Pete and Patty's accusing eyes, along with several patrons' stares of outright disapproval, so I bustled on into the inn and chalked it up to my imagination.

I stopped off in the kitchen for a diet soda and some pretzels before climbing the stairs to go to my bedroom. I felt my muscles beginning to stiffen, a gift from the unexpected and highly unpleasant exercise during the afternoon. I decided to spend an hour, or maybe even two, indulging in one of my favorite pastimes – soaking in a steaming hot bath. Almost every night of the week I submerged my body into near-boiling water and read a novel. I doubted very much that I would have the requisite concentration to read, but the heat would clear my head and set the stage well for my planned activity – mystery solving.

Grabbing a towel and stripping off my dirty clothes, I piled my hair on top of my head and lowered myself into the hottest water I could tolerate without passing out. My bath was a sacred ceremony not a think tank, so I forced all errant thoughts of my strange weekend from my brain and let Calgon take me away. By the time I emerged – one and a half hours later – I was clean as a whistle, shriveled as a prune, red as a lobster, and ready to rock. My brain was clicking on all cylinders and I was more than up for the task that lay before me.

Wrapping up in my favorite fuzzy towel, I padded back to my room, cursing the picture window that dominated the entire back portion of the Martin's Nest. It made for a wonderful view of the lake and surrounding landscape but it offered little in the way of privacy. Pete reminded me on more than one occasion to take my clothes to the bath to change into, but it quite often slipped my mind. After my little display of temper in front of the guests, a peep show would certainly add fuel to an already burning fire so I hoped no one spotted me. At least, if they did, it would infuriate Patty and that was always fun.

One of many personality inconsistencies was demonstrated by the difference between my daytime and nighttime attire. During the day I never veered far from my standardized dark uniform but the night – the night was something else altogether. I was barely out of diapers before I began displaying a passion for lingerie – the brighter and more flamboyant the better. Satin, silk – even a feather or two – were all a part of my boudoir wardrobe. While dark clothing was preferred in the light of day, the darkness itself brought out a wide array of vivid colors including fuchsia, lime green, hot pink and orange.

Tonight I chose a more sedate number in my repertoire to reflect my introspective mood. After shimmying into the baby pink silk pajama set, I grabbed a pen and paper from my desk and sprawled across my bed to start the arduous process of dissecting the past two days. But all my plans were indefinitely delayed when I pulled back my covers to grab a pillow for support, and found a neatly folded piece of notebook paper, my name written across it in block letters. My heart skipped a beat and I quickly cautioned myself not to get too excited. It might very well be a message from Patty asking me in her oh-so-condescending way to pick up my room. But I didn't think so, because Patty didn't call me "Gracie," which was the name written across the paper. Besides, I recognized the writing from the note that had been pressed into my hand the night before; it was Merc's - I was almost sure of it.

How could he have gotten into my room? I probably should have felt violated in some way but, in all honesty, I didn't really care if he had to gas the residents of the inn to gain entry. All I cared about was that he had gone to a considerable amount of trouble to get a message to me.

A thought suddenly tore through my mind and I jumped up, paper in hand, to look around the room, in the closet and under the bed, to make sure that he was no longer on the premises. My room was empty of all welcome interlopers, but I still said a quick prayer of thanks that I had a quirky bend toward pretty nightclothes and ripped open the note.

Dear Gracie,

I first want to apologize for making a complete jerk of myself on our date this morning (Oh, joy! He had called it a "date"). *I have no excuse for my behavior but to say that I was nervous, and I thought the champagne might help ease the jitters.* (How sweet! He was nervous…that was about the cutest thing I ever heard!) *Would you meet me behind your boathouse at midnight? I would like to see you. I need to talk to you about something.*

Yours,
Merchison

Would I meet him?! Hmmm, let me think for a minute . . . uh . . . YEAH!!! Wild horses couldn't keep me from being at that boathouse at midnight. I read the note once, twice, three times before finally putting it away so that I could start getting ready for my late night rendezvous. "Late night rendezvous!" That sounded so romantic. I was over the moon with excitement.

I threw open my closet and began frantically combing through my wardrobe, thankful for the unusually low nighttime temperature that would allow me to top anything I wore with a hoodie. I dreaded the advent of summer. I was definitely a cold-weather girl because the lower the temperature, the more material I could put between my body and the outside world.

After picking yet another black getup I did what I could with my steam-ruined hair, pinched my cheeks until they were sore but rosy, and re-waxed my lips, making a mental note to hit the drugstore for some more cherry-flavored lip balm because apparently I was going to need it – fingers crossed!

I could feel it in my bones. Tonight was the night. I would finally get the kiss I'd been waiting for, ever since at six years old my Barbie had met my friend Kim's Ken for a dream date.

I heard Pete and Patty saying good night to the guests and, one by one, doors being locked as patrons settled in for the night. I was eternally grateful that my brother and his wife were early-to-bedders, because though I had the run of the place and was plenty old enough to walk the property at night, I could do without the suspicion that it would certainly arouse in them should they see me heading out for a midnight assignation. Pete was just the kind of guy who would say something like, "A boy who would ask to meet you in the middle of the night is out for only one thing." Ha! I should be so lucky. With two dates in one day under my belt, I hadn't even managed a simple kiss on the lips. I certainly didn't see my date tonight turning into a full-on, hands-down, free-for-all night of love. I did have my hopes for that kiss though – I really did.

Dressed down and made up, I was ready to slip out of the inn like a thief in the night with my pseudo-guardians sleeping soundly, blissfully unaware of my planned tryst. As I waited for the clock to tick down the final minutes, I drove myself crazy with all the questions for which I had no answers. This time, though, my thoughts no longer included the mansion residents and their confusing, mysterious ways. My mind rested solely on the beautiful, elusive boy I was waiting impatiently to meet. Why did he want to see me? Could it be possible that he actually, truly liked me? How did he get into the inn, unseen, to leave the note? Why, oh why, hadn't I broken with long-standing tradition and cleaned my room before I left this morning?

Try as I might, I couldn't come up with a single solid answer to the questions swarming around in my brain like an angry nest of hornets. I knew I was just going to have to wait and see. I'd never been good at waiting. I'd always preferred instant gratification. Maybe this whole weekend was designed by some higher power to teach me patience. If so, it wasn't working. I was just getting more and more frustrated each time I realized that the answers I sought would not be provided on my time schedule but rather someone else's.

After what seemed like an eternity, the big and little hands on the clock finally reached an acceptable time to head to the boathouse. As quietly as I could manage, I slipped down the stairs and out the back door, circling around to the side of the inn and down the hill to reach the designated meeting place behind the small building that housed Pete's prized *Mastercraft* boat.

The adrenalin that propelled me forward suddenly evaporated when I realized that Merc had not yet arrived. The moon and stars weren't visible due to heavy cloud cover and unfortunately the dim lighting mounted on the end of the pier didn't do a thing to illuminate my rendezvous point. I had hoped Merc would be waiting for me, but when he didn't emerge from the dark woods I slipped closer to the corner of the boathouse so that the darkness wouldn't completely envelop me. I didn't really know the boy I was clandestinely meeting. If he was in some way dangerous, I was serving myself up to him like a Christmas goose on a platter.

The first seeds of worry began creeping into my mind as snippets of conversations I'd had with Locke and Willem regarding Merc played back in my head. But I willfully chose to push those recollections to the back of my brain in favor of Mrs. B.'s more positive reinforcements of him. Any other time I would have chosen Willem's advice over the old lady's – hands down. But when it came to Merchison Spear – because I wanted to believe only good of him – I chose to lean on Mrs. B.'s words. But even Mrs. B. had said Merc might be dangerous, so I couldn't help feeling mildly apprehensive while waiting for him in the middle of the dark night.

I had almost given up hope of his coming when I heard him calling me from somewhere within the inky thicket of trees. I wondered why he didn't just come to me but then I realized that he probably didn't want to take a chance of being seen by Pete or Patty, so I nervously began making my way toward the dreaded woods. I hesitated just a moment before plunging into the pines, wishing I had some breadcrumbs to throw behind me in case I got lost. I was definitely no Nature Channel junkie, but even to my untrained senses something seemed off. Not an owl hooted or frog croaked. Not even a cricket had the decency to chirp to soothe my frayed nerves.

I called out into the night. "Hey, Merc – where are you? It's dark as pitch. I can't see a thing." I must have sounded scared because his voice was silky smooth in what I felt sure was an attempt to calm me.

"I'm right over here, Grace. You'll be fine. Just follow my voice. I've got a surprise for you."

Oh – a surprise! How romantic! But the thrill was short-lived. Since I was counting, I knew that I had taken exactly six steps when a force so strong it nearly swept me off my feet seized my body. It felt as if a giant magnet had taken control of my limbs and was pulling me forward, deeper and deeper into the black abyss of trees. I wanted to fight the compulsion by planting my feet in the clay earth, but my limbs were frozen solid. With the slick pine needles under me, I slid along like a skier on rough waters, hitting rocks and pinecones on the way to God knows what destination. Wet branches and limbs slapped me in the face, and my hair was caught and pulled over and over again. I desperately wanted to scream, but when I opened my mouth I found that my vocal cords were completely uncooperative, only allowing a raspy squeak of "help" to escape.

Though my body and voice were worthless at the time, my brain had never worked better, nor had my senses. I immediately became aware of a putrid, rotten odor hanging thickly in the air – the same gag-producing smell that had overcome the woods during my picnic with Locke earlier in the day. Along with the stench came the sound of my name being chanted over and over in sadistic stereo by what sounded like hundreds of voices, none of which were Merc's.

I was surprised to find that while the imagined danger of my daily life muddled my brain, sending it into senseless counting exercises and repetitious nonsense, real danger galvanized my grey matter. Everything was happening very quickly, but my marvelous mind was slowing it down allowing me to formulate a plan and, in short order, put it into action.

I knew that as unpleasant an experience as this magnetic ride was, it would be nothing compared to what gruesome fate awaited me at the end of the line. I just didn't think something like this could possibly end well, so with a will I never knew I had in me I forced my limbs and vocal cords to simultaneously obey. Bending my knees deeply, I used every ounce of strength I had to lunge sideways and grab hold of the trunk of a large knotty pine. At the same time I let out a bloodcurdling, ear-splitting, I'm-being-murdered

scream that rang out through the woods, giving rise almost immediately to a host of freshly awakened woodland responses.

Finally loose from the force, I spun around, ready to run in
the direction of the boathouse, but instead I collided head on with
an immovable wall of stone. As strong arms wrapped around me,
I realized that my flight to freedom was not interrupted by an
inanimate block of cement but by a living, breathing body that
was carrying me up through the trees and into the midnight sky.

Chapter Eleven

ANGEL

THE SENSATION OF BEING CARRIED INTO THE AIR ONLY LASTED A MOMENT — just long enough for me to fully make the connection between my mortality and the hard cold ground. But that was enough to completely overwhelm my circuitry and send me into a shock so profound as to render all subsequent thought incoherent, thus inconsequential. Everything happened so quickly that even if my brain had been functional and able to catalogue the event, I doubt seriously that the speed with which we moved would have allowed for any observations or impressions past a blur before my eyes and wind on my face.

Simply put, one minute I was running for my life and the next I was lying in my bed, staring up into the heavenly green eyes of an angel — his countenance full of curious concern, as if trying to decide whether I was alive or dead.

Of course, as my brain and eyes began to focus I realized the face was not that of an angel but instead belonged to the boy I'd left my room to meet only a short time ago. I didn't dare speak to him because I was still trying to make sense of all that had happened since walking toward the woods. I felt like I was seeing the world through a funhouse mirror and nothing I looked at was exactly as it appeared.

I closed my eyes again and reopened them, wanting to make sure that the boy of my dreams would still be there after I blinked. Without warning, images of the frightening incident in the woods flooded through my brain and I began to feel an overwhelming sense of gratitude toward Merc for saving me from an uncertain but surely horrible fate. Unfortunately, the benevolent emotions were only a momentary thing, and when I played the mental tape all the way through to the end my brain exploded with white-hot rage as I remembered the danger I'd been put in and whose note had brought me to the brink of disaster. With every ounce of strength in my weakened state I could command, I drew my hand back and slapped the dark boy's awe-inspiring face. And finally, after all these years, I understood the reason behind violence.

It had always been a mystery to me – why men went around punching each other with abandon. What lay behind the primal need of man to inflict bodily injury on man? I'd seen it on television and observed it firsthand on school grounds and military bases, yet I could never comprehend the compulsion that caused one human being to drive a fist into the face of another.

Well, now I knew. It was an amazingly cathartic experience – if only temporarily. All the confusion and frustration of the last two days – maybe even the last two years – was packed into the slap I'd delivered to Merc's gorgeous face. A sense of euphoria swept through my body like a drug. Of course, that euphoria was quickly supplanted by guilt, and I guess that was the difference between the bully on the playground and me.

Sitting up on the bed, I put my elbows on my knees and pushed my face into my hands, suddenly ashamed of the violence of my rash action. I finally got the nerve to peek up at Merc through my fingers, wondering why he had, thus far, not made a sound in response to my strike. Thankfully, he didn't seem angry or indignant. The look on his face was pure shock mixed with more than a touch of hurt.

"Why did you do that, Gracie? Did it make you feel better?" His gaze was penetrating, as if he was attempting to read into my mind. There was a quiet desperation in his tone I didn't understand.

My palm stung from the blow I'd delivered, and I lowered my eyes away from his stare, pretending to study my lifeline. I didn't want to look at him. I felt real shame, all my machismo washed away with regret.

"I'm not really sure," I finally admitted. "I'm just really, really sick to death of being lied to. Nobody will tell me the truth, but I'm smart enough to know something strange is going on with Mrs. B., Willem, Locke . . . and you." I stopped and took a deep breath before continuing. "Who are you really, Merc? And who are the old folks and Locke? Don't say you don't know because I know you do." I looked up at him with eyes full of reawakened defiance. "And while you're at it, you can tell me who tried to hurt me tonight – and who was chasing me this afternoon, too."

"Look, Gracie," he jumped into my tirade. "I can answer some of your questions, and some of them I can't. I'm trying to figure out some things, too. You aren't the only one who is confused and . . . scared."

I could tell that last admission had cost him. All evidence of the cocky charmer of last night and the smooth operator from the morning were gone. He looked almost as lost as I felt – maybe more so. It could have been my Joan of Arc persona resurrected or perhaps a never-before mothering instinct come to life, but I wanted to reach out to him – help him and take his pain away.

I laid a gentle hand – the same hand that had moments before struck him – on his shoulder. "It's okay, Merc; really, it is. I'm so sorry I hit you. I was wrong to do that." It was a first for me – admitting wrong. Surprisingly, it felt good to do it. "You know, Merc, since we both want to figure out what's going on, why don't we work together to get some answers?"

I held my breath, waiting for his rejection – expecting his rejection. And he did hesitate, but only for a moment.

"Yeah . . . maybe. I guess that would be all right."

He didn't sound the least bit enthusiastic but I was excited enough for the both of us. Finally! Some action!

"Great!" I exclaimed.

Maybe I was displaying a bit too much emotion because he looked a little taken aback by my enthusiasm.

"So where do you think we should start?" he asked. His voice was tinged with stress, obviously dreading the possible answer to his question.

"How about with the things we already know? You could tell me about yourself, Merc. The real, unvarnished truth of how you came to be on Mrs. B.'s property with the others."

I jumped up from the bed and retrieved the pen and paper I'd planned to use earlier in the evening to make my investigative list. "I want to do this right," I explained when he looked questionably at the items in my hand.

He just shrugged indifferently and slid farther onto the bed putting his back to the padded headboard and crossing his arms.

"So . . ." I said, pushing him to get started on his story. I had the sneaking suspicion that he was coming up with an edited version of his life, right there on the spot. I wasn't going to have it.

"Uh, uh, Merchison – don't even . . ."

"Don't even what, Gracie?" His look of innocence was so overdone that I laughed out loud.

"Don't even try to leave things out. No secrets. Okay?"

"I'm not sure I've known you long enough to lay my whole life out on the table for your perusal. I'm assuming you know that turnabout is fair play, right?"

Ugh! He'd found my Achilles heel. I wanted to know every little thing about him but I had no desire to tell him all my deep dark secrets. Of course, that was because I had no deep dark secrets – not really. I'd led a pretty boring life and except for my trips to the shrink there was nothing the least bit interesting about me. Not that my OCD was all that fascinating, either, but it did set me apart from the average gal – just not in a good way. I would have to do my best to keep Merc talking about himself so that he wouldn't have the time to talk about me.

"Why don't you start by telling me how you came to live in Tallassee on Mrs. B.'s property?"

"It was my uncle's idea for me to move to Tallassee, and he arranged for me to live in the guesthouse."

Oh, surely he knew that brief explanation wasn't going to cut it. I didn't want to push him too hard so I tried a little gentle prodding.

"Your uncle – is that who raised you?"

He seemed surprised that I'd made that assumption. Of course, he didn't know that Locke had filled me in on a few of his details - like that he was an orphan.

"Yeah . . . yeah . . . my uncle took me in when I was five, after my parents died."

"Oh Merc, how awful for you." I reached out to touch him, to comfort him, but he suddenly seemed so detached, as if he was lost in another world. I hesitated to break into his concentration, even with a touch.

"It *was* awful," he finally agreed. "My parents died when our home burned to the ground. I was there that night but I got out. They didn't."

Looking at him now, he seemed much older than his nineteen years, as if the weight of the world was on him. This time, I couldn't help myself. I put my arm around him and pulled him close to me. To my surprise, he didn't pull away but laid his head on my shoulder. I could feel the heaviness of his heart and it ripped through me as if it was my own pain. For the first time in my life, I was experiencing genuine empathy for another person and it left me deeply shaken.

Neither Merc nor I moved for quite a while, but finally he lifted his head from my shoulder and looked directly into my eyes, his stare full of bewilderment.

"I've never talked to anyone about that night – until now. I'm not really sure why I told you. I usually just lie or avoid the subject."

I was moved, so much so that I could scarcely speak. I'd never been anyone's confidante before. I was touched that this strange, beautiful boy had trusted me.

A feeling descended upon the room after he spoke those words – a sense of "specialness." It was as if we were supposed to be there together, talking and sharing – and planning. I knew I wasn't by myself in the feeling. Merc was touched by it, too, and that was the best part. I didn't feel alone anymore. I began to experience real hope for the first time, and my heart felt as if it might explode with joy.

I could have sat there with him all night. We wouldn't have even needed to say a word. But I felt like he wanted to talk, that he had things he needed to get off his chest. So I pushed, ever so gently, for him to continue. I put my pen and paper away, not wanting to make him uncomfortable by my note taking. I wasn't worried. I didn't think there was a chance I would forget a single thing he had to say.

"You must have been really scared the night of the fire. How did you manage to get out of the house – if you don't mind my asking?"

He appeared to consider the question for a minute and then replied. "I don't mind you asking, Gracie. Though we've only just met, I know we are supposed to be having this conversation."

My heart thrilled at his admission. So he did feel it, too. It wasn't exactly déjà vu; I didn't think we'd done all of this before. It was just a sense of "rightness," for lack of a better term. It was right that we were together - sharing confidences. I didn't know where it all would lead but I was willing to sign up for the ride.

"I feel the same way, Merc." I said, smiling shyly at him, marveling at whatever miracle had brought me to this point in my life.

"You asked me how I got out of the house that night. I'll tell you, but you should be prepared, Grace. The answer is going to surprise you. In fact, I'll be shocked if you believe me. The night of the fire changed everything in my life and not just because my parents died."

"I will believe you, Merc," I pledged. "I know I can trust you. So just tell me. How *did* you escape?"

"An angel carried me through the fire and out of the house."

Had I heard him right? Had he said that an angel saved him? How was I supposed to respond to that? The silence felt heavy in the room but then, after a moment, the thought occurred to me that I might have assigned the wrong meaning to his statement.

"Do you mean a Good Samaritan came along and rescued you, Merc? That's amazing. You must have been so grateful." I knew that wasn't what he had meant. Deep down inside, I was sure he had meant he was saved by a halo-wearing, harp-playing, winged son of the Most High, but I was trying to buy a little time to formulate a response that wouldn't sound too sarcastic or shocked.

He let out a loud gush of air and rolled his eyes. "No, that is not what I meant and you know it."

He was on to me but I was ready for him. If Merc was crazy, he sure played sane well. He seemed completely lucid to me. But he had been through a horrible trauma at a very early age. It would be perfectly understandable if his terrorized, childish eyes misinterpreted the events and people from that night. I wasn't going to belittle him or judge him. I was going to be the ideal girlfriend (fingers crossed). I would listen to his story and help him deal with the pain in the best way that I knew how.

"Yeah, I guess I did know what you meant but I wanted to be sure," I admitted. "So I've never known anyone who has met an angel. Tell me about it."

He studied my face, trying to decide whether I was being sarcastic or not. I carefully arranged my features to reflect only serious interest in what he had to say. In truth, I really was curious.

It had begun to rain heavily outside again and with only one dim lamp burning in the corner of my room the scene was set perfectly for Merc's tale, which, told in his low serious voice, took on the feel of a ghost story.

He settled back against the headboard and began. "The night of the fire, I'd gone to bed early. I was at the tail end of chickenpox and was still running a slight fever. I'd been asleep for hours when I was awakened by the sound of my mother screaming my name."

I felt Merc slipping into a kind of trance as he told the tale. He was reliving each horrendous moment in his mind, and the pain of those scenes was etched into his flawless face.

"At first, I thought I was having a nightmare brought on by the fever and medicine. But the smoke had already overtaken my room and I was finding it difficult to breathe. I began yelling for my mom and dad, and I heard them crying out for me, but after only a few moments I could hear nothing but the horrible noises from the fire." He said the last words so low I had to lean in toward him to hear them. "I'll never forget those sounds as long as I live – the sounds of death and destruction."

This time Merc reached out for my hand and I grabbed it, trying to convey every bit of compassion I could through my touch. I didn't say a word – I couldn't. I just kept listening to the sounds of Merc's heart breaking all over again.

"I was so scared and confused that I just froze to the spot. I literally couldn't move but when I could no longer hear my parents calling me, I knew." He stopped for a minute and when he continued his voice was choked with emotion. "I knew they were dead. They wouldn't have left me any other way." He shook his head, as if trying to clear the images from his mind. "So I put my blanket over my head and crawled underneath my bed, desperately trying to escape the smoke and heat . . . and noise – that awful noise." His voice regained some of its strength for just a moment as he confided, "I knew I was going to die, Gracie, and because I knew my parents were dead, I was okay with that. I just didn't want to burn up. I could see the flames outside the door of my room and I prayed – I prayed so hard – that I would die before they made it to where I was."

Deflating again, he rubbed his eyes, as if fighting the urge to cry. Who could blame him? Tears were pouring down my face. I could see the image in my mind of Merc as a young child, wrapped in his blanket, under his bed, awaiting death.

"I was just about gone – overtaken by the thick, acrid smoke," he finally continued, "when the whole room lit up with the most unbelievably beautiful light. The smoke was gone, the heat was gone and only a sense of peace and love surrounded me." Merc's beautiful green eyes reflected the wonder of the moment. "I thought I was in Heaven. I really did. And I excitedly crawled out from under the bed, ready to search for my parents, who I knew must have been there as well.

"As I scrambled to my feet, the light in the room began to gradually dim and I realized that I wasn't alone. Standing in front of me was an exquisite boy. He was dressed all in white and had long bright gold hair. From his waist hung a braided belt and from that hung a jewel-encrusted scabbard that contained an ancient-looking sword, its hilt covered in giant rubies and diamonds. And on his back, Gracie, were magnificent . . . wings."

He looked up at me as if daring me to contradict him. I wasn't about to; I was spellbound by his story. If it was a hallucination or misinterpretation, it was very specific.

Why couldn't his story be true? After all, I was raised to believe in God, and I did. But trusting in a vague concept of a benevolent Father in the sky was much different than believing a concrete story about a winged, mythological creature – wasn't it? I held my breath and prayed that the object of my affection wasn't crazy and that I would have the good instincts to know real from fantasy.

"I'm listening, Merc," I encouraged. "Please go on. I can't imagine how you must have felt. I would like to know what happened next."

Satisfied that I wasn't going to turn against him or laugh, he kept talking. "I wasn't really scared at that point – or even surprised. I guess kids are resilient that way. I'd been to Sunday school as a child and had been taught all the typical Bible stories. As we get older, we stop taking things so literally but at six years old I assumed every story I'd been told was true; so a beautiful angel standing in front of me during such a horrific ordeal really didn't seem outside the realm of possibility to me," he reflected.

"The angel was an imposing figure, for sure, but I wasn't intimidated. I think it might have been because of his eyes. Even though he looked to be about sixteen or seventeen years old, his eyes were ancient and filled with such torment that, for a moment, I actually forgot my own tragic circumstances. I wanted to do anything I could to console this conflicted creature."

Merc suddenly jumped up saying he needed to stretch his legs a bit, but I suspected he didn't want me to see just how difficult the memory of the angel's misery was for him to relive. He paced silently for a moment or two and then sat back down on the bed and continued talking.

"I reached out to comfort the angel by laying my hand on his cheek and what happened next, neither of us expected. The second I touched the angel's face my mind was filled with the most horrible images you could imagine. Fires, wrecks, murders and disease were all transmitted from his brain to mine and in that instant I understood what caused the angel so much grief. My young heart bled with the weight of his eternal pain. I wanted to move my hand to escape from the horrendous images but I was strangely compelled to keep watching. Somehow I knew that by sharing his memories I was lessening their tragic hold over him.

"At the very end of the vision, I saw a brief glimpse of another angel – a female – and she was being carried off on the back of a winged creature that I was sure was evil. That vision, in particular, pierced my mind with such hopelessness and despair that I cried out loud, grabbing hold of the boy angel for support."

Merc's speech slowed as he dragged the memory from his mind. "That was when he gently, regretfully pulled my hand away from his face. He kissed my palm and, with eyes full of gratitude, he thanked me for the gift I had unwittingly given to him. He then said it was time for me to go and though I begged him to let me stay, he insisted that it was not my time to be with him or my parents. I wanted to know why, but he only said that I had much still left to do. He told me that I had very special talents, and I was destined to help many souls." Merc stopped for a minute, considering his next words. "He also told me that I was to have a great love in my life who would help me with my cause. He said that if I stayed with him, my love would have to walk the world alone and that she would suffer greatly in my absence. At six years old, I didn't care about all that." He shook his head and laughed wryly. "I wanted to stay with him and go to my parents but he insisted that one day

I would understand. He then thanked me again and wrapped me in his arms.

"The next thing I knew, I was standing in my neighbor's front yard, wrapped in a blanket, watching swarms of police and firemen going in and out of the burned-out hull that was once my house. After a few minutes, a very kind policewoman gathered me up and put me in a patrol car, taking me to the station, where I slept until my uncle picked me up the following afternoon."

The whole time Merc was talking, I was watching his face, checking for any signs that he could be pulling my leg. Studying his serious features I realized almost immediately that he was telling the truth. I wasn't sure how I knew – I just knew. My common-sense girl screamed for the justice of being heard, but I clamped down on her mouth pretty hard. She had no place in my heavenly new world. I'd just been given – in my mind – evidence of another realm, and my brain was fully open to it.

It was a pretty earth-shattering revelation – to say the least. The existence of angels – real angels – rocked the core of my uneventful, ordinary life. I would have to be an idiot to question Merc's veracity. In one short weekend, I'd gone from reading supernatural romance to living it, and there was no going back for me. Merc was quickly becoming my magnificent obsession and whatever he said, I was going to believe. I didn't think I was being gullible. The events of the past two days proved the truth of Merc's story. There was no reasonable, logical explanation for the magnetic force that had grabbed hold of my body or for the faceless entity that had saved me from the same. Clearly there were other-worldly forces at work and I was only glad that the boy sitting next to me on the bed appeared to be operating on the side of right.

I was listening very carefully to my heart, and it was telling me that this boy was special, and not just because he was beautiful. He was going to leave a mark on this world, and I was going to be with him when he did it – if he would have me. He hadn't said that I was the one he was destined to love – the one the angel had spoken about – but in my heart I knew that I was and in my heart I knew that he knew it, too.

It was Merc's turn to study me. He was obviously trying to figure out what was going on in my brain – my reaction to the things he had said. I wouldn't make him wait for long; I turned to him and smiled. "That's the coolest thing I've ever heard."

Surprise colored his face. "You mean you believe me?"

I thought for a moment before answering quietly, "Yeah, I think I do."

He was amazed. "I can't believe it. I wasn't expecting you to buy a word of it, Gracie. I mean, you hardly know me, yet you are willing to believe such a fantastic story." His bright green eyes held mine steadily, and in a voice saturated with emotion, he murmured, "Thank you. Thank you for trusting me."

I blushed from head to toe in response to his warm gaze. I was almost too distracted to ask questions but I finally pulled out of the haze.

"Merc, I'm so glad you told me what you did. I really am. But your story didn't really answer the question of what's going on right here – right now. At least, I don't think it did. Something or someone tried to hurt me tonight, and I need to know who – or what – it was."

Still sitting next to me on the bed, he casually rubbed my arm, sending chills down my spine – good chills.

"I told you from the beginning, I don't understand everything myself, Gracie. I do think that all of this is connected to me and to the angels."

My head shot up in shock. Did he say angels - as in more than one?

"Uh, Merc . . . what do you mean angel*ssss*?" I drug out the "s" to emphasize the plural form. "Why do I feel like you left something out of your story?"

He flashed his million-watt grin a little sheepishly. "I didn't really mean to leave anything out. I never said I was finished. I was just taking a little break, seeing how you handled the first part before I got to the weird stuff."

I jumped up from the bed and turned – hands on hips – to face him head-on.

"The weird stuff? Are you telling me that I haven't already heard the weird stuff?" My voice cracked with dismay. "If meeting an angel isn't weird, please – by all means – tell me what is."

He looked a little nervous, as if he might be reconsidering full disclosure.

"I'm kind of thirsty. Do you think we could sneak down and get something to drink?" he asked sweetly, intentionally manipulating me with his gorgeous dimple and pleading green eyes.

I highly suspected that he was stalling for time, possibly giving me a chance to recuperate from one bombshell before hitting me with another, more earth shattering, revelation. I didn't mind because this time I was surer of him than before. I believed that he would be honest with me now that he understood that I wasn't going to duck and cover at the first sign of strange.

I was very curious about what further secrets he had to reveal. I couldn't imagine anything more staggering than the angelic admission, but clearly I had much to learn about Merc's world and I was ready to be taught.

Chapter Twelve

HEAVEN AND HELL

WE SNEAKED DOWNSTAIRS TO THE KITCHEN, GIGGLING LIKE FOOLS, AND grabbed a couple of sodas and a bag of chips to snack on. I hadn't even thought about eating in hours and that alone bore witness to my altered state of mind.

As we tiptoed back to my room, I felt Merc's large hand on the "medium" of my back, and I almost purred with satisfaction. If the girls from Homeroom 12 could see me now, they would expire from envy. I made myself a mental note to add that scenario to my growing list of things to daydream about while falling asleep.

As Merc and I sat cross-legged on my bed, we crunched on chips and drank our sodas, neither bringing up anything controversial as we snacked.

I finally polished off my drink and turned toward him, ready and willing to hear what info qualified for "weirder than an angel." Seeing that I was itching to talk – really talk – he gushed out a breath that sounded like a capitulation and ran his hands through his thick dark hair.

"You think you want to know everything about me, Grace, but you may not realize what you're getting yourself into. Once you know things, you know them. You can't really 'unring the bell,' if you get what I mean."

"It doesn't seem to me that I've got much of a choice here, Merc," I said quietly. "And even if I did, I would still choose to know everything." I stared down at my empty soda can, too shy to look him in the eye. "Would it make sense to say I feel like I'm supposed to be here . . . with you? Like my life has been building to this point and this night is the culmination of all that has come before." I paused for a moment, struggling to put into words the feelings that were swirling around in my brain and in my heart. "I mean, I've never seen angels, Merc, or done anything particularly special. In fact, my life up until now has been unremarkable – to say the least."

My eyes stung with tears of embarrassment but I kept going – determined to be as honest with Merc as he had been with me. I peeked up at him through wet lashes, hoping I wouldn't see pity on his face.

His expression was not only full of love but also so strangely familiar as to have me wondering if we had shared a past life. My heart missed several beats as he reached over and tucked a stray curl behind my ear and then laid his warm palm against my cheek.

"Nothing about you is unremarkable, Gracie. You are absolutely mesmerizing. I could stay right here in this room with you forever and be perfectly satisfied. But there is still so much that you don't know about me, and I would never want to do anything to hurt you." His voice dropped to a whisper. "I know what you're feeling, Gracie, because I'm feeling it too. But we have to be careful – really careful. Strange things are happening. Things I don't understand."

I was so surprised – so blown away – by his words that I could only dumbly nod and sigh, hypnotized by his liquid eyes and warm touch. My brain completely skipped over the part about strange things happening and my getting hurt.

In a flash his beautiful eyes changed from warm to searing hot and, with a gentleness that seemed at odds with his almost violent gaze, he bent toward me and put his lips on mine – changing my life forever.

I would have expected fireworks, maybe even to see a star or two, but I wasn't prepared for the loud click in my brain that signaled the other half of myself snapping neatly into place. It was as if I'd spent the last seventeen years missing a vital part of my makeup that was suddenly and permanently restored to me the moment Merchison Spear's lips touched mine.

Those were my thoughts and they sounded insane even to me – insane but true. With Merc's kiss, every insecurity and negative thought disappeared. I was no longer angry with my parents. In fact, I understood my mother's need to be with my father. My sister-in-law – always so irritating, even borderline evil – now in my altered mind's eye was angelic in her kind and loving patience with me. The kids at school, my teachers, and my brother all took on different personas in the light of the dawn of my new understanding. Like Snow White who'd been given new life when kissed by her Prince Charming, I'd been given the same by the lips of my love. But even my Prince Charming had changed in that moment. Though he was as gorgeous as before, I no longer objectified that beauty but only cherished it as the corresponding half of my own spectacular new whole – a whole that feared nothing, despised nothing and resented nothing.

Unfortunately, Merc might need a little convincing. While my newly christened lips were beaming with the happiness of my awakened reality, he didn't look so good. I would love to say he was breathless. I could have lived with stunned. But preoccupied – that wasn't what I'd been hoping for at all. Yet that was exactly what Merc was. After our kiss, he turned his head to the side as if he had heard a sound, and then without as much as a "thank you ma'am," he ran to the window and ripped open the blinds.

"Merc . . . uh . . . what are you doing?" I struggled to reconcile my recent past with my present.

"I'm sorry, Gracie. This is not the way I wanted you to find out."

"Find out what? What are you talking about?" I was almost yelling now, with no thought of the ears that might hear.

"I really am sorry," he mumbled. And with that, right in front of my disbelieving eyes, my Prince Charming threw open the window, climbed over the ledge, and jumped.

Under normal circumstances I would have stopped to check my pulse and wait for the inevitable signs of heart failure, but not this time. This time I had not a single thought for myself. Every fiber of my being cried out for the boy I had just watched plunge to his almost certain demise. Well, maybe death wasn't a certainty; it was only three stories to the ground. But catastrophic injury was a definite possibility. I was stunned. Merc hadn't paused or even looked unsure or frightened. I was scared enough for both of us as I raced to the window and peered over, fearful of what I might see below.

With no lights to illuminate the back of the inn, I was spared the sight of my heart's desire in a mangled mess on the hard ground below my window. I needed to see, though, so I ran to my bedside table and grabbed the flashlight I kept in the drawer for use during the frequent power outages inherent to an area rife with thunderstorm activity. Thankful that Pete had changed the batteries in it recently, I flipped on the switch and leaned over the sill as far as I could, shining the light straight down on the ground below.

I hadn't realized I was holding my breath until, seeing only empty dirt and pine needles, I let out a loud whoosh of air, relieved that neither Merc — nor any of his body parts — was within view. I was frustrated and puzzled, wondering how Merc could possibly have made that jump unscathed. I began swinging the bright beam from left to right in an attempt to catch a glimpse of his departing silhouette but was only further disheartened when he was nowhere in sight.

The less sage, more insecure, pre-kiss girl of an hour ago would have wondered if I could have possibly been so lacking in make-out mojo as to cause Merc to run for the hills, never to return. But I wasn't that silly young thing anymore. I was confident and assured and completely convinced that, despite my sad lack of technique, Merchison Spear was as crazy for me as I was for him.

Even so, there was nothing that could be done about his sudden departure. So with a final look around I reached up to close the window, and that was when the piercing female screams of "Help!" coming from the direction of the lake cut through the silent night. Shocked, I again leaned out the window and just as I did the inn's perimeter lighting clicked on, illuminating the ground from the building to the woods.

Instinctively, I looked in the direction from which the screams came even though I knew whoever was doing the yelling was out of my line of sight. I didn't see anything but trees and at first I thought the movement I saw in the distance was a waving branch from a thin pine. As my eyes became accustomed to the landscape lights, I realized with a start that I wasn't looking at a lone tree but a lone figure – tall, thin and robed – standing just at the edge of the woods some twelve to fifteen yards from the back of the inn.

My breath left my body but my eyes never moved from the spot on which the hooded figure stood. I stared in fascinated horror as the creature raised its hideous head to pierce me through and through with its malevolent, glowing, blood-red eyes. It lifted its arms, extending its bony, decrepit hands out toward me, as if welcoming me into its demonic fold.

I wanted to scream but I couldn't. I wanted to run but I couldn't do that either. Once again, I felt my body taken over by a compulsion too strong for me to fight and I immediately knew that the thing standing at the edge of the trees – beckoning me toward it – was one and the same as the evil magnet of the woods from earlier in the night. Just as I had been paralyzed in the woods, I was now motionless with fear and anxiety, unable to fight the force that literally lifted my body up and over the windowsill and dragged me through the night air toward the waiting monster's arms.

No words exist to express the depth of my terror at that moment, slowly moving through space, closer and closer into the clutches of evil personified. I wanted to close my eyes to block out the leering jack-o-lantern grin that decorated its hideous face but, unable to look away, I saw every scar and crevasse of the repulsive visage, every moment with more perfect clarity.

Illuminating Gracie

I was so focused on the horrific object in front of me that I never saw my savior until his arms wrapped around my waist, dragging me away from the vile creature and back into the safety of my bedroom. I didn't think it was possible for me to be more confused, but I was when I saw the face of the boy who'd rescued me.

It wasn't my beloved - my knight - my prince. It was Locke Wingard, and yet not Locke, all at the same time. There was something distinctly different about him, though I was helpless to explain the change. It might have been the startling moments that led up to my saving that caused my eyes to detect a glow emanating from around Locke's body.

Maybe it was the illumination of appreciation that I was seeing; but I didn't think so. Locke really seemed to be alight from within. His iridescence faded rather quickly, though, and pretty soon I was left with only the memory of a glow and a nagging thought that I was somehow missing an obvious piece in a puzzle I was trying to solve. But the mystery would have to wait because a more urgent question was pushing its way toward the forefront of my cerebellum.

"How . . . how . . . how," I stuttered. "How did you do that?" This time I was going to get some answers. Locke had wrestled me from the demon's grip, midair. No way, no how was that possible. I wasn't sure what he was – maybe some kind of high school superhero? But one thing was for sure: before he left the room, I was going to know.

Locke turned and leveled me with a cool, amused stare. Gone was the good ol' boy routine and in its place a personality, I suspect, more in line with his true character – that of an arrogant jackass.

"What . . . what . . . what . . . did I do?" He laughed.

God! Why did I waste a slap on Merc when I should have been saving my energy for a full-on punch across Locke's condescending face? Well, at least his response had, if only momentarily, diverted me from going into shock as the result of my terrifying demonic flight.

"Don't you dare make fun of me, you jerk," I screamed. Then to my absolute horror I burst into deep wracking sobs, an obvious delayed reaction to my close call with the devil.

138

"Hey, hey, hey . . . don't cry," he said, while patting my back awkwardly. Despite myself, I turned into his arms and buried my face in his chest.

"I don't get anything that's going on," I sobbed. "And I am really, really scared. Please, Locke, please . . . tell me what's happening to me. Who or what was that thing?"

I finally looked up at him with tears coursing down my cheeks. I guess, despite his over-blown ego, he was a softie at heart because in his eyes I saw genuine compassion. He stroked my hair and murmured soft words of comfort before gently pushing me away.

"Okay, okay, Grace," he said softly. "I guess you're right. You do deserve some sort of explanation. It's like this . . . "

And with those words, all hell broke loose. The inn was suddenly alive with noise. I heard men yelling, women screaming, and doors slamming.

"What in Heaven's name is going on?" My brain was immediately assaulted with images of a demonic invasion. I flew to my bedroom door with Locke right on my heels, ready to fling it open and investigate the chaos coming from the other side.

Though bedlam ruled, I still managed to remember that it was very, very late – or really, very, very early – and there was a boy – no, a young man – in my bedroom. I quickly turned to Locke, putting my hand up in the universal signal for STOP.

"Stay here," I commanded. "My brother and sister-in-law don't need to see you leaving my room."

He rolled his eyes. "Ridiculous! I'll meet you downstairs," he said. Before I could respond, he walked over to the window and just like Merc had before him climbed over the sill and jumped.

"WHAT . . . THE . . . WHAT?" I screamed to no one in particular. This time I didn't even bother with racing to the window and looking down. I knew Locke wouldn't be there. I mean, the boy rescued me from midair, so I shouldn't be surprised if he jumped from the third story. In fact, at this point, nothing should surprise me. I shrugged my shoulders and walked out of the room to see what was going on.

Leaning over the hallway balcony, I immediately noticed that all the lights had been turned on around the inn, but there was not a soul in sight. I could hear the buzz of voices coming from outside so I flew down the stairs and out the front doors to investigate.

Of all the sights I expected to see, a wet Merc being attended to by not one but two visiting airheads was about the last thing on my list. I would rather have been greeted by the sight of the entire bed & breakfast group floating through the air toward the Devil himself than my beautiful Romeo caught in the clutches of the Doublemint Twins. But there he was, smack dab in the middle of the two blonde bimbos, their ample bosoms visibly heaving through soaked wet T-shirts. I wanted to throw up right on the spot but instead I stood on the deck of the inn – right next to the barbeque grill – and did a little heavy breathing of my own. I was seething with anger as I watched their every movement and though I didn't join the group of folks now milling around the pier, I heard enough of their talk to get the gist of the story.

The sleaze sisters had commandeered the inn's fishing boat in order to row across the lake and meet up with two boys from town. Apparently, all went well on the first crossing but problems arose for the girls on the return trip. One or the other of them (they're interchangeable) stood up to wave to her townie boyfriend and the small boat flipped, throwing both the girls into the dark lake. Since neither had the foresight nor intelligence to secure life vests for the voyage, they were in serious peril when they hit the water.

At that moment, I was wishing they were still in the water. Not a particularly charitable or Christian thought – but a truthful one. More disturbing still was that as I stood steaming and staring into the melee, I couldn't help noticing how perfect Merc looked sandwiched in between the two blondes. Weak and disheartened, I felt all my newfound confidence drain away even as I scolded myself for the lack of faith I had in Merc – and in me. Only minutes before I would have bet my life on Merchison's devotion. Maybe I'd just been caught up in the powerful grip of first love, but in that bedroom with Merc by my side I felt as if we would be together forever. And now all those dreams were being washed away by a pair of mindless miscreants in tight, wet T-shirts.

From a distance, I looked on as the twins' grateful and indulgent father shook hands with Merc, thanking him for his timely intervention in the girls' plight. I suddenly wondered how Merc had managed to be in the right place at the right time to play hero. Thinking back, I recalled how he had seemed to hear something just before his unexpected exit out the window. From inside my bedroom at the back of the inn, it seemed impossible for him to have heard the girls scream. I certainly didn't hear anything. In retrospect, his hasty retreat had me wondering whether he had been running away from me or running to them. And as much as I detested the thought of Merc playing savior to the twins, that thought was preferable to his leaving my arms because he was turned off by my kiss.

So many thoughts and questions were racing through my mind I could barely concentrate on any one thing. I tried to catch Merc's eye, but he never looked in my direction. I wanted to slink quietly back to my room and lick my wounds in private but I was honestly too scared to be by myself, terrorized by the thought of what lay in wait for me.

Since the errant object of my devotion was clearly more interested in the twins than in me at the moment, my thoughts turned to Locke. Would Merc feel differently if he knew what tragedy had almost befallen me? Maybe he would pay a little closer attention to me if he saw his rival by my side. Or more likely than that, the blonde wunderkind would offer to take one of the sisters off his hands and they would all ride off into the sunrise together. That sounded like a more plausible ending to the evening. I'd be left to fend off the monster alone while the girls entertained the two boys that I'd mistakenly imagined were interested in me.

As I struggled to remember my number sequences, I knew my thoughts were even more erratic than usual. But I didn't realize how close I was to completely losing it until I felt a warm breath on my neck, followed by a chuckle in my ear. I nearly jumped out of my shoes.

"Do you know you are literally shaking all over, Grace? I could hear your teeth chattering from ten feet away."

It was Locke, of course, and I could only feel relief when he put his arm around my shoulders and squeezed.

"I d-d-don't know what you are t-t-talking a-buh-buh-bout." I could barely get the words out. I could feel my limbs trembling and see my world going white . . . again. Delayed stress was taking over as I lost my senses one by one.

"Grace? Grace?" Locke's voice was getting farther and farther away as my blanched vision slowly narrowed to a point. I was dimly aware of being lifted off my feet.

The last thing I remember before losing consciousness was Patty's cry of alarm. "Grace? Oh, my goodness! She's fainted! Has she been drinking?"

Chapter Thirteen

I NEED TO KNOW

I WOKE TO A CACOPHONY OF VOICES ABUZZ ALL AROUND ME. I CONFESS to feigning unconsciousness for several minutes longer than necessary. It's amazing the things one can overhear when folks don't think you are listening to them.

"What I'd like to know is why both boys were skulking around our property in the dead of night," I heard Patty whisper.

"I'm sure there is a perfectly good explanation for their presence," came Pete's diplomatic reply – ever the statesman.

"You don't think *both* those adorable boys were at the inn to see Grace, do you? I mean, can you imagine?" One twin sniped, as the other giggled.

I couldn't believe how loud everyone was talking. My ears seemed to pick up each separate conversation with ease.

"I wish Grace could stay on her feet," Merc said, with sweet concern in his voice.

"You wouldn't think she'd have such a delicate constitution," Locke observed.

Hey! Wait one minute! Was that arrogant buffoon taking a shot at my weight? That jerk!

"What happened to make her pass out, Locke?" Merc sounded angry now – accusatory.

"You would know if you hadn't been so busy playing hero to the twins," Locke shot back.

Hmmm . . . Locke could be lovable sometimes.

"What was I supposed to do, let them drown?" Merc groused.

"They wouldn't have drowned. They have built-in flotation devices." I heard Locke snicker and I almost laughed out loud, giving myself away. Merc wasn't laughing though.

"Very funny. Stop stalling. What happened to Gracie? Why does she end up on the ground every time she's around you?" Merc was really mad now, and I knew I should open my eyes and take control of the situation before it got out of hand.

"It's neither the time nor the place for this conversation, boy." Locke was as mad as Merc now, with not a stitch of the previous humor in his voice.

Surprisingly, Merc backed down or at least didn't fire back, opting for silence. I blinked my eyes open, trying to appear as if I was just coming round. I slowly turned my head to the side and was puzzled to see only the two boys next to me. I was lying on the sofa in the great room of the inn, obviously having been carried there by either Locke or Merc.

"Uh . . . where is everyone?"

"Just relax, Gracie. Locke and I are right here. No worries." Merc was fanning my face with a magazine. He looked anxious – even alarmed. I wondered if he could possibly be so distressed about me; I hoped so.

"I thought Pete and Patty were in here . . . and the twins." I tried to rise to look around but Merc gently pushed me back down on the couch.

"Pete and Patty have gone to take care of the fishing boat, and the twins are down by the lake, probably waiting to get chewed out by their father. Pete said you pass out a lot, so they weren't too worried. He did say for you to keep your feet up for a while, so PLEASE keep your feet up." He sat down on the end of the couch, lifting my legs and then dropping them back down on his lap.

I was completely perplexed. I could have sworn that everyone I'd heard talking while I was faking unconsciousness was standing right next to me. *Curiouser and curiouser.*

I must have looked confused because Locke repeated Merc's suggestion, making it sound more like a command. "Relax, Grace. You don't look so good."

Merc ignored Locke and, dropping the magazine on the floor, grabbed my wrist and began checking my pulse.

"This is twice you've fainted this weekend. You really need to go to the doctor," he said.

"Ha!" I sat straight up on the couch. "I knew you were there!"

Merc looked bewildered. "You knew I was where?"

"You were in the woods when I was on the picnic with Locke . . . when I fainted. I heard you two talking, but when I came around and asked Locke where you were, he said I was hallucinating."

I glared at Locke, who had the good grace to blush before attempting to lie again.

"When you fainted on the deck a few minutes ago, I told Merc about your passing out in the woods on our picnic."

"Stop it! Just stop it! No more lies. The three of us are going to talk. Now!"

Merc patted my arm condescendingly and at the same time leveled a warning look toward Locke. I would have said more, but Patty and Pete came strolling into the room.

"Grace, welcome back to the land of the living," Pete boomed.

"How are you feeling, honey?" Patty asked, rushing to my side and giving me an uncomfortable hug.

"I'm fine . . . really fine," I assured them. "You know me, a little excitement and out I go."

"Yep, we do know you," Pete agreed. "And we know you need some rest, Grace. Why don't you say goodnight?" He turned to

Merc and, sticking out his hand, said, "I can't thank you enough, Merc. You averted what could have been a real tragedy."

"Oh, I don't know. I don't think it was the twins' time to go," Locke jumped in, causing my brother and his bride to look at the blonde boy with wary surprise.

"Well . . . still," Patty said haltingly. "Things could have turned out really badly if Merc hadn't intervened." She looked pointedly from Merc to Locke and back again. "Which reminds me, boys. What were you two doing here so late?"

"Patty!" Pete and I cried in unison.

"I was just curious," she mumbled and sniffed while giving her long blonde locks an unnecessary toss.

I watched Merc with amused interest as he attempted to explain. I was pretty curious about a few things, too.

"I went to get a CD from my car tonight and I realized that Grace had left her wallet in there. I was afraid she might need it, so I decided to bring it by to her. It was so late when I got here, it seemed like a better choice to hide it on the property and call her in the morning to tell her where I put it." He slung an arm around Locke's shoulder before adding, "Locke just came along for the ride. We were hunting for a place to leave the wallet when I heard the girls scream."

Man, I forgot what a good liar Merc was. He'd certainly tied everything up in a nice tidy package, and Pete and Patty bought the whole thing.

"Well, you certainly can't fault your timing," Pete laughed. "And it was amazing how you managed to get both girls to shore. You must be a really strong swimmer."

Patty wasn't looking at Merc. She was eyeing Locke and I'm sure wondering why he hadn't gotten wet. Locke was oh-so-aware of Patty's eyes, and I saw him bristle at the obvious silent comparisons being made between him and the hero of the hour. I'm sure he would have said a word or two in his defense if he could have thought of something to say without discrediting Merc's version of events. He was stuck with the story, and he didn't like it one bit. To make matters worse, Merc had to throw a little dig in his direction.

"It *would* have been nice to have a little help, but Locke here isn't much of a swimmer, so I made him stay on the banks. I didn't want to have to end up saving three people." Merc's sideways grin told me he was enjoying the other boy's discomfort way too much.

"Yeah, yeah, yeah. You're just a real stud. How ever can I compete?" He threw Merc's arm off with a shrug. "It's late, let's go. The sun will be up soon and Granddad will be worried."

I wanted to argue with him – to demand that they stay and give the promised answers. They both had some major explaining to do, but it would have seemed too odd to Pete and Patty so I kept quiet. I was also scared to death, but that couldn't be helped either. Most girls I knew would probably cry to their family or call 911. But that just wasn't me and for good reason. Over the years I had developed somewhat of a reputation for fabrication or, at least, exaggeration and I didn't see any good coming from reporting the bizarre incidents that had happened over the last few days. I would just end up in a home away from home – complete with designer padded walls and security bars on the doors and windows. Even worse, I would be whisked away from my new love faster than you can say, "Loony Tunes," and I wasn't about to let that happen. I had the right to remain silent, and I was going to.

Under great protest, Merc swept me from the couch and into his arms. I normally wouldn't have stood for such an action – too horrified to enjoy the ride for concern of my crushing weight. I certainly didn't need the assistance, either, because in truth after my quick blackout recovery I'd never felt better. But I wasn't above playing the fading flower should the act be of some romantic benefit to me and, thanks to my active day, I was actually feeling a few pounds lighter as well.

Eyes bulging with curiosity, Pete – always the practicing pseudo-parent – reminded us that I needed my rest as he passed us on the landing, a none-too-subtle hint that Merc was to stop, drop and roll on out, not stay in my room for an early morning chat. But in my mind that wasn't my dear brother's call, and if Merc wanted to tuck me into bed he was welcome to. In fact, I would encourage it. After all, along with my obvious amorous intent, I had more to worry about than just the average cover monster. I had a real life demon calling my name.

Chapter Fourteen

CRAZY TRAIN

MERC HAD SCARCELY CLEARED THE THRESHOLD BEFORE WE WERE BOTH talking at once: me, demanding answers regarding his sudden and astonishing exit, and him, wanting to know the details of what had happened to me after he left. Abiding by the "ladies first" rule, he insisted that I begin by telling him what had caused my emotional breakdown into blackness. Trying to appear as in-control as possible and failing miserably, I hit the highlights of my near nabbing at the magnetic claws of the Devil – or devil-like being.

Merc was so shaken by the story that I found myself attempting to backpedal – to mitigate in someway the horror of the happening. I watched as his gorgeous face morphed into a mask of anger and his electrifying green eyes darken with a rage that frightened me very nearly as much as the demon did. I attempted to calm the situation by reminding him that I was perfectly fine and that Locke had been there to save me. In hindsight, that probably wasn't the best way to go.

"Locke? Locke!!! Great, just great! While I'm out in the lake saving the twins' worthless hides, Locke is saving the one person that I do really care about."

He was pacing the length of the bedroom with long, angry strides, muttering Locke's name over and over again. "Grace, I know it seems like Locke is a nice guy and all, but I really don't trust him. I wish you would keep your distance from him until I can get some things figured out." He stopped pacing and came to stand directly in front of me, putting his hands on my shoulders and melting me with his pleading green eyes. "I just couldn't take it if something happened to you, Gracie. Believe me, I will never leave you unprotected again, at least not until I find out what we are up against and deal with it."

I was completely hypnotized – entranced – by his heartfelt declaration. He was pledging his devotion to me, and it was almost more than I could take in. In a daze I touched his glorious face, wanting to make sure he was real. As my hand grazed his cheek, he lifted his own hand and placed it over mine and, turning it over, kissed my palm. The sweetness of the gesture took my breath away and, no longer able to contain myself, I stood slightly on my tiptoes and kissed the boy I knew, in my heart, I was meant to be with forever.

Enthralled in the kiss, we both jumped when a voice dripping with sarcasm burst through the haze of our passion.

"Sweet Gabriel! The declining morals of today's youth!" It was Locke, and he was casually leaning against the closet door, arms crossed over his chest, sardonic smile on his angelically beautiful face.

"Locke!" I cried, jumping back from Merc, more embarrassed than guilty. "What in the world? Where did you come from? How did you get in here?" I shot him questions in rapid-fire succession.

"Yeah, how *did* you get in here . . . Locke? Where *did* you come from?" Merc spat the words out through tightly gritted teeth.

My blonde savior barked a laugh before turning toward me. "It wasn't hard, Grace. I've got skills."

Clearing his throat, he continued as he swung around to address Merc. "And as far as where I came from . . . do we really want to get into that here? Now?"

Puzzled, I glanced toward Merc, who looked as if he wanted to hit something, namely Locke's face. But he ignored his pointed question and instead, sounding both tired and frustrated, asked, "Why are you here?"

"I would think the answer to that question is fairly obvious. I bet Grace knows why." He turned to me expectantly.

"No . . . not really," I hedged, though I wasn't being completely truthful. "I hope you're here to finally tell me what's going on. What that thing is that's trying to get me."

I couldn't believe I was behaving so calmly and rationally. I think both boys were surprised at my cool demeanor, as well. I was probably in shock – my mind trying to protect my body from completely shutting down.

"You are the *man* with all the answers," Merc pointed out to Locke. "That 'thing,' as Grace calls it, has to have something to do with you."

Locke seemed shocked and insulted that Merc had drawn that conclusion. "Why would you think that?" he asked.

"Now who's asking the obvious? I mean, considering what you do for a living . . . uh, sorry . . . poor choice of words. Considering your occupation . . . well. . ." Merc let the sentence trail off.

"Ahhh, I get it. You think that I'm the bad guy. That somehow my function is evil."

"Well, isn't it?" Merc demanded.

The conversation between the two guys was completely over my head. I mean, they were on a totally different plane, and I didn't intend to listen to another unexplained minute of it.

"You two – cut it out! I'm not going to be treated like a stupid speck on the wall. That grotesque monster is coming after me, not you," I said, looking directly at Merc. "And not you," I continued, turning my attention to Locke. "Ergo . . . I should be told the 100 percent unvarnished, unaltered truth!"

I fixed both boys with the most ferocious glare I could manage but after they paused for one moment to stare dumbly at me, they went right back to their argument.

"Let me remind you, Locke, I have first-hand knowledge of your *function*. Remember my parents?" Merc spat, not missing a beat over my mini-tantrum.

"Of course I remember your parents, Merc. I saw them just the other day. They couldn't be happier."

Merc stumbled backward onto my bed, his face a portrait of shock and confusion.

Did Locke just say he'd seen Merc's parents?! I thought they were dead. Immediately my mind flashed to the mental images I'd created while Merc was telling me his story. Had it all been one big lie? I felt like I'd been socked in the stomach. But as I looked over at Merc, I realized that whatever I was feeling paled in comparison to the storm of emotions going on inside of him. He looked as if he had seen a ghost. I took a few steps toward the bed, wanting to offer Merc any comfort I could, but suddenly I froze as a conversation I'd had with Locke flashed through my mind.

Full of outrage and feeling like an avenging angel, I went on the attack. "Why would you say a thing like that, Locke? You know full well that Merc's parents are dead! You told me so yourself. Why would you be so cruel?"

Locke was taken aback by my rage, and for once he looked uncertain as to how to proceed. Tempers were flaring and emotions running high, but he clearly hadn't planned on a brawl with a babe. I wasn't backing down, so he stepped around me and stooped down to crouch at Merc's feet. He was whispering something to him, and I strained to hear his words.

"Merc, I'm not who you think I am. Or, at least, what I am is not what you think it is."

Well, that made no sense at all, but I kept listening, hoping for some clarity.

Merc raised his head from his hands, and to my shock there were tears rolling down his cheeks. I felt the buildup of tears in my own eyes, and I swallowed hard trying to keep them at bay.

"Did you really see my pa-pa-parents?" he sputtered out, disbelief and revulsion clear in his voice.

I jumped back as if I'd been kicked. This was getting waaaaaay too weird.

They both looked at me, and Locke reached out his hand. I reluctantly took it and he guided me to sit down on the bed next to Merc.

"I think it's about time we put the cards on the table." Locke said quietly, regret tingeing his tone. "It was never my intention to cause you suffering – neither of you. If you will just listen, I'll try to explain as much as I can."

Finally, finally, finally – the truth! I just hoped I was ready for what he had to say. I had a strong feeling – maybe even a premonition – of impending disbelief. But I'd come this far, so I might as well press forward with this odyssey into the outlandish.

Merc raked his fingers through his hair and unashamedly wiped the tears from his eyes. "What about Pete?" he mumbled to Locke. "He was pretty clear about wanting me to leave. Maybe we should take off and meet up with Gracie somewhere in a few hours."

Lordy, the last thing I wanted to do was to put off this conversation for a single second, but he did have a point. I shuddered to imagine what my brother would say should he come in and find not one, but two guys in my room. He'd think I was making up for lost time in a big way. But I had a strong feeling Merc wanted to get me out of the way so that he could talk to the other boy alone, and I was relieved when Locke said he had the problem covered.

"Pete and Patty won't be a problem," Locke promised, and I could have sworn I saw an actual twinkle in his eye.

"What do you mean, 'they won't be a problem,' Locke?" Merc demanded with so much concern it made me nervous.

"Oh, calm down, for Heaven's sake. I didn't do anything bad to them. I just suggested that they get some good rest and sleep late in the morning."

Why did every communication between Locke and Merc seem like a code? I stifled a yawn and decided to let that one slide in favor of the bigger picture. If Pete came in, I'd deal with the consequences. What was he going to do – ground me?

I watched as Locke helped himself to a bright pink pillow from my bed then flopped down on the floor. Taking that as our cue that he was ready to talk, Merc and I followed suit and got on the floor with him. Deciding to err on the side of caution, I jumped up and ran to lock my door. There was no sense in making things too easy for Pete.

As I sat down with the pair of boys, I was struck by their opposite beauty – one so dark and the other so light, yet equally, ethereally exquisite. Up until two days ago, the only prerequisite I had for a boyfriend was that he wore a smaller waist size in *Levi's* than I did; blow, blow sweet winds of change.

"So where should I begin?" Locke asked. But before I could say anything, Merc stopped me.

"I think it would be best if I finished telling Gracie my story before we get into your . . . uh . . . who you are." He struggled to figure out just what to say.

'That makes sense to me," Locke said, now seemingly eager to get along. "What were you talking about when you were interrupted by the twins screaming?" He made a face, as if remembering something unpleasant. "Oh, yes, never mind. Why don't you tell Grace what happened to you after the fire."

It seemed apparent that Locke had at least some knowledge of the conversation that took place between Merc and me earlier in the evening – the one about the angel. Was it possible that Locke had been hiding in my room when we were sharing confidences? I wanted to confront him, but I was afraid it might stem the flow of confessions and I didn't want to do that. One look at Merc told me the same thought had crossed his mind but he, too, chose to keep silent on the subject. Instead he turned to me and began talking.

"As I told you, Gracie, I was pulled out of my burning house by an angel. A tough story to swallow, I know, but the truth."

Locke made a grumbling noise, but Merc, save for a raised eyebrow, ignored it and continued. "After that night, I lived with a man who called himself my uncle. He really was no relation to me, but saying he was my uncle made things easier."

"If he wasn't your uncle, Merc," I asked, "who was he?"

"He was a man who took care of kids like me – kids who had been exposed to the power of angelic beings." Merc's voice took on an instructional tone. "You see, once someone comes in contact with an angel, his or her physical makeup is subtly – and sometimes not so subtly – changed forever. I began showing signs of those changes almost immediately after the fire."

"What kind of changes?" I asked warily. I was fascinated but also more than a little apprehensive to hear his answer.

"I became stronger, for one thing – almost right away. I could run faster, too. Even my eyesight improved. I no longer needed the glasses that had been prescribed for me the year before. It was like I'd become Superman overnight," he explained.

"Faster than a speeding bullet!" Locke laughed, and for the first time, I had hope that the boys might actually become friends.

But Merc again ignored Locke's remark and continued. "I can tell you, even though I was grieving the loss of my parents, the super strength was pretty heady stuff for a young kid. I was lucky on so many levels to have Theodore to guide me through everything."

"Not to mention how blessed you were to have the angel pass on such gifts to you," Locke pointed out.

Merc cut his eyes to him. "I would have preferred to have my parents."

"That wasn't the angel's choice, Merchison. Your parents died because it was their time to go – plain and simple. Even as a child, you understood that much."

"How could I possibly understand? I was just a kid – a kid who had lost his parents in a brutal, terrible way. I was in shock!" Merc shot back angrily.

What was going on? How did Locke know so much about the death of Merc's parents? None of this made any sense to me. I thought I was going to get answers and instead I was more confused than ever. I felt like I was on a runaway train. I didn't want to get off. I just wanted to slow it down.

To my surprise, Locke didn't meet Merc's tone with a hostile one of his own. Instead he reached out and put a hand on his shoulder. "You *should* have been in shock, but you weren't. You understood because your heart was completely open at the time, unsullied by anger or resentment. You can thank your parents for that. You were a special child, and they raised you with unconditional love, and that love allowed you to see the situation for what it was. Only later did you become closed to the truth. Open your eyes now, and you will see what I'm saying is right, Merc."

As I watched the perplexing exchange between the two boys, something happened before my very eyes that, were I not there to see it, I would never have believed to be true. Locke began to glow. It wasn't a faint luminescence such as I'd seen before – something I could deny to myself. It was a full on, open-twenty-four-hours, glow-in-the-dark light, and it was radiating from Locke's body. Even his eyes seemed to take on a life of their own, elevating their beautiful but normal blue shade to a color I didn't believe existed on any human level.

"Oh, oh," I cried, while jumping from the floor to the bed, desperately trying to put some distance between the strange new Locke and me.

Merc mimicked my action, though not in fear. He didn't seem to be the least bit surprised by the incandescent elephant in the room. He was solely focused on me and my shocked reaction.

"It's all right, Gracie," Merc assured me. "I promise you, it's okay – no one is going to hurt you. Please just let us explain."

I couldn't imagine what possible explanation there could be for having a human neon sign in my room. I couldn't manage even the smallest coherent statement, so I dumbly nodded my head and, carefully maintaining space between Locke and me, listened to their unbelievable words.

"Grace, we've talked about the angel that saved me," Merc started, speaking slowly and soothingly, like one would talk to a young frightened child. "But I left out one vital bit of information about that night." He barked out a short, rueful laugh and swung his head from side to side. "Believe me, I wish I had time to sugarcoat this – to let you get used to the idea of angels before laying this on you. But circumstances require that I just come right out with it." He seemed terribly hesitant as if he were trying to work up the nerve to say what he needed to.

"I don't know why you are making such a big deal out of this," an exasperated Locke jumped in. "This should be good news. Dare I say even glad tidings of great joy! Most people would love to meet a heavenly being – would consider it an honor. Gracie Marie Bennet . . . I'm an . . ."

"Hush, Locke, I need to tell her!" Merc grabbed my hands in his and said the words I knew before they left his mouth. How stupid did they think I was?

"Gracie . . . Locke was the angel that saved me." He seemed to deflate like a balloon, and I realized that this secret he'd been keeping from me, if only for a few short hours, had been weighing on him heavily.

Calmly – almost eerily so – I squeezed Merchison's hands reassuringly and then turned to Locke – or whatever his angelic handle truly was – and studied him, taking in every inch of his heavenly body.

Just what response should I make to this revelation? There was no precedent for such an announcement – at least not in my world. Had I been some loyal handmaiden of the Old Testament I might have recorded my every moment, both prior to and following the blessed event, and having done so ended up memorialized in a book bearing my name. But I was a twenty-first century girl and, as such, much more likely to be committed to an institution than committed to print, should I decide to make known my visit from a divine being. So I decided to follow my standard operating procedure. I would watch, listen, and gather information and use those insights in the way most beneficial to me. I was excited about this metaphorical journey I was about to undertake and the fair pair of lads with whom I was to travel.

If I had to choose one thought as outstanding among the thousands buzzing in my brain at that moment, it would have to be the possibility of my having special powers as a result of my contact with Locke. As a girl who had spent her life well below the curve – physically speaking – I was thrilled to think that through my contact with the blonde angel, I might become some kind of heavenly Wonder Woman. I felt certain that my hearing and eyesight were already improved and prayed my other senses would soon follow suit. I even had a few superhero uniforms and monikers in mind. If Locke or Merc could count mind reading among their talents, they would surely get a big laugh out of the daydreams bouncing around in my brain.

Easy girl, I cautioned myself. I didn't want to get too fired up with crazy thoughts that might never come to fruition, because, knowing my luck, there was some kind of celestial legal loophole that would prevent a mean-spirited minx like me from being elevated to a loftier status in the universe.

What I really should be focused on was the demon angle. I'd yet to see a superhero that'd not been kept busy by the machinations of a villain, and my archrival had already made his presence known. I needed to learn exactly what or who this "Magnet Man" was, and why he was so intent of drawing me to him. I felt like my two new guy friends had much more knowledge on the subject than they were sharing with me. An inquiry regarding the life-threatening boogeyman should be at the top of my agenda, but I just had to ask one question first.

"So if you're an angel – where are your wings and halo?"

Locke and Merc looked at each other and then at me before bursting out in loud laughter. I hadn't realized I was making a joke, but it felt so good to lighten the mood that I found myself joining in.

Wiping a tear from his sparkling eye, Locke finally replied. "I can't exactly walk around Lake Martin in my true form, Grace. I would be even more of a traffic stopper than I already am."

"Oh, pleaaase," Merc exclaimed, rolling his eyes.

"So do you create a human form or do you possess someone?" I asked, honestly curious.

"Angels do not possess people," Locke replied stiffly. I noticed that he and Merc gave each other a quick nervous look that was undoubtedly layered with meaning I couldn't begin to decipher.

"So . . ." I encouraged him to continue.

Locke exhaled with a great, dramatic gush of air. "I appear on earth as a dialed-down version of my heavenly self. You couldn't withstand the magnificence of my true presence. But I have essentially the same features in both realms."

"The magnificence of your true presence?" Merc scoffed. "You've got to be kidding me."

Anxious to keep the boys from bickering, I jumped in. "I get it – kind of 'Locke lite' – a shadow of your true self. That makes sense. I have to say, I'm relieved to know there isn't some poor guy inside of there," I said, pointing at his chest, "that's dying to get out."

Again, the guys looked at each other before Locke said quietly, "Grace, angels don't take over the bodies of humans, but demons do."

An ice-cold shiver of apprehension ran down my spine. I didn't dare speak out loud the words that would make my fears real. I chose instead to make light of Locke's comment. "Oh, I know that. I've seen *The Exorcist*. If my voice lowers a few octaves and I start spitting out pea soup, I hope you guys will be able to exorcise me." I laughed but quickly shut up when I realized that neither of the boys was joining in.

"Grace," Locke started, and my earlier apprehension tripled at the sound of my name spoken with such gravity. "There is something we need to talk about."

Merc quickly cut him off. "Why don't we continue this talk at lunch. The sun is rising. We should go."

I looked at him as if he'd lost his mind. I had the sense that he was trying to protect me, but I wasn't going to stand for it. "Forget it, Merc. You two aren't going anywhere. Tell me what you are worried about. I know it has something to do with the demon." I hesitated, trying to get the courage up to ask the real question. "Is that thing . . ." I stopped again before choking out the last words, "trying to possess me? Is that it?" I felt my body begin to shake but managed to get the quaking under control. I was no longer the girl who had to count to control my fear. I'd been touched by an angel and I would fight back the urge to run and hide.

Merc moved closer, wrapping his arms tightly around me and pulling me toward him. "It's okay, Gracie. I told you before; I'm not going to ever let anything hurt you. Ever!" he promised vehemently.

"I'm not sure you can keep that promise," Locke said. "At least not by yourself."

Merc looked like he wanted to rip Locke's head off. "I can take care of Grace. I don't need your help." His green eyes darkened to gold in anger. "In fact, I'm not even completely sure you are on the right side of this thing."

Locke struggled to keep control of his own temper. "Look Merc, I know you hold a huge grudge against me because of your parents, but you need to know it was just their time to go."

I had heard Locke say the same thing to Merc before, but at the time I didn't understand it. Now I did. Merc blamed Locke for his parents' death, and that wasn't good. I was going to have to find some way to help him put those feelings aside if we were all going to work together. I wanted us all to work together because I knew beyond a shadow of a doubt that I was in grave danger, as was Merc because of his vow to keep me safe. I didn't know the extent of my new love's powers and I certainly had no idea of my own, but common sense was telling me that in a fight against evil, it was a really good idea to have an angel in your pocket, if you could get one.

Merc seemed to question Locke's loyalties, but I didn't. Every instinct I had told me that the gorgeous blonde boy, despite all his quirks, was a card-carrying member of the Heavenly Hosts; therefore, one of the good guys. I just had to convince Merc of Locke's sterling status – not easy because of the angel's involvement in Merc's parents' death. I was going to have to open up a dialogue on the subject and hope the boys could work it out.

"Locke, I know you were there the night Merc's parents died. Did you, in any way, cause their death?"

Merc, who had calmed down – if only slightly – leaned forward, listening intently for Locke's response.

"Of course not," came Locke's immediate reply. His face softened and he looked directly at Merc and repeated, "Of course not. Your parents were wonderful people. They were simply needed elsewhere. I know it's hard for you to believe, but there is a plan for everything and your parents' demise was a part of that plan. In order for you to fulfill your destiny, they had to be taken." He reached to put a light hand on Merc's shoulder but seeing the look on the dark boy's face, thought better of it. "I'm so sorry. You know it wasn't my call, but I trust the one who makes the decisions, and you should, too."

"Wait a minute," Merc cried. "Are you saying that it was my fault that my parents had to die? That they were killed so that I could do something important?" He looked horrified, and I didn't blame him.

"No, no . . . you misunderstand me." Locke shook his head vehemently. "Or maybe, I'm just doing a poor job of explaining things. Your parents and you and Grace . . . and everyone else on this earth have a destiny. Your parents' destiny was fulfilled, but yours has yet to be. All of our fates are intertwined, yet at the same time, separate. Please believe me when I say that your mom and dad understood this; though they loathed the pain it would cause you, they knew it was for the best."

"So they knew they were going to die?" Merc asked, disbelief coloring his voice.

"I didn't say that. Look, Merc, we are getting into areas that no person on Earth is meant to know. The only reason I've told you as much as I have is . . . because . . . I owe you." His last words were stilted and strained.

I turned my attention from Merc's face to Locke's and was surprised to see tears forming in his beautiful eyes.

"What do you mean, you owe me?" Merc demanded in confusion.

Locke, at that moment, bore no resemblance to a supernatural being – an angel. He simply looked like a boy who was tired and sad.

"Angels all have jobs to perform, and one of those jobs is to usher people into the next world. Believe me, it's a thankless task in many ways. The people that are being taken away are not the problem." He stated flatly. "Without going into details you're not meant to hear, I will say that everything negative is gone for those who die. Their soul is transformed, and they are jubilant beyond description – immediately; at least the good ones are." His voice grew somber. "But the loved ones of the souls taken – that's another story. Because they are left on Earth, they are subject to all the pain and suffering that death brings." He stopped for a moment to gather his thoughts, and I suspect his emotions, and then continued. "Angels have their feet in both worlds, so to speak, and can be affected by the grief and pain of the human existence. The night of the fire, I was struggling mightily with the burden of the job I was asked to perform. I'd been working that detail a millennium and, frankly, it was getting to me. The heartbreak and sorrow of human loss was crushing my soul and I no longer had . . . " He stopped and started again. " I had always been able to handle the pain because I had someone . . . " Again he quit speaking, and for a moment I thought he wasn't going to be able to continue. Finally, he turned to Merc and said, "And then I saw you."

Merc and I sat mesmerized, listening to Locke talk. My heart ached for his pain, and I knew Merc, too, was moved by his words. It was obvious that the angel had suffered a great loss – a loss that, all these years later, he still couldn't bring himself to talk about. I hoped one day he could share his grief with us, and we could find a way to help him.

Locke's voice broke into my thoughts, as he spoke directly to Merc. "I couldn't understand how you could even see me." He shook his head, remembering his confusion on that night. "But you did and you looked at me with such love . . . such compassion. There was no fear or anger in you – only acceptance and wonder. And then you raised your little hand and touched my cheek, and I felt all the pain of a millennium of human suffering drain away from me."

Merc's brows pulled together as he concentrated hard on the shared memory.

Locke continued, "At first, I was scared – afraid that the suffering had been transferred to you. But I looked into your eyes, and that's when I knew." He paused for what I was sure was dramatic effect.

Enthralled in the story, Merc and I cried in unison, "Knew what?"

Locke reached his hand out and took Merc's. "I knew you were special; that you had a tremendous gift and an important role to perform."

Merc looked at him warily. "And what role is that?"

Locke chuckled, "That knowledge, my friend, is above my pay grade. All things will be revealed to you in time," he said, sounding more like a gypsy fortune-teller than an angel. "Right now, there is nothing more important than keeping you and Grace safe."

He would get no arguments from me there! I couldn't agree more. I *was* a little depressed at the thought of my new love's role in the big scheme of things. I suddenly felt very insignificant. As usual, Locke picked up on my mood and thoughts right away.

"You, too, have an important role to play, Grace. We all do."

His statement triggered a thought in my head. "And what about the old folks – Mrs. B. and Willem? I know they must be a part of all of this. They would have to be. What role do they play?"

Merc seemed equally interested in my question and Locke's answer to it, but as usual, the angel was cryptic – giving no real response.

"It's not my place to say. But I'll tell you this much – they're on our side. And that's a good thing because we are going to need all the help we can get."

"So I'm guessing that you aren't *really* related to Willem," I said, raising an eyebrow in his direction.

"We are all brothers and sisters, Grace," Locke replied piously.

"Yeah, uh huh . . . sure," Merc mumbled sarcastically.

"Angels sure play fast and loose with the truth," I pointed out, having a little fun by yanking Locke's chain.

"All in the name of love, my dear." He smiled and Merc and I laughed together.

Locke walked over to the window and looked out. "The sun's coming up. We need to get down to business. I can't keep the whole inn sleeping all day long, you know. People will get suspicious."

I decided to let that remark pass because I didn't really want to know what he meant.

"What do you have in mind?" Merc asked before adding, "The most important thing is how to protect Gracie. Nothing – I mean nothing – better happen to her." His look was fierce but filled with loving concern. My arm was beginning to turn blue from the multiple times I'd pinched myself for assurance that I was awake.

"I could just hang out with her." Locke offered. "No demon is going to get past me." He grimaced and straightened his shoulders, doing his best to demonstrate the truth of his statement.

Merc bristled with anger. "I don't think so. If anyone is going to 'hang out' with Grace, it will be me. I am more than capable of taking care of her."

Though spending my every waking moment with Merc was certainly a tempting prospect, I didn't particularly want to be cast in the role of helpless victim, 24/7. The occasional bit part as damsel was fine with me, but as an ongoing theme, I didn't care for it much. I far preferred to be a full-fledged partner rather than an ongoing problem for these two boys.

"I thought I would be getting powers of my own. Why can't I take care of myself?" I asked while silently praying that my question wouldn't backfire on me, leaving me alone to deal with the Devil.

"There's no way to know how profound a change you will undergo or how quickly the change will happen," Locke pointed out. "We can't depend on anything we have so little control over."

"Besides," Merc added, "it will take you quite awhile to learn how to use any gifts you may receive. Believe me, it's a very big adjustment. It takes a lot of hard work and practice to learn to control the power. That's what Theodore does," he pointed out. "He works with kids in channeling their new energy in the right direction. If not properly taught, people can get hurt and disasters can happen."

"But can't you and Locke teach me?"

Both the guys nodded vigorously, but it was Locke who answered my question. "Certainly we can, but it's not an overnight thing. Like Merc said, it takes hard work and discipline . . . and . . . time."

"And that's the problem," Merc took up where Locke left off. "We don't have the time. The dark side is after you right now. So we have no other choice but to watch you every moment of every day until your powers are completely established."

"Even then we have to be very careful." Locke jumped back in – the boys tag-teaming me now. "I don't recall a demon making himself so visible to a human in hundreds and hundreds of years. For some reason, they want you bad, Grace. We cannot let our guard down for a minute."

Ice water flooded my veins at his words. Would I spend the rest of my life running from the Devil? Could this really be happening? I assigned a whole new meaning to the phrase "taking the good with the bad." I should have known that since my "good" was fantastic, my " bad" would be equally awe-inspiring. But, despite it all, for the first time in a long time, I felt alive. I wouldn't have traded my right *now* for my life of a week ago, for all the money in the world.

"What about calling in some reinforcements?" Merc asked. "I could get in touch with Theodore and have him send some of my brothers and sisters to help. For that matter, couldn't you call down a few of your kind?"

Locke's face shifted slightly, and to me, he seemed a little embarrassed – or maybe uncomfortable with the subject. "No, it doesn't exactly work like that," he hedged.

"Well, how does it work then?" Merc was raising his voice, and I saw the conversation heading in the wrong direction fast.

"That's not any of your business," Locke replied stiffly.

"I'm beginning to wonder if I might have been right all along. Maybe you're working with the demon."

"Whoa, Merc. That's not fair," I said quickly. "Let's not turn on each other. Locke is an angel; of course he's on our side."

"You need to remember your Bible, Gracie. Demons *are* angels – just not good ones," Merc said evenly.

"WERE angels," Locke corrected. "Not ARE angels."

"Hah! Semantics!" Merc threw back. "Potato, Po-*tah*-to," he spat, using the alternate pronunciations.

"Lord, give me strength to deal with humans!" Locke spat back.

"Enough, you two!" I shouted and then lowering my voice, continued. "Please, I have enough to deal with without having to keep breaking you two apart."

Both boys looked back at me with shamed faces and began mumbling profuse apologies. With very little effort, I worked up a tear or two to drive home my point. It worked in all the books.

"Really, you guys, I am completely freaked out by all of this. If I can't count on you to stay calm, well . . . I don't know what I will do." I finished up with a light sob, which seemed to bring on the right response.

"She's right, Locke. We've got to stop arguing and deal with the problem. But you need to understand that I have a right to be concerned about who you are. I've spent the better part of the last fifteen years learning about demons or fallen angels or whatever you want to call them, and I know enough about them to know that they are very tricky and can take on many different personas. I wish there was some acid test that would relieve my mind, but to my knowledge, there isn't."

Locke closed his eyes, maybe to regain composure or maybe to pray – I wasn't sure. After a moment, he turned his attention back to us and smiled broadly. "I think I have an idea. There *is* someone who can convince you I'm one of the good guys."

"And who might that be?" Merc asked, clearly a little suspicious.

"Willem," Locke responded simply, but his voice held a tinge of amusement that I found puzzling.

"Willem? Why in the world would I believe anything that old man says? I don't even like him."

For some reason, Locke seemed to find Merc's reaction really funny, which only made him madder.

"What are you laughing at? This is serious business, and if you aren't going to take it as such, I will find a way to take care of Gracie by myself. I don't really need you anyhow."

"Wait," I pleaded. I turned and put my hands on either side of Merc's perfect face. "Please Merchison, let's listen to what Locke has to say. I like Willem, I really, really do. I would bet my life on his being a good guy."

Strangely, Merc seemed mesmerized by my touch and he slowly nodded his head in agreement. "Okay, I'll talk to Willem."

Turning to Locke, he said, "I'm not sure how the old man can help, but I'm willing to listen to him." He grabbed my hand and pulled me toward him. "I'm not leaving Gracie here alone with you, though. We will all have to go to the mansion."

"Sounds good to me," I chirped, relieved at the turn of events. "I need to talk to Mrs. B., anyway."

I should have been tired – exhausted really – but I wasn't. Though I'd not given it much thought, once I did, I realized that I felt like a million bucks. Energy coursed through my veins, strengthening my limbs and fortifying my brain with a surge of raw power such as I'd never felt before. It was happening, just like Merc and Locke said that it would, and I couldn't wait to see what I was capable of accomplishing with my improved body and mind.

As superhuman as I felt, I was still a slave to the earthly realm, so I begged a few moments of privacy from the boys and ducked into the powder room to freshen up for my visit to the mansion to see the old folks. I brushed my teeth and hair and changed into a different pair of jeans and yet another black T-shirt. As was my custom, I accomplished all of the above with scarcely a glance at myself in the full-length mirror that hung on the back of the bathroom door.

Finally, with a sigh, I squinted my eyes to soften the impact, and peeked over my shoulder to gain access to the dreaded view of my ever-expanding backside and was shocked to see a slim yet slightly rounded derriere reflecting back at me. Startled, I whipped around and stepped a foot closer to the glass to ensure that my eyes weren't playing tricks on me. Still not fully convinced of what was in plain sight, I lunged for the dimmer switch on the powder room lights and cranked it around to the highest setting.

In astonished delight, I turned this way and that, all the while sucking in my stomach and pooching it back out again, trying to create some combination of moves that would result in my recognizing the near perfect vision that stared out at me from the silvered glass.

Once getting over the initial shock of seeing my altered body, I began to take notice of the many subtle changes in my overall appearance. My hair – always a mousy shade of light brown – was a beautiful dark blonde shot through with strains of strawberry and even platinum. My eyes were not the dull greenish blue of my memory but rather a magnificent aqua, reminiscent of the most beautiful of azure seas. Everything from my pug nose to my blotchy skin was slightly adjusted. It was as if I'd spent my life being slightly out of focus and then, through some magical or divine intervention, my knobs were turned and my image sharpened and perfected.

I was particularly taken with my bust line, the measurement of which was always more impressive on paper than in appearance. Until today, my pillow-like bosoms had made me look like everyone's grandmother – but not anymore. Though still impressive in mass, they had somehow shifted and rearranged leaving plenty of room between them and my now lithe waistline. I'd gone from a stodgy adobe hut to a brick house in a matter of hours. I made myself a mental note to buy a bigger mirror.

I grasped for an explanation of my transformation, though in all honesty I didn't care what it was. Be it devil or angel, Heaven or Hell – or something in between – whatever or whomever the architect of my metamorphosis might be, I could only adore them for the magnificence of their timing. I now looked like a girl capable of wooing and winning a guy like Merchison Spear.

As to be expected, my instant makeover was a major motivator for me to linger awhile longer behind closed doors – pruning, primping and admiring my recent renovations. Though I found it difficult to tear myself away from my own dazzling vision, I was equally excited to see the reaction my heavenly modifications would bring about in the two gorgeous guys who waited for me outside the bathroom door. So for the first time in years I tucked my T-shirt into my jeans and, ecstatically happy with the result, blew a kiss at the mirror and headed out.

Chapter Fifteen

TOUCH

My heart was nearly beating out of my chest with anticipation as I presented myself to the boys like a debutante at her first ball. I eagerly waited for their stunned gasps of amazement but was terribly disappointed and perplexed when neither made a single comment regarding my changed appearance. I didn't know whether to be insulted or relieved. It was completely odd that they didn't seem to notice my slimmed-down silhouette or refined features, but nothing about this weekend came close to being normal; so I inwardly reveled at my outward appearance and chalked it up to par for the very strange course my life had taken.

I was tempted to wake Pete and Patty from their "assisted rest," just so I could see the look on their perfect faces when they saw that the family's ugly duckling had, overnight, become a beautiful swan. But fearing it would lead to far too many questions that would take far too long to answer, I opted for writing them a note to explain where I'd gone and saving my little surprise for later.

"Okay, boys," I said saucily. "Let's roll; daylight's burning!"

They both grinned at me and Locke said, "We're going to have to take your car, Grace; neither Merc nor I drove over here."

"What . . . why?" I whined, disappointed. I was really looking forward to riding in a convertible with the two best-looking guys around. I no longer had to worry about being a thorn among roses; I had some petals of my own now.

Merc started to say something, but Locke quickly cut him off. "Willem dropped me by last night. But Merc . . . well, I guess he wanted a little exercise because he ran over here. Right Merc?"

The dark-haired boy looked a little confused and studied Locke's face for a moment before finally agreeing. "Yeah, right; I gotta keep in shape ya know."

I thought the whole exchange was a little weird, but I chose to overlook it in favor of inwardly celebrating the knowledge that Merc had gone to so much trouble to see me.

"My goodness!" I exclaimed. "You ran all the way here? That was so considerate of you, Merchison." I batted my newly thickened eyelashes, reveling in the feeling of power my altered appearance gave me.

"Sooooooo considerate," Locke chimed in false agreement, making a face that made me laugh out loud. "You're such an angel . . . NOT!"

"No, I'm not an angel," Merc agreed. "And dang glad of it. If I was a magnificent being like yourself, I couldn't do this." And right in the drive of the Martin's Nest, to my stunned delight, Merc whipped me into his strong arms and planted a big kiss on my lips.

I quickly forgot where I was or who might be watching and wrapped my arms around his neck and drew him close. What had started as a retaliatory smooch had morphed into a passionate embrace that took my breath away. I could have kissed him for hours had I not remembered the very irritated angel on my shoulder.

One sneak peek at poor Locke's humiliated face confirmed that Merc's jab had hit home. I hoped that my gorgeous new boyfriend had been motivated by more than just a need to get at his rival. I felt bad for Locke and reluctantly pulled away from Merc and turned toward the dejected-looking boy.

"I'm sure Locke has a girlfriend in . . . on . . . uh, another plane. Right, Locke?"

He picked an imaginary piece of lint off his shirt, not willing to look me in the eye. "No, not really – not anymore," he mumbled. "I've been busy with my job and stuff," he explained, sounding like a regular guy, not a heavenly being.

The cylinders of my brain were clicking away as a plan began to emerge from my mind. Amazingly, even with all the chaos – good and bad – surrounding me, I could still find time to think about matchmaking. My one and only friend, March Ann, was the most beautiful girl I'd ever seen and with her blonde hair and blue eyes, she could well be Locke's twin. Would a match between the two stunners be a possibility? Were earth girl/heaven boy unions even sanctioned? I would have to give the idea some serious thought in between my make-out sessions with Merc and my close escapes from the Dark Lord of the Underworld.

From what Locke had said earlier, I gathered that he had at one time loved and lost, and the pain of that parting still weighed heavily on his heart and mind. If I could engineer a romance between Locke and March Ann, then it might go a long way toward keeping the blonde angel satisfied and by our side.

I did have one concern about my plan, though, and it was a pretty petty one, for sure. I'd come a long way in a short time in the self-esteem department, but jealousy still raised its ugly head long enough to remind me that introducing March Ann to Locke would probably also mean introducing March Ann to Merc and that could create complications for me. The boys at school went positively gaga over my best friend, though she never deigned to look their way. What would my love's reaction be upon seeing my gal pal, the goddess? Would he be enamored of her, too? Oh well, I wouldn't be able to keep Merc to myself forever, so it might be best if I push her toward Locke anyway – and pray she prefers blondes!

We were halfway to the mansion in my old raggedy car before Locke said another word.

"You know, angels don't really need physical love the way humans do. We are on a higher plane where those desires are irrelevant." He was back to sounding all pious again, and I realized that the holier-than-thou act was nothing more than a defense mechanism.

"Is that right?" Merc asked, sounding doubtful.

"Yeah, it is. Of course, you wouldn't understand."

"I know, I know – I'm just a mere mortal," Merc said, "not capable of understanding the workings of the gods."

"God . . . not gods," Locke corrected him. "And while I don't think mortals are meant to understand everything while they are on earth, you are not a mere mortal – far from it."

"Why do you keep saying that? I don't understand what you want from me – what I'm supposed to do."

"Let me ask you this, Merc. Why do you think Theodore sent you to live here in Alabama? Do you even know?" Locke asked.

"Yes and no," came Merc's confusing reply. I turned and looked at his flawless profile, the sun illuminating every perfect feature. I couldn't keep a civil thought in my head if I stared too long at his strong jawline and high cheekbones, but at least from the side I couldn't get lost in his dreamy green eyes.

With a sigh, I pulled the mirrored visor down in front of me and studied my own, now lovely, face before asking, "Yes and no – what does that mean?" We had talked about Theodore, but Merc never explained to me why he had sent him to live in Alabama.

He reached out and put a hand on my leg and gave it a squeeze, sending chills of pleasure through my body.

"Gracie, I told you about how Theodore took care of children who had been given supernatural powers because of their contact with angels. He taught us how to use the gifts we were given to our advantage and to the advantage of mankind."

"Kind of like heavenly superheroes. That's so neat!" I enthused.

"Yeah, neato!" Locke sniped sarcastically. "But, that doesn't explain why you are here.

"Patience, angel boy, I'm getting to that." Merc explained. "Our whole focus in life with Theodore was to learn to fight evil – to channel our powers to battle the dark side – namely demons."

"Are you saying that you were sent to Alabama – alone – to fight a particular demon?" Locke, who was leaning forward into the front seat, sounded appalled.

"No, not exactly. Coming to Alabama was kind of a rite of passage for me. At nineteen each one of Theodore's 'kids' is required to go off on his or her own for one year. It is a test of our training and skills. When we return, after the year is completed, we are considered full-fledged members of "The Company." We can then be sent out alone or in groups to deal with evil wherever it's found."

"And how do you know where to go?" I asked. I was fascinated with every word out of his mouth, yet at the same time, strangely depressed. It didn't sound as if there was much room for a love life in Merc's world.

"For my year alone, Theodore assigned me to Tallassee, Alabama, and specifically to the bungalow on Mrs. B.'s property. When I become a full-fledged fighter, I'll still look to Theodore for assignments but I'll also participate in locating demon trouble."

"Is it hard to find?" I was asking all the questions but I could hear Locke's shallow breathing in my ear; he was listening intently to every word. I felt sure he was a good guy – a real angel – but if he wasn't, he was getting a lot of information from the enemy camp.

"No, it's not too hard to find if you know what you're looking for. Of course, you have to know how to separate real demon issues from satanic panic," he laughed.

"What in heaven's name is *satanic panic?*" I asked, testing the feel of the phrase on my tongue.

"Oh, you know – a couple of cows die for unexplained reasons or a cat is found mutilated, and the next thing you know people are screaming demon. But most of the time, there is a much simpler explanation for that type of thing. Besides, true demons are much stealthier – not as obvious."

"That's an understatement," Locke jumped in. "Demons rarely present themselves in their true form." He stopped and thought for a moment before continuing. "In fact, I can only think of one recent incident in which a demon showed himself in all his terrible glory – and that was last night outside of your window."

It was a strange reaction Locke's statement caused in me. Not fear, as any sane person would expect, but red-hot rage that boiled up in my veins, spilling over into my system and flooding my body with unholy power. I felt as if at that very moment, I could have taken down ten demons and eaten a sandwich while I was doing it.

"Is that so?" I asked with bravado that, for once, I truly felt. "Well, bring him on. I'm not worried about the Magnet Demon, or any of his freakish friends. I'm more than ready for a fight."

Merc's eyebrows shot together, and Locke sat up even farther in his seat, both boys shocked by the vehemence of my words.

"Whoa now, little missy, you just calm yourself right down. You're not going to be fighting any demons anytime soon, so you can just forget it. If there's any battling to be done, Merc and I will do it."

"Locke's right, Gracie," Merc hastily agreed. "We need to keep you as far away from this thing as possible. You are nowhere close to being ready for a confrontation with a devil. If I have my way, you will never have to fight one of them."

Just my luck! The boys finally find something to agree on. I found it terribly insulting and more than a little irritating that they would choose this time to align against me.

"Why?" I demanded. "I'm not going to be dead weight in this thing. I'm stronger – I can feel it. Everything about me is different."

Why couldn't they see what was right in front of their faces? I was a changed girl – no longer the dumpy, dowdy, dishrag of a gal I was three days ago. Were they so caught up in their own competition that they failed to notice what was happening to me? I thought I was the object of their mutual admiration. Apparently not!

"So let me get this straight," I started, not even trying to hide my anger. "I'm supposed to sit by and watch two people I care for put their lives in danger to protect me; yet despite my newfound power, I'm not to participate in my own preservation. Does that about sum it up?" I looked from one of them to the other, very aware of the curious expressions they each wore. It was patently obvious that neither knew what to make of my swagger.

We had turned off the highway onto the dirt road that led to the mansion before Merc finally summoned the courage to answer my blustery query. 'That sums it up precisely, Gracie," he said, showing for the first time in awhile the arrogance I'd noticed in him when we'd first met. "To attempt to get involved will only put all of us in more danger. You wouldn't want that, would you?"

Locke was nodding his blonde head in agreement with Merc's every word.

I paused to think for a minute before saying, "That reminds me, Locke, I have a question for you." I turned around in my seat so I could face him eye to eye.

"Fire away!" His smile was full of cockiness that I didn't think he really felt.

I'd noticed that when Locke got nervous, he blinked his eyes rapidly. I was well versed in compulsive habits, and I knew one when I saw one. How strange to see such a human quirk in an angel, I thought, and was suddenly reminded of what I wanted to ask him.

"Merc said that I could put both of you in danger, but how can I put you in harm's way if you are an angel? I thought angels couldn't be killed."

"Grace, there are some things that . . . "

I cut him off before he could finish the sentence. "Bull, Locke!"

"Excuse me – what did you say?" Shocked and offended, he stared at me with his big, blue innocent eyes – the blank gaze that I had come to find so exasperating.

"Don't even start that business of claiming we can't know something because we aren't from the heavenly realm. I don't believe you. You just use that as an excuse to keep us in the dark."

I never took my eyes from Locke's face, but I heard Merc's quiet chuckle. I guess he was enjoying my confrontation with the angel.

"You don't have to believe me but it's true. I can't tell you everything. But I'll say this: While death is not a part of the angelic existence, there are fates worse than death for angels, Grace."

"Such as?" I wasn't going to let him back me down, so I ignored his hurt tone.

"Such as being permanently separated from our heavenly home."

Merc, who had parked in front of the mansion and turned off the car, twisted around in his seat to face Locke. "Like the fallen angels . . . and Lucifer were?"

Locke's face became a mask of stone, but his eyes reflected the pain of centuries of loss. My eyes, on the other hand, were cast downward in shame for my unfeeling words and uncharitable thoughts. I felt even worse as Locke confirmed Merc's statement, his voice trembling in remembered grief.

"Yes, exactly like that. Their fate was infinitely worse and far more enduring than death."

I'd read all the stories from the Old Testament and knew as much as most about Satan and his followers' ejection from the Garden. But I'd never given a moment's thought to what pain that action might have caused in those left standing – the angels on the side of right. Clearly, Lucifer's expulsion was a painful chapter in Locke's existence. It was written all over his face.

I reached out and took his hand. "Did you have friends that fell from grace, Locke?" I asked quietly, hoping I was using the correct terminology.

"No, not friends . . . brothers and sisters, together since the beginning of time. You can't possibly understand the depth of heartbreak and sorrow Lucifer's betrayal caused in our world."

"But I thought Lucifer and his followers were evil incarnate. Are you saying you all were close – like a family?"

"Of course. That's exactly what we were – a family. And Lucifer was the head of the family – next to the Father, that is. He was the Morning Star – the brightest and most powerful angel in Heaven. We all looked up to him. That's why he was able to take so many down with him when he fell." He shook his head as if he still couldn't believe what had happened. "He became so powerful that he thought he was on the same level as the Father – and he convinced many of my brothers and sisters of that, as well.

He leaned back against the seat of the car and covered his eyes with his hands. Reliving the ancient memory was taking a toll on him, and I found myself wishing that I hadn't prodded him to recall the devastating details.

"It was a terrible time that turned brother against brother and sister against sister," Locke continued with his eyes closed. "And even though throughout the years the fallen ones have become increasingly evil – with no redeeming qualities or hope – it's still hard to forget the way it once was when we were all together and peace reigned."

In a weekend full of extraordinary events, nothing should have surprised me, but what happened next did. Merc flung open his car door and instead of coming around to my side or heading to the mansion steps, he slipped into the backseat with Locke. As I watched in stunned silence, he placed his hands on either side of the tortured boy's face and, closing his own eyes, he began quietly speaking to Locke with low words that were unintelligible to me. The gesture was so intimate and unexpected that I felt unsure of whether to leave the car or to stay, but the decision was made for me when Locke reached out his hand and grasped mine.

I was dimly aware of the darkening sky and distant roll of thunder that signaled yet another storm brewing, but my focus was on the two entranced boys sitting in the car with me. Tears rolled down both their cheeks, mirroring the large drops meandering down my face. After about five minutes, Merc dropped his hands into his lap, and Locke opened his eyes that were now back to a normal, but glorious, light blue – no longer darkened with the grief of past pain and loss.

After a moment, Locke dropped my hand and turned to face Merc. "I don't know what to say to you – how to thank you." The words were simple enough, but the depth of emotion behind them was profound.

Merc tried to downplay the moment; however, I could tell he was deeply affected, not just by Locke's gratitude, but also by the whole experience. His face was drained of color, and I could now see a shadow of Locke's past pain reflected in his eyes, telling me exactly what had happened. As a child Merc had lessened the angel's pain by touching his face, and just now he had done the same for Locke again. I wasn't fooled, though. My sweet love had taken on those horrible memories at an awful cost. He tried to cover it up – to hide the torturous truth from Locke and me. But I did see it, and it ripped my heart in two.

I'm not sure what motivated me to reach out and place my hand on Merc's cheek. It was probably a strong desire to comfort him – to wipe away the grief I saw etched into his face. But as my hand drew close to his tear-stained skin, it was caught in a current of electricity that instinctively made me want to pull back. After getting over the initial shock, I let my fingers lightly graze his cheek, and when I did, I nearly cried out loud at the images that assaulted my brain. I didn't completely understand the visions, but I felt every heartbreaking emotion emanating from them. Betrayal, denial, anger and heartbreak simultaneously burned through my brain, catching my heart on fire and suffocating my soul.

"What's happening to her?" I heard Locke cry.

"I'm not sure . . . unless . . . " Merc stumbled, before finally saying "Gracie, talk to me. Are you okay?" He yanked my hand away from his face and a cool rush of relief swept through my body like a summer rain, washing away the terrifying and bewildering pictures and emotions.

Like a shot, Merc was back in the front seat of the car, pulling me into his arms and apologizing over and over.

"I'm so sorry, Gracie. I had no idea that could happen to you."

Though the images and emotions had disappeared, the memory of what I'd felt and seen stayed with me like a bad aftertaste, leaving me barely able to communicate.

"It's okay, Merc. It's not your fault," I mumbled, too shaken to offer anything more comforting than that.

"What's not his fault? Would somebody please tell me what's going on?" Locke demanded. He had leaned so far into the front seat that he was practically in my lap.

"Just give her a minute to catch her breath, Locke."

"I'm fine – really I am. I'm just confused. What was that I saw?" I had a pretty good idea, but I needed to hear him say it.

"Of course, I can't say for sure, but I'm guessing you were made privy to Locke's memories and the feelings attached to those recollections." Now that Merc realized I was, for the most part, unharmed, his voice had lost its tone of frenzied distress.

"What?" Locke shouted. "Are you serious? You're telling me that Grace has the same abilities that you do? That she is able to heal hearts through her touch? That she can ease suffering by the laying on of hands?"

"It looks like that might be the case," Merc confirmed, sounding like a proud papa.

"This is amazing, Grace – just fantastic news," the blonde angel gushed, all his previous concern for me out the window. "In all my existence, I've never known any human but Merchison to have the gift." He was rocking back and forth in the back seat, so excited that he could barely contain himself, and Merc was just as thrilled.

"Everything makes sense now. This is why we were all brought together," Merc rationalized. He fixed me with his bright green eyes – his gaze telegraphing adoration and approval. I should have been on Cloud 900 but instead I was at Ground Zero.

With jaded eyes, I studied the two gorgeous boys – one dark, one light, both equally fantastic – both good to their core. In the cramped quarters of my beat-up old car, they were huddled together – head to head – singing my praises. And, all the while, they were positively glowing with good will and charity. I tried my best to glow, too. I even attempted to emulate an Old Masters Madonna– serene and beautiful in her holiness, with the peaceful smile of martyrdom painted on her calm face. I was having trouble pulling it off.

This was supposed to be a good thing? They had to be kidding me. Was this my "superpower?" What happened to leaping tall buildings or racing trains? Of all the gifts I could have been given, I'm stuck with taking on other people's heartaches? I've got plenty of heartache of my own. Hadn't anybody upstairs been watching me these last few years? In case they hadn't been paying attention, I needed to let them know that I didn't do stress and pain well. I resorted to things like counting and checking and belligerent behavior of all kinds.

But how was I going to say that to these two guys? How could I tell the boy I'd fallen so fast and hard for that I was a selfish shrew of a girl, unwilling to sacrifice my meager and tenuous hold on sanity in order to help my fellow man? If I refused to practice this terrible talent of healing hearts and souls, would I be forced to return my other improvements, as well? Would I go back to looking like my old chunky self before I ever even had the chance to show off my improved curves? I didn't even have to ask myself the most important question. I knew with absolute certainty that in Merchison Spear's world, there was no room for cowards. If I didn't embrace my fate, I would lose him. Of this I was sure.

I had no intention of losing my miracle man because of my inability to "act" holy. After all, I was no slouch in the thespian department. I'd been playing normal for years. So if I now had to act the part of spiritual healer – replete with flowing robes and snakes to handle – in order to keep my man, I'd give an Oscar-worthy performance. I was going to have to invest in some new makeup if I was going to pull off a glow, though.

Locke and Merc talked among themselves, apparently giving me the needed time to absorb the blessed news that had gotten them all excited. If I'd hit my mark, I was outwardly displaying the perfect blend of delighted surprise and modest self-deprecation, wanting to appear thrilled with the revelation of my gift yet aware of my unworthiness to have received it.

Finally, trusting myself to speak, I broke into the guys' conversation, trying hard to keep the dread from my voice. "So are you two sure about what you're saying – that I have the power to heal people emotionally?"

"I think so, Gracie." Merc confirmed. "When I touched Locke, I saw images of the fight between good and evil that took place in the beginning. I felt all the hurt and pain that the angels were feeling. I especially felt Locke's . . . uh . . . Lochedus' emotions."

The use of Locke's angel name caught me off guard. "Is that what you want us to call you from now on, Locke? Do you want us to use your real name?" I was stalling a bit. If I had any doubt about what I'd seen when I touched Merc, it was gone. The pictures in my mind made sense now, and I could no longer deny the role I'd been picked to play.

"No, I don't think so . . . no sense in changing things now." Locke looked at me through narrowed eyes, and I got the feeling that he was a little suspicious of me. This wasn't the first time I'd felt he was reading my mind. I looked uneasily back to Merc, willing him to continue talking.

"Anyway," he began again. "The second you touched me, Gracie, all the images and feelings were gone. Well, I guess I still feel a small amount of residual emotion," he corrected himself. "But for the most part, I'm back to smooth sailing. It was amazing." He turned the full power of his gaze upon me. "YOU are amazing."

Lord, what a tangled web I was weaving. I was suddenly waging my own internal war between good and evil, and evil was winning the day. I was reminded of the boys' warning that demons came in all manner of disguise, and I wondered if the "Benevolent Madonna" look I'd adopted qualified as a mask. I suspected that it did, but I kept it plastered on anyway. Crossing my fingers that I wouldn't melt in the rain, I followed the boys into the mansion, feeling more like a fraud than I ever had before.

Chapter Sixteen

BACK IN BLACK

"GET ON IN HERE, KIDS," WILLEM SAID BRIGHTLY, OPENING THE GIANT mansion doors wide and ushering all of us through the foyer and into the den.

"A phone call would have been nice, young man. We were getting worried sick about you." The old man scolded Locke, playing to perfection the doting grandfather.

"You can eighty-six the act now, Willem. I've told them everything," Locke confessed, throwing himself onto the sofa and propping his feet on the coffee table in front of him. I followed suit by perching on a nearby chair, but Merc continued to stand awkwardly in the doorway of the room, unsure of how welcome he was in the home.

"I'm not sure what you mean by 'everything,' son." He was trying to catch the boy's eye, but Locke was casually flipping through a magazine he'd grabbed from the coffee table. It looked to me as if he was trying very hard to avoid Willem's gaze.

In an attempt to alleviate the tension I felt building in the room, and inside of me, I asked with false brightness, "So where is

Mrs. B.? I was wondering if she needed me to do anything for her today?"

Merc walked over to where I was sitting and grabbed my hand, giving it a quick but firm squeeze. "We aren't here on a social call – or to work," he said, clearly wanting to skip the small talk and get right down to business.

"Then why are you here?" Mrs. B.'s raised voice preceded her into the room, causing all but Willem to jump.

Merc was the first to recover his tongue. "We are here to get some information. Gracie is in danger, but we aren't sure from whom. Locke seems to think you can help with that, Willem." Making it clear by the tone of his voice that he didn't really believe Locke's assertion.

Willem couldn't hide his shock or concern. "Gracie, what has happened? Has someone harmed you?"

All eyes turned to me as I stumbled out a response. "No, I'm okay. But something weird did happen to me." Something weird was still happening to me, but I didn't say so. I felt strange, different somehow – probably a residual effect from the emotional roller-coaster I'd just ridden on. I was angry with both boys – furious really. I felt blindsided by the "gift" I'd been awarded and livid at their assumption that I'd go peacefully, like a lamb being led to the slaughter, into a new lifestyle that would require me to take on the woes of the world. I tried to ignore my rising panic and frustration and concentrate on what was going on in the room.

At that moment, Mrs. B. was studying me in a way that was making me uncomfortable. There was definitely something about the old woman that just creeped me out. I wanted her to stop looking at me like a bug in a glass jar.

"We would appreciate your being a bit more specific, please. What exactly happened to Grace?" The old woman asked.

God! I thought disgustedly. *What business is it of hers?*

"Grace had a run-in with a demon. She's fine. Let's not belabor the point. We have more important things to talk about." Locke waved his hand dismissively.

Locke's offhanded attitude regarding my near miss with a devil was infuriating. One would think that type of thing would be front-page news, not a footnote. I would have taken his head off had Merc not beat me to the punch.

"That is the point, you idiot! Gracie's safety is what matters. It is why we are here." Ever the knight, Merc jumped to my rescue, but now I found myself wondering why. Did he really care about me or was he just trying to recruit me for my pain-taking talent?

"We all want Grace to be safe," Willem said gently, as always, trying to unruffle ruffled feathers. "How can we help, Locke?"

Merc jumped in. "Lochedus," he corrected, using the angel's real name as proof of his complicity, "seems to think you know a way to convince me he's one of the good guys." He dragged his hand through his hair and let out a big whoosh of air. "Although I don't really need any proof – not anymore." He turned toward Locke, who was staring at him in surprise. "I guess I've known all along that you were a true angel, but I just have a few trust issues. I'm sorry about that. When it comes to Grace, I just have to be careful."

Locke was nodding his head, not at all offended by Merc's earlier outburst, but it was Willem who verbalized his agreement. "You're right to be cautious. Demons are very good at deception. I'm not sure you'll take my word for it, but let me assure you that Lochedus is most definitely who he says he is."

Merc seemed surprised at Willem's conciliatory tone. I guess he still expected him to be mad about the whole drinking thing. I wasn't surprised. Willem had such a kind heart and didn't seem like the type to hold a grudge. Of course, his gentle demeanor could be a masterful cover for a sinister soul. When it came right down to it, I didn't know him any better than I knew the rest of them.

"I do believe you – and Locke," Merc conceded. "I've run into a few demons in my time, but not many angels. I guess Locke just wasn't what I expected – or remembered," he laughed, obviously ready to play nice now.

A slightly indignant snort came from the angel in question. Though I'd never seen him leave the sofa, the blonde "boy" had somehow magically produced a large bag of brightly colored candy and was tossing them, one by one, into the air and catching them in his mouth. His cavalier attitude was making me see red, and I had to fight myself to keep from walking over to the couch and smacking him.

Merc shook his head and chuckled in a way that made me think he found the boy's attitude funny. I didn't find it a bit humorous and I certainly didn't appreciate my hero's quick conversion to "Team Locke."

Mrs. B. had been uncharacteristically silent throughout the exchange, but naturally her muteness was just the calm before the storm.

"So, I see you've chosen to let the cat out of the bag, boy." She had turned on Locke with daggers for eyes, her hands on her ample hips. "One would think you would consult with us before taking such a drastic step."

Locke, no longer the lounging clown, saw her tone and raised it by yelling. "Why should I consult with you, woman? Honestly, you have no idea what position you are in, do you?"

As always, Willem immediately stepped in between the two before things got worse. "Now, now – everyone just calm down. Bickering will get us nowhere." He turned toward Merc and I watched him study the dark boy for a minute before asking me, "Gracie, would you mind if I have a few moments alone with Merchison?"

What was I going to say? No? I didn't much like the idea of Merc talking to Willem privately because I was tired of secrets, but something inside of me kept me from arguing with the old man.

"Sure, go right ahead," I responded grudgingly, dreading the thought of being left alone with Locke and Mrs. B. I didn't feel particularly comfortable with either one of them. When I'd first met Locke, he had seemed so easygoing, but I knew now that it had all been a big act. Things were much different than they originally appeared. I could only assume I didn't know the whole story regarding the old folks either, and I would feel light years better having Merc by my side until I felt on steady footing. But then, did I really know him?

Merc and Willem excused themselves, saying that they were going to go to the bungalow and talk. Without Willem to referee, Mrs. B. and Locke started sniping at each other almost immediately. I was glad for their argument because it kept the focus away from me. I think I was particularly uneasy around the old lady and the angel because both seemed to have some kind of pipeline into my mind. I couldn't stand the thought of their knowing what I was thinking because at the moment my thoughts were a little strange, at best. Over the years, I'd become pretty adept at hiding my innermost musings, but something told me that my usual mental maneuvers would be in vain when dealing with Mrs. B. and Locke.

I would have liked to have some time to myself to analyze what was going on inside of me. There was a fast growing darkness in my head that I didn't understand, and nothing felt right or good. I had always been wishy-washy in my emotions – up one moment, down the other; terms like manic and bipolar had been littered around me since puberty. But until now my moods had never been extreme enough to actually qualify for the diagnosis. As I stood listening to the young man and old woman bicker, I began to wonder if my shrink might have missed something.

I desperately tried to reanimate my mind by recalling every exciting detail of the weekend, but nothing seemed to raise the shades of my mind. Just as quickly as one could flip a switch, my brain had gone dark. Every good thing that had happened since I first turned on the mansion's dirt road was re-evaluated and re-characterized. Every kind act now had an ulterior motive – every positive thought a sad misinterpretation.

I struggled to hide the horror going on in my head. The sea of despair was rising quickly, and it would be only moments before the waters of depression covered me completely, and I'd be drowning in the wake of the sudden loss of the light. I scolded myself for my moments of jubilation and confidence – the brief periods I'd felt sure of my strength and convinced of Merc's love. How could I have been so stupid? How could I have believed, even for a moment, that my life could change completely in the space of a weekend? I tried to pinpoint just what had caused my drastic shift in outlook. Even in my wretched misery I knew that there was something abnormal about the suddenness with which the depression had seized my soul. Could the transfer of Locke's emotion onto me have caused this dreadful malady of the mind?

Every action I now painted with a sinister brush, sure that I'd been the victim of a scheme or joke or, even worse, a delusion. With dread washing over me, I excused myself to the powder room and once there was in no way surprised to see the same substandard reflection I'd been gazing upon for years. I wanted to crawl in a hole and die or slink quietly out of the mansion, back to the world I'd always known – back to my comfortable misery. Maybe, I reasoned, my depression would ease when I left the house that had started it all, and distanced myself from the people who had altered my reality. Grasping at straws, I decided to make a run for it and, carefully avoiding a second glance in the glass, I left the room and headed for the door.

"Are you going somewhere, dear?" Mrs. B. asked in a kind tone I was unused to associating with her voice. To my chagrin, she'd been waiting outside the bathroom door for me. Locke was nowhere in sight.

"I need to go. Could you tell the guys I'm sorry? I've got somewhere I've got to be." I edged closer to the door, hoping to get away before Merc or Locke realized my intention.

"There is nowhere you need to be more important than here, Grace." I didn't have the energy to put up a fight when she gently but firmly took hold of my elbow and walked me down the hall into the library.

"I've sent Locke to the bungalow to be with Merc and Willem. We need some time alone," she said mysteriously, though I only half heard her through the haze in my mind.

I was so completely engulfed in the depression that I couldn't even speak, only mutely follow. I felt as if I'd fallen into a deep, dark well from which there was no escape. Yet in the pitch of my mind, a small, small voice was calling out to me – offering me a lifeline – if I could only find the courage to reach for it.

From across the room, the old lady studied me quizzically and after only a few moments she began to speak.

"Grace, I know this will be difficult for you, but you need to try very hard to listen to me. You are going to want to retreat into yourself, but you mustn't. You need to fight to stay cognizant. Fight as if your life depended on it – because it does."

Her voice was like a bee buzzing around me – irritating me – annoying me. I didn't want her to talk. I just wanted the quiet of my head. But with my vitality zapped and the darkness encroaching, I had nothing left inside of me to resist her. Why was she bothering me? Why wouldn't she just shut up? I longed for the initiative to get away from her, but I was stuck listening to what at first seemed to be the nonsensical ramblings of a crazed old woman.

She closed the library doors and came over to sit next to me on the sofa, taking my hand in hers. "Grace, please try to concentrate and listen to what I'm saying. You need to understand that what you are going through is only temporary. You can and will pull out of this, but you are going to have to make some real effort. You cannot . . . " She paused, clearing her throat. "You *will not* get lost in the darkness. You are strong. You have the inner resources to come back. You have an opportunity in front of you that is fleeting, and if you miss your chance, I can promise you that you will spend your life regretting it. Fight, Grace! Fight the demons inside."

What was the old woman talking about? What did she know of my darkness? My brain fought to close the door on her voice, but she was persistent and continued talking in the same low, calm voice, repeating over and over that I needed to listen to her, that I needed to concentrate, that I needed to fight. I rallied long enough to angrily push her away.

"Leave me alone, Mrs. B. I just want to go home. I need to get away from here!"

I no longer cared about the job or the money; it had probably all been a ruse anyway. I only cared about escape. The pressure inside my head was debilitating, and I felt the only refuge from the unrelenting stress was to sleep – to slip into unconsciousness and stay there, protected from the pain. But even in my condition, I knew sleep would be impossible under the roof of the mansion, so I wanted to flee back to the safety of the bed and breakfast where I could lock myself in my room and throw the covers over my head.

I didn't even allow myself to consider how Merc would feel when he got back from his private talk with Willem and found me gone. Merc was just an illusion, or at least Merc's feelings for me were an illusion, every bit as fleeting and migratory as my fickle reflection. I couldn't allow myself to sink any deeper into the fantasy of a future involving the boy that I first confused with a dream. My hold on sanity was at best tenuous. To entertain crazed illusions of grandeur wherein I shared a supernatural life with a God-like love would only drive me further into the arms of madness.

I had never been suicidal, largely because I was a coward, but at the moment I would have given anything for a shot of hemlock followed by a chaser of cyanide. No fate could have exceeded the anguish I was currently experiencing. And just when I thought it couldn't get any worse, the whispers began.

They started quietly – murmured innuendo and muttered accusations, spinning like a merry-go-round of the mind, rising and falling in tone and timbre, riding through my head on the steeds of my insecurity and fear.

You couldn't possibly think that a guy like Merc – so handsome, so gifted – could love you, one voice whispered.

He must be using you. They probably all are. They want you to take on the pain so they won't have to, a second joined in.

You're nothing special – why would he want you? Questioned a third vicious voice.

These weren't the utterings of my fractured personality – voices who were at times themselves diabolical in their insights. The demonic round circling my brain was the product of a foreign entity, though strangely familiar. With a jolt, I knew where I had first heard the voices, and the realization was stupefying. These were the same bodiless intonations I had heard in the woods when I was being pulled closer and closer to the Magnet Demon. Had the devil of the woods succeeded in taking over my mind and body?

In terror, I began frantically listening for the voice of the old woman, no longer the enemy but possibly my savior. However, each time I thought I heard a dim echo of her voice the demons would grow louder and drown out her ever-weakening cries.

"Help me! Help me, Mrs. B.!" I screamed, fearing my pleas were only internal manifestations of my panicked thoughts.

The chaos built to a fevered pitch, and then I gasped out loud when suddenly everything stopped, and for one blissful moment silence reigned in my brain. But relief was short-lived because in the still of that moment a singular, petrifying voice rang out. *Don't you know who the old woman is? Of course you do, my dear. Look into her eyes and behold your future.*

As the sound of his words faded from my ears, my mind cleared, and I was once again cognizant of my surroundings. I found myself staring into the ancient face of the old lady. Only this time I looked at her with freshly opened eyes. I could no longer hide from the truth that was staring right back at me with a mixture of fear and defiance – the look I'd perfected many years ago as a defense against school bullies. I stared in horrified fascination into the old aqua eyes that now begged me for a mercy that I was ill prepared and unwilling to extend.

If ever there had been an appropriate time to pass out in my life, it would have been at that moment but naturally my body and brain chose the most mind-blowing moment of my existence to remain fully alert and functioning. Thankfully, my vocal cords kindly provided a needed release, and I began to scream as if the whole world was being blown away – because my whole world had, in the space of a heartbeat, disintegrated into ash.

Chapter Seventeen

HERE I GO AGAIN

I WAS AWARE OF THE HORRIFIC HURT ETCHED INTO THE OLD WOMAN'S face. Although it should have mattered to me . . . I mean, it really should have; I didn't care. All I wanted to do was run. I jumped up from the sofa and headed for the door as fast as I could move.

"Please, Grace, please," she begged. "We need to talk."

"No, we don't," I screamed. "I can't breathe! I need to get out of here . . . NOW!"

"It's not safe. At least let me get Merc or Locke to drive you."

"No! I want to be by myself. Tell them not to follow me; I mean it."

"It isn't safe. You are in great danger, Grace," she repeated, her pain and fear evident in every word.

But I wasn't listening. After all, what could be worse than this? I flew to the car and, relieved that the keys were still in it, cranked up and tore off as fast as the old Cutlass could go. Wet mud and gravel slung from my tires as I banged in and out of potholes and dodged fallen limbs. I was driving way too fast down the red dirt lane, and I fishtailed – barely holding the car on the road – as I turned from unpaved to paved road. A steady rain beat down on the roof, and between the flapping of old wipers, *Black Sabbath* blaring, and the residual gravel beating on the underside of the engine, I could barely hear myself think. I tried to concentrate on driving, putting out of my head the life-changing truth of what had transpired behind the walls of the old mansion. But this was no garden-variety realization; the revulsion and horror of the secret self revealed was more than I could block from my over-taxed mind.

Looking for a more forceful way to get control of my nerves, I bit hard on the inside of my cheek, the pain causing a welcome diversion from my agonizing reality. I banged my fists hard against the steering wheel and screamed until my throat gave out. I considered the simple solution of driving into a tree or over a bridge, but I feared with my luck, I would render myself partially disabled rather than permanently released from the torture of my existence.

I decided not to go back to the inn and be forced to field questions when I had no answers to give and no energy with which to give them. Instead, I chose to go off the grid, speeding down the narrow highways and bi-ways, daring a lawman or woman to give chase and give reason for me to make an already terrible situation worse.

Without really thinking about it, I headed toward Fort Toulouse, a National Park outside of Wetumpka that my class had visited just a few days after my fateful first appearance at All Saints High. Trying to divert my mind from what had just happened at the mansion, I cast my brain backward to the events of the time.

I remembered that day in February well, as one of hideous discomfort – the perpetual new girl in the class providing a source of instant entertainment and mildly mean fascination to the thick-as-thieves good ol' boys and Dixie darlings of the junior class. I also recalled that windy February Monday with some fondness as the day that my one and only friend strolled casually into my life.

But even though several months had passed since the field trip to Fort Toulouse, when March Ann rescued me from my solitary lunch eaten on a lonely slope of grass next to the gift shop, I still had no more insight into what made her tick than when first she said, "Hey, honey!"

I was extremely standoffish with March Ann in the beginning, thinking her interest in me had to be a prank – a spite-spirited punk devised by the reigning royalty of the class to put the new girl in her place. But slowly I began to accept her as every bit as much of an outsider as I was. After careful consideration, I decided that her exceptional beauty had created a vacuum around her, making her untouchable and therefore just as lonely as me.

The interesting thing about March Ann was that she didn't seem to mind her loner status and, in fact, reveled in it – putting as much distance between her and the All Saints in-crowd as possible. She always had a kind word for the unpopular, the geek, the nerd, but barely acknowledged the existence of the hip kids – treating them with as much disdain as they treated those not deemed good enough to gain their favor.

As the "uncoolest" of them all, I became March Ann's best friend, and with that title came her protection from the marvelous masses. If a girl shot a sideways glance at my clothes, March Ann would be there to cut her to the quick – leaving her unsure of what had happened and running for the door. If a boy approached me – ready to yank my chain – my beautiful best friend was there to run more fierce interference between us than the boy had ever encountered on a field. She was the only one to understand my anger with my parents and my irritation with my sister-in-law – commiserating with me yet never allowing me to wallow in my pain. In short, she was everything a girl could want in a BFF and I would have given anything to have her with me at the moment.

Maybe that's why I chose to run to the park. If I'd been a normal teenager, I could have called her on my cell phone and poured out the whole unbelievable story. I would have begged her to meet me and help me wade through the issues in my brain. But as punishment for my defunct website rendezvous, my parents had moved the computer to the family room and taken my cell phone away. They tried to return the phone several months ago but in my stubbornness I refused their offer – unwilling to admit that I really didn't have anyone to call anyway. Now I was wishing I'd accepted the cell so that I could ring up my sole supportive friend and cry on her always-available shoulder.

As I wheeled my car through the gates of Fort Toulouse, I was pleased to see that, probably because of the rain, the park was fairly deserted. I knew it would be only a matter of time before the guys tracked me down. Merc would be demanding and frantic, and Locke, with his heavenly connections, would make short work of locating me. My head was in such an awful place that I was convinced the boys had some monstrous motive for seeking me out and I felt certain that after all the trouble they had gone to in order to meet me the first time, they would do all in their power to get me back under their spell.

A tiny muffled voice in the very core of my being was whispering that I was wrong about everything, but by now I had no faith in what that voice had to say. I had completely lost my center, and my thoughts were reeling around in my head like a pinball – every instinct and idea banging against the corners of my mind in chaotic fashion. What I now knew to be true simply couldn't be; therefore, I had no choice but to question my entire mental platform – the very basis of who I was. Despite my OCD and ADD and all the other "Ds" in my personality, I had never doubted my intelligence. I might have made jokes about my alleged cerebral defects, but inside I'd always been exceptionally proud of my mental acumen and had used it on many an occasion to batter those I felt in every other way to be my superior. Now the one shining star in my otherwise lackluster crown of merits was being called into question, and I could no longer depend on my brain's reasoning abilities to determine yea from nay.

When my brain ever so quietly whispered that the boys were honorable, that they meant me no harm, that Merc truly loved me - I couldn't trust its convictions. The louder voice overwhelmed my hushed instincts, using my insecurities and doubts as clear and convincing evidence of the boys' sinister intent.

No conscious voice directed me toward the park, and I didn't really have any particular area of the property in mind when

I arrived. For a few minutes I just slowly drove around the winding roads and past the visitor center, finally parking in the lot adjacent to the campgrounds where folks pulled in their campers and RVs for the night.

In a daze I parked, got out of the car and began walking toward a path marked *The William Bartram Trail*, so named for a naturalist from the late 1700s who passed through the area collecting specimens of plants and recording data of his findings. My mind flashed back to the morning of the field trip, and I shuddered at the memory, recalling the uncomfortable, solitary trek I'd taken down the trail while simulating note-taking in a sad attempt to cover up my own embarrassment over my solo status.

It was against every long-held belief and habit I had to work out my problems through physical exertion, yet now my feet seemed to take on a life of their own and before I knew it I was halfway down the lonely way, soaking wet from not only the steady rain, but sweat. Though it was not my nature to enjoy nature, for a short time I actually lost myself on the trail, surrounded by the beauty of the elm, cedar and red bud trees. The light rain didn't really bother me at the time, and though the sun wasn't visible through the cloud cover, I began to feel as if being out in the fresh damp air was doing my brain a bit of good.

I stopped for a moment, craning my neck to see up through the trees to the sky, trying to decide whether to turn back or keep going. In just that instant – like a light switch being turned off – the heather gray heavens darkened to a deep sultry ash, and a now-familiar odor whipped through the pines like a physical force, assaulting my senses and turning my stomach to jelly. I knew right away what was going to happen, and I was also immediately aware of just how stupid I had been. But self-awareness, as usual, came too late for me, and I was not even surprised – though certainly I was terrified – when my body was again gripped in the magnetic force of the demon.

I veered my head wildly, straining in vain to catch a glimpse of the monster that I knew lay behind the horrible pull. Although he did not make his physical presence known to me as he had the night before outside my window, the mental images replaying in my head were every bit as gut-wrenchingly terrorizing as when I had beheld the Devil in all his terrible glory.

The strange power now seemed magnified, as well – much greater in strength – and I got the sense that the malevolent presence behind it was angry, no longer willing to toy with me, its patience at an end. Time and time again, I was hurled into the air and brought back down with tremendous force, my body battered by the limbs of the large trees blocking my path of ascent and descent. Much like the first two times, I was momentarily paralyzed with the terror of what was happening to me, but finally – thankfully – I began to feel a pool of adrenalin build within my core, its liquid fortitude rushing from its center source to every muscle and sinew of my body. Instantly I remembered how I had first escaped the devil's magnetic attraction, and deciding to repeat the same move, I hit the ground in a crouch and used my powerful new leg muscles to lunge to the side and escape from the path of the unholy attraction that towed me toward my doom.

Once away from the immediate danger, I ran in the direction of my car, trying to make it toward what I hoped was safety. Though my limbs were far stronger and more agile than they had ever been, I had only gone a few dozen yards when, once again, I was seized by invisible manacles and dragged upward through the thick woody barrier of limbs toward the near-black sky.

Amazingly, I wasn't panicked, and as if my brain was in slow motion, I planned a course of action and followed it through. I looked ahead of me and picked out the largest, sturdiest limb in my path. I jumped, grabbing hold of the rough bark arm, and swung my body up and over it, landing gracefully on my feet. At lightning speed, I moved toward the opposite side of the massive trunk and used it as a shield against the magnet, pausing long enough to catch my breath.

It was in that moment of rest that it came to me how wrong I had been about everything. The dastardly voice of doom had fled my

head, leaving only the finally combined pieces of my own personality –
now made whole – my dominion absolute. I was no longer confused
but rather infused with the supremacy of certainty that had eluded
me. Joan of Arc was back and she was raring for a fight.

More power and the understanding of that power poured into
me with a vengeance, and with a wave of my hand, I stopped in
its tracks the force field of malice that sought to entrap me. As
I poised gingerly on the sturdy oak limb, I mentally prepared to do
battle against the menace that had made clear its malignant intent.
I stepped farther into the demon's line of sight and lifted my hand
again to send my own weapons its way.

I didn't get the chance to see what destruction my first genuine
supernatural act would cause against my opponent because suddenly the sky was alight with a blinding flash, and a loud, vaguely
amused, strangely familiar southern soprano trilled, "GET THEE
BEHIND ME, EVIL ONE! LEAVE THIS PLACE AND LEAVE
THIS GIRL ALONE!"

Immediately, all the electrical pull and malodorous odor
evaporated into thin air, and the darkened sky turned a brilliant
shade of cerulean blue. Almost more disappointed than relieved, I
turned to face the interloper who'd dared to steal my virgin thunder. I had to grab hold of the trunk of the tree for support when
my indignant spin brought me inches away from the twinkling
blue eyes of my best friend March Ann Mayham, dressed not in her
usual designer jeans and baby-T, but in full angel regalia – replete
with sparkling white robe and bejeweled sandaled feet. She, like
Locke, didn't sport wings, but I didn't have to be told that even
without aerodynamic appendages, my friend was indeed a being of
the heavenly kind.

Chapter Eighteen

AWAKEN THE GUARDIAN

ALL THE LITTLE HINTS AND CLUES CAME TOGETHER IN MY BRAIN IN a second and it all made perfect sense to me; of course March Ann was an angel. I mean, before the weekend, I had no experience with the supernatural, so I wouldn't have suspected such a thing was possible. But now that I knew about the true existence of the heavenly realm and the messengers of God, it was easy for me to accept my best friend's role in a divine plan – a plan involving me and all those I'd made the acquaintance of in the past two days.

I wondered if March Ann had perhaps always been my guardian angel – not the loudest of the voices in my head, but the one that most often made sense. I marveled at her now, standing so sure and strong next to me, looking like a warrior princess ready to protect me from the devilish demons that meant me harm. Had she seen me through other tough times, as well – quietly posting guard over my soul, allowing me to dip my toe into the shallow pool of insanity yet never fall headfirst into the deep water? I'd come close so many times in so many ways to losing it completely, but something always prevented me from taking the final plunge. Could that something have been March Ann?

I suddenly felt shy, not knowing how to react or what to say to the amazing creature I called my friend. It was probably her roguish wink and impudent smile that loosened my tongue.

"March Ann, I . . . I can't believe it's really you. How did you know?" I stopped and rolled my eyes at my own foolishness. "Sorry, stupid question. You know because, well . . . because you're an angel. Wow!"

She laughed – a musical wind chime of merriment – and then hugged me close to her. "Yep, that's right," she confirmed. "I'm an angel, and we need to get out of here - pronto!"

"Okay . . . where to? Are we going back to the mansion? I was so stupid. I can't believe I just ran away. Merc and Locke must be so worried." I secretly wished the boys were somewhere nearby, but my hopes came crashing down with March Ann's ominous reply.

"Merc and Locke have their hands full with problems of their own right now. We'll have to meet up with them and the old ones later. I have to get you somewhere safe."

Problems of their own? Is that what she had said? My heart was in my throat - suddenly terrified that Merc might be in danger. In fact, I was petrified at the thought of any of my new friends being hurt. Why had I left them? Guilt washed over me in waves, but instead of paralyzing me, it was a call to action. If they were in trouble, I needed to be there. I wasn't sure exactly what I could do to help, but I was infused with the confidence of new power and ready to cut my teeth on any battle in which my loved ones might be in peril.

"We've got to go back. I've got to get to Merc; he needs me."

"Absolutely not." March Ann crossed her arms over her chest with finality. My friend had always been stubborn, but somehow just knowing she had wings hidden somewhere gave teeth to her obstinate answer. I could be pretty bull-headed myself though, and

I was absolutely determined to get back to the man I loved and the people I cared about.

"I mean it, March Ann – halo or no halo – I'm going back to find Merc, Locke and the old folks. If you won't take me, I'll get there by myself." It was hard to stamp my foot on top of a tree limb, but I gave it my best shot.

March Ann merely raised a sarcastic eyebrow and without another word scooped me into her arms and jumped from the tree. I closed my eyes, not wanting to see the ground coming up to meet my expensive orthodontia work, but rather than hitting the expected dirt I felt my body being lifted upward toward the sky.

It had never been a big dream of mine to fly, so I didn't find the whole "bolting through the sky at light speed" especially exhilarating. It certainly wasn't what I would have imagined it to be. There was no looking down at the ground with wonder at the people who looked like ants, or admiring the beautiful landscape from miles above. There was simply a sensation of being lifted into the sky and seconds later the reverse sensation of descending to the ground. It did take me a moment to get my bearings and realize that we'd not gone very far at all. We were, in fact, still on the property of Fort Toulouse.

March Ann had landed us dead in the middle of Fort Jackson – a structure I remembered from my class field trip and history lessons as being built by General Andrew Jackson toward the end of the Creek Wars in the early 1800s. It wasn't anything like the forts I'd seen in the old John Wayne movies I'd watched with my dad. It was small and very, very primitive, but it was easy to see why March Ann had picked the place; it was impossible to sneak up on. It only amounted to a couple of small barracks and a fire pit, but the strategic location and setup was perfect.

Regardless of the rains, there should have been some employees hanging around. Strangely, there wasn't a soul in sight, and I began to get the uncomfortable and claustrophobic feeling that I was in the wrong place at a very wrong time.

After straightening my soaking wet clothes to the best of my ability I swung toward March Ann, who was carefully studying the layout of the place.

"Are you going to let me in on what you're planning?" I asked stiffly, still miffed by her pushy show of angelic strength and cavalier treatment of my feelings.

"All in good time, my dear. I know this isn't the most comfortable of places, but it suits my purposes for now – so just hang tight."

I watched as she scooted around the small area – looking into the barracks and climbing onto the armaments. She seemed particularly pleased with the fire pit and I prayed she wasn't planning to do any cooking.

She certainly seemed in very good spirits – reveling in whatever was to come. Her devil-may-care swagger was even more pronounced than usual and had me wondering if her attitude was a bit of hyperbole designed to put me at ease. Actually, I would have been more comfortable if she had shown some concern, considering what she'd intimated we might be up against, but to me it seemed like she was playing a game. I guess things were easier if you knew what kind of power you were packing.

I thought all things considered, I was hanging in pretty well myself. I'd had one heck of a weekend, and I was still standing. I'd learned I could deal with an awful lot without losing my mind, and that was something. Of course, I'd chosen not to even think about the worst revelation of the day. Even my brain had its limitations, so I refused to admit to myself the one thing I knew I couldn't deal with. I needed to maintain my sanity in order to survive what was coming, and the only way to do that was to stow away the devastating realization of Mrs. B.'s true identity. I might never be able to look that piece of info in the face – not and keep lucid.

"What are you concentrating on so hard?" March Ann asked, biting into an apple that had somehow materialized out of thin air.

"Gee, I don't know, March – maybe thinking about how my best friend is an angel." I resisted the childish urge to knock the apple from her hand, settling instead for a light punch on her arm, which she ignored. "You would think sometime in the last four months you could have squeezed that little tidbit of news into the conversation. Or maybe I was wondering if the man I'm in love with is in danger. Or . . ."

"Okay, okay," she laughed. "I get your point. You have a lot on your mind."

"Ya think?" I said sarcastically before getting serious. "Really, March Ann – I need to know what's happening with my friends. I can't just sit around this creepy old fort when they could be in danger. Why can't we go find them and help them? I mean . . . you're an angel, for gosh sakes. Isn't that what you do? Save people?"

She tossed her picked-clean apple core nearly thirty yards into a trash bin next to the barracks door. Giving me an impish smile, she answered, "Angels do a lot of things, but mostly we follow orders, and my orders are to keep you here and safe."

For some reason, her lackadaisical attitude was rubbing me the wrong way and I found it impossible to keep quiet. "Well, I don't follow anyone's orders, and I'm leaving," I declared, with about as much confidence as I could muster under the circumstances.

I had almost made it to the front gate when I was unceremoniously picked up into the air and dragged backward to the top of the same picnic bench I'd been sitting on before.

"Hey, cut it out, March Ann. I mean it. I can't just sit here." I was near tears, more from anger than upset. There was nothing I hated worse than feeling helpless.

The color in her cheeks flamed, and it wasn't hard to see that the golden girl of the hour was fighting back her own rage. "Look," she said, with impatience and frustration ringing in her voice. "I don't like this either, but we have to stay here and wait for my brothers. You're just going to have to calm down and trust me."

Her plea for trust fell on deaf ears because her words brought a whole new issue to light. "Your brothers? This is the first I've heard of you having brothers. You told me you only had sisters," I reminded her pointedly. "I guess that was a lie, too."

"Of course it was," she said simply, not even bothering to deny her deceit, which only served to fan the flames of my ire.

"I guess angels don't feel the need for honesty," I shot back. "Good to know."

"You know nothing, and for now you just need to sit down and shut up!"

I couldn't believe she was talking to me in such a hateful way. I wanted to jump down her throat, but I was getting the uncomfortable feeling that it wouldn't be a good idea. She was clearly as stressed as I was, and I wondered if she was more worried about things than she let on. Instead of swapping barbs with her, I settled for quietly pouting and waiting to see who showed up to help us.

The time crawled by in silence. March Ann seemed to have no problem sitting stock still for hours, but it was driving me crazy. Where were my friends? Where was Merc? I was sick with worry and finally decided that I had to do something to pass the time, or I was going to lose my mind.

An idea came to me that it might be a good thing to test my abilities. With March Ann right on my heels, I walked outside the gate and looked around, trying to devise a course of action to carry out my plan. Under my former friend's cool amused gaze, I ran from one end of the fort to the other and was shocked to find that it only took me a second or two to accomplish the task. I thought about challenging the angel du jour to an arm wrestling match, but we weren't speaking so I was forced to play solo. I jumped, climbed, pushed, pulled and toted for over an hour, never once even getting winded.

Maybe it was the passing of time or just extreme boredom that finally caused me to break down and bury the hatchet. "You know, March Ann, you could teach me a few things about how to protect myself. I can see that I'm stronger and faster, but I haven't got a clue what to do with what I've got. How about it?" I asked, sweetly smiling, going for a look of helpless sincerity. "Will you help me?"

It took her a minute to consider both my olive branch and my request, but finally she answered, surprising me with her response. "I don't need to teach you anything, Grace," she said, standing up from where she sat cross-legged on the grass and crossing over to where I was standing. "Once the guys get here, we'll do the ceremony and then you will know everything."

Taken aback, I stepped away from her, wanting to put some distance between us. "What ceremony? What are you talking about?"

"Calm down, Grace. I thought Merc or Lochedus would have told you about it. They probably thought there would be more time. But now we're under the gun, and we have to get it done – for your safety."

I didn't know why, but warning bells were going off in my head. I tried to slow my racing pulse and think rationally, but it was hard. "I'm calm. Just tell me what you're talking about, please."

We walked back into the fort and sat down on a weathered old bench next to the fire pit, and she began to explain. "When you came in contact with Lochedus, you began to change. But your transformation won't be complete until you are brought into the fold." She turned, studying me quizzically, before adding, "You've probably noticed that your powers and abilities have been stronger sometimes more than others, right?"

"Yeah, that's right. Uh . . . I think I sort of look different, too, at least some of the time." I was embarrassed, but I forced myself to go on. "This morning when I looked in the mirror, I had changed. I was actually . . . pretty." I hung my head down, not wanting my stunning friend to see the color flood my cheeks. "But now, well . . . I think I'm back to my same old unattractive self."

Excited, she jumped up from the bench and kneeled at my feet, grasping both my hands in hers. "Exactly! That's what I'm talking about, Grace. You won't change permanently until you go through the ceremony. Afterward, you will never feel unlovely again." Almost as an afterthought, she added, "And you will also be much stronger and faster – all your gifts will be amplified and consistent."

My heart soared, all my irritation and distrust now a thing of the past at the mere mention of my being beautiful. "Well, what are we waiting for then? Let's get this show on the road!"

She laughed merrily and wrapped her arms around my waist – hugging me close. "Slow down, Cupcake! You're going to be ravishing soon enough. We can't do anything until my brothers get here, which should be any minute now.

She hopped up and dug her hand into her back pocket, fishing out a cell phone. "Excuse me for a moment, won't you? I need to call my brother Monroe to see what's keeping them."

Puzzled, I watched her walk away. She must have really wanted some privacy, because she left the fort for parts unknown. It struck me as kind of strange – an angel using a cell phone. One would think she could use heavenly telepathy or something. But I guess she subscribed to the "when in Rome" theory. I strained to see if my new, improved hearing could pick up any traces of the conversation she was taking such pains to conceal; but I wasn't able to hear a thing. Her chat with the mysterious Monroe must have been a short one though, because it wasn't long before she strolled back through the gates to my side.

"That sure didn't take long," I said, while holding my hair up off of my neck. The humidity of the afternoon was killing me, and I was ready to get the party started. "So did you talk to your family? Will they be here soon?"

"You know, Grace, patience IS a virtue. We haven't been here all that long. I know you're just worried about your maaaan." She drew out the word "man" while giving her shoulders a little shimmy for effect. "But Merc and the mansion gang are going to be just fine. Stop worrying – you're harshing my mellow."

I rolled my eyes and half-heartedly laughed at her attempt to lighten the mood; I was worried and had a tough time following her silly lead. Maybe angels were accustomed to drama and danger, but I wasn't. I had led a somewhat sedentary lifestyle up until now, and my induction into the world of the supernatural had been exhausting, not to mention worrisome, not to mention terrifying. It was easy for March Ann as a daughter of the Most High to laugh in the face of peril, but I was new to all this stuff and flying blind. You'd think an angel would have a bit more empathy.

After a moment of quiet, an idea popped into my head that got me a little excited.

"Say, March, does Locke have a cell phone?" He had never mentioned one, but we hadn't had too much time together, so it was possible that I just didn't know about it.

"I don't know - maybe. Why?" She replied, more puzzled than I thought she should have been.

Lord, for an angel she was pretty dang dense. I guess common sense wasn't always a part of the seraphic package. "Why do you think? I want to check on them. I'm worried sick."

For some bizarre reason, my concern seemed to really make her mad. "Locke, Locke, Locke! Merc, Merc, Merc! Give it a rest, sugar. Don't you trust me to take care of you?"

She was actually pouting, which I found faintly amusing. Apparently being angelic didn't stop one from behaving like a typical temperamental teen. But, I didn't get a chance to point out her less-than-mature behavior because a distinctly male voice interrupted her rant.

"Someone got up on the wrong side of the cloud today."

I gasped in shock because one minute March Ann and I were alone in the deserted fort and the next we were looking at five gorgeous young men – any one of whom could grace a Paris runway. I stared in open-mouthed shock as the boy who I assumed was the leader gave me a quick, uninterested once-over and returned his attention to March Ann.

"You're looking unusually fetching today, sister." He smiled winningly.

My friend was having none of his flattery. Though she'd not said so, I assumed these were her brothers and they were not on time.

"Save it, Monroe. Why are you late? Did something happen?"

The boy, a bleach-blonde surfer type with misty green eyes and a brilliant smile made whiter by his deep tan, stepped back a pace from his seething sister. "I'm sorry. We encountered a few problems," he explained. "Nothing we couldn't handle." He seemed nervous and I was impressed. Clearly, my best friend wielded some kind of power in the higher realm. She obviously outranked her band of brothers, who stood quaking in their sneakers.

March Ann said nothing, only glared at the group, prompting Monroe to start a fresh round of apologies. It was refreshing to see this merry group of men all groveling at the knees of their mistress. *Lordy!* What that must feel like. March Ann was a lucky girl. Uh . . . make that blessed girl . . . make that blessed angel. I was going to have to learn the lingo.

For the second time in a short time, March Ann excused herself to speak privately with her brother. If I'd been alone, curiosity would have surely gotten the better of me, and I would have found a way to accidentally "overhear" their conversation. Unfortunately, she'd charged her other four "siblings" with the task of entertaining me while she was gone – a ploy I was sure she devised to prevent me from doing the very thing I would have done had she not ordered her brothers to keep me occupied.

Under normal circumstances I suppose I would have been thrilled to be left in the hands of four such fabulous-looking lads; however, my thoughts were otherwise occupied, focused solely on Merc, Locke, Willem and Mrs. B. and whatever troubles might have befallen them in my absence. That didn't keep the boys from doing everything in their power to get my attention, and after a while I began to get rather annoyed at their transparent attempts to attract me.

They did and said all the right things – each introducing himself with varying degrees of gallantry. There was Edmund – a tall, muscular, olive-skinned boy with curly dark hair, piercing blue eyes and a roguish smile. His exaggerated Southern accent and country-boy shtick would have had many a girl weak in the knees, but my knees were just fine, and I gave him no more than a quick smile and a "how do you do."

The second brother to make my acquaintance was Clifford – a hulk of a guy who looked as if he'd been carved from stone. His dark hair was cut military short, and he had the bearing and bone structure to pull it off. The "nice to meet you, ma'am," he threw at me could have easily been followed by a salute, and I had to force myself not to respond with a "roger that" or "hooah."

The other two boys – Kenny and Donald – were auburn haired, medium-built twins, who were as remarkable looking as their brethren and equally uninteresting to me. The quartet made up a veritable smorgasbord of manly delights, yet I might as well have been swapping shakes with a Sunday afternoon canasta group for all the fascination they held for me.

After finally giving up on getting anything more from me than a distracted answer and a half-hearted smile, someone produced a football, and the boys began playing a game of two-hand touch that quickly deteriorated into a no-holds-barred free-for-all that looked more like a wrestling match than a ball game. I couldn't help getting tickled a few times at the boys' antics. It was funny to me that even angels acted like idiots to gain a girl's favor. I probably would have been a little more interested and a lot more flattered if I hadn't known they were merely following the directions of their undisputed leader – March Ann. It wasn't my beauty compelling them to show out, it was my guardian angel and that knowledge kept me from really enjoying the horseplay designed for my benefit. Actually, I don't think I would have enjoyed it anyway, because the later it got the more worried I became about my friends who were miles away and possibly in peril.

The sun was on its downward path, and though I didn't have a watch on, I figured it was about six o'clock. The rain had finally cleared out completely, leaving the atmosphere muggy and uncomfortable and my clothes sticking to my body. I couldn't figure out where the afternoon had gone, the hours eaten up with no real progress to show for the passage of time.

I was beginning to get extremely aggravated with March Ann, who had been gone for what seemed like forever, leaving me alone to deal with the three-ring circus she called her family. I wasn't sure they were her true siblings or rather her relations in a more spiritual sense, but the more time I spent with them, the more I began to see a resemblance among all of them that ran deeper than their startling good looks. It wasn't anything obvious, but more of a feeling that I got in my bones when sharing space with the group or any one of them individually.

While I had never noticed this uneasy sensation in my gut over the past four months with March Ann, I began to feel it almost immediately after she blew onto my branch earlier in the day. I knew I was being ridiculous; after all, these were the good guys – Heaven's storm troopers – but the odd feeling was there, nevertheless, and it was getting more pronounced with each passing minute.

I had walked every square inch of the small fort at least ten times and was ready to climb the weathered old walls. It was kind of amazing that the place had remained standing over the years, because it looked to me like a stray spark or carelessly thrown cigarette could have taken the fort down in a matter of minutes. But it was full of rich history, and I spent some time reading the literature I found lying around the place, just to pass the time. But soon I'd read every word and walked every corner and was tired of waiting.

I debated my chances of escape. Though I knew they weren't good, I decided to go for it. I was sick and tired of sitting around doing nothing and I was going to get back to the mansion or die trying. I waited to make my move until the brothers were all gathered around an old radio listening to the replay of a college football game. Timing was important, so on the fourth down when the Crimson Tide was at the five-yard line I, too, ran for the goal – for me the back gate of Fort Jackson.

Chapter Nineteen

IRON MAIDEN

As was so often the case, Bama made it to the end zone; unfortunately, I was turned back at the door.

"Just where do you think you are going?"

I was so busy looking behind me that I failed to see what was directly in front of me – a heartbreakingly beautiful, hopping mad March Ann. She was dressed from head to toe in gold – some sort of lamé, I supposed – and it clung to every curve of her body as if she'd been turned upside down and dunked into a melted pot of the 24-karat metal. Even her eyes were no longer blue but a citrine color more familiar on a cat's face than a human's. The plunging neckline of her gown combined with the slave bracelets on her arms and four-inch-heeled sandals on her feet screamed one word, and it wasn't Hallelujah! It was SEX.

Confusion, anger, hurt and jealousy were all present and accounted for in my mind. I was completely unnerved. I was no expert on angels – far from it – but my every instinct told me that this was no seraphic choir robe March Ann was rocking. The gown was better suited for a much warmer locale and if that was the case I had made a drastic error in judgment – an error that could well cost me my life. Or worse.

I was smart enough to know how badly outnumbered and out-powered I was, and deciding that discretion was, indeed, the better part of valor, I kept quiet, choosing instead to watch, look and listen for any activity that could help me confirm or deny my suspicions.

I carefully cleansed my face of any surplus horror and wid-ened my eyes to innocent effect. "I was looking for you, of course!" I tossed back as casually as I could, praying that she couldn't hear my heart pounding loudly through my chest. Opting for a quick change of subject, I added, "You look amazing! I thought I was the one being inducted into the Heavenly Hall of Fame – not you."

Her shoulders dropped from their defensive position, sure of my gullibility and hungry for compliments. She dimpled prettily and spun around showing off the back portion of her dress that was cut even lower than the front. "You don't think its too much, do you?"

"Of course not," I replied sarcastically. "It's just perfect for a religious ceremony." I was reminded of March Ann's penchant for skimpy clothing. She'd always shunned the boys who fawned all over her, but she had certainly worked hard to knock the socks off those she turned away.

I laughed ruefully, unable to keep the irony from my tone. "What will I be wearing? Let me guess – sack cloth and ashes?" I was will-ing to put down money that the same motivation that caused my friend to seek attention would also cause her to dislike that attention being focused elsewhere. I could probably parade around naked next to a fully clothed March Ann, and not a single boy would notice me, but I would still like to, at least, be dressed to have a fighting chance. After all, this little shindig was supposed to be about me.

"Oh, I have something very special for you." As if on cue, Monroe walked through the back gate. He was wearing, of all things, an immaculately cut tuxedo, and his hair was heavily gelled and slicked back, giving him the look of a 1940s movie star. Over his shoulder was a garment bag that, I presumed, concealed March

Ann's "something special." I reached out to grab the bag, anxious to see what she had purchased for me to wear, but Monroe gracefully twirled to the side, dodging my grasp.

"No, no, no," she scolded. "You're filthy. We have to get you cleaned up before you put on this little beauty." She relieved Monroe of the package and marched ahead, leaving us to follow in her wake.

"This isn't exactly the Hilton, M.A.," I called after her, using her initials to shorten her name. "Where am I supposed to get a bath, may I ask?"

She came to a stop outside the door of the first small barracks. "You're right, this isn't the Hilton, but I did the best I could with what I had." With that, she yanked open the beat up old door and walked through it.

Puzzled, I followed mutely behind, and when I crossed the threshold, I nearly fainted. I blinked my eyes, rubbed them and blinked again – unable to reconcile what I was seeing with what I knew to have been there only a short time before. Gone were the dirt floors, which were now covered wall-to-wall with a sinfully plush intricately patterned Aubusson rug. The low-beamed ceilings were no longer in sight, masked by a series of overlapping strips of beautiful silk fabric that draped in a circus-tent manner. The swaths of silk met and tied in the center to form a rosette from which a sparkling cut-crystal chandelier hung. The walls, too, were covered in the same shimmering silks, all in varying shades of teal and aqua and all accented heavily with thick borders of gold and silver. The plank-board beds had been taken away and were replaced with a rose moiré-covered fainting couch, a mirrored dressing table, and piles and piles of large and small velvet pillows.

The only other item in the room was a large claw-foot tub. As I drew close to its edge, I realized it was filled with steaming hot water, bubbles and pink rose petals whose scent filled the air in a most enticing way. A brass bracket ran across the top of the tub and on it sat a champagne flute filled with something sparkling and a plate of strawberries dipped in both white and dark chocolate.

Speechless, I took in my surroundings, struggling for a response to such unexpected decadence. Finally ready to form syllables, I looked up and saw not March Ann but a dark haired, dark eyed beauty of obviously Middle Eastern descent, dressed in a sari that perfectly matched the genie's bottle I had somehow fallen into.

"Who are you?" I demanded. "Where did March Ann go?" A bizarre thought darted through my head – something about human trafficking and harems – but it only took a moment to discard the errant idea and get back to waiting for an answer. The girl just stared at me, not bothering to respond, which of course made me mad.

"Hey . . . did you hear me? I said, where is March Ann?" This time I took a step toward the girl and in doing so began to notice a few things. She had all the makings of a truly extraordinary look-ing young woman. Her features were delicate, yet at the same time proud and refined. Her lips were full and her eyes large and heavily fringed with dark lashes. Her figure, though well covered in her sari, was obviously voluptuous – possibly the lauded 36-24-36. In short, she was everything I had always wanted to be. Yet something about her was very, very off.

Though my patience was wearing way thin, the dark girl's meek posture kept me from barking at her again. The poor child, despite her mysterious and alluring appearance, had no more between her ears than an Afghan hound. So, with very little trouble, I managed to dial back my distinct distaste for all girls gorgeous in favor of a heavy serving of Southern condescension now that I realized she was no direct threat to me.

"Honey," I began, the endearment dripping from my freshly sweetened tongue. "Can you tell me your name?"

In the silence that followed, I allowed myself, without flinch-ing, to study her amazing features and try to put a finger on just what was missing from her makeup. As with my initial assessment, I found no fault with her appearance, but on closer inspection I decided that what she was missing was life. Her skin may have been flawless, but it was sallow and waxy with no color or glow. Her hair, although thick and chestnut, was drab and limp, and her large, topaz eyes were devoid of even the slightest sign of spirit. If I were given to Biblical phrasing (and perhaps at this point, I should be), I would say the girl had no soul.

"Her name is Sarah, and she isn't doing her job!" March Ann was back but I wished she wasn't because I could see immediately the fearful response her return brought out in the silent young woman.

I was kind of proud of myself at how quickly I dropped my long-held prejudice against pretty women. I was in March Ann's face in a minute, defending Sarah, though I didn't really know why I was doing it. I sensed something in the girl that made me want to help her. It was the same feeling I got when I saw a PSA about abused puppies. I had a real need to stand up for the underdog, perhaps because I related to them so well.

"And what exactly is her job, March Ann?" I had unconsciously stepped in front of the shrinking violet, who I could feel trembling against my back.

"She should already have you out of your clothes and into the bath. We have a time schedule to keep."

"You can't be serious. I don't need anyone to 'get me out of my clothes,' thank you. I've been undressing and bathing myself for years."

"Oh, I see. So what you are saying is that Sarah is useless, is that right?"

I could sense a trap being set, and I wasn't about to step into it. March Ann's treatment of the frightened young woman was just one more nail in the coffin of my faith in her, but for my safety and Sarah's, I'd better think through my every move and word.

"No, that's not what I meant at all. I can bathe without assistance, but I need Sarah to help with my makeup, hair and clothes." I turned toward the shaking girl and was gratified to see, for the first time, life come into her beautiful eyes and the light of gratitude shining from them.

I watched as my "friend" raked *her* eyes up and down my body, "tsk, tsk, tsking" with disapproval. She even picked up my hands and studied my nails with a look of disdain before commenting,

"I'm not so sure you can bathe yourself, but you can try. Just please be thorough."

I watched self-satisfaction spread across her face like war paint and I fantasized about dragging my unkempt nails down her silky smooth cheek. But I knew that violence would get me nowhere when she was clearly the stronger of the two of us, so I merely jerked my hand away and turned my back to her in silent protest. Still, I had no intention of disrobing with an audience, and she must have known it, because she pulled Sarah away from my side and told me to get started.

After making sure that a towel and robe were within arm's length, as quickly as I could I discarded my muddy shoes and clammy clothing. As I sank into the deliciously hot tub of bubbles, I strained to hear the conversation going on just past the layers of silk that operated as a divider between the bath and the rest of the small room. I could hear March Ann and Sarah talking, but they were speaking in a strange language that I didn't believe for a minute was part of any earth dialect; so I surrendered to the heat and fragrance of the tub and began reviewing all that had happened to me over the afternoon.

Any examination would have been remiss without going back in time and thinking over my entire relationship with March Ann. It's strange how clear hindsight can be when one has the luxury of looking back; I had no problem seeing how I'd been set up from the very beginning. I knew now that March Ann had not been my champion at school, shielding me from the barbs of mean girls and boys. In retrospect I saw her defense of me in a whole new light.

I was pretty sure that I had not actually been the victim of any bullying at school, but only a gullible girl who'd been fooled by the fabricated tales of the manipulative March Ann, who sought to isolate me from the crowd. She even twisted my hurt over my parents' perceived defection to suit her needs, fanning the flames of my pain and convincing me of their betrayal. I was ashamed of how easily I had been taken in by her ploys and castigated myself over the mental weakness that allowed her plot to take root within me.

As directed – if only for my own pride's sake – I scrubbed, shaved and buffed my body, hoping against hope that my knight in shining armor would show up to save me from the evil queen. But I also had no intention of waiting around for someone else to do the saving. That's what had gotten me in trouble in the first place.

I probably should have been drawing all kinds of parallels between Sarah and me by then, but I had a hard time seeing past her gorgeous face to the obvious similarities of our positions. We were both being held against our will, but so far in my case it wasn't quite so obvious. Everything had been done under the guise of "helping me." But I wanted to leave, and I was being prevented from doing so. In my book, that made me a prisoner.

I didn't know what Sarah's story was yet, but it was as plain as the nose on your face that she wasn't a willing participant in the scenario. My best bet was to enlist her as an ally, but in order to do so, I had to get her talk and that wouldn't be easy.

Once I was satisfied that my nemesis had left the room, I rushed with the rinsing of my hair, toweled off, and robed up. Pushing through the layers of silk draping, I found Sarah quietly standing next to the divan, a stack of boxes and vials piled on a tray next to her. I tried to channel my heretofore unidentified inner-Mother Theresa to appear as non-threatening and compassionate as possible because the girl looked scared to death, and I needed her to open up to me if I was going to get anywhere with my plan.

"Sarah," I started, in a quiet, hopefully non-intimidating tone. "I'm sorry that I raised my voice to you earlier. This is a very stressful situation for me, and I'm afraid I took it out on you. Please forgive me."

She didn't respond, but I thought I detected just a glimmer of surprise – or maybe confusion – in her eyes. It was enough to keep me going.

"I don't want to be here," I stated flatly. "And I don't think you want to be, either. I thought, together, we might be able to find a way out."

Okay, I wasn't much for subtlety; but I didn't think time was our friend. I decided to cut to the chase, despite a decided lack of verbal response from the dark-haired beauty.

"I don't think March Ann and her 'brothers' are who they pretend to be. My friends are in trouble, and I need to get out of here. Will you help me?"

It was unnerving – watching and waiting for a response from the girl. I had almost given up all hope of her cooperation when, miracle of miracles, she spoke.

"They are evil – all of them. I will help you, but you must take me with you."

My heart plunged to my toes and then leapt to my throat. So I was right. March Ann was bad; not my guardian angel but an iron maiden, determined to imprison me and mold me to her will. Now that I had established that, I had to figure out when and how I was going to make my escape, and apparently how I was going to take Sarah along with me. One teeny, tiny, little bitty part of me warned that taking the enticing girl with me meant – if all went as planned – Sarah's meeting Merc, and that thought gave me a moment's pause; but I pushed my insecurity back down inside where it belonged and got down to the business of getting to know my sister-in-arms.

I sat down on the divan and pulled her down with me, anxious to pry from her now loosened lips information about our captors.

"I need to know what you know, Sarah. How long have you been here? Who is March Ann?" I was whispering frantically, scared I'd be overheard by some supersonic, evilly enhanced ear.

She rubbernecked around before answering in a shocked and equally frantic whisper. "You mean you really don't know . . . who she is?"

We sounded like two schoolgirls swapping hushed confidences, but the subject wasn't boys or grades or who made the cheerleading squad; it was something far more serious, and my blood ran cold at her tone.

"No, I don't," I said, before taking a deep breath and asking the obvious question: "So, who *is* she?"

"YOU HAVEN'T EVEN PUT HER MAKEUP ON YET?!" Sarah and I both nearly jumped off the couch when March Ann's exclamation pierced the air.

Praying that she hadn't heard our murmured conversation, we both jumped into action, with Sarah frantically opening boxes and me reclining and closing my eyes, ready to be primped on.

I knew my new friend was too terrorized to speak, so I took the lead. "It's your fault, M.A." I kept blabbing, despite March Ann's look of disbelief. "If the bath hadn't been so perfect, I wouldn't have stayed in it so long. Sarah tried to get me out, but I was loving it way too much." I mentally patted myself on the back before adding, "So how long do Sarah and I have to get me presentable?"

"The ceremony begins at midnight, which gives you less than three hours. You cannot be late."

My Lord, how long did she think it would take me to get ready? Clearly she thought I had a lot of work to do. I bit back a sarcastic reply and settled for an "Aye, Aye, Captain," and a sardonic salute.

After throwing a few harshly spoken, unintelligible directions Sarah's way, March Ann whisked from the makeshift salon and spa and left us to our own devices.

When I was sure she was well away, I turned to Sarah and asked, "What language were you two speaking?"

Sarah's smile was "Mona Lisa-esque" as she quietly replied. "She speaks to me in the language of angels. She thinks I know no other."

Well this was certainly an unexpected turn of events! "My stars, honey! Are you saying you're an angel?"

I probably should have come up with a slightly more dignified response to her admission, but I was nothing if not spontaneous. Besides, I was shocked and worried. If Sarah was an angel and being held against her will, then that meant Locke was not all-powerful, and all my friends were at risk. I had a brief urge to start counting something, but I powered past it with a renewed sense of strength and determination. I tried to look at the positive side of things. If Sarah was an angel, she must certainly have some heightened abilities that would prove useful in what was to come.

"Yes, I am an angel." She said it so simply that my mind immediately paged backward to Locke's arrogant demeanor and I was forced to reevaluate my initial perception of the angelic personality. Of course, for all I knew, Sarah could have been just as obnoxious as the beautiful boy angel before all her bravado was drained away by the malicious skullduggery of one March Ann Mayham.

"Okay, okay . . . glad to hear it. Your powers should help us." I smiled encouragingly, trying to instill in her a sense of confidence that I could see she was lacking.

Her eyes filled with tears but she said nothing. My stomach churned, knowing the answer to the question before I even asked it. "Sarah, what's wrong?"

"My powers are gone – stripped from me along with my wings." She reached up to wipe a tear, and her hand was trembling violently.

Even in my disappointment, my heart went out to the poor, sad young woman. What she must have been through. I wondered how long she'd been under my former friend's control.

Thinking it was the thing to do I reached out to comfort her, but just then without a word Sarah jumped up and began pouring cream into her hand and massaging it onto my face.

"She is nearby. We must make her think we are getting ready," she whispered at last.

I hadn't heard a thing, but I knew she was right. We needed to go through the motions. I leaned back on the couch and surrendered to her ministrations. She worked quickly and quietly – adding touches of this and globs of that – and before long I felt as if I had a mask on my face, so thick was the makeup she had applied. I didn't want to criticize her because I knew she'd had plenty of that during her time of captivity, but I didn't want to look like a clown, either.

"I hope you're applying that stuff with a light hand," I said gently. "I've never been much for makeup." I shrugged, to soften my words. "Of course, it doesn't really matter much anyway because we don't plan to stick around for the Witching Hour. But if we are going to have to save Merchison, Locke and the old folks, I'd rather do it looking good."

I winked at her, trying to provide some levity to calm her down. But there was also truth behind my words. I did have my pride, and it would be bad enough to see my friends again with a gorgeous ex-angel by my side, much less if I were decorated like a Christmas cookie.

Sarah studied my face and then grimaced – not a reaction one particularly wants to get after being made over. "I'm sorry but M-M-March Ann," she stumbled over the name, "was very specific about how I was to ready you for the ceremony." She frowned again before adding, "Have you seen your dress yet?"

Something in her tone sent me flying to the garment bag I'd seen Monroe hang from an invisible nail on the wall of the "spa." I held my breath and prayed it wasn't as bad as I suspected and unzipped the bag.

The few dresses I'd been forced to choose for myself over the years had been required to fit a certain very stringent set of guidelines, and I knew the dress March Ann picked for me would probably not fall within my past parameters of acceptability. However, nothing prepared me for the horror that lay behind the garment bag's zipper. To begin with, it was red – the very antithesis of my preferred and limited color palette – and on top of that it was, of all things, made completely of sequins.

This time, I was the one who couldn't manage to speak, struck dumb by the sheer shock value of the dress. I guess I shouldn't have been surprised by anything, but March Ann's audacity on my behalf took my breath away. I didn't know whether the gown was chosen specifically to humiliate me or just because it was appropriate for a demonic debut, but either way, my ex-BFF surely must have known I would guess her game the second I laid eyes on the monstrosity. That fact alone told me all I needed to know about my status at the fort. I was a prisoner – and I would be forced to participate in some midnight ritual, the end result of which was no doubt the loss of my soul.

I heard a strange clacking sound that took me a moment to realize was my own chattering teeth. A buzzing began in my head, and I really thought I was going to lose it completely.

It was Sarah who came to my rescue by laying a calming hand on my arm and speaking to me in her low, melodious voice. "It's going to be okay, Grace. You are exactly where you are supposed to be, and everything is going to be fine."

My head jerked up in surprise at the familiarity of her murmured consolation. She had used almost the exact same words as Willem had the night I met him. And just as Willem's assurances had given me strength on Friday night, so, too, did Sarah's words now provide me the needed comfort and fortitude to persevere.

I slowly turned my head in her direction. "What did you say, Sarah?"

My intensity seemed to take her aback because her response came out as a question. "You are exactly where you are supposed to be, and everything is going to be fine?"

I grabbed her by the shoulders gently – just to really get her attention – and stared straight into her eyes. "Who told you to say that to me – to use those exact words?"

Obviously befuddled, she responded, "What do you mean? I just said what was on my mind." She seemed shaken, so I guess I was a little more intense than I had intended.

As a rule, I didn't believe in coincidences, and I certainly didn't believe this one now. "You just said the exact same thing to me that the old man – Willem – said when I met him. Why is that?"

Sarah shook her head back and forth, as if she was trying to clear her brain. "I don't know, but you're kind of scaring me. Who is Willem?"

I couldn't help but feel a little bad about my outburst. The color that had been gradually seeping into Sarah's skin had drained away, and her eyes again looked haunted. By way of explanation and apology, I took a steadying breath and in as few words as possible I explained the remarkable events that had taken place in my life over the past few days.

The further I went into my story, the more animated Sarah's face became until, no longer being able to contain herself, she burst forth with a question. "This angel – Locke – are you sure that was his name?"

"Sure, I'm sure," I said, before remembering, "Oh, well, Locke is his earth name. He goes by a different angel name."

This time Sarah was the one to grasp my shoulders, but so firmly that it actually hurt.

"Hey, hey, easy, girl – what's wrong?"

"What is Locke's angel name? Tell me!" She demanded.

Wow, she had gone from Little Miss Meek to Sarah the Hun in a flash.

Peeling back her fingers from my smarting shoulders, I searched my brain for the answer she was so desperately seeking. "Uh Locust, I think . . . no wait . . . Lochedus."

She jumped up from the couch, spilling all manner of makeup, boxes and pots onto the floor. "Lochedus . . . did you say Lochedus?" She was just short of shouting. Her eyes were bright with unshed tears, but only for a moment because soon they were coursing down her cheeks unchecked.

"Yes, Lochedus . . . that's it . . . I'm sure of it," I whispered while pulling her back down next to me and putting a finger to my lips to remind her to keep her voice down. "Why? Do you know him?" Talking about your small worlds!

It took her a moment to get enough control to speak, and when she finally did, what she said left me mute with shock and awe.

"Lochedus was my partner – my mate for all existence . . . until . . ." She left the sentence unfinished, but she didn't have to complete it; I knew what she meant. Lochedus was to be her mate – until she somehow fell into the hands of the enemy.

"Ohhh . . ." Not exactly a response for the quotation books, but I didn't even know how to respond to what she'd said. The hairs on my head were probably standing straight up as I was overcome with the knowledge of a greater hand – a divine hand – in control of everything that had happened, and everything that was going to happen. I felt humbled by the knowledge, but at the same type empowered by it. And I was more determined than ever to play out my role to the best of my ability, assured of a blessed result because it was preordained.

Chapter Twenty

SHOULD I STAY OR SHOULD I GO

NEITHER SARAH NOR I SAID A WORD FOR AT LEAST A FULL TWO MINUTES — Sarah lost in her thoughts and me in mine. When we finally looked into each other's eyes, it was with a mutual respect and resolve, ready to do whatever was necessary to return to our loved ones.

I wanted to ask her about so many things, but our time was slipping away and we were both aware of it. As if by verbal agreement, though no words passed between us, she whipped the towel from my head and began combing, twisting, and twirling my hair until she was, at last, satisfied that its up-do style would meet March Ann's requirement. We both knew that until our time for escape came, our best bet was to give all indications that we were following along with the demon girl's plan.

I continued praying that Merc and Locke would show up and save us but, fearful for their safety, I also prayed they would not.

Sarah seemed calm – abnormally calm - and so irritatingly cheerful that I had to ask her what was up. "Do you know something

I don't, Sarah? I'm shaking in my shoes here, but you . . . well, you seem calm as a cucumber."

It wasn't just her demeanor that had changed. She seemed to be suddenly glowing with a light I'd come to recognize as angelic. "I know you're excited about Locke . . . uh, sorry . . . Lochedus, but listen, girl, we have to live through this thing if you are ever going to see him again."

She smiled demurely in a way that made me suspect she did indeed possess insider information.

"What? What? Tell me!" *Grrrrr!* What was it with these people . . . these angels and "angels-lite" (my name for those touched by an angel)? They were always keeping secrets, and I didn't like it because those secrets usually involved or affected me!

"It took me a little time to figure it out, but now I know," Sarah offered, with a perfectly bland, curiously familiar expression on her face that made me want to scream. Talk about your cryptic statements!

"You know what?" I asked, with poorly concealed irritation.

She had her back to me, taking out the disaster of a dress I was expected to wear, but I could have sworn I "heard" a smile in her voice when she confessed mysteriously, "I know who you are."

I was stunned, stupefied and a few other things, as well. I didn't bother responding but only walked around to stand in front of her with the demand for explanation clear in my eyes.

"It would take too long to go into it now," she hedged. We just don't have the time. Suffice it to say you are much stronger than you think you are."

"Stronger . . . how?"

Her answer was immediate. "In every way. You are physically, mentally and perhaps most importantly, emotionally capable of great things. You've allowed evil to infiltrate your mind and almost break your spirit, but there is hope for you and because of that, hope for many."

Her little speech didn't inspire me; it only made me mad. I thought I was going to be told I'd run with angels; instead, I'd been given a pep talk straight out of the Parent's Handbook 101. What kid hadn't been told how much more he or she was capable of than he or she was doing? I'd been getting that rhetoric since fifth grade with nothing to show for it but a "C" average and some annoying habits.

"Really, Sarah? Is that all ya got? My mother gives that talk a lot better."

Sarah must have had the same ability to read between the lines as Locke did, because she caught on immediately to what was bugging me.

"Gracie, you are *very* special." She shook her head from side to side as if to say, *silly, silly girl.* "You have powers and abilities far greater than you know, but – and this is a big but – the only way for you to tap into your strength is for you to believe in it and to believe in yourself. You have to find a way to put aside the doubt and fear that has crippled you in the past."

The beautiful dark-haired angel reached out her hands to me and for a second I thought she was going to hug me – something I wasn't keen on because I was still a little peeved. But she surprised me by putting her hands on either side of my face. At her touch my mind was flooded with images of Merc and me together; but we were changed – elevated and perfected somehow. We were no longer trapped by the confines of earthly existence - free from the restricting weight of humanity. Merchison and I were filled with love for each other and for all God's creatures and creations. Birds were singing, and I could not only hear the beauty in their songs but also interpret their glorious sounds. I could talk with the trees, and Merc laughed with the flowers and all was more than right in the strange, wonderful world in my mind.

Sarah tried to break contact, but I was greedy for more and flattened my palms against her hands to keep them in place. It took me only a moment to wish I'd let her leave because suddenly a dark shadow fell over my dream, turning it into a horrendous hallucination that sent shivers through my body and pierced my heart with hopeless despair.

Nothing in my experience could prepare me for what now floated through my mind like the Ghost of Christmas Future. A sickening prediction of my life ran in fast-forward, complete with ill conceived multiple marriages and punctuated by long stretches of utter solitude. Drug and alcohol addiction and eating disorders plagued my years and my life culminated in a pitiful ending as a lonely, sad, fat old woman – horribly familiar and unloved save for one, whose love I was unable to return.

The vision ground to a halt, as weak with disgust and disbelief, I allowed Sarah to finally drop her hands from my face. I thought I was going to be physically ill, but I lacked the requisite energy for even that relief. I sat staring into space, refusing to answer the insistent pleas of the young angel I had only moments before promised to help free from her awful fate. Who had I been kidding? I couldn't even help myself, much less help her. Depression bore down on me like a two-ton weight, preventing me from doing anything more than sitting motionless and breathing in and out.

I heard Sarah's whispered entreaties and felt her gentle, concerned ministrations but simply couldn't respond, in either word or deed, to her hushed appeals. Somewhere in the back of my brain I knew that I should be preparing to participate in the midnight ceremony, if for no other reason than to keep March Ann from hurting Sarah. But no amount of knowledge could help me scale the wall erected in my head upon seeing what lay ahead for me in the future.

At some point, I felt Sarah lift me like a ragdoll from my seated position and begin the thankless and difficult task of squeezing me into the hideous red creation March Ann had chosen for my debut. I was so sick at heart that I didn't even care what participating in the demon ritual would mean for me, because I'd been to the mountaintop and looked over and what I'd seen was no Promised Land – just a lifetime of misery and pain.

I was dimly aware of a frantic Sarah counting down the minutes until midnight. As if in a trance, I nodded blankly at March Ann when she dropped by the barracks to check on our progress. I gave some thought to the phrase "a fate worse than death," and decided that if the images I'd seen played out in my head were to be believed, then whatever my ex-best friend had planned for me would have to be preferable to my bleak future. I wouldn't fight it, but go willingly into that dark night. After all, the prophetic vision had laid waste to any ideas I might have once entertained regarding a loving family or friends mourning my disappearance. Just as I'd always suspected, I was alone in the world, and I always would be. My parents had deserted me, and my brother and his wife only tolerated me. I need spend no time worrying about their concerns over my sudden and unexplained departure.

And then there was Merc. My heart sank even lower as I whispered his name. Beautiful, perfect, heavenly Merchison Spear was not coming for me. I was still confused about why he had walked into my life to begin with. Was it because of some latent power I possessed to take on the burdens of humanity? The only reason I found that idea at all believable was that it would be a plausible explanation for Merc and Locke's interest in me. Well, I didn't want to be some human tuning fork for bad emotions; I had enough heartache headed my way without taking on the woes of the world.

My mood swings had been so drastic over the past two days that I wondered yet again whether my shrink had missed the boat with my diagnosis. While I'd done very little counting over the weekend, I was exhausted with the back and forth of my emotions, and felt as if I was losing my mind altogether. When March Ann pranced in, announcing that we only had another hour and a half until the big show, I was so drained and listless that I couldn't even fake excitement.

"What's wrong with you, girlfriend?" she chirped way too cheerfully. "You look like your best friend died or something."

I wondered if she intended the irony rife in that statement but I didn't care enough to comment.

"I'm dressed, aren't I?" I snapped back, tired of the whole shooting match and wishing there was a way to duck out the back and run away from everything and everybody. But where was I to run? Pete and Patty were probably worried sick about me – not out of any real concern but because that's how they were "supposed" to feel when a family member went missing. Still, I didn't want to go home to the same old situation because, good or bad, I wasn't the same person I'd been forty-eight hours ago, and I didn't think I could pretend to be.

"I thought you'd be excited. Have you even looked in the mirror?" she pushed, characteristically oblivious to my mood.

I hadn't noticed a mirror in the tiny room and probably would have avoided it had I seen it. But despite my best efforts to the contrary, March Ann was determined that I behold the monster that was me. Grabbing my hand, she pulled me through a series of hanging veils to the far east wall where a full-length mirror hung and pushed me in front of it, all smiles, confident that I'd be thrilled with my transformation.

I'd had an image in my head throughout the evening of what I would look like all dolled up and painted into the sequin gown, but my imagination had utterly failed in doing the real thing justice. I was, to steal a phrase, a sight for sore eyes. My hair was pure trailer park bouffant, and my makeup a salute to drag queens the world over. My bloated body – wrapped in the awful dress – bore a striking resemblance to a summer sausage stuffed in its casing.

At that moment, the vision of my horrific future collided with my vision in the mirror and it proved too much for me; I broke down in a torrent of tears. Instead of getting angry, as I would have expected her to, March Ann gently wrapped me in her arms and pulled my head to her chest, letting me cry.

"Honey, what's got you so upset?" She seemed genuinely concerned about me and her compassion was my undoing.

Maybe I'd been wrong about her all along. So what if she had a love for trashy dressing? Did that make her a demon? She was the one who had saved me on the trail – not Merc and not Locke. She'd never really been anything but nice to me. Besides, it was Sarah's touch – not March Ann's – that had brought on the spectre of terrible things to come. That should tell me something, shouldn't it?

With March Ann's encouragement, I poured out the details of the prophetic vision and was surprised to see empathy and understanding in her eyes. The chill that had hardened my heart toward her began to melt, and I grabbed onto her kindness like a lifeline in stormy waters

"I don't understand anything," I wailed. "I thought Merc would have been here by now. I should have known all along that he didn't really care about me."

From the corner of my eye, I caught Sarah's disapproving, disbelieving glare, but I chose to ignore it, and she was far too scared of March Ann to say anything out loud.

Sarah's fear should have been ample proof of my former friend's questionable allegiances, but I was looking at things in a different light now, and that light cast doubt on everything the beautiful dark-haired girl said and did.

Something kept me from confessing everything to March Ann, though. I didn't tell her what I suspected about Mrs. B. because, in truth, I couldn't bring myself to say the words. I also didn't tell her about the plans I'd made with Sarah to take off, but since running was out of the question now it didn't matter anyway.

March Ann must have seen Sarah's expression too, because she suddenly turned sharply and barked, "Leave us." The dark-haired angel, who had once again lost her sparkle, nodded resignedly before scurrying from the room.

"Look, Grace," March Ann began once Sarah had gone. "I didn't want to have to tell you the truth. I wanted to protect you from it, but I see now that I have no other choice."

I felt the stirrings of life boil up from within as my anger flared. "The truth? I don't think any of you know what the truth is. You all have come into my life and turned it upside down, and I don't know what or whom to believe."

She patted my hand, trying to calm me down. Reaching into a bag she'd brought with her, she pulled out an apple and handed it to me. "You must be starving; you didn't touch the strawberries. You'll feel better when you eat something."

I was caught off guard by her abrupt change of subject, but I acquiesced and took a bite of the proffered fruit just to keep her talking.

Satisfied I was eating, she began to speak. "I know you must be frustrated, but you can believe in me, Grace. I *will* be honest with you. But that doesn't mean that it's going to be easy for you to hear what I have to say."

"I'm a big girl. I can handle it," I shot back. "Just as long as I know what 'it' is." I took another large bite from the apple for effect.

She sighed and smiled, giving me a patient, pitying look that made me feel like a child throwing a tantrum. "Look, Grace," she began. "Merchison and Lochedus . . . and the old folks, too . . . well, they are all working together to keep the truth from you. It's why they aren't here right now. They don't want you to go through the ceremony because when you do, you will be like them. You will know everything."

Her words had a ring of familiarity to them, but I couldn't quite place where I'd heard them before. I let them sink in before asking, "What do you mean by 'know everything,' March Ann? Know everything about what?"

I could practically see the wheels turning in her head as she tried to formulate an answer. Maybe I knew more about what was going on than she did. While I hardly thought I was destined for greatness, something *had* happened in the car today when I reached out and touched Merc's cheek – something that had thrilled and fascinated both of the boys. They'd said I could ease the pain and suffering of others. But at what cost to my already damaged psyche? One thing was for sure, I'd been kept in the dark most of the weekend, and while Merc had supposedly poured out his heart and soul to me, I'd still come away with the feeling that he was holding something back. Had I let my blinding attraction to him overwhelm my common sense? Had that been his plan all along?

The taste of the apple turned bitter in my mouth as my face burned bright with the memory of our kisses. I cringed at the thought of Locke and Merc planning a seduction in order to gain my trust. Had they flipped a coin in order to see which one would get stuck with the onerous task of seducing me? Rage replaced embarrassment as I swore vengeance on the boys who had humiliated me. If they thought they could use me like a toy for their own nefarious schemes, they had another "think" coming.

I pulled myself back to the present in time to hear March Ann say, "You have a gift, Grace – a very special one. But your ability is a double-edged sword. By your touch, you can ease the suffering of the mentally afflicted. That suffering doesn't just disintegrate, though." Her beautiful eyes filled with tears as if she were truly feeling my pain.

"It doesn't? What happens to it?" I had a sinking feeling inside because I knew the answer before she said it.

"All the pain and hurt is transferred to you, and eventually it will destroy you."

My mind bolted backward to the terrible vision Sarah had accidentally allowed me to see. I was putting the pieces together now, and it was all beginning to make sense. I could relieve the masses of their pain, but in doing so, I would destroy myself. I would turn to alcohol, food, drugs and sex in a misguided attempt to escape the suffering. No wonder Merc and Locke were so keen on me; I would be their scapegoat. Well, no way. I wasn't anyone's fall guy, and I didn't appreciate being played for a sucker.

"So that's what I saw in the vision? I saw what will happen to my life if I go along with Merchison and Locke?"

"You got it, hon, and now you understand why I've had to keep you away from them – to protect you from them."

I nodded as if I understood, but her words bothered me. "Wait, have Locke and Merc been trying to find me?"

March Ann looked like she wished she could take her words back, but she simply shrugged and said, "No, not really. I haven't seen them. But I have to tell you, Grace, if they did come looking for you, I would stand in their way. They will only use you and hurt you. You don't want that, do you?"

Despite myself, I was disappointed. I struggled to focus on the positive. "Tell me what will happen to me after the ceremony." I was searching for a silver lining – anything to make me feel a little better.

Her face lit up with an excitement that fell short of being contagious. "Oh, it will be wonderful! We will truly be sisters. You will be strong and beautiful like me, and you will know all the secrets of the universe. You are one of the chosen few, Grace. You should be very grateful."

I *should* be grateful. Maybe I'd finally be picked first in kick-ball. Yeah, I should be thrilled, but I wasn't, and I was pretty sure I knew why. I couldn't completely excise the little itch in the back of my brain telling me that something was wrong.

And then it happened. *Click, click, click* – all the info in my beautiful brain dropped into the right slots and everything made sense. My line of reasoning followed your basic a + b + c = d equation: If my gift was to take away the pain of others, then that was a good thing – for lack of a better term, a "holy" thing. And if Merc and Locke were proponents of my exercising that gift, then they were on the side of good. And if they were on the side of good, March Ann must be evil. And if March Ann was evil, then the ceremony was a trap.

I'd not been asked to sign any contracts in blood (yet), but I had a strong feeling that the result of the ceremony could well be the same as if I had – the loss of one soul, barely used.

Chapter Twenty One

ROUND AND ROUND

To my relief, March Ann excused herself to make last-minute preparations, leaving me with about an hour to decide what I should do. Even though I'd teetered like a see-saw between believing March Ann and believing Merc and the others, my common sense had never let me stray too far from the truth – that truth being that I was smack dab in the middle of a demon conspiracy.

My temper, pride and depression may have caused me to temporarily fall for March Ann's party line, but in my heart I'd known since the beginning of this mess that the vixen I'd once thought was my friend was not of the heavenly sort. Even though I may have taken great offense to some of the mansion gang's tactics, that didn't mean I was ready to sign on the dotted line with Beelzebub. I had one hour to come up with a plan to keep that from happening.

I would have loved nothing more than to dip back into the tub and spend a while ruminating over all the events that led to my current predicament. But as tempting as it was, the idea was far from practical. Instead, I opted to spend a few minutes on the couch trying to clear my head from all but the most important details of the weekend.

I decided right away that I'd been terribly unfair to poor Sarah and that the first thing I needed to do was to try to find her and include her in my plan of escape. She would probably take a bit of convincing because I hadn't exactly earned her trust, but hopefully she could use her angel powers – whatever those might be – to divine my good intentions, and I wouldn't have to waste too much time persuading her to leave.

The way I saw it, nothing good could come from sticking around long enough to participate in the "demon do," so my best bet would be to wait until just before midnight and make a mad dash for the woods. I didn't know what, if any, power my new angelic friend had maintained throughout her captivity, and any tricks up my sleeve would be child's play compared to what we were up against. Running seemed to be the safest alternative.

I made the decision to leave the barracks under the auspices of trying to find Sarah for help getting into my gown. Instead of walking out the front and into the center of the fort, I applied a little super-pressure to a boarded up back door and was gratified to see the nails fly easily from the frame – an indication that I'd maintained a higher level of strength than I'd realized. Energized by the ease with which I'd pried open the door, I stepped cautiously onto the dark path . . . and right into the arms of a tall robed figure.

"Oh . . . oh . . . I'm sorry," I immediately apologized, and launched into my prepared explanation. "I was going to look for Sarah. I needed help with my makeup and hair. I've made a mess of things." I was mumbling almost incoherently the story I'd planned to use should I get caught – which I had. My knees nearly gave out when I heard the deep calming voice of the robed man.

"Shhh, it's okay, Gracie. It's me, Willem."

Breathless with relief and surprise, I allowed him to lead me back into the room I'd just left, and I watched as he closed the door behind him.

"Are you all right, love? Have they hurt you?" His voice was like a symphony to my ears. But, there was something different about him – jarringly different. I was just too nervous and scared to figure it out.

I began crying almost immediately. The rush of relief was overpowering. "How . . . how did you find me? Where is Merc?" I squeaked out through my tears. If for no other reason than political correctness, I should have asked about Locke and Mrs. B., too, but my heart was so filled with terror for Merchison Spear, I could think of no other.

Willem was far too much of a gentleman to mention my appearance, but his red face spoke volumes. He ignored my question about Merc completely and only said quietly, "You are in grave danger, Gracie. You are going to have a hard time running in those . . . clothes, but we don't really have time for you to change. I'm sorry."

"Not a problem," I assured him, while at the same time reaching for the hem of the offending dress and ripping it up and over, so that it no longer confined the bottom half of my legs. "There," I said, proud of my ingenuity. "I should have a little more room to move now."

If possible, he blushed even more furiously. "That will work, I guess. Let's go."

Hand in hand, we made a break for the back gate and were almost there before I remembered. "Oh, no! I forgot about Sarah! We have to go back." At his look of confusion, I gave him a much-abbreviated version of my introduction to the girl angel.

Hesitating, Willem's bushy gray brows pulled down into a hard "v." "Are you sure this, 'Sarah' is not a demon?"

Just the touch of Willem's hand had cleared my mind and I suddenly had no problem separating good from evil. "I'm sure," I assured him, knowing there was no time for further explanation.

"Then, let's go get her. We'll have to hurry." He grinned mysteriously before adding, "The two devils guarding the back gate are taking a 'nap' right now but I'm sure they'll raise the alarm as soon as they regain consciousness."

I did a quick double take toward the old man who suddenly didn't seem so old, looking at him with a newfound respect. I would have loved to ask him how he managed to knock out the demons, but there was no time for that now. Maybe later; if we were lucky.

I bit my lip and confessed, "I'm not really sure where Sarah is. Maybe in the building next to the one I was in." I pointed to the rear of a small barracks, which was identical from the outside to my makeshift spa.

"I guess there's no way to find out but to try," he said, surprisingly calm under such tense circumstances.

There was obviously quite a bit about the old man I didn't know. I wondered if he was some kind of "undercover angel." I hoped so, because even excluding March Ann's two "brothers" – who lay comatose at the gate – we were still outnumbered. On top of that, I'd never been in any kind of physical confrontation in my entire life. I would have been out of my mind with fear but, as usual, Willem's mere presence put me at ease. He seemed fully in control and though cautious he didn't seem scared. That, in and of itself, was a comfort to me.

Just as we'd made it over to the boarded up rear door of the second barracks, a large young man sped past us, running in the direction of the back gate. On a moonless, cloudy night, I shouldn't have been able to make out a thing, but my improved vision gave me the ability to see him well enough to realize that he wasn't one of March Ann's family members I'd met earlier in the day. I held my breath, waiting for the inevitable hue and cry to go out as the unidentified demon discovered his fallen comrades. In the unexpected quiet that followed, I turned to Willem in puzzled relief, only to find my partner in anti-crime nowhere in sight. I didn't have time to panic because it was only a second before he was back by my side, with a small tear in his dark T-shirt and a strange smile on his face.

"Where did you go?" I demanded in a furious whisper. "Did you see that guy run by? I thought we were caught, for sure."

"I saw him," he confirmed flatly. "He joined his brothers at the back gate." Willem absentmindedly brushed a bit of dirt off his jeans before adding, "There are more devils here than we planned for – we best be getting a move on."

I hadn't missed William's use of the word "we." I assumed he meant his presence here was part of a group effort that also included

Merc and Locke. I suppose Mrs. B. was a member of the gang, as well, though for the life of me I couldn't figure out what her role in the endeavor could possibly be. I also couldn't fathom why Willem was sent in alone to save me, leaving the angel and "angel-lite" behind to cool their heels. It was becoming increasingly clear to me that Willem possessed more than a passing acquaintance with the supernatural but, even so, it still didn't make much sense that he came alone when he didn't have to. There were only a few possible scenarios that could explain the old guy's solo save: the first being that the two younger, more powerful boys were waiting somewhere outside the fort to make their entrance at the most opportune moment; the second, and by far most worrisome explanation for their absence, was that they were otherwise detained – tied up, imprisoned, hurt, bleeding, dead.

I had to bite the inside of my cheek to keep from crying out loud at the awful thoughts in my head. I took a moment to study Willem as he crouched next to me in the dark, trying to evaluate his expression for any signs of the overwhelming grief or worry I felt sure would be there had Merc or Locke fallen in the line of duty. I saw only a calm determination etched into his face and I chose to, without question, accept that as a confirmation of the boys' safety.

I continued to watch in fascination as Willem, with barely a flick of his wrist, silently pulled the battened down door off its hinges and, looking much more seasoned than senile, stalked into the room – SWAT style – scanning from left to right, searching for anything breathing, either friend or foe. Staying close together, we saw at the same time that the room was quiet as a tomb and completely empty. Frustrated, we looked around hoping to see some sign that the angel had been there but came up empty-handed.

"I'm honestly not sure what to do, Gracie. I want to help the girl, but it is most important that I get you out of here. I don't think we have much more time before the demons realize you're missing."

It wasn't really like me to be so brave and selfless, but I suddenly couldn't bear the thought of leaving the dark-haired angel behind. I had never had anybody depend on me before, and the way

Sarah had looked at me when she thought I was going to help her escape was seared into my brain. She needed me and I wasn't going to let her down . . . again.

"We can't just throw her to the wolves, Willem. I'd never sleep another good night in my life. We have to find her."

Instead of arguing, Willem surprised me as his old face creased in a huge smile. "I knew you would say that, Gracie. You've got a fighter in there." He pointed to my chest, and as he did, I felt it swell with pride. "So, what's our next step?"

He was asking me?! I didn't want to leave Sarah, but at the same time, I had no idea how to go about saving her. From the look on the old man's face, I was about to find out, because he didn't wait for an answer but instead lowered himself into a crouching position and peeked cautiously through the boarded-up slats of the front window.

"Gracie?" He whispered, barely turning his head, his eyes never leaving the narrow band of vision in front of him. "I've got some bad news."

My heart sank at the grimness of his tone. "What is it? What's wrong?" I half whimpered. Did I really just ask that question? I *must* be crazy. Everything was wrong. We were in the middle of an old fort, waiting to be caught by a devilish band of demons intent on making me one of their own.

"Uh, honey, please don't panic but I think we've found Sarah." He scooted to the side just enough to allow me visual access through the boards, into the center of the fort.

I couldn't believe what I was seeing. It *was* Sarah, and she was bound, gagged and tied onto some type of altar, which sat on a raised platform in the middle of the courtyard. Behind the platform was a wall of fire that stretched from one end of the dais to the other. The blaze was operating apart from the norm – not following any natural law but hanging like a curtain from an invisible rod, from some twenty feet into the air down toward the ground.

Willem and I sat staring mutely in horrified fascination as the pulsating flames parted and two figures – unaffected by the bizarre tongues of heat – walked through them. March Ann's odd choice of attire somehow now made sense to me, as she in her gold lame gown and Monroe in his tux sailed to the "podium" like two Hollywood megastars gliding down the red carpet to graciously accept their award. But the onlookers in the crowd were no paparazzi or wannabe winners; they were chanting, robed demons, raising their voices in a monotone mantra of bloodlust, ready to bear malicious witness to whatever evil deed their Mistress of Ceremonies had in store.

With a slashing wave of Monroe's hand, the chanting stopped, and March Ann nodded her head, acknowledging her loyal subjects.

"Thank you all for being here tonight," she began, in her high-pitched drawl. "This evening is the culmination of many years of preparation. Together we shall right the wrongs of our past, and before this night is over, we will have secured the weapon necessary for our eventual domination over all in heaven and on earth."

Following her proclamation, she joined in with the chanting of the masses – her voice being heard over all the rest. She spread her arms wide, and her followers immediately formed a large circle that encompassed the whole scene. Willem and I continued silently watching as seemingly without provocation the strange blaze mimicked the actions of the hooded demons by following in their footsteps and forming a ring of fire around them all.

Round and round the devils danced to a doxology of death – singing their praises to a Mistress of Evil I'd once thought was my friend. To say the scene was surreal would be the understatement of the century.

Willem's face was creased with concentration as I, in wordless horror, waited for him to break the silence – unsure of what to say myself. After several minutes of watching the scene unfold, he closed his eyes and began wordlessly moving his lips as if in silent prayer. At times, he appeared to be fighting some internal struggle by arguing back and forth with himself or maybe with some unseen entity or even God.

I couldn't help but panic, thinking if the only tool in Willem's arsenal was a silent supplication to an absent Almighty then

I might as well be sitting next to a raving radical ready to die for the promise of seventy-two virgins and a couple of camels. But when his eyes opened, I saw no signs of lunacy reflected in them. What I saw was steely resolve that, to me, gave blessed assurance.

"Gracie, they are going to use the girl as a sacrifice to Lucifer. I can't let that happen." He turned to look me straight in the eye, wrapping his hands around my arms rather forcefully. "Sarah is Locke's mate. I can't let them hurt her. But I can't let them hurt you either; so when I go to Sarah, you must run – as fast as you can – for the back gate."

I didn't remember telling Willem anything about Sarah's relationship with Locke, but I just chalked it up to one of the dozens of things I didn't understand and focused on the rest of his statement.

"I can't leave you here to fight by yourself, Willem! No way!" I wasn't itching to battle demons, but I loved Willem. I felt a bond with him that I didn't even understand, and I wasn't about to run away and leave him to die alone – or worse.

"You must, Gracie. They are using the girl to get to you. I cannot let that happen."

"Why? Why do they want me? Please . . . I need to understand." I had never been so frustrated in my life. I wanted to scream, to cry, to flail out at Willem, but I knew none of this was really his fault. If he had made any error in judgment, it was simply that he hadn't given me enough credit or control – none of them had. In their effort to protect me, they had crippled me and left me ill prepared to deal with the forces assembling against me.

"I know you're tired of hearing this, love, but there just isn't time for explanations right now." He jerked his head in the direction of the demons and added, "Something doesn't make sense about all of this. They have to know you're not where you're supposed to be. They also have to know you have help. They must be expecting something, so we have to do the unexpected."

Strangely, I wasn't really all that frightened. I couldn't identify what I was feeling, but it wasn't fear. Maybe it was acceptance; whatever was going to happen would happen. Part of that acceptance was about Willem – his cool but loving demeanor giving me strength I'd never envisioned myself having. That didn't keep me from wishing Merc and Locke would show up to save the day. I knew there were depths to the old man I hadn't even begun to plumb but as we sat facing a courtyard full of devil's advocates, an angel or two wouldn't have hurt.

I was torn in two directions, and no matter how hard I listened for my heart's advice, I could hear nothing but the monk-like chanting going on outside the barracks walls. I turned to study Willem and saw that the bright burning blaze, shining through the gaps in the boarded up window, cast an odd patterned shadow across the old man's face and illuminated his eyes that looked frighteningly haunted and somehow different. I was startled by the quick peek into his otherwise stoic visage and shaken to realize that he, too, was battling his emotions. He must have had to work hard to cover this part of himself, not wanting to frighten me or cause me more stress. I wanted to hug him and tell him that everything was going to be all right, but I didn't want to embarrass him or give away that I'd seen into his soul. When I took a second look, all traces of the conflicted, torn old man were gone, replaced by a seasoned warrior who somehow looked years younger and confident once again.

A crescendo was building in the courtyard as one of the chanting minions stepped from the fiery ring to the front of the platform and in one fluid motion shed his robe and leapt onto the stage with his bare muscles rippling, to stand nude – save for a tanned loincloth – directly next to March Ann. I recognized the boy immediately as one of March Ann's brothers, Clifford. Because he had seemed an affable enough guy, I found it hard to believe that he would take part in anything too evil or grotesque. It took something short of a minute to disprove my theory completely. Within 25 seconds of his leap on stage, the demonic Mistress of Ceremonies produced a wicked-looking dagger and slit his throat ear to ear, carefully catching every drop of his blood in a large jewel-encrusted chalice.

Until that very moment, I never really, truly believed that I was in lethal danger. I guess I was in pure denial, because while

I understood everything that was going on, in theory, I simply could not wrap my head around the reality of the situation. Seeing someone's head cut clean off tends to change a person though, and it certainly changed me.

The only muscle in my body that seemed to be working was my throat that was convulsing in spasms, fighting back the bitter bile that threatened to spill out onto the ground at any moment. I was grateful that the only thing I'd eaten in hours was the bite of apple March Ann had foisted on me mid-lying-lecture in the barracks cum boudoir.

Willem's whispered prayer I'd thought benign took on urgent, new meaning in light of the bloody demonic ritual taking place in front of my eyes. After all, if the existence of true demons was more than mere myth, then should it not follow that there was a man (or woman) upstairs to hear prayers? That logic now seemed airtight and I was suddenly uttering every Bible verse and children's Sunday school ditty that my traumatized mind could recall. Willem, on the other hand, seemed not at all surprised by the horrific turn of events but only more determined than ever to get me away from the action.

"It's time, Grace. You have to leave – now!" His tone brooked no argument, and I would have been more than happy to oblige had my legs been willing participants in the plan. "Gracie, love – you have to go!" He repeated more urgently.

"What about you, Willem?" I whined. "I can't leave you by yourself." My legs were regaining their strength, but I still couldn't seem to make a move toward the door. For some strange reason, my father's voice was in my head repeating over and over his favorite quote from the Irish orator, Edmund Burke: "All that is necessary for the triumph of evil is that good men do nothing." My subconscious was giving Mr. Burke the benefit of the doubt by assuming a universal definition of the word "men," thereby including me – as a woman – in the admonition. I guess my brain was sending a message to my body to stay and fight, and part of me really wanted to, but there was just enough resistance in me to allow Willem's insistent pleas to win me over. To make matters even more urgent, Mistress March Ann, on the backs of several male minions, disembarked the stage and began a slow, deliberate advance straight for the barracks where we were hidden.

"You must go – now! You are faster than they are . . . and stronger. But there are too many of them. You must go now. And Gracie, whatever you do, don't go back to the mansion."

"Okay, okay, I got it." I promised, and then took one step toward the door before stopping dead in my tracks. "Wait … what did you say? Why can't I go back? I need to find Locke and Merchison so that they can come back here and help you."

"I'm sorry, Gracie, but please just do as I say and stay away from there. Now go!"

There were tears in Willem's eyes as he pulled me toward the back door of the barracks. Confused, torn, and unable to speak, I gave him a quick, crushing hug, turned and fled the room.

Guilt coursed through my body, slowing my pace, which was still much faster than I ever imagined possible. I cringed at the sounds I heard coming from behind me, but kept running as Willem had instructed. The horrendous odor of sulfur burned my nose and I knew that meant, though I saw no demons, they were hot on my trail and had not bothered with whatever masking agent they normally used to cover their smell. The cat was out of the bag, and the lines were drawn.

The woods and river were only a blur as fear triumphed over guilt, quickening my step even more. With super speed on my side, my feet were barely touching the ground, so it took me a moment to realize that I was no longer earthbound. I was being lifted into the sky by no power of my own. Figuring the jig was up, I opened my mouth to scream but before I could expel a lungful of terror, I was tossed willy-nilly even higher into the night sky, only to land squarely in the arms of a fierce-looking, yet familiar winged man. I was almost unconscious with relief, yet still a teeny bit disappointed that it wasn't Merc's arms I'd fallen into.

Now fully seraphic, I assumed Locke would be worried, solicitous, caring, kind and concerned – all those things one expects from a good angel. I did not think he would be mad.

"I can't believe you left Willem there by himself!" His mouth drew a hard line across his face and his eyes were piercing pinpoints of anger.

"Huh? What do you mean?" I was so shocked by his intensity that I couldn't even come up with a real response. Instead of heading back to the fort, he began to fly straight up into the stratosphere. By the time I realized how high we were, my own anger had flared, and I didn't even care. After the day I'd had, I was in no mood to put up with Locke's mouth. "What did you expect me to do?" I fired back. "I don't know how to fight!" Guilt exacerbated my ire, leaving me with little ability to apply reason to my behavior or judge the wisdom of angering an inflight angel. "I was headed to find you and Merc," I yelled, before going on the offensive. "By the way, *Lochedus*," I spat out his angelic name as a reminder of his responsibilities. "What took you so long, and where *is* Merc?"

He ignored my questions completely. "Lord, you humans! Doomed to repeat the same mistakes over and over again. Now you listen to me, Gracie Marie Bennett," (apparently two could play the "name game"). "Without you, Merchison has no chance, but you two together are unstoppable."

Shock seized my stomach, and I thought I was going to be sick. "Merc? Merc is in danger? Where is he? Take me to him now!" For a moment the blonde angel looked confused, and then he corrected himself. "Not Merc – Willem. Without you, *Willem* has no chance. Now, stop asking questions and get ready."

"Are you going to help us? There are dozens of demons in that fort." I told him. "And someone has to save Sarah!"

As soon as her name left my lips, I realized my mistake, but by then it was too late for me to take it back or bring up the subject more tactfully. I was falling like a huge dead weight, at what seemed like a million miles a minute, straight toward the ground.

I was proud of the fact that I didn't panic. I guess somewhere in my head I had enough faith in Locke to know he wouldn't let me hit the dirt. He sure took his sweet time about it, though, and I was only a second or two from impact when he broke my fall.

I would have been furious, but one look at his face told me I should be happy just to have been caught at all. The poor guy was in much worse shape than I was.

Locke's face was white as a sheet of paper, and the arms that held me were trembling so violently that my own teeth were chattering. Thankfully, he flew only a short distance before sitting down next to the riverbank in a thick grove of pine trees. Wasting no time with formalities, he got right to the point. "Why did you bring up Sarah? What do you know about her?" His eyes were full of distrust, but I tried not to take it personally because I knew he was upset.

I did take personally the death grip he had on my arms and, wincing, I pried his fingers from around my biceps. "Hey, easy — I'm delicate. I bruise!"

He gave me a skeptical look that I found mildly insulting before repeating his question. "What do you know about Sarah?"

Rubbing the circulation back into my maimed limbs, I answered. "I know she is being held by the demons." He didn't say a word, just stood, staring at me with a blank expression on his face, so I continued. "I also know she is your mate, or at least she *was* your mate before she was captured."

His face crumbled and for just a second he actually looked as old as he probably was — his countenance etched in a sorrow as ancient as time. "I failed her, Grace. Everything that has happened to her is my fault." A primal sob welled up from deep within him, bringing tears to both our eyes. I slapped mine away with windshield wiper efficiency because we didn't have time for a pity party. I'd been counting on him to help save Willem and Sarah — to swoop in and do some angel tricks to save the day. Now it looked like I was going to have to take the lead on the mission.

"Well, I don't know if that's true or not, Lochedus," I stated flatly. "But I do know that she needs you now. So does Willem. So stop feeling sorry for yourself and get it together!"

My stern words seemed to do the trick because he began to regain his color and focus. "Is Sarah okay? Is she hurt?"

"She seemed in reasonably good health to me," I said, not sure exactly how one would go about judging that type of thing in an angel. "She was being used as a slave, I think. Not an ideal situation for her, but at least she was alive."

"So she wasn't . . . one of them?" He asked, hesitantly, his voice sounding, for the first time, hopeful.

"No, no," I quickly assured him. "She's definitely not a demon . . . or possessed or fallen . . . or whatever." I awkwardly answered, trying to make the point that she hadn't crossed over to the other side, but not knowing how to do it.

He closed his eyes for a moment and mumbled something that sounded like a prayer. Then a slow smile spread across his face that was so bright and beautiful that it reminded me of a sunrise. "Well, what are we waiting for? We have some demon tail to kick!" His laughter echoed across the water, and as if the happy noise pushed the clouds away the full moon was suddenly visible. Its light danced across the water and made the world no longer seem quite so sinister. I didn't even mind when he, without permission, grabbed me into his arms and took off – wings flapping like a giant bird.

Before we even got to the fort, we could see the flames burning from the demon ritual being performed on the grounds. Locke flew low and slow and landed right outside the back gate.

"Are you ready?" He asked, and as I turned to answer, I got yet another shock – probably the most profound of the weekend. I wasn't looking at Locke because there were no signs left of the affable teenager I'd spent time with for the past two days. In front of me stood the angel Lochedus – winged son of the Most High – warlike and frightening in all his terrible glory.

He was massive – somewhere between seven and eight feet tall – and muscular beyond belief. His hair was longer and his features sharper, and though he was still beautiful, he no longer bore any resemblance to the boy next door. His wings were huge and though soft and downy, they somehow made him look even more masculine and threatening than he already did. The glow emanating from his skin was blinding, and I found myself having trouble looking directly at him.

But I was very aware of what he expected of me, so I ignored his transformation as best I could in favor of answering his question. "Am I ready? Is that a joke? Of course, I'm not ready. I have no idea what I'm doing." I forced myself to stand my ground and look at him without squinting or flinching. "Do you care to give me a hint or a secret code or something to help me stay alive past the next few minutes?"

"You'll know what to do, Grace. You just have to have faith."

For the millionth time this weekend, I debated the wisdom of hitting an angel and, yet again, decided against it. "Pardon me if I'm not willing to just take your word for it. You haven't exactly been forthcoming or truthful with me." I shielded my eyes and attempted to look him up and down to drive home my point. "Clearly, you've got a few more weapons at your disposal than I have. Can't you just wave a magic wand or cast a spell or something to make me stronger?"

"Don't be ridiculous, Grace. I'm neither your fairy godmother nor a witch. I possess no magical powers. I'm an angel, and I'm telling you that you have everything you need right here," he said, pointing to my chest. "Now stop stalling. You will defeat the enemy within."

He was pushing me toward the gate, and I was beginning to panic. "Hey, wait – where are *you* going to be?"

"I'm going to get Sarah, of course. I've been waiting nearly 500 years for the demons to let down their guard so that I can get her back."

Digging my heels in even further, I exclaimed, "Please, Lochedus, we need a plan. I need a plan. I keep telling you, I don't know what I'm doing. I won't make it ten steps inside the gate before getting caught."

Blowing out a great gust of air that actually blew my hair back from my face, the angel acquiesced, "Oh, okay – listen up. I'll clear a path between the gate and Willem and Sarah on the platform.

Once you get to the stage, everything will become clear and you'll know what to do."

Ha! That was a joke. Nothing had been clear from the moment I'd turned onto the dirt road of the mansion, but I figured arguing with the angel would be fruitless – even possibly dangerous – so I closed my eyes, tossed a prayer into the great beyond and readied myself for battle. At least I wouldn't have to worry about losing Lochedus in the melee; he was twinkling and glowing like a disco ball, and suddenly biting at the bit to breach the fort.

I was kind of hoping we could quietly sneak through the back gate and get as far as we could toward the dais before being noticed. I should have known that my ostentatious angel friend had something different in mind. With a great whoop of a war cry, he grabbed me under his arm and leapt over the back wall of the fort, square into the middle of the ceremony.

Chapter Twenty Two

FAITH

I HAD NOT EVEN A MOMENT TO CATCH MY BREATH AND PREPARE FOR MY trial by fire, because before Lochedus could even sit me on my feet the two of us were covered stem to stern in demons. A short time ago when I was in the fort, I would have put the body count of devils at no more than twenty-five, but now there seemed to be an endless supply of robed rebels, all absolutely focused on doing us in.

Lochedus was impressive – no doubt about it – and with what seemed to be minimal effort he disposed of literally hundreds of Satan's sons and daughters. I wasn't too bad either, if I do say so myself; it was as if another entity had taken hold of my body and was punching, choking, and hurling demon after demon – sending them back to the fiery darkness from whence they came. I guess that was what was happening, because once they were rendered immobile, they simply disappeared with not even a pile of ashes to memorialize their remains.

As the old song goes, though, all good things must come to an end and so, too, did our march toward victory. One minute Lochedus and I were hip-deep in howling hellions, and the next we were tied up, flat on our backs, side by side, sharing a stage with Sarah and Willem.

It had all happened so quickly right in the middle of the fray. March Ann had simply appeared, standing on the platform directly behind the trussed up old man and beautiful raven-haired angel, a wicked smile stretched across her face and an even wickeder dagger in her hand. "STOP OR THEY DIE!" Her voice rang out across the courtyard.

At first, I didn't think the raspy, growling baritone words came from March Ann's mouth, so different was their sound from anything I'd heard from her before. As every soul froze mid-swing – including Lochedus – I looked around, confused and wondering from whom the horrible directive was issued. I saw but one lone figure standing on the stage, knife in hand held directly against the neck of the angel known as Sarah, and I knew the chilling command could have come from no other.

It only took one sideways glance in Lochedus' direction to know continuing to fight was out of the question. Not that I would have wanted to prolong a struggle that could endanger either Willem or Sarah, but giving up seemed unthinkable, as well. The decision wasn't mine to make, though, because even with Lochedus by my side, our chances were negligible. Without his aid, a victory was impossible. I could only hope and pray that Lochedus had a Plan B he hadn't bothered sharing with me.

My ears were still ringing from a final sucker punch from a short, muscular devil, so I was only vaguely aware of being carried on the backs of the crowd to the altar-like table on top of the platform. It all seemed like a particularly horrifying dream.

My only dim ray of hope came from the look plastered on Lochedus' face – an expression that could best be described as dreamy. He looked, if possible, almost pleased with the situation, but I feared his comfort came only from being at long last near his mate rather than from any real chance we had of escaping the dire situation. As I slowly swung my head – the only thing mobile on my body – first left, then right, I saw that I shared the center of the stage with Willem, who was flanked by Sarah as I was by Lochedus.

March Ann and Monroe had stepped to the front of the stage and were leading the increasingly loud mantra that was like clanging symbols in my head. The continuous chanting had become pure torture. Though it caused no physical pain, the emotional battering from the pagan anthem was so intense that I had to bite my tongue to keep from screaming, "Shut up!" to the grisly crowd. At least the gibberish covered up the loud whispers going on between Willem and Lochedus.

With muscles bulging, the huge blonde angel strained at his bindings to see over me and make eye contact with Willem. "Somehow the demons have gotten their hands on the Lariats of Longinus," he spat through gritted teeth.

When he saw the look of confusion on my face, he explained. "The Lariats of Longinus are the only ropes an angel can't escape from." He continued to struggle, his face red and glowing from effort and irritation.

Strangely, his ire didn't seem to be directed at the demons, but rather at the old man lying on the altar next to me. "Look what you've done, Willem! And after everything I've done to help you. What were you thinking?"

I turned just in time to catch a sheepish look cross Willem's face before an angry one replaced it. "I was thinking I wanted to keep her away from all of this," he hissed back loudly as he jerked his head in the direction of the crowd. "And what do you do? You bring her right back into the middle of it."

They were speaking to each other in the strange "angel language" I'd come to recognize, but up until that very moment, not comprehend. I must have crossed over a threshold, of a sort, and entered a new realm of being; despite the seriousness of the situation, I couldn't help but feel a sense of pride – and with that pride, duty. I'd gone back and forth all weekend between the old, phobia-laden me and the new, significantly braver and stronger me, but I was pretty sure the changes were now etched in stone, and I was ready to say goodbye to damaged Grace forever.

"He didn't *bring* me anywhere," I bristled. "I wanted to come to try to help you . . . and Sarah." My statement might not have been technically true because even though my spirit had been willing, my flesh was weak. In other words, I'd been scared spitless. But even as I lay strapped on an altar and surrounded by Satan's playmates, I didn't regret Lochedus' insistence that I breach the fort and fight.

I could see the veins pop out on Willem's arms and neck as he fought the ties that bound him – trying to get enough play in the straps to reach out and touch me. I was worried about the stress on the old man - afraid his heart would simply give out. His skin had taken on a pasty look and his breathing was labored. I started to tell him to relax, that I would find a way out of the situation, but before I could say a word March Ann lifted her hands in the air, the chanting came to an immediate stop, and she began to speak.

"Brothers and sisters - the Master draws near." Her high-pitched voice was back and no less frightening than the possessed gravelly growl from earlier.

The demon fatale had covered her gold gown with a cloak the color of bright blood, making her look like a deranged Red Riding Hood. Every eye in the place followed her as she turned and walked around the four altars on which we lay. She circled us seven times, all the while chanting in a voice that grew increasingly discordant and maniacal. With each lap she took, her appearance seemed to change, and by the seventh round, she was no longer the gloriously beautiful fallen angel, but little more than a putrid-smelling pile of rotting flesh, covered in warts and strange hair growths with horns grotesquely protruding from her head and an odd rope-like tail hanging down from under her cloak.

When she – or it – finished round number seven, it pulled the dagger from the recesses of its cloak and dragged it slowly across our four bodies, drawing and mingling our blood onto the point of the vicious blade. After cackling in deranged mirth, the red robed monster raised the knife to its twisted semblance of a mouth and lapped up every drop of our wasted blood. It then began making a reverse trek by walking backward seven times around our altars while continuing the mind-numbing devil's song.

Staring down the barrel of my obvious and imminent mortality, it would have been an excellent time to feel sorry for myself, but I'd lost my taste for self-pity. I did, however, have regrets – more than a few. My mind was filled with the *shoulda, woulda, couldas* of the past eighteen years of my life and I mentally swore if I made it through the night, I would spend the rest of my existence making up for the mistakes I'd made. I'd wasted so much precious time with anger and selfishness. I wouldn't squander another second.

Just as before, when the monster made its rounds it began to change. But this time the transformation did not bring the expected result. As all looked on, the demon became, easily, the most breathtakingly perfect male specimen one could imagine. Over the weekend, I'd met Merc and Locke and March Ann's demon brothers – all awe-inspiring, each in his own way. Even the old man was quite handsome for an elderly gentleman. But this boy – the one that once was March Ann – was like no other found on earth. He was dark and light, delicate yet strong, and frightening with the terribleness of his beauty.

"Beladona!" I barely heard Lochedus's strangled whisper, but the extraordinary-looking demon hadn't missed it.

The golden-eyed, dark-haired devil flashed his brilliant white smile at my angel friend. "Hello, brother. Were you expecting someone else?"

"I should have known," Lochedus muttered disgustedly.

The dazzling demon turned his attention away from Lochedus and toward the crowd that now bowed before him. The circle of fire that surrounded the group and the blazing curtain behind the stage began slowly closing in on us creating a suffocating, smokeless, blanket of heat that sapped the oxygen from the atmosphere, leaving Willem and me gasping for air.

I heard Sarah trying her best to comfort Lochedus. "You couldn't possibly have known it was him, my love. I've been with the demons for ages, and I never knew who he really was."

"Please forgive me, Sarah. I've failed you miserably – again."

"There's nothing to forgive, Lochedus. Nothing that has happened is your fault. It is simply meant to be."

There was something in the angels' exchange that scared me. Maybe it was acceptance, or resignation, perhaps. Whatever it was, it set off alarm bells in my head and sent a message to my brain that said it was all up to me now. I couldn't depend on the angels or Willem or Merchison. If I was going to live to take out my new lease on life, I was going to have to face the demons alone.

"Release me!" I demanded, sending shock waves across the crowd.

Beladona's head swiveled dramatically. "Well, well, well . . . release you, huh? Now, why would I want to do that? I have you right where I want you. And just as soon as your coward of a mate shows up, I'll be taking you both to meet the Master."

His words should have struck fear in my heart. I should have been quaking in my Converse; but I wasn't. If I had to label my feeling at that moment, I would have called it excitement. A thousand angels – good or bad – couldn't be wrong. He had to have been talking about Merchison when he mentioned my "mate." Merc must be my man for life. Of course, having a fabulous, gorgeous, super-powered boyfriend would do me no good whatsoever if I were not alive to enjoy him.

The arrogant stance and mocking words of Beelzebub's beautifully evil buddy opened a valve in me that I couldn't have shut off if I'd wanted to. "Look, pretty boy, you may think you're all that, but I've seen you in your birthday suit and you bring a whole new meaning to the phrase, 'Beauty is only skin deep,'" I jeered, trying to match his sardonic tone with a brazen attitude of my own. "Don't tell me you're afraid of one little girl. Why don't you just untie me so we can have a little one-on-one time?"

"Grace!" I heard my three friends gasp in horrified unison. But I just ignored them because, for once, I didn't need anyone else's advice or approval. I only needed one thing – for Beladona to release me from the ties that bound me.

The evil angel produced the now-familiar knife and pressed it, rather forcefully, into my throat. "You dare speak to me in such a way? Perhaps you would like to meet my master sooner rather than later."

He had my attention now. I fought to keep the terror from my tone, sensing that my fear was exactly what he was going for and would get me nowhere. "Ooooo . . . big man! You can threaten an incapacitated woman. Veeeery impressive!" I forced a note of sarcastic humor into my voice – normally natural to me but difficult under the circumstances.

The payoff was as dramatic as it was immediate. Beladona sliced the cords from my body and dragged me off the altar and onto my feet to stand directly in front of the mob.

"Do you really think you – alone – can face down the demons?" he sneered.

The bizarre blaze burned all around me as Beladona's psychotic laughter echoed in my ears. If he'd had a fiddle, I would have thought it was Rome that was burning. My friends' cries were muffled and distant amidst the madness, and I could only depend on my inner voices – at last on the same page – to support the path I'd chosen. I knew the time for second-guessing my decision was over and terror would serve me no purpose. I'd lived the first eighteen years of my life riddled with doubts, fears and insecurities, and they made poor companions. I'd been brought to this place and time for a reason and, for once, I was going to live up to my potential or die trying . . . literally.

"I'm standing here, aren't I?" I bluffed. I was sure if I wished or prayed hard enough I would be given whatever strength I needed. I truly believed, for the first time, that I had it in me to be great.

I looked out over the crowd that had grown considerably in a few short minutes. I couldn't see the faces of the demons, but I could hear their bloodthirsty growls and imagine their teeth and claws digging into my flesh and tearing my body apart. I couldn't dwell on that type of thing; if I lost focus I might never regain it - then all would be lost.

"Who will be first to challenge the girl?" Beladona bellowed, scanning his followers for the first taker.

The throng cheered as a figure stepped forward boldly responding, "I will, My Lord."

So it was to be more like a cage match than a lynching. That was a relief! My confidence was at an all-time high, but I would be lying if I said being ripped apart by an angry demonic mob sounded like a good time to me. At least I would be able to face the monsters one at a time. That plan seemed much more doable.

I took a deep breath and sized up my giant foe, grateful to feel a strong surge of pure energy flow through my body. Over the voices of the crowd, I could hear the encouraging shouts of Lochedus and Sarah. I was concerned that I'd heard nothing from Willem, so I took a quick look around and nearly lost my footing when I saw his body lying motionless on the altar. I wasn't sure how old he was, but he suddenly looked ancient, no doubt direly affected by the night's tragic events. Seeing the old man in such a weakened state filled me with anger as well as a sense of urgency, and I faced my opponent more ready than ever to destroy him.

"Prepare for battle," Beladona roared, sounding like the bodiless voice on a video game.

With no training of any kind, I did the only thing I knew to do. I crouched into a fighting stance I'd seen in karate movies and prayed for some unseen force to take hold of my body and manipulate my limbs. I steeled myself for the first strike, having no idea that the wind would be knocked out of me without a single blow exchanged.

When the robed figure that had challenged me didn't budge, only stood motionless, waiting for me to make the first move, I decided to surprise him by ripping off the hood that had thus far obscured his face from my view. I wanted to see what I was up against. It seemed like a good idea at the time.

Having been slapped square in the face with the existence of demons, I was kind of prepared for anything. I wouldn't really have been all that surprised had my opponent howled at the moon or flashed a set of incisors made for puncturing jugulars. Over the past two days, I'd been levitated by a magnetic ghoul and flown through the air on the wings of an angel. Could vampires and werewolves really be that far behind? I was expecting fairy tale monsters – even ready for them – but I was in no way, shape, form or fashion prepared for what I found when checking under the demon's hood.

The face revealed was not grotesque or pale or trimmed in fur. It was an exact replica of my own, and the force of my horrified disbelief sent me reeling backward as if I'd been kicked in the stomach. I grappled wildly trying to retain my footing and caught myself by grabbing hold of Lochedus' huge, muscular arm.

"Grace, are you okay?" he asked, not sounding nearly as worried or surprised as I felt he should.

I swung around to face him. "Okay?! Of course I'm not okay. Did you see . . . I mean . . . oh my Lord . . ." I was stuttering and stammering and furious with Lochedus, who despite his bindings seemed very much in control.

"Grace," he began patiently, and so quietly I had to strain to hear over the chanting that had started back and was louder than ever.

"Don't *Grace* me," I shot back, not willing to listen to his explanations. "I thought I was special – that I was going to be a demon fighter! This has all been some kind of trick. That's not a demon," I pointed angrily toward the front of the stage – toward my evil double. "That's me!"

Willem's weak-as-water voice came from behind me. "You are special, Gracie. Listen to Lochedus . . . please . . . for me."

I turned and stared at the old man. He looked awful, like he was going to die at any minute. I rushed to his side and began furiously trying to untie his ropes but it was impossible to set him free. Tears of frustration and confusion poured down my cheeks. As I looked down on his sweet face – my vision blurred from crying – a jolt of recognition shot through my body. I didn't really understand it completely, but I knew that my connection with this old man went deep. I wanted so badly to pick him up in my arms and just run with him – away from this terrible place, far away from the danger, and pain, and confusion. But I couldn't leave. Whatever fate awaited me – awaited us – depended on what happened here and now.

"Tell me what to do, Willem," I begged. "I'm scared. Am I evil? Is that why I have to fight myself?"

He winced as he tried to roll his head from side to side, "No, no, sweet girl. You could never be bad. But you must fight your own demons before you can fight the demons of the world."

I lay my head on his chest, trying to put off the inevitable. I wanted to ask about Merc but I was scared to, afraid of what he would say. Had Merc been hurt or worse? Did he really exist at all, or had I just made him up in my disordered mind? I felt my faith draining away.

"Don't you do it, Gracie," he pleaded. "You've come such a long way and just have a little further to go. Fight for your happiness and fight for our life together."

I pulled away quickly. "Wait . . . what . . . what do you mean – *our life together?*"

"Pardon me," Beladona whispered in my ear. "I believe you have an opponent waiting, dear one." His voice was sugary sweet – nauseatingly so – but his breath in my face bore the stench of death, an easy reminder of his true nature.

I stiffened my spine and whipped around to face him. "I'm coming, I'm coming," I said, with much more enthusiasm than I felt. I wanted to say a quick, though hopefully not final, goodbye to my three friends. But when I turned back around I was flabbergasted to see the altars empty. I couldn't believe it. I'd only taken my eyes off of them for just a second, yet in that moment they had simply disappeared.

"What did you do to them, Beladona? Where are they?" I was livid and shaking like a leaf.

The wind was blowing furiously and though the fire had ceased to spread it still crackled wildly against the dark sky. The scene had all the elements of a fantastic nightmare, but I knew I wasn't asleep. Then again, I thought I might be moments away from a permanent slumber.

Beladona ignored my question and pushed me toward my waiting foe. I fought to get my head in the game, trying to remember Willem's parting plea and trying to forget his unexplained disappearance. I breathed deeply and centered myself, inwardly searching for the secret to my success. It came not in a flash but in a quiet word in my soul – faith. Hadn't that been the theme of my weekend? To have faith in myself, to believe in my own abilities and to trust a Higher Power that had cared enough about me to send me help? I could do this. I was sure of it. I was exactly where I was supposed to be, and everything was going to be all right.

Chapter Twenty Three

AMAZING GRACE

OF COURSE, ALL MY HEADY RESOLVE WENT STRAIGHT OUT THE WINDOW when before I could even shake hands and come out fighting, the demon wearing my face grabbed hold of my throat and squeezed so hard I thought my eyes would pop from my head. I grasped at its hands, trying as hard as I could to break its hold, but to no avail. I couldn't breathe, and I couldn't see; I could only think, and thank the Lord for that, because despite the pain I was in I managed to dredge up from the recesses of my brain the image of a Krav Maga demonstration I'd seen performed at Barksdale Air Force Base in Louisiana. The instructor had acted out the most expedient method for breaking a chokehold, which was to bring one's arms up between those of their opponent, and quickly and forcefully knock their arms apart. I don't know which one of us was more surprised by my miraculous maneuver, but it had given me an edge – be it ever so slight – and allowed me the ability to make an offensive move of my own. Before the monster could regroup and re-attack, I used the strongest part of my body – my head – to butt it off its feet and then used my other advantage – my weight – to knock the breath clean out of the devil by jumping on top of its chest. Knowing I had the upper hand and figuring I wouldn't get a second bite at the apple, I used all the strength I'd been recently awarded to twist the demon's head off its body.

And, just like that, it was over. No muss, no fuss. One minute, the attractive-for-a-demon monster was trying to kill me, and the next – after a slight pfffttt and a puff of smoke – it was gone. Unfortunately, just as I was patting myself on the back for my stealth and praising the Lord above for no blood, I became aware of yet another monster stealing quietly up behind me. I didn't have to take this one's hood off to see it wore my face because it had done it for me. It made no pretense toward disguise and made no effort at subtlety. In a matter of moments we were in full-on wrestle-mania mode, and to make matters worse, when I thought I had it whipped, it tagged its waiting twin partner and I had to go a few rounds with it as well. I eventually came out the victor, but just as before there was another "Gracie" waiting in the wings.

My demonic double sauntered onto the stage looking for all intents and purposes to be a better version of myself. "She" preened and pranced and walked the "runway" with a style and confidence I, to date, had never possessed. She glided to within a few feet of where I was standing and, with a theatrical shrug of her shoulder, shed her dark robe of Satan to reveal a stunning little hot pink number that, if I was being honest, I would have to say jibed with my wishful taste to a T. With her nose in the air, she held out her hand and crooking one finger beckoned me to her. Momentarily nonplussed, I acquiesced to her command and cautiously approached my beautiful doppelganger as the audience whooped and catcalled – excited and enjoying the show.

The only thing I can say in my defense for what happened next was that I was temporarily taken with the vision of what I'd always wanted to be – stunning, slim, seductive and secure. As if in a trance, I moved closer to my dream girl and, in doing so, became aware of a sour, rotting odor that soon I realized could only be coming from her. Sickened and suddenly unstable on my feet, I turned to run but not quick enough to avoid the demon's skeletal paw grabbing me from behind and hauling me back toward her with a vicious yank.

I desperately flipped through the flashcards in my mind, frantically searching for another long-forgotten tip or trick I might have inadvertently picked up that would aid me in my battle for supremacy. Nothing came to mind that might help me in freeing myself from the stinking witch that held me tight. As I looked over my shoulder into her face, she grinned at me. Her teeth were rotting and yellowed, her eyes bloodshot and rheumy, and it took everything that I had not to be sick on the spot.

I finally decided my only choice was to "take it to the mattresses." In other words, to fight as down and dirty as I possibly could with no regard for rules or etiquette or those watching from above or below. My first defensive action was to blindly reach behind me and grab hold of a handful of her hair and yank it with all my might. Unfortunately, my strategy didn't work out so well, because as I pulled on her dark golden curls, my hand came back holding not just a few strands, but an entire head of hair. I dang near passed out, thinking with my new super-strength I had actually beheaded the hellion. With a glance through my spread fingers that covered my horrified face, I peered toward my nemesis and was relieved yet repulsed to see not a headless torso but a hideous old woman, bald save for a few sprigs of greasy hair. Her tortured eyes were fixed on the wig I held high in my hand and for one blissful moment I thought her de-wigging would be her undoing. But it quickly became apparent that more than a haircut would be required to take down this succubus; with a bellow of pure rage, she charged me like an angry rhino and before I knew it I was flat of my back, gasping for air.

I thought about, if only briefly, sticking my fingers into the demon's eyes, but quickly decided that the strategy might prove more detrimental to me than to the demon. I had a weak stomach, and the smell of decay wafting from the balding devil was already perilously close to making me ill. Biting her ear – or any other of her body parts – was also quickly vetoed for much the same reason. Frustrated and more than a little grossed out from the spittle dripping onto my face from her snarling fangs, I finally went with a simple move and head-butted her in the face, hearing the satisfying crunch of her broken nose when I did it.

She shrieked in rage and disbelief, and I, being reasonably intelligent, saw this as the perfect time to go on the offense. As she leaned back and away from me – as if to howl at the moon – I grabbed hold of her shoulders and using her backward momentum to my advantage, hurled my body up and over, landing on my feet to stand directly behind her. I'm not sure who was more surprised by my black-belt move, the crowd or me, but it was a game-changer for sure and following its execution the audience seemed to show me a little more respect.

I decided to test my new skills and show out a little too, by bending backward and grabbing hold of the demon's throat, lifting her up and over my head. Feeding off the momentum of the chanting assembly, I twirled around like a shot putter and hurled the screaming demon into the arms of her brethren. I heard the jeers turn to cheers, and I felt like Rocky fresh from his victory against Apollo Creed. I danced around the stage with my arms held high, sure that the battles were over, and that I, Gracie Marie Bennet, had come out on top. Too late I remembered that "pride cometh before a fall," and I was to fall many more times before my bloody day was through.

The line of demons seemed endless; I didn't think they would ever stop coming. Some were sneaky and others in my face. They came alone and in twos and threes. As I walked through the valley of the shadow of death, I was surrounded by evil. But every time I thought I'd had enough – that I simply could not go on – I would feel rather than see the presence of another.

Sometimes it was Lochedus and other times Sarah, giving me the tools and encouragement to persevere. Though a battle it was, I had moments of great joy and relief. Conversely, within the fight came valleys of bone-jarring despair the likes of which I'd never known. It was in these times of tremendous anguish and fear that my invisible helpmates most greatly assisted in the fight – never letting me down, fighting through me and for me.

My battle seemed to go on forever, and the sun was setting on that Monday night before the last demon went down. Bloody, but unbowed, I ran around the fort, checking every nook and cranny, hoping against hope to find my friends so that we could celebrate the victory.

The last place I looked was the small barracks that March Ann had transformed into a harem-like boudoir. I figured that if any demons were holed up in hiding, they would surely be there, so it was with trepidation that I swung open the beat-up old door. To my surprise, once again the old barracks had been changed, but not back to its original state. The once jewel-colored devil's nest was gone, and in its place was a room bathed in glowing white light.

I couldn't see if there was anything or anyone in the room because the area was so bright it actually hurt my eyes and prevented me from staring into it for too long. It seemed strange and a little frightening to me that I hadn't noticed its pulsing incandescence from outside the building, so I hesitated before finally taking one faltering step past the threshold, discovering immediately that I'd been right to be concerned. As I placed my foot just inside the door, my body was literally sucked into the room with a "whoosh" that left me breathless and shaking with anxiety.

I had no time to think or formulate some type of plan for escape, because my body began to betray me. I felt like a giant balloon was being blown up in my stomach and my chest became tighter and tighter, cutting off my oxygen and forcing me to fight just to breathe. It was as if the room itself was alive and was crushing me from the inside out. Barely maintaining consciousness, I turned toward the door, praying for the strength to run out of it, and in horror realized that it was not where it was supposed to be.

I crumpled to the ground in exhaustion and disbelief. So this was to be the end of me? I'd foolishly thought that because I'd battled the demons and won, my perfect new life would be mine for the taking. How wrong I had been.

I continued to struggle and fight the unseen force for as long as I could but finally simply gave in, unwilling and unable to do any more. And that's when it happened. Sweet relief flooded through my lungs, and my body was filled with the most incredible feeling of warmth, love and peace one could imagine. Was this what death was like? If so, I was ready because it beat anything earth had to offer. I did have some misgivings about meeting my maker dressed like a contestant on "Dancing with the Stars," but hopefully a white robe could be furnished before my audience with the King.

I was contemplating my place in the great scheme of things when my name was called – "Gracie." The musical voice – singing my name - came from behind me and was familiar. I felt vaguely annoyed to be interrupted right in the middle of my rapture, but I was filled with too much love to stay mad for long.

"Sarah?" I whispered, suddenly tongue-tied with awe. Just as I had known immediately the trilling tone of Sarah's voice, I also recognized the angel's sweet face as she came walking through the light as if she had been there all along. But there was something very different about her. The most obvious change was her wings, which were magnificent and, while more delicate than Lochedus', still impressively large and heavily layered with rows and rows of pearlescent feathers. The stunning angel radiated all over with color that was, at once, golden and pink and tinged with violet. Had it not been for her smile – so filled with love and acceptance – it would have been almost impossible to look at her.

A nervous bubble of laughter welled up from within me at the errant thought that this time yesterday I was laboring under the false impression that her soul mate, Lochedus a.k.a. Locke, was interested in me. What a hoot! Not that I cared, because I had eyes only for Merchison Spear, but it was still kind of funny to think that any man – or angel – could possibly choose me over this fabulous creature.

When she was under the demon's sway, she had been a mere girl of about my height, but now that she had shed her mortal coil for the wings of an angel, she towered over me by at least a foot – maybe more. I wanted to ask her where everyone was and ask her if this was Heaven, but she pressed a finger to my lips and cooed, "Shhh." When an angel asked you to be quiet, you buttoned your lip, and I did, giving myself over to her completely to do with me as she pleased.

She took me into her arms and cradled me like a baby, all the while singing comforting words in her glorious, impossibly high, angelic voice. I was almost comatose with relaxation when she laid me onto a cool surface that I could feel but not actually see and began ministering to me, gently tending to my cuts and bruises not with ointments or bandages like a human would but with feathery touches and tender massage. She even stripped off the final vestiges of the horrible red gown and then slipped over my head a white Grecian-style slip of a dress that glowed and twinkled and shimmered with iridescent, unrecognizable color.

I never saw a bath or basin, yet I felt the cool wetness of water as she bathed my feet before slipping onto them a pair of simple gold sandals. She combed her hands through my hair and ran a finger around my eyes, cheeks and lips – gently outlining their shape with the lightest of hand. And then, as if things weren't strange enough, she backed away from me and softly blew her breath – which smelled like an amazing blend of honeysuckle, lilac and roses – into my face and up and down my body, clearing my mind of any traces of residual worry or care.

Throughout the whole process, she never said a word, but when she was finished, she gave me a huge smile and said, "Well, that should just about do it."

I wanted to ask, "Do what?" but it seemed kind of inappropriate and ungrateful. I was in the presence of an angel, that much was obvious, and I didn't really know what was expected of me. It wasn't the same as when I was with Locke. Most of the time, the boy angel didn't really intimidate me, probably because he spent most of his time irritating me. Sarah was different. She radiated heavenly goodwill and unconditional love and was so clearly "holy" that I didn't feel right badgering her for information.

I decided it wouldn't be rude to express my appreciation, though, so I did. "Thank you so much, Sarah. I don't know what you did to me, but I've never felt better!" That was certainly the truth; I felt fantastic. I looked around for a mirror, to check and see if I looked as good as I felt, but there wasn't one around.

"Yes, thank you, Sarah." The gratitude expressed came from a woman who simply appeared out of the light. I straightened my spine, not wanting to look like a slouch in case the woman was someone important in the heavenly realm. She certainly looked important. She was an older lady of indeterminate age and was poised and elegant and very, very lovely. Her solid white hair was cut short and chic, and she was dressed much like I was; in a simple Romanesque robe, only hers was cinched at the waist with a braided gold belt that matched the sandals on her feet. Everything about the woman screamed authority and strength, and I found it difficult to look away from her. Her sparkling aqua eyes were openly apprais-ing me, as well, and just a tiny spark of the old Gracie flared at her frank stare. I wasn't dumb enough to open my mouth, though, so I just stood there waiting for her to say something. When she finally spoke, it wasn't to me.

"You've done a wonderful job, my angelic friend." The woman was speaking to Sarah about me, and again I felt just a little jolt of irritation. In any other circumstance, I would have pitched a fit over being talked about like a piece of meat, but I had to con-sider that this might be the way things were done in Heaven. If this was indeed the kingdom in the sky – and it certainly seemed a good possibility – then I ought to be so relieved and grateful that I'd made it this far that I'd be willing to tolerate almost any indignity.

The older woman and Sarah spoke quietly and rapidly only to each other before finally exchanging hugs and kisses of goodbye. Part of me wished that Sarah wouldn't leave me alone with the lady, but I supposed I didn't have much say so and figured it was just a part of the process. I hoped I would see the beautiful angel again and wondered if I would be seeing Lochedus since he was an angel and I was obviously in Heaven. I watched wistfully as Sarah turned to go and quickly thanked her again for her help before she quietly disappeared into the whiteness, leaving me alone with the mystery woman.

Chapter Twenty Four

STAIRWAY TO HEAVEN?

"P ERHAPS WE SHOULD MAKE OURSELVES COMFORTABLE," THE WOMAN SAID.

A moment ago, the room had been devoid of furniture, but now there were two throne-like chairs a few paces to my right, and I followed her to them, politely waiting for her to take a seat before I did. I guessed that was how the room worked, kind of like "wish-craft" – one need only desire something for it to be there.

Though my mind was anywhere but woodwork, I traced the arm of the chair nervously waiting for the woman to take the lead in our conversation. For a full five minutes, she said nothing – only studied me carefully – until finally, not being able to take it any-more, I broke the silence.

"Should I be saying something? Confessing my sins, maybe?" It was just a guess because, never having been to Heaven, I had no idea what was expected of me. I hoped my demonic conquest would prove enough to erase my past bad behavior and keep me going in the right direction. My suggestion seemed to bring some amusement to the older woman, but I wasn't sure that would do me a whole lot of good.

"You don't care much for silence, do you, Gracie?" She asked.

Deciding it would be a waste of time to be subtle because she could probably read my thoughts anyway, I answered honestly. "I'm just trying to figure out how to proceed. This is all new to me. Do you mind telling me who you are?"

"Sometimes, the best way to learn what you need to know is to be quiet and listen." She smiled in a Cheshire cat kind of way – the way people who held all the cards smiled.

I felt my internal temperature rise a degree or two but said nothing. If I were going to be forced to play her game, I would try to play it well. I began to study her as carefully as she had been studying me and after a few minutes I began to recognize subtle things about her facial features that I found familiar. Her strong jawline was vaguely reminiscent of my father, and the slight unevenness of her full lips made me think of my mom. But mostly it was her eyes. The aqua shade was a blend of my dad's bright blue and my mother's sea green, and their shape was big, round and 100 percent me. My heart lurched to the front of my chest, and my breath caught in my throat. Who was this woman? I had read stories about near-death experiences where the nearly departed had met future children and grandchildren. Could that be what was happening? I was dying – no pun intended – to ask, but the woman had all but told me to shut up and she didn't look much like a person who liked to repeat herself, so I continued to sit and stare at her just as she was staring at me. The light in the room had dimmed to a low, pulsing glow and I found myself subconsciously counting the number of palpitations in an effort to pass the time without speaking.

"Heavens! You aren't going to start that business again, I hope."

It took me a minute to realize that the woman was talking to me, although I don't know why; there was no one else in eyesight.

"Excuse me?" I said, as politely as I could manage.

"The counting - you had all but stopped it this weekend. Did you know that?"

So the mystery lady had tipped her hand a bit. She'd been keeping tabs on me. I wasn't sure what kind of response she was expecting, so I just went with a light pat on my own back by way of an answer. "Yeah, I guess I was too busy fighting demons to worry about counting," I preened.

There was no sense in missing an opportunity to remind her of my victory against the bad guys. If this was some kind of entrance exam into Heaven, and she was the proctor, I would probably need to lean on my success as this weekend's warrior, because, Lord knows, I hadn't done much in the way of good deeds prior to then.

"Always thinking, always planning, always plotting," the elegant old woman remarked, while looking down at her beautifully manicured white-tipped nails. She looked a little bored or maybe mildly disappointed, and I wanted to say something in my defense – something to make the woman sit up and take notice of me - in a good way. My mind was abuzz with excuses and explanations for everything I'd ever done, along with promises to do better. I had just about outlined in my head a speech to deliver to the lady in the hopes of swaying her toward my side when she waved her hand in a cutting motion. Suddenly every thought I had seemed to freeze-dry, crumble and fall out of my brain, leaving me with nothing whatsoever to say.

"Peace, Gracie – be still." She said "peace" in a way that didn't sound so peaceful. It was more like a command, and while I wasn't sure exactly what she meant by her words, I decided to adopt as calm a countenance as I could muster while I waited for her next "suggestion."

She surprised me by scooting her chair so close to me that our legs were touching. Without saying a word, she lifted both of her hands to my face and began rubbing, rather forcefully, across my forehead and down to my temples where her fingers made small circles. After a bit, I felt myself beginning to relax a little. It wasn't the same zoned-out, high-on-love, all-is-right-with-the-universe kind of vibe that I'd felt with Sarah. It was a more reserved, in-control sensation, which kind of made sense because the white-haired lady seemed much more down to business than my beautiful angel friend. Perhaps I was picking up on her spirit.

"Gracie, you've come a long way in a short time. I'm very proud of you."

Well now, this was unexpected and seemed high praise indeed, coming from this woman. I was willing to bet she didn't dole out compliments lightly.

"Before you start fashioning your halo, dear, let me finish." She scooted her chair back a bit and took my hand, pulling me up to stand with her. We were almost the exact same height, so I had no problem facing her eye to eye, but she had other plans.

"Come, walk with me," she said. As soon as the last word was out of her mouth, we were standing in the middle of a lovely, flower-covered field on a perfectly cloudless day. A light breeze rattled through the leaves of a gloriously blooming cherry tree, and a bird sang happily on a nearby limb. It was slightly disconcerting to be in one place one moment and another the next, but I was getting pretty good at the surreal and I just let the change of scenery roll off my back.

We walked in silence for a while before she finally commented, "I was getting rather tired of all the white. This is much better, don't you think?"

"Yeah, sure it is, uh, I mean uh, yes, ma'am, it certainly is," I corrected myself quickly.

A strange smile crossed her face as she said, "What have I told you about uh, uh, uh?"

I stopped mid-stride, not believing what I had just heard. But then, as if I'd had a little outside "help," the thoughts and memories came crashing through my brain like waves on a tumultuous ocean. "You . . . you, but how . . . and why?" What was the purpose of such an elaborate charade? There was no denying what was staring me in the face. This woman was Mrs. B. – the same voice, the same eyes, but so very, very different.

I was just this side of ticked off and fighting hard not to be. I felt duped - played like a fiddle . . . and to what end? Had I been a pawn in some Utopic chess game devised as a diversion for those greater than man? If so, the heavenly hosts must have more in common with the gods of Olympus than the giants of the Old and New Testament.

I lost the battle raging inside of me and finally asked accusingly, "I realize you must be somebody important in . . . in . . . wherever we are, but could you maybe tell me why all the lies – the subterfuge? Do you all just enjoy making people feel foolish?" I was hurt over everything, but most of all, my mind was on Merchison. Was he a part of the game? Of course he was. And Willem – I had been crazy about Willem. Why would he want to fool me?

Maybe I wasn't really in a waiting room for Heaven. Maybe it was Hell I was headed to, and the precursor to the fiery furnace was an elaborate bag of tricks designed to make a girl feel like she had a chance in life (or death) right before the rug was snatched out from under her. Nice!

"If you're not careful," the woman pointed out, "you'll be right back in as big a mess as you were before the weekend started. Why are you so ready to pass judgment? Have you ever thought about just asking me?"

Was she kidding? I had spent the past two days doing nothing but asking what was going on. I had been lied to over and over again and now . . . the ultimate lie. Everything had been a sham. I didn't trust myself to speak, afraid that if I opened my mouth, I might find myself on the express route to Hades.

"Just calm down, Gracie. I understand that you may be a little upset, but I promise you there is a very good explanation for what I've done – for what we've all done. And it all comes down to what was best for you."

Ah, the parental party line. I was well familiar with that one. I gave her a sardonic look to match my sarcastic words. "Sure, sure – you did it for my own good. Like I haven't heard that one before." I stopped short of rolling my eyes, only to see the woman actually roll hers.

"Try not to be so jaded, my dear. If we are going to get through this little talk, we are both going to have to exercise some patience."

In silent protest, I let her get a few paces ahead of me before reluctantly catching up. I hadn't noticed a pier leading out to a small pond until it was right in front of us, but there it was, and I followed her to the end of it and sat down next to her – both of us hanging our feet off the edge. We sat looking out over the lime green water, lost in a silence that was anything but comfortable. At first, I thought I'd heard wrong because it didn't make a bit of sense, but after hearing the second sniff, I turned away from the water to look at her profile. I was right; she was crying, and the sight of the tears rolling down her face threw me for a complete loop.

I didn't usually get all mushy at the sight of tears. In fact they normally made me uncomfortable and even a little irritated – probably because I assumed that, like me, most girls and women used tears to manipulate. I'd found there was nothing like a bogus breakdown to get a little sympathy swinging my way. But it took just one look to know there was nothing disingenuous about this lady's display of emotion, and I suddenly wanted to comfort her and relieve her of her pain.

"I'm . . . sorry," I stammered out awkwardly, not really sure what I was apologizing for but wanting to make things better. "I don't mean to be ungrateful or unkind; I just don't understand a thing about what's going on. And . . ." I forced myself to continue, even though doing so would require me to let my guard down. "I just liked everyone so much – Willem and Locke and . . . Merc," I finally croaked out. A huge lump formed in my throat, but I didn't even worry about it. If I didn't have a cause to cry, then there wasn't a porch in Georgia.

"And Mrs. B.?" she asked almost shyly. We both knew that she and the old lady were one in the same but we'd yet to address the issue head on.

"Things were a tad complicated between me and Mrs. B. but I think we could have eventually been friends," I answered as honestly as I could, not wanting to hurt her feelings but not wanting to lie, either. A thought popped into my head, so I added, "I was looking forward to working on her autobiography. She definitely seemed like an interesting woman. One of a kind."

I guess she decided to take the bull by the horns, because though she never came right out and said, "I'm Mrs. B.," she spoke with the assumption that we both knew. "When I said I was working on my autobiography, I wasn't lying, Grace. And when I said I needed your help with it that was the truth, too."

I couldn't just skirt the issue. I simply wasn't built that way. I had to put it right out on the table. What did I have to lose? "So you *are* Mrs. B. – Wow! I don't mean to be rude, but you sure have changed a lot." I stopped for a minute, praying I hadn't said anything wrong. When she only nodded her head in assent, I decided to go for broke. "And who are you to me?" I asked. "I mean, I know this sounds crazy, but are we . . . " I paused for a minute, trying to figure out how to ask the question. "Are we related?"

She reached out and took my hand before answering. As she gave it a steady squeeze she answered, "Gracie, you are a very smart girl. I think you know who I am. You knew at the mansion yesterday, and you know now."

I closed my eyes to soak it all in – to try and accept what, in my heart, I did already know. I should have been floored – shocked to my shoes, breathless with disbelief – yet somehow I just wasn't. Maybe it was because I had really known all along. I still had plenty of questions, though, and it seemed if I was ever going to get the answers, now – in this strange spring wonderland – was the time.

"So," I began haltingly, "you are like from the future or something? Is that right?"

She laughed softly before answering, "Something like that, Grace."

"Okay, I can handle that. But here's what I don't get. If Mrs. B. is me from the future and you are me from the future, how can you two be so different?"

That was about the best I could do. It was a confusing question, but it was a confusing situation. I hoped she could clear things up for me.

"Up until this Friday, Gracie, you were headed in a very wrong direction: angry with your parents, with Pete and Patty, with the world. But even more than all those put together, you were angry with yourself. To tell you the truth, I was hoping that when I inserted myself into the situation I would be able to see just where all your pain and insecurity was coming from, but I never really figured it out. Maybe it was Dad's drinking or perhaps all the moving around; I'm just not sure."

I blanched at hearing her call my father "Dad." Intellectually accepting that she was me was not the same thing as understanding it in my heart, I guess. She didn't seem to notice my reaction, and I shook it off, starving to hear more.

"The Mistress of the Mansion – Mrs. B. – is where you were heading had Lochedus not intervened. The bitter old woman was at the end of a very sad, very lonely life. Broken marriages, addictions and anger marked all of her days; yet at the very end of her life, one man still loved her – had always loved her. And because of that love, she . . ." The beautiful old woman stopped and put a soft hand on my face before correcting herself. "We . . . have been given a miraculous – an unprecedented – second chance."

It was a lot of information to take in, and I wasn't anywhere near complete understanding, but I was getting closer. "So what you're saying is if I don't change, I'll end up like Mrs. B., but if I mend my evil ways, I'll end up like you. Does that about sum it up?"

She didn't miss the slight sarcasm of my comment but clearly decided to ignore it because she must have known I meant no harm. I was just trying to deal with things the best way I knew how.

"Precisely." Her smile was a little mocking but I, too, could be forgiving. I didn't want to waste time sparring, though fighting with my future self would have certainly been an interesting challenge. I still had too many questions, and I didn't know how long we had together.

"Things are starting to make a little sense to me now," I said. "I had to fight my own demons so that I wouldn't end up like Mrs. B. . . . right?"

"Correct again. You really are so clever," she said with a sly smile. To compliment me was to compliment herself.

We fell into companionable silence. After a while I asked, "Why were *we* so lucky? Why was Lochedus willing to do this for us?"

"A good question, to be sure, and one for which there isn't just one answer."

"Does it have something to do with Willem? You said one man loved Mrs. B.; that would have to be Willem."

A slow, beautiful smile that spoke volumes spread across her face. She loved Willem. That must mean that I, too, would one day love Willem. *But what about Merchison*, my heart cried out. I was so sure we were meant to be together.

I looked to my older self – searching her eyes for the truth. Her steady, love-filled gaze told the tale.

"Willem *is* Merc! Isn't he?" I thought back to the change in the old man that I'd seen at the fort – that something different I couldn't explain. When I'd first met the old man his eyes were blue, but when he came to save me from March Ann they had changed to bright green - just like Merc's – or at least Merc's some of the time. My heart was so full I thought it would burst. Merchison Spear would stand by me forever, my love for life. I didn't think I could ever be this happy. I couldn't wait to see him again.

"Slow down, girl. There is still much for you to know," the woman cautioned. "You must understand that nothing is written in stone. You and Merc have many hills to climb and they will not be small ones. You *cannot* depend on him – or any other man. You must depend on *you*."

She squeezed my hand firmly. "And Grace . . . don't make it too easy for him. He's a man – much like every other." She winked before adding, "Just with a few extra skills." I wasn't sure how to interpret that last comment, so I let it go, but I took her words to heart and planned to mull them over more carefully later.

Finally she stood up, and I followed suit, walking with her off the pier and around the pond. We were almost all the way back to where we started when she began speaking again.

"You asked me why Lochedus was willing to do this wonderful thing for us and the answer is not a simple one. First, he felt he owed a debt to Merchison – one he very much wanted to repay. And he also knew that you and Merc were the keys to finding his lost mate." I started to break in, but she held her hand up to stop me. "Let me finish, please, because the third reason is, by far, the most important."

I couldn't imagine what could possibly be more important than repaying a debt to Merc and finding Sarah, but I guessed I was going to find out. As we came full circle around the pond, the clouds began gathering in the sky, blocking the sun and cooling the breeze that now sent a slight shiver down my spine. I waited for my older self to gather her thoughts and, when she finally did, she stopped walking and turned to me with such a serious look in her eyes that it caused a stab of apprehension to run through me.

"What I have to tell you, Gracie, is not meant to scare you. It is meant to prepare you for what is coming." She paused, I suppose, for effect before taking in a deep breath and continuing. "The world is headed for some very dark times. You will see and experience things in your lifetime that our parents never dreamed existed – dark things – evil things."

The stab of apprehension I'd first felt was rapidly blossoming into full-blown panic, but before I could ask for clarification on what she'd said, she again held her hand up to stop me from speaking.

"Please, let me finish," she said. "I know, in your mind, everything that was said to you this weekend was a lie; but trust me, Gracie, it was not. I know that Merchison spoke to you about the man that reared him – Theodore – and his group of followers." She paused and after a minute I realized that she was waiting for me to confirm her statement.

"Yes, he told me about the 'angel lite' group he'd been living with until he moved to Alabama. I assumed what he said was made up for *my own good*." I raised my fingers into the air to simulate quotation marks.

She raised a beautifully shaped eyebrow, smirking at my use of the term "angel lite." "Well, I believe Theodore refers to his group as simply 'The Company,' but the name does not matter. What does matter is the function of the group."

I had to ask: "And that function would be?

"Saving the world, of course!"

I checked her face to see if the comment was made tongue-in-cheek; one look in her direction told me that she was dead serious.

"Save the world from what?" I asked, disbelief heavily coloring my words.

"I told you already, dear - evil." She said the word simply, as if I was just supposed to take that for an answer without knowing anything more.

"Uh," I started, and then could have bit my tongue out. "I mean . . . do you mind being a little more specific, please?"

She shook her head. "I really can't get too far into it. It's not my place. But suffice it to say that the Devil himself will unleash onto earth every manner of evil creature; things that cannot be killed by normal, human means. That is why the rules separating Heaven from Earth have been bent almost to the point of breaking. Angels have been allowed to pass on some of their powers to humans in order to protect the world from true chaos."

"How does any of this have anything to do with me?" I asked, praying that some mistake had been made. Surely, I couldn't be expected to participate in killing the horrendous creatures she spoke of. I mean, sure, I conquered my own demons, but this . . . this was something else entirely. "You should know better than anyone I'm not cut out for slaying dragons —or whatever. It's just not me," I said, almost begging her to agree.

"Gracie, this has everything to do with you - and with Merchison." She said his name almost like a prayer, and I knew she was every bit as much in love with him as I was – probably more, because she'd been with him so much longer.

"But, but."

"NO buts, Grace. You met Mrs. B. *She* is the result of living a life of selfishness and greed, never thinking about others, only ever thinking of herself. You have this chance, Gracie. Don't blow it. A life without love and service to others is empty and meaningless and, in your case, devastating to this world. You and Merc will lead the way!"

"Oh, my God!" I gasped. "You expect me to be the leader in some battle against the Devil? My Lord, woman!" I nearly screamed. "Until Friday, I couldn't even sleep at night until I'd checked under my bed and in my closets ten times. You've got the wrong girl. Nobody should know that better than you."

She waited to make sure I'd finished my rant and calmed down before answering. "I have a theory about all that checking and rechecking. Would you like to hear it?"

"Why not?" I answered flippantly to try and disguise how interested I really was in what she had to say.

"The demons stand a far better chance of victory without you in the way. I think it's possible that they began targeting you years ago, keeping watch over your progress and playing on your already damaged psyche."

My mouth dropped open in surprise. Strangely, I wasn't horrified by the idea but rather relieved. For years, I'd felt a constant presence around me like someone was watching me. I didn't even put up that much of a fight when my parents insisted I see a shrink, because I was afraid that something really was very wrong with me. But when I actually got to the doctor's office, I couldn't bring myself to tell him that I heard noises and saw glimpses of shadows. I was way too claustrophobic to take a chance they might lock me in a small, padded room.

Now I was being told that all my crazy delusions might not have been delusions at all. I suddenly felt stronger and more in control. Unwittingly – or maybe intentionally – the woman next to me had said just exactly what I needed to hear. I felt almost giddy with relief and overcome with a desire to stick out my tongue at someone – anyone – and say, "Ha, ha! I told you so!" I wanted to delve further into the topic of my justifiable fears, but my elder alter ego was wrapping things up so I hastily pushed for a few more answers.

"If Locke – Lochedus, I mean, wanted Merc and me to be together, why was he trying to discourage me from seeing him?" I felt my face flush a bit, but I persevered because I really wanted to know. "Why did he flirt with me and ask me out? It doesn't make any sense."

"Merc has his own issues to deal with and he is definitely being tracked by demons. Lochedus and Willem were simply trying to protect you until they could get Merc's problems under control." Her mouth twitched a bit like she just remembered something funny. "Also, when Locke took on the guise of a human, he fell prey to all the human frailties, not the least of which was pride and lust." She laughed out loud before saying conspiratorially, "The little shirtless show he put on was really too much, wasn't it?"

"I'll say!!" I agreed and then joined in her laughter as we hugged each other tightly. I couldn't believe how calmly I was taking everything.

We talked on for what seemed like hours, but she was very careful not to say anything more about my future, at least not specifically. She was full of wisdom about how I should behave and how to get the most out of my life, but her advice seemed more along the lines of a self-help manual rather than from firsthand experience. I listened to every word, though, figuring this was a once-in-a-lifetime scenario and I should feel grateful for being given the upper hand in how to proceed in the world.

We were discussing how, once again, my plans for summer employment had changed, when she suddenly turned sharply, as if hearing a noise. For a split second, her face took on the look of a woman hunted, or frightened maybe; but it quickly changed and when she turned to me again it was to place her hand on my cheek. "How could I have not known how beautiful I was?" Her eyes filled with tears, which in turn caused mine to do the same. "It's time for me to leave. Please remember everything I've said to you, and most of all . . . remember . . . I love you." She reached out and hugged me again before softly adding, "You have a beautiful light inside of you, Gracie; let it shine."

I wanted to beg her to stay because I wanted to know so much more. That wasn't the only reason, though. "I love you, too," I whispered, knowing in my heart that I meant it. "Please . . . can't you stay?"

She was shaking her head before I even finished my plea. "No, it's my time to go." She stroked my hair and cooed, "You'll be fine,

I promise. Remember Gracie - you have everything you need inside of you. Having a soul mate is wonderful and a blessing, but you must love yourself before you are able to love another. You have to be strong now and depend on your own inner resources that were gifts from your Father above."

Suddenly the entire area was drowned in bright light. I couldn't see anything anymore but I yelled into the whiteness, "I need to find Merchison. I don't know where he is! Where do I go?"

From out of the light came the last words I was to hear from the woman – from me. "Follow your heart, Gracie. It will never lead you wrong."

With her final utterance, the bright light vanished and I was sitting alone in my car in the parking lot of Fort Toulouse, listening to the tap, tap, tap on my windshield from the dripping wet leaves of the giant oak tree limb hanging directly overhead. Doing as my older self suggested, I cranked my car to head toward the only place my heart could direct me – the red dirt road where my miraculous weekend began.

Chapter Twenty Five

SWEET HOME ALABAMA

EVEN ON THE DARK, RAINY NIGHT, THE WORLD LOOKED BRIGHT AND beautiful to me, filled with so many possibilities that had never been there before. I was no longer handicapped by hatred and bitterness and I could finally see the God-created artistry of the scenery surrounding me. The gift I'd been blessed with was one that I intended to enjoy and put to the best use I possibly could. I vowed not to let fear and insecurity ever stop me from living life again.

I was fascinated with my improved senses that allowed me to see, hear and even smell things in a brand new way. The red clay hills lining the highway now seemed like mighty miracles, and I was amazed that I'd never once noticed these unusual mounds before tonight. I saw the charm in the architecture of the small town of Wetumpka and the beauty of its quaint bridge as I prepared to leave its borders. Maybe I was just drinking the Koolaid of the angels, but even the cows in the wet pastureland looked lovely to me as they stood grazing next to the majestic oaks and graceful birch trees.

I sang to the top of my lungs, deciding to forego my usual dark music in favor of the up-tempo soft rock I hadn't listened to in forever. I wasn't giving up Ozzy for good (eating the bat *was* an accident!), but the night seemed to call out for a more peaceful melody than "War Pigs." I thought about my dust-covered guitar that lay – untouched in months – under my bed and promised myself that I'd drag it out when I got home and reacquaint myself with the pleasure of its company. There had been a time when making music meant the world to me and soothed my savage beast within. I'd been pretty good at both playing and singing, but over the past few years, I'd lost my love of the lyrical along with so many other things that had once brought me comfort. I would welcome those joys back into my wheelhouse one by one.

My mind began filling with reminiscences, many of which caused me some shame, though not enough to change my mood. The memories brought me a strong desire and determination to right the wrongs of my past and an excitement for the promise of tomorrow. I was looking forward to talking with my parents and apologizing for the many times I'd behaved like a psycho brat. Perhaps, a bit selfishly, I couldn't wait to hear the surprise in their voices when they realized their erstwhile child was a brand-new person complete with a host of super talents to match the new attitude. That thought stopped me short and had me wondering whether I would actually be allowed to share my "angel-lite" status with my "'rents." I hoped I could spread the news, but even if I couldn't tell the whole truth and nothing but the truth, the change in my attitude would be enough to thrill my folks to pieces.

I thought it might be a good idea to take it slow when it came to Pete and Patty. Having experienced my vertigo-inducing mood swings firsthand, I was afraid that they might misinterpret an over-the-top personality change as a slide into alcohol abuse or drug addiction. And who could blame them should they be suspicious of my mercurial moods, because I'd certainly put them through their paces over the past few months. I would have to introduce myself to them all over again and bit by bit earn the trust I'd never been interested in securing before. Patty and I would probably never be best friends, anyway – we were just way too different – but our dissimilarities were no reason to treat her badly or make fun of her. I'd have to work on that - eventually.

I glanced at the clock on my dashboard and was shocked to see that it was almost 3:30 a.m. I knew I needed to find some time to get a little shut-eye before cramming as much studying in as I could to get ready for my Lit test on Wednesday morning. When I thought about going to school, I didn't immediately make plans to try and ditch like I usually did; I was actually kind of stoked about it. I knew it was going to take some work to change people's minds about me. I mean, Rome wasn't built in a day and neither was the wall I'd constructed around myself to prevent any meaningful contact with others of my age. I could easily see now that I'd pushed people away and that while there were cliques in every school, there were also many opportunities for friendship – opportunities that I'd been too scared and too insecure to take advantage of. I wasn't frightened of rejection or ridicule now. Of course, I wouldn't have much of an opportunity on school property to reintroduce myself to my classmates, because the summer break had all but begun, but the lake community was a small one and I'd probably bump into my fair share of folks in and around the area over the next few months. That is, if I wasn't out snaring demons with my love.

Naturally, I was excited about what the future held for Merchison and me, but I cautioned myself not to place too much emphasis on our fledgling relationship. Now that I knew that we were meant to be together, I didn't plan to force the issue – much. I'd seen too many girls in too many schools make complete idiots of themselves by falling all over a guy. I guess one benefit from living on the fringes of society was that you got a bird's eye view of what *not* to do in a relationship. I made up my mind on the spot that I would never make a nuisance of myself nor sell myself short. If a guy was too stupid to know how lucky he was to have me, then he was not intelligent enough to be my boyfriend. Period - end of discussion.

Not that I thought I would have to go to any extremes with Merchison Spear anyhow, because what we had was spiritual, even – dare I say – ordained, and above and beyond the normal high school dating scene. Even so, I planned to follow the old woman's advice and stick to my principles with the boy. If he wanted me, he was going to have to toe the line. Strong words from a girl who'd never had as much as a kiss on the cheek from a guy until this weekend but if I was going to be a brave new girl in a brave new world, I was going to do it right – right from the start.

I did rather look forward to showing off my beautiful beau to the kids at All Saints High. I guess that type of pride thing didn't really jibe that well with my "angel-lite" persona, but as the old saying goes, "Progress not Perfection." I was a different creature – inside and out – no doubt about it, but I was also still the same in many ways. After all, I wasn't without a redeeming quality or two to rub together before my transformation. I hoped to blend the old me and new me and end up with the best combination possible.

Apparently I was to have some major responsibilities to go along with my new powers and that was about as cool an idea as they came. Surprisingly, that thought didn't cause me any particular distress, though maybe it should. I guess bravery came with the territory because I sure as heck wasn't courageous before the "touch."

Suddenly, I found myself spoiling for a fight against evil. I wondered what type of things I would be doing. I hoped it would be more than just touching people's heads and taking on their pain; that didn't sound too exciting. I pictured Merc and me fighting side-by-side, vanquishing evil wherever it might rear its ugly head. I guessed there was the possibility that the performance of my duties might conflict with my schooling. Unfortunate, yes, but a price I was willing to pay.

By the time I'd made it to the familiar dirt road that led to the mansion, the steady rain had picked up and was threatening to become a full-blown storm – again. As I bumped along the dark wet road in the old Cutlass, I couldn't help but remember my maiden voyage down the messy path. Before long I was laughing out loud at the mental images created by my trip down memory lane. The girl who'd battled the elements on Friday night in no way resembled the young woman who now sat behind the wheel. The pitch-black woods were no threat to me - nor was anything else I might find down the road. My life had been transformed because of what happened down this muddy lane and I, for one, could only celebrate its soggy beauty while slowly making my way toward the man of my dreams.

Because I was nervous about seeing Merc again and preoccupied with my thoughts, I crept along and, at first, thought nothing of the fact that the house wasn't where I remembered it being. It had been a long, trying day, and the windswept darkness, I figured, was throwing me off my navigation. Slowing to almost a standstill, I shined my lights on high and low beam yet saw nothing but trees and moss and country lane.

I'd gone almost a mile farther down the road before I began thinking I'd somehow missed the mansion. I hadn't checked my odometer, thinking that this time it would be a cinch to simply drive until I reached my destination. But as it turned out, it wasn't all that simple. For thirty minutes, I crept up and down the dirt road searching for any sign of the big house. Several times I started back at the main road and made a yard-by-yard reconnaissance of the property, completely puzzled by my inability to find the old place. I even drove back to the start of the main highway thinking that, perhaps, I'd turned at the wrong set of lighted poles. But despite a thorough search of both sides of the road, I only ran across the one grouping of bright white sticks.

After turning for the third time onto the rocky red lane, I began to feel a little bit like Dorothy heading down the yellow brick road. The hair stood up on the back of my neck as the strangeness of the situation began to set in. Had a tornado picked me up on Friday night and set me down in the middle of Oz? I thought the more likely scenario was that when the older version of me vacated this mortal realm, she had taken her house with her. There was just one problem with that: Without the mansion as my base, I had no idea where to look for Merc. I had never even seen his "pied-a-terre," and if I couldn't find the French fortress, how was I supposed to find his little apartment? I tried to hold on to my hard-won confidence but it was really hard to remain calm and upbeat in the face of such a massive let down.

I couldn't sit in my car all night. I knew that. I just didn't know what I should do or where I should go. My investigation of the property had turned up a big, fat zero and no amount of searching was going to change that. I felt the cold fingers of dread trip down my body, and the familiar beginnings of panic seize hold of my heart. Just a short time ago, I'd felt such excitement for the future and couldn't wait to see what tomorrow would bring. But I had assumed Merc would be by my side, and now I didn't know where to find him.

I was about an inch away from losing complete control - breaking down and bawling - when a revelation hit me square between the eyes. I had spent all day and half the night fighting the worst kind of demons and here I sat – alive and well and able to tell the tale. Yet of all the devils I'd fought, none was so vicious or so soul-destroying as the one that lived deep inside of me that whispered, "You aren't enough. You need someone else. You can't make it – even for a second – on your own." This demon would feed on my fear and sip on my self-loathing until nothing was left inside of me but an empty hole incapable of being filled. Instinctively I knew I could not let that demon live. It would bring all its brothers and sisters in to stay, and it would be as if I'd never conquered a single one. I couldn't let that happen. I wouldn't let that happen. Momentarily depressed but ultimately determined, I wiped my eyes, turned up my tunes, and threw the car into drive.

As I reached the end of the empty way, I prepared to turn right and resignedly head home but something – a pull of some kind – seemed to guide my eyes toward the empty pastures on the opposite side of the highway. Maybe it was my keener vision, or maybe my headlights hit just the right spot, because for the first time I noticed a narrow dirt road – barely wide enough for a car – directly across from where I sat.

There would have been a time - say two days ago - when I would not have even considered crossing the road to explore an unmarked, unlit trail. It would have been a proposition – in my mind – for peril. But I was a little bit wiser and a whole lot braver now and ready to explore what lay just across the highway. I didn't see headlights to the left or right of me, so I shot across the way, fishtailing slightly and kicking up mud and rocks as I accelerated a little too zealously in an effort to move before I changed my mind. For the first hundred yards or so pastures flanked the road I was on. Gradually trees began closing in and before I knew it dense woods surrounded me. Mother Nature – always a fickle female – in a sudden uncharacteristic display of compassion blew the last of the storm clouds away, leaving a dazzlingly brilliant full moon and a blanket of stars that through the interlacing, moss-hung limbs of giant oaks filtered light in dappled patterns onto the auburn lane.

The night and uncharted path, which once would have seemed ominous to me, now held a powerful allure that drew me in and pulled me deeper and deeper toward an unknown destination. I had no idea where I was going, but I did know that I was supposed to go there. The attraction was the antithesis of the evil magnet wielded by the demon, because the closer I came to the source of the draw, the calmer and more assured I was.

There were many side roads and trails that ran off the main path, but I never hesitated with indecision even once. I let my instincts guide me and each time I came to a crossroads I knew immediately in which direction to proceed. When the way became too narrow and littered with natural debris to continue, I slammed my car into park, got out and, without a look backward, began to run through the dark woods, surefooted and fearless in my flight.

I moved through the dense growth of trees swiftly, dodging wet branches and brambles when I could, but oftentimes simply plowing right through them. I gave little thought to my gown or hair or muddy sandals because all that mattered to me was getting to that person, place or thing that beckoned me – pulling me as silently as a whispered prayer – through the night.

After running for what seemed like hours, the thicket of trees began to thin, and the dark, star-lit blanket above me mellowed to a misty shade of purplish-blue. I cleared the last group of pines just as the sun peeked its head over the horizon, turning the eastern sky into a blaze of pink and orange hues and the clearing into a magical utopia of fiery color.

I had arrived, and the sight before me was so breathtaking that I could only sink to my knees in humble adoration of the master architect of universal design. The area before me was so immaculately rendered that most would assume it to be the product of careful planning and artful arrangement, but I knew better. The glory of this early morning display was proof positive the ground I walked on was not created by an ancient massive boom in outer space. Only the hand of a being far, far greater than myself could even dream of such natural majesty.

After a few minutes of quiet wonder, I rose to my feet and began walking through the field of flowers – each bloom more lovely and colorful than the next – until I reached the bank of a gently rolling pond framed by a wide variety of gracefully bowing shade trees. I removed my ruined sandals and luxuriated in the feel of the cool green liquid against my tired feet. I tried my best to revel in the earthly Eden alone, but I'd be lying to say I wasn't disappointed. I'd been so sure Merc would be waiting for me like my personal pot of gold at the end of the rainbow. Without him I felt like a part of me was missing.

For years I'd felt fragmented – my pieces scattered in the wind. Yet with every passing hour of the weekend, my life – my soul – became more cohesive; the puzzle that was me coming together to create a complete and miraculous picture. But there was one vitally important part still missing and though I might be far better off now than I had ever been before I would never be truly whole without it – without him.

I looked to the heavens, at first in silent supplication, and then to shout in frustration. "You said to go to Merchison," I cried. "What have I done wrong? I followed my heart and this is where it led me. Why is he not here? "

"I *am* here, Grace," a quiet voice answered.

"Merc!" I was in his arms in a flash, crying and laughing and abandoning all past plans for decorum, kissing him over and over again.

It took us both a little while to even get to a mental place where we could talk and begin to make sense of things. As it turned out, Merc had been almost as much in the dark as I was, and the weekend for him had also been one of confusion and change. While I'd been fighting my demons, he had a few run-ins of his own and he was still having trouble even remembering everything that had happened. Thanks to his upbringing, Merc might have had the upper hand over me - knowledge wise - in regards to devils and angels and all the saints and spirits in between, but his understanding of our role in the world was as limited as mine.

We were both on the same page regarding our relationship – steadfast in the knowledge of our future together but hesitant to skip from Point A to Point Z without enjoying all the rites of passage that led from one step to the next.

I was proud of myself for how willing I was to take it slow. A week ago I would have probably scared Merc off with my desperation to hold on, but that wasn't me now. I didn't feel a driving urge to grab hold of him and not let go, because I knew that would be a mistake. I wanted to savor every stage of the game and experience all that life – jointly and separately – had to offer. I didn't expect every minute of our time together to be bliss, and I was almost as excited about the bad times as I was the good because with bad times comes strength and endurance.

I wasn't really shooting for sainthood, though, so I could change my mind tomorrow on everything – clinging hold of the gorgeous guy by my side with both hands and feet. I'd probably wind up parading him around Tallassee's town square like a character from Disney on Ice while winking sarcastically at the school's most eligible bachelorettes just to get their goat. I've always been a moody minx, and that part of me is here to stay; I know where I'm heading and I'll get there eventually.

"What are you thinking about so hard?" Merc asked, while brushing a stray curl away from my face.

"Oh, I was just hoping that the 'suggestions' Locke gave Pete and Patty were still at work because, otherwise, the sheriff is probably out looking for me by now."

My brother and his wife had, indeed, briefly flitted through my mind but that wasn't what I'd been thinking about when Merc asked. I wanted to keep the mystery alive, and I didn't feel particularly compelled to share every thought in my head with him. It was going to be strange enough to be with a guy that we both knew was meant to be my mate; I would have to use every trick in the book to keep him on his toes.

"It might be a good idea to check in with them. Don't you have an exam tomorrow?"

It seemed odd to be talking about such mundane things after the weekend we'd had. "Yeah, I do actually. But . . ." I hesitated, reluctant to bring up anything that would mar the beauty of the day.

"Yes?" he answered, sitting up from where he was lying next to me on a soft bed of green grass.

"I was just thinking about what Mrs. B. said to me – about fighting evil. Aren't we supposed to be battling demons for a living?" I smiled coquettishly, trying to keep the mood light, even though there was no way around the seriousness of the subject.

Merc wiggled his eyebrows and gave me a wicked grin that said he had more important things than demons on his mind "Not today. Maybe tomorrow. It's not like the bad guys are going anywhere. You need to check in with your family and I have a few things to do, then we should spend a little more time getting to know each other better."

It was hard to argue with that kind of superior logic. "So, you think we are okay for right now?"

"Of course, my beautiful Grace." He assured me. He smiled and his eyes twinkled like pure gold in the morning sun. "As long as we are together, you don't have a thing to worry about."

A thrill of satisfaction shot through my system as I leaned down and kissed the man I would follow into forever.

Epilogue

THE GARDEN

LOCHEDUS AND SARAH SAT QUIETLY TOGETHER AT THE EDGE OF THE pond. There was no need for them to speak because their souls were in constant communication. A deep sense of satisfaction traveled between the two of them. Their mission had been accomplished and they could, at last, be together again. Neither was particularly surprised when the wind began to pick up, creating peaks of white on top of the water, and jagged streaks of lightning bolted across the darkening sky. Lochedus closed the tiny space between him and Sarah, getting as near to his mate as he could. He had heard his brother approach and wanted her to feel safe.

"You're getting rather predictable, you know, Beladona. But it's going to take more than a little thunder and lightning to ruin our mood today." Lochedus squeezed Sarah's hand and smiled, not being able to resist twisting the knife into his brother just a little.

"Gloating, huh?" Beladona observed cheerfully. "Isn't that a little . . . un-angelic."

"I suppose it is," Lochedus agreed amicably. "But ever so satisfying."

"Well, I hope you two enjoy your little victory," the dark brother said while brushing his windswept hair from his eyes. "Because the celebration won't last for long."

Lochedus stiffened and Sarah put a gentling hand on his shoulder before whispering, "Don't let him bait you, love. What he says means nothing."

"Don't let him bait you, love," Beladona mimicked. "Listen to your woman, brother. You don't want to start anything with me. Run on back home to Daddy."

Like a lioness protecting her cub, Sarah jumped to her feet, shaking all over with righteous indignation. "You are the one that needs to go back to where you came from, Beladona. Go straight to Hell!" Now that she was back with Lochedus, she had no fear of the devilish captor who had kept her locked away for so many years.

Unperturbed by the beautiful angel's outburst, the raven-haired demon winked at her before answering, "Don't mind if I do, *love*, but don't you worry, you'll be joining me there soon."

Lochedus was suddenly tired of it all. He was tired of the fighting and the threats, of the thousands and thousands of years of pain and conflict. With a resigned sigh and a heavy heart, he turned back to the demon he had once considered a brother and a friend. "You really don't take defeat well, Beladona. It's over. Just accept it."

Beladona looked at the two angels in genuine confusion. "Defeat? There was no defeat. Not for us." He took a few steps closer and lowered his voice to almost a whisper. "You may have gotten the girl and your mate, but at what price, dear brother? Surely you know the consequences of your actions."

Lochedus wished he had the self-discipline not to ask, but he didn't. "What consequences, Beladona? What are you talking about?"

"Did you really think you could tamper with time and upset the natural order of things without paying a price?" He shook his head, looking almost regretful. "You've opened the doors to unspeakable evil, my friend, and made ready the path for those things best left in Hell."

"You're lying, Beladona – as usual." Lochedus felt Sarah trembling by his side and put an arm around her shoulders to try and calm her down. "If you were speaking the truth, you'd be a lot happier about it," he reasoned.

A strange look crossed over the handsome demon's face, and it took a second for him to answer. He drug his fingers through his thick hair before finally saying, "You're forgetting, Lochedus. I was once an angel just like you."

"What's your point?" Lochedus asked wearily.

"Just that some of the fallen ones still believe we have a chance for reconciliation."

Lochedus couldn't believe what he had just heard. He knew it was a trick but the tiny part of him that had always hoped for the same thing was compelled to hear what Beladona had to say.

Sarah felt no such compulsion and ready to get away from the evil one, she began pulling at Lochedus' arm – hard. "Please let's go home. I'm ready to go home."

Torn between doing as his mate asked and hearing out Beladona, Lochedus searched the demon's eyes for the truth. "If you have something to say, just say it. We are leaving."

"It was all a trick, Lochedus. The Master wanted the gates of Hell open and that's exactly what happened. Now the world will suffer in a way neither of us wants. If we work together . . ."

Sarah was frantic now. "Please, my love! You know you can't trust him. He tells nothing but lies."

His soulmate was crying now and Lochedus' heart tore with every tear. Relenting, he turned to the dark one and said, "Sarah's right, I can't believe a word you say and we have to go."

"Please, Lochedus," the demon begged. "We were close once. I've only done as the Master ordered – only what I had to do to survive. But this is my chance for redemption. I will help you, brother, and believe me you are going to need help."

The blonde angel only shook his head sadly and along with Sarah unfolded his wings, resigned and ready to fly away from the garden he adored and the world he loved. His brother's final plea resounded in his head. Could it be true? Could there be a reunion? And what about the things that he'd said were going to happen in the world? He had so much to think about and so much to discuss with the others. He sighed loudly as he watched Sarah – graceful yet mighty – lift off first and, spreading his wings, prepared to follow her. But it was not to be.

Flying was not something the angel had ever had to think about before; it just came naturally to him, like breathing. But he was sure thinking about it now because try as he might, he simply could not leave the ground. Over and over again, he willed his wings to work - to do what they had been doing for his entire existence. But no amount of running starts or prayers sent above could lift Lochedus from the ground.

Suddenly terrified, he called out to Sarah and he was way past frightened when his mate did not return to offer him aid. A deep fear – a primordial panic – seized hold of him, turning his insides to ice. He felt weak as a kitten - his mighty angelic strength sapped from his body leaving him an empty shell of what he had once been. Like Samson shorn, Lochedus – whose wings held his power – was now little more than mortal.

"Looks like Papa might not be too happy with you, brother, and even your woman has deserted you." The dark demon walked to within an inch of the shaken angel, and leaned in close. "So *Locke* . . . " He used the human name like a weapon designed to humiliate. "I've just got one question for you."

Barely able to speak, the terrified, beaten angel could only manage a weak, "What?"

The demon's voice deepened as he asked, "How do you like me now?"

Lochedus stumbled backward, falling to his knees and clutching his sides while his stomach rolled in very human waves of unfamiliar nausea. One by one, the dominoes of understanding fell into place, along with the knowledge of his own blind arrogance – arrogance that had allowed him to overlook that which he should have known from the start.

With dreadful clarity, the pageantry of proof paraded through his mind. The underage drinking, the mercurial moods and the strange appearances and disappearances illustrated in perfect play-back the inconsistencies of the past few days.

Hardly daring to breathe, the earthbound angel looked back up at the demon through grief-stricken, terrified eyes and watched as a shockingly familiar one-dimpled smile spread across the devil's face and his eyes, full of malicious merriment, changed from citrine gold to brilliant green and back again.

ACKNOWLEDGEMENTS
A very special thank you to:

MY HUSBAND, DANA, FOR BEING MY TOUGHEST CRITIC AND MY BEST friend; my son, Temp, who is the light of my life; Jere Beasley, Sr., without whose daily support and encouragement I would never have finished this book; Sara Beasley, for her continuous prayers on my behalf; my brother, Chip Cheek, for listening to my daily readings and encouraging me every step of the way; Kim Rhyne Carr, for almost 40 years of friendship - going through the wars with me by daily sharing my triumphs and disasters and for her PR skills; my dear friend, Reece Mracek, for always making me laugh and for her insight, encouragement and compassion; Dr. Jim Mracek, for his friendship and for always taking care of me and my family so that I can be free to write; Barbara Fowler, for her editing skills and kind-hearted willingness to roll up her sleeves and dive into a first-time author's manuscript; Wendi Lewis, for her unerring eye for detail and amazing editing abilities; Janie Bell Slaughter, Laura Kern Williams, Amy Gaddis Singletary and Diane Bailey for their support of my endeavor – above and beyond the call of friendship; Joyce and Cecil Spear, for their loyal and loving family friendship for over forty years; Barbara Holman, for reading an unpolished manuscript in one weekend; tiny Sidney Murray, because she never fails to make me smile; Woody Woodman, for exemplifying Christ's love through untiring service to others and for always having a mint handy; Ronnie Taunton, for his huge heart and for being there to help my family in any and every way; Guy Johnson, for his many skills and willingness to share them in service to others; for all our close friends at St. James United Methodist Church and especially the members of the Stanley Frazer Class for their abiding love and support.